THE LION AND THE UNICORN

(ARK ROYAL, BOOK XV)

CHRISTOPHER G. NUTTALL

The characters and events portrayed in this book are fictitious. Any similarity to real persons, living or dead, is coincidental and not intended by the author.

Printed in the United States of America.

ISBN: 9798677208072
Imprint: Independently pubished

Cover by Justin Adams
http://www.variastudios.com/

Book One: Ark Royal
Book Two: The Nelson Touch
Book Three: The Trafalgar Gambit
Book Four: Warspite
Book Five: A Savage War of Peace
Book Six: A Small Colonial War
Book Seven: Vanguard
Book Eight: Fear God And Dread Naught
Book Nine: We Lead
Book Ten: The Longest Day
Book Eleven: The Cruel Stars
Book Twelve: Invincible
Book Thirteen: Para Bellum
Book Fourteen: The Right of the Line
Book Fifteen: The Lion and the Unicorn

http://www.chrishanger.net
http://chrishanger.wordpress.com/
http://www.facebook.com/ChristopherGNuttall

All Comments Welcome!

AUTHOR'S NOTE

As always, I have done my best to make this book—the start of a new *Ark Royal* trilogy—as stand-alone as possible. However, the war depicted within this pages started in the *Invincible* books (available from online sellers now) and the character Richard Tobias Gurnard was first introduced in *Life During Wartime*, a semi-novella within *The Dogs of God: Science Fiction According to Chris* anthology. You don't have to read it to know what's going on, but it helps.

CGN, 2020

CONTENTS

PROLOGUE

ADMIRAL SUSAN ONARINA KNEW, without false modesty, that she'd been in some pretty uncomfortable—even hellish—places in her long career, from middy country to jail and even boarding school. And yet, the Alpha Black facility—located on the very edge of the solar system, within an asteroid that wasn't listed on any charts—was the worst place she'd ever been. She tried to avoid it, as did all sensible officers. The asteroid's inhabitants were either servicemen on short-term deployments, medical scientists too intent on their work to notice their surroundings, or infected humans who were no longer in command of themselves. The asteroid was far worse than jail.

She squeezed her eyes shut as she stumbled through the chemical shower, the acidic liquid stinging her skin. Rays of ultraviolet light poured down on her from high above, followed by lasers that were designed to sweep her body clear of the slightest trace of bacteria. She forced herself to keep moving as robotic arms pressed against her to collect skin and blood samples. The lights seemed to get brighter as she passed through another series of airlocks, wondering—not for the first time—if the precautions were more than a little excessive. Blood samples, urine samples, stool samples... she shuddered as she kept going, trying to ignore her awareness that she was being probed on a molecular level. She'd seen the alien virus—*the* virus—at work. If anything, the facility director wasn't being paranoid *enough*.

And I suppose it makes sure I don't come out here more than once or twice a year, she mused, as she stepped through the final airlock. Warm water—clean water—cascaded down, washing away the traces of chemicals that had survived the earlier showers. *The director doesn't want anyone looking over his shoulder.*

Susan breathed a sigh of relief as she dried herself with a disposable towel, then walked into the locker room. Her clothes were waiting. They felt like paper against her skin. She found it hard to feel like a serious person in the outfit, even though she knew her dignity was not the important issue on the asteroid. The garments were designed to be torn away, if the medics needed to tend to a patient. She understood the logic. She just didn't like it.

She took a long breath, then opened the door to the antechamber. Admiral Paul Mason, Director of Alpha Black, jumped to his feet and snapped a salute as she entered, then held out a mug of tea. Susan took the mug and sipped it, gratefully. It was navy tea, strong and sour, but it washed the taste away perfectly well.

"You'd think we could spring for better tea," she said, as she poured herself another mug. "Or even proper milk."

"You know what it's like," Mason said, dryly. "Billions for untested research equipment that never does what it says on the tin, not one penny for better food and drink for the workers."

Susan nodded, brushing her dark hair back over her shoulder. "It's good to see you again," she said. They'd been lovers, once upon a time. "I take it you haven't gone mad yet, trapped out here."

"Not yet, but I'm still trying." Mason winked, then sobered. "We may have had a breakthrough."

"The beancounters will be pleased," Susan said. "They're still talking about defunding this facility and spending more on warship production instead."

"That would be a mistake," Mason said, urgently. "We're not going to out-produce the virus."

Susan nodded, curtly. "I agree," she said. "The key to victory—or even simple survival—lies in pushing technological and biological research as far as possible."

She stared into her empty mug, remembering hours after hours of endless arguments with the bureaucrats and politicians. *They* felt the money would be better spent on tried and tested technology, on warships and starfighters rather than potential war-winning weapons. Susan understood their concerns—she'd read *Superiority,* they'd all read *Superiority*—but she also understood the virus didn't need to concern itself with economic issues. Its society, insofar as it even existed, was communistic to a degree no human society could match. It didn't have to worry about keeping the population alive and reasonably contented. It could simply churn out an endless series of warships and point them at its foes. And there was no way the Alliance could match the virus ship for ship.

And we have to worry about zombies within the ranks, she reminded herself. *One moment, someone is perfectly loyal and trustworthy; the next, they're agents of an alien power.*

"Like I said, we've made something of a breakthrough." Mason took her mug and put it in the sink. "If you'll come with me."

Susan nodded and followed him through a maze of corridors. The facility was almost completely barren, save for a handful of childish paintings pinned to the wall that somehow made the corridors look worse. One of the researchers had kids, she supposed. The poor children were probably back on Earth, perhaps in a naval boarding school. She winced in sympathy. It was never easy to be separated from one's parents, even if there was no actual danger. The parents hated being apart from their children too.

She frowned as they stepped into a large compartment. The rear bulkhead was transparent, allowing the guests to peer into the environmental compartment. A handful of naked people—men and women—wandered aimlessly around the chamber, their bare skin marred with unsightly growths and protrusions. Susan had seen horror—she'd seen people injured or killed in active service—but there was something about the scene in front of her that chilled her to the bone. The infected were no longer wholly human. Their will was no longer their own. The virus had them in its thrall. An alien intelligence seemed to hang in the air, pressing against her thoughts…she told herself, savagely, that she was imagining it. And then the infected turned to face her.

Susan glanced at Mason. "Can they see us?"

"They shouldn't be able to." Mason sounded worried, a far cry from the cocky midshipman she'd known years ago. "The bulkhead is opaque, on their side. But they seem to know when someone is looking at them. We don't understand it."

"I see." Susan calmed herself with an effort. She'd faced all sorts of challenges in the past, from incompetent commanding officers to naked racism and sexism. She'd face this one too. "Are they secure?"

"We think so," Mason said. He ignored the sharp look she sent him with the ease of long practice. "That said, they've been quite good at testing our defences. A couple of bioresearchers got infected; we're not sure how. Thankfully, we caught it in time to flush the virus from their systems. Others…the Russians had a breakout at their facility, one that forced them to trigger the nuke and vaporise everyone. Apparently, one of the guards got seduced. We don't know how that happened either."

Susan shuddered. Bioweapons research was *the* big taboo. The tailored biological weapons that had gotten loose during the Age of Unrest had killed hundreds of thousands before they'd been stopped. No one, even the *really* weird independent asteroid colonies, cared to push the limits any further. And yet, governments had continued research into bioweapons on the grounds it was the only way to develop defences against biological warfare. They were right, she acknowledged sourly, but it didn't sit well with her. It was only a short step from defence to attack.

She turned her gaze back to the infected prisoners. "Is there nothing that can be done for them?"

"The infection's too far advanced," Mason said. "Their brains have been literally *riddled* with the virus's command and control structures. One of the zombies"—he indicated a middle-aged man—"actually has a bullet hole through his brain. It hasn't slowed him down any. Sure, we could purge the infection, but we'd kill them in the process. Once the infection reaches a certain point, it's unstoppable and euthanasia is the only solution."

He stepped forward until he was almost touching the bulkhead. "We've had some success in slowing the infection, or even purging it, but not after the tipping point is reached. It seems to laugh at our genetically-engineered immune systems. We're working on nanotech solutions, but so far we haven't come up with anything practical."

Susan turned as an older woman bustled into the room. "Admiral? I'm sorry I wasn't at the airlock to meet you."

"It's quite all right," Susan assured her. "Doctor Velda Womack, I presume?"

"Just call me Velda," Velda said. "I'm the director of research in this facility."

Susan smiled at Mason, who shrugged expressively. "It's a pleasure to meet you," she said, deciding not to point out that Mason was in formal command of the facility. Velda wasn't the first civilian she'd met with an inflated idea of her own importance. "I understand you have a briefing for me?"

"Yes, Admiral." Velda walked over to the wall and tapped a console. The bulkhead turned opaque. A holographic image appeared in front of them. "The face of the enemy."

"Living cells," Susan said. She still found it hard to wrap her head around the idea of a sentient *virus*. The previous alien enemies she'd faced had been humanoid, for a given value of *humanoid*. "It's almost beautiful."

"It's also almost certainly artificial," Velda said. "There's remarkably little junk DNA, if you'll pardon an outdated and imprecise term, in its structure. Even the most enhanced human has a *lot* of junk in his genetic code. The virus was created by someone, we're sure, and got out of control."

"And they might be still out there," Susan said.

"It's possible," Velda agreed. "It's also possible they were simply the first victims. We may never know."

She indicated the display with a single finger. "We've been looking for ways to fight the virus on its own level. It isn't easy. It's capable of overwhelming most immune systems fairly quickly, unless the victim receives medical attention within the first few hours. We think it's actually adapted to face humans, as the time between infection and mental collapse has grown shorter. It may not be intelligent as we understand the term, but it's clearly very resourceful. Once the air is infected with viral base cells, total infection is just a matter of time."

"I am aware of this," Susan said, stiffly. "We lost a handful of colonies to biological attack."

Velda adjusted the display. "We've been experimenting with manipulating the base cells ourselves. They're really quite remarkable, in so many ways. We came up with a way to use modified base cells to break down the viral...biological computer network, for want of a better term. It would be a terminal blow to their cohesion. We think it would shatter the infected hive mind into a collection of individuals."

"We think," Mason put in. "We don't know for sure."

"No one ever does," Susan said. She looked at Velda. "Are you sure they can't adapt?"

"We believe they wouldn't have time to react before the base cells die," Velda said. "The virus requires a high concentration of base cells within the atmosphere to maintain the hive mind. We'd be smashing it like... like building blocks, in a manner that should make it impossible for the network to be rebuilt. The rate of infection would be reduced sharply, if not curtailed completely. Or so we believe."

"It can't be that simple," Susan said. "What's the catch?"

"We can hit a planet, easily enough," Mason said. "Taking out a ship would be a great deal harder."

Susan's lips twitched. "And they can deploy counter-infection protocols of their own," she said. "They may slow the spread of our infection..."

"Our BioBomb," Velda said. "We'd be fighting fire with fire."

"Clever." Susan studied the hologram for a long moment. "How do you know the...the BioBomb won't turn into a worse threat?"

"It relies upon viral base cells," Velda said. "If we released it here"—she waved a hand—"it would die swiftly. It isn't capable of infecting us or adapting to its surroundings. One might as well transport a human to the bottom of the sea and expect him to survive long enough to learn how to breathe water. In a sense, we've actually created a predator. It's designed to prey on the virus."

"I hope you're not going to suggest we infect ourselves with a downgraded virus," Susan said, dryly.

"That *is* how the first vaccines were created." Velda shrugged. "No, we're still working on medical defences. It might be possible to turn our blood into viral poison, but doing that *and* keeping the infected person alive has so far proven beyond us."

Susan nodded, curtly. "I read the reports," she said. "They didn't make comforting reading."

"No," Velda agreed.

"In theory, we should be able to disrupt their networks if we unleash the BioBombs," Mason said. "At the very least, we should be able to give them a nasty fright."

"I'm not convinced the virus has emotions, as we understand the term," Velda said. "All of our attempts to communicate have failed."

"This is a war of extermination," Susan agreed. She glanced at Mason. "I'll discuss it with the First Space Lord and COBRA, then take it to GATO if they agree. Until then...start producing the BioBombs. I want them ready for deployment as soon as possible."

Mason looked disturbed. "What has this war done to us?"

Susan nodded to the opaque bulkhead. "We either fight, using every weapon at our disposal, or wind up like them," she said. She understood his fears, but...she knew she couldn't afford to let sentiment blind her. "There's no other way."

CHAPTER ONE

"WELCOME TO NELSON BASE," Midshipwoman Nancy Ryland said. "Admiral Onarina is waiting for you."

Captain the Honourable Lord Thomas Hammond nodded as he stepped through the airlock. The summons to Nelson Base had caught him by surprise, forcing him to make his excuses to his wife and board a shuttle on very short notice. His wife hadn't been pleased—she'd been hosting a garden party—but she'd understood. Duty came first, even if her husband had only just returned from Luna for a month of shore leave. Thomas felt a twinge of bemusement as the midshipwoman turned and led him down the corridor. He'd spent the last year at the academy, helping to impart lessons from previous engagements to officer cadets. He would have preferred another ship, but the navy hadn't bothered to take his preferences into account before assigning him.

"Please take me to a washroom first," he said. "I need to freshen up."

"Yes, sir," Nancy said. "There's one just outside the admiral's office."

Thomas sighed inwardly as he followed her, feeling old. Nancy looked to be the same age as his daughters, give or take a few years. He wondered, idly, if she viewed the assignment to the admiral's office as a reward or a punishment. There was something to be said for endearing oneself to one's superiors by serving as their aides, but it wasn't active duty. The navy wouldn't promote someone past a certain point unless they'd served at least a year on active duty. Nancy would probably be assigned to a ship in a year or two, unless she had no ambitions to rise higher. Thomas found that incomprehensible, although he supposed it was possible she was biding her time until a good match came along. Or that she just wanted to do her bit for her country.

He put the thought out of his mind as they passed a giant viewport. Earth floated in front of him, a blue and green marble in an endless sea of stars. It took his breath away, even though he knew the planet was far from peaceful. The virus had infected large swathes of the planet's population, unleashing a nightmare that might never end. The BBC maintained a positive outlook, as did most of the other national and international news channels, but he'd read the reports from more pessimistic analysts. The virus was steadily grinding the human race down. It was only a matter of time, some feared, before it broke through the defences and infected the remainder of the planet. There were even people talking about a mass evacuation of Earth.

Which is logistically impossible, he thought, as they stopped outside a washroom. *We've been shipping people off-world for the last century, and we've barely made a dent in the global population.*

Thomas took a breath and stepped into the washroom. The summons really *had* caught him by surprise. Admiral Onarina wasn't known for being a martinet—she didn't have a reputation for reprimanding officers who didn't wear dress uniforms—but he simply hadn't had time to find anything more than his academy tunic. He splashed water on his face, then stared at himself in the mirror. He'd had a lifetime of genetic tweaks—it was one advantage of being born into the aristocracy, then going into naval service—but he still looked old. His brown hair was starting to gray, his skin looked a bit wrinkled. He was almost tempted to visit a cosmetic surgeon and have everything tightened up, but he wasn't *that* vain. He'd certainly never thought well of men—and women—who made themselves look like teenagers, even though they were parents and grandparents. They'd always seemed like people who'd never really grown up.

He dismissed the thought with an irritated shrug as he brushed down his uniform, then headed for the hatch. Nancy looked as if she'd been waiting patiently, when he stepped into the corridor. Thomas was mildly impressed. It was unlikely she'd been remotely patient—he certainly hadn't been, when he'd been at the beck and call of everyone who outranked him—but she hadn't had a choice. He wondered, idly, if she had orders not to leave him alone for very long. It was unlikely—Nelson Base wasn't a top-secret facility—but he had to admit it was possible. These days, friend could turn to foe very quickly. Who knew who might have been infected without even knowing it?

"This way, sir," Nancy said. "Admiral Onarina is waiting."

Thomas felt a little fresher as Nancy pressed her fingers against a keypad, then opened the hatch. Admiral Onarina's office was surprisingly small, although still much larger than the ready room on his last command. A simple desk, a set of chairs, a comfortable sofa, a small cluster of pictures on one of the bulkheads...Admiral Onarina, it seemed, didn't believe in luxury. Thomas approved. He'd met too many officers who seemed intent on turning their quarters into apartments that wouldn't have shamed the Ritz.

Admiral Onarina rose as he entered. "Thank you, Nancy," she said. "Please bring us tea, then leave us."

"Aye, Admiral," Nancy said.

"Please, take a seat," Admiral Onarina said, as Nancy left. "We have much to discuss."

Thomas sat, studying Admiral Onarina with interest. She was taller than he was, with dark brown skin, long dark hair and darker eyes. The Order of the Garter was clearly emblazoned on her chest, a vote of confidence from the highest in the land. It was unlikely she'd reach First Space Lord—she didn't have the family connections to climb to the *very* top—but no one doubted her competence. He wondered, idly, what she'd been doing since she'd reached flag rank. He'd heard rumours, but none had been substantiated.

Nancy returned with a tray of tea and biscuits. Thomas allowed himself a flicker of relief as the midshipwoman placed the tray on the desk, then retreated. He wasn't in trouble. The admiral wouldn't have offered him a drink if she intended to rake him over the coals. He'd been fairly sure of it—he'd have known if he'd done something worth a bollocking from an admiral—but it was nice to have confirmation. And yet, why *had* he been summoned? He couldn't think of a good reason. A promotion? It was unlikely Admiral Onarina had called to promote him personally.

"I'm sorry for cutting your leave short," Admiral Onarina said. She actually managed to sound regretful. "You're being reassigned."

Thomas raised his eyebrows. He'd assumed he'd be spending at least another six months at the academy, if not remaining there for the rest of his career. It was quite possible, he'd thought, that the navy had seen the academy as the last stage of his career. He'd probably missed the chance to jump up to commodore, if not admiral. Family connections or not, there were limits. A stalled career might never be restarted.

Admiral Onarina leaned forward. "The war is going poorly," she said. "The blunt truth is that the enemy outnumbers us. In the last two major engagements, they brought enough ships to outnumber the defenders two-to-one. Intelligence believes they're planning to continue thrusting towards us through at least two tramline chains, simultaneously. If they do, we will be unable to stop one thrust without giving the other thrust a chance to break through and wreak havoc."

Thomas sucked in his breath. He'd seen the reports—and he was a past master at reading between the lines, particularly when the news broadcasts were so vague it was brutally obvious they were concealing something—but he hadn't realised it was so bad. The naval reports hadn't been anything like so grim. And yet...he took a sip of his tea, trying to remain calm. Admiral Onarina wouldn't have summoned him, a lowly captain, to discuss the war. She had something else in mind.

"We cannot hope to out-produce the virus," Admiral Onarina continued. "We're pushing our industrial nodes to the limit, despite the risk of a general collapse, but it isn't enough to keep the virus from crushing us through sheer numbers. Our only edge is that our technology is slightly—slightly—more advanced. We at Special Projects have been working hard to develop newer and better weapons systems that will give us a chance to turn the tide. We've had some successes, but—so far—we haven't developed a silver bullet."

"I see," Thomas said. "We may come up with something revolutionary..."

"We may," Admiral Onarina agreed, grimly. "There are problems, of course. The naval commanders don't want to risk betting everything on an untried weapons system. They're concerned about discovering, the hard way, that a brand-new invention works perfectly in the lab, but fails spectacularly in the real world. Quite a few of the concepts that have come out of Special Projects—and the Next Generation Weapons program—have proven unworkable, at least until the kinks are worked out. However, we have made a number of advances and improvements to weapons tech."

She tapped her terminal. A holographic starship materialised above the deck. Thomas leaned forward, drinking in the details. She was oddly designed, a cross between a giant battleship and a light cruiser. Thomas frowned as his eyes traced the flattened cylinder, bristling with weapons pods and missile tubes. The drive section looked unusually large for a ship of her size. He didn't like the look of it. The section struck him as a huge target. There'd be drive nodes embedded into the hull itself, but if the drive section were shot off, the ship would be effectively dead in space. His eyes narrowed as he spotted the tiny gunboats clinging to the hull. Had the designers tried to combine a carrier with a battleship and a cruiser?

"HMS *Lion*," Admiral Onarina said, when he looked at her. "Our first battlecruiser."

Thomas blinked. The Americans had experimented with a battlecruiser design, if he recalled correctly, but their prototype hadn't worked out. She hadn't had the acceleration of a cruiser, nor the armour to fight beside the battleships. Most navies preferred to deploy destroyers, cruisers, carriers and battleships. Hybrid designs tended to have all the weaknesses and few of the strengths. And...

"She carries missiles," he said, bemused. It made no sense. "They'd be blown out of space before they reach their target."

"We've been improving missile design and technology ever since we realised they might still have a use in modern war," Admiral Onarina explained. "*These* missiles are designed for long-range engagements, their seeker heads crammed with ECM generators and suchlike to make targeting them difficult...although, sadly, not impossible. They carry improved warheads too, far more deadly than starfighter torpedoes or kinetic projectiles. A battleship that took a direct hit would be seriously damaged. A cruiser would be blown to atoms."

Thomas sucked in his breath. "But enemy point defence would still pick them off...?"

"Perhaps," the admiral said. "The missiles are designed for multiple roles, as you can imagine. They are capable of going ballistic for a time, relying on the gunboats to provide guidance, or simply travelling at speeds that make them difficult to hit. They're even capable of travelling in evasive patterns, just like starfighters...expensive as hell, I have to admit, but right now expense isn't an issue. We're gearing up to churn out hundreds of the missiles."

She altered the display. A smaller ship appeared beside the battlecruiser. "HMS *Unicorn*. Officially, she's a corvette, although she's actually bigger than a standard design. She's a combination of recon ship, sniper spotter and a few other roles. Ideally, she'll be providing targeting data to *Lion's* missiles, allowing *Lion* a chance to open fire from a distance and then vanish back into stealth before the enemy can react. She's also capable of operating independently, if necessary. She has shorter legs than the average destroyer, and she's not designed to stand in the line of battle, but she does have enough point defence to provide cover for her mothership."

Thomas nodded, slowly. "The concept sounds good."

"On paper," Admiral Onarina agreed. "Practically, we want—we need—to make sure the prototypes are tested to the limit before we commit to building more. It took months of arguing to convince the Admiralty to assign funding and resources to construct even *one*, then the project was delayed twice as shipyard workers had to be assigned to other projects and then reassigned back to *Lion*. Ideally, she would have left her slip six months ago."

She met his eyes, evenly. "I would like you to take command of HMS *Lion*."

Thomas felt a thrill of excitement. There was nothing, absolutely nothing, like starship command. He wasn't blind to the politics—or to the danger of being made the scapegoat for the project's failure, if it failed—but he couldn't resist. If he declined the command, the navy would never offer him another. And besides...he lifted his eyes to the hologram. He was a conservative when it came to naval technology—most serving officers were all too aware of the risks of taking untested weapons into combat—but he had to admit the concept *sounded* good. It remained to be seen just how well it would work in the real world.

"It will be my pleasure," he said. An untested ship, fresh off the slips... there'd be challenges galore. It wasn't uncommon for ships to develop problems as they were put through their paces—it was why the navy insisted on shakedown cruises before putting a ship in the line of battle—but many of those problems could be anticipated and corrected. *Lion* was a new design. It remained to be seen what would go wrong when she powered up her drives for the first time. "Do we have a mission?"

"Not yet." Admiral Onarina grimaced. "There are a handful of possibilities, and I want you ready for deployment as quickly as possible, but nothing is set in stone. There's some...*disagreement*...amongst various senior officers about just how *Lion* should be employed in combat. Some of us believe she should be held in reserve until we have enough additional units to prove decisive, others feel she and her classmates will not be enough to turn the tide on their own. Your first priority is to get *Lion* ready for combat. We'll have orders for you then, never fear."

"Yes, Admiral." Thomas found himself smiling. "It will be one hell of a challenge."

"Quite." The admiral's lips thinned, just slightly. "You'll be partnered with Captain Mitch Campbell, who'll have command of *Unicorn*. You may have seen him in the news reports. He's going to be promoted when I meet him, but you'll have command of the two-ship flotilla and you'll be breveted commodore for official correspondence. I'm afraid this doesn't come with a pay raise."

Thomas had to laugh. "Why am I not surprised?"

"Captain Campbell is a hard-charging young man," Admiral Onarina said. "He's very good with small ships, but—so far—hasn't served on anything larger than a destroyer. He was also injured during the last set of engagements and spent several weeks in hospital. I expect you to keep him under control."

"Admiral?"

"He's very hard-charging," she said, again. "Aggressiveness is a useful trait, as you are aware, but there's more at stake here than a lone corvette. No one doubts his bravery, and his crew loves him, but—frankly—I'd be concerned about giving him anything bigger than *Unicorn*. He really needs more seasoning before taking command of a cruiser, let alone a battleship or carrier."

"And the media might make that difficult," Thomas said. He vaguely recalled watching broadcasts about Commander Campbell. "They've been promoting him as a major hero."

"He is a hero," the admiral said, bluntly. "He deserves the medal and promotion. But he also needs more time to mature. The media may have made that impossible."

Thomas nodded, curtly. He'd studied history. Naval heroes were *heroes*, a tradition that stretched all the way back to Lord Nelson and Francis Drake. The time when movie stars and football players had been regarded as heroes and role models was long gone, so far removed from the modern world that it was impossible to understand why anyone had ever taken it seriously. Who *cared* what someone whose only skill was kicking a football around a field had to say about *anything*? Naval heroes—and army heroes—were far more significant. And yet, it was easy to start turning them into icons… icons who inevitably had feet of clay. Everyone knew Theodore Smith had been a drunkard. It hadn't kept him from saving the entire human race.

And it's also very easy to get a swelled head, he thought. *This might not end well.*

"I'll keep him pointed in the right direction," he promised. "And we'll be a long way from the media."

"Always a good idea," Admiral Onarina agreed. She stood, signalling the interview was over. "Nancy will escort you to your shuttle."

"I'll have to call my wife first," Thomas said. He stood, brushing down his uniform. "She needs to know I'm going back on active duty."

"Nancy can arrange a private call," the admiral said. "You can leave immediately afterwards."

"Aye, Admiral," Thomas said. It was inconvenient, to say the least, and his wife would not be pleased. But he'd signed away his freedom when he'd joined the navy. "And thank you."

"Thank me when you come back," the admiral said. Her expression was hard. "A great deal is riding on this project, Captain."

"I understand," Thomas said. "I won't let you down."

CHAPTER TWO

THE HOSPITAL ROOM FELT LIKE A PRISON.

Commander Mitch Campbell sat in the armchair, trying to read the latest reports. The medics seemed determined to keep him in the ward, even though he knew himself fit for duty. He'd only been *slightly* injured in the engagement. There'd been others who'd been far less lucky when HMS *Pelican* had come under enemy fire. Mitch knew, without false modesty, that he'd done well. Even the BBC said so. He'd been brave and lucky enough to emerge a hero, at a time when the country desperately needed heroes. But it wasn't enough to get him back into space.

He glowered at the datapad. He'd fired off requests for reassignment to everyone he'd thought would listen, trying to call in favours from old friends and commanding officers in a desperate bid to escape the hospital. He would have been happy to serve as an XO, even if it meant taking a technical demotion; he would have been happy to be assigned to an orbital patrol vessel or solar guardship, if it meant getting out. And yet, no one had seemed inclined to help. The datapad was crammed with everything from military reports to email spam offering him services he neither wanted nor needed, but nothing that so much as hinted he might be getting a new assignment.

The war isn't over yet, he thought, as he stood and paced the room. He was self-aware enough to know he wouldn't be welcome, or advanced, in a peacetime navy, but there *was* a war on. *They'll reassign me soon enough.*

The hatch bleeped, then hissed open. Mitch rolled his eyes without bothering to turn and look at the intruder. The nurses were nice—he'd flirted with them outrageously—but they couldn't give him what he wanted. They couldn't give him a ship. He was tempted to cut the monitor from his wrist and leave the sickbay, even though it would have landed him in real trouble. The doctors and nurses would probably be glad to be rid of him. Mitch had read his own medical reports. He knew he was no longer in any real danger. The best thing he could do, both for himself and the country he served, was go back on the front lines.

"Commander Campbell?"

Mitch turned, raising his eyebrows as he saw the newcomer for the first time. She was young and attractive, wearing a midshipwoman's uniform that suggested she was permanently assigned to Nelson Base. He felt a flicker of sympathy, mingled with contempt. People who wanted to be uniformed bureaucrats tended to lack vision, in his experience; they rarely grasped the potentials and limitations of the personnel under his command. He hoped, for the midshipwoman's sake, she didn't *stay* on the base. In wartime, her career would stall and promotion would become a thing of the past.

"That's me," Mitch said. He outranked her and technically she should have saluted, but he was on medical leave. He didn't really care. One advantage of serving on corvettes like *Pelican* was a degree of informality that could never be permitted on a fleet carrier. It was astonishing how many people blossomed when they felt free to speak their minds. "What can I do for you?"

"Admiral Onarina requests your presence," the midshipwoman said. "I've been sent to escort you."

Mitch raised his eyebrows, even as his heart leapt for joy. The admiral wanted to see him? It had to be good news. If he was in trouble…he frowned inwardly as he grabbed his jacket, silently relieved he'd dressed after his morning shower. He'd hoped a show of personal grooming would convince the headshrinkers there was nothing particularly wrong with his mind. *Pelican* might have been shot up so badly she'd been sent to the breaker's yard, but her commander was alive and well. And so were most of her crew.

"You'll probably have to sneak me past the guards outside," he joked, at least partly to see how she'd respond. He'd paced up and down outside the room before the nurses had told him to get back inside and stay there. "Did you bring a disguise?"

The midshipwoman looked unamused. "The doctors have cleared you to leave."

Mitch nodded. The midshipwoman was definitely young, then. Too young and inexperienced to know when someone was teasing. The doctors wouldn't have let her take him out unless he'd been cleared first. He checked his appearance in the mirror, put a hand through his brown hair to smooth it as much as possible, then followed the midshipwoman through the hatch. A pair of nurses at their workstation nodded as they walked past. Mitch smiled cheerfully. They might have been his wardens as much as his caretakers, but they could hardly be blamed for following orders. The doctors had seemed convinced the damage had been worse than he'd thought.

He put the thought out of his mind as they walked through a series of airlocks that separated the hospital wing from the rest of the orbiting structure. Ultraviolet light beamed down on them, making his skin prickle uncomfortably; tiny sensors checked their blood for the slightest hint of the virus. He was tempted to point out that he'd been in a facility *designed* to prevent infection from spreading, but there was no point. The guards had strict orders. They couldn't let *anyone* through unless they submitted to the bioscreening. The odds of infection might be low, but the virus had managed to slip zombies through the defences before. Better to be paranoid now, he told himself, than sorry later.

The midshipwoman stopped in front of a large hatch and keyed it open. Mitch stepped forward, coming to attention as he entered Admiral Onarina's office. He couldn't help a thrill of fellow-feeling. She was a commoner, just like he was, but she'd reached the very highest levels through guts, determination and an unflinching refusal to be deterred from doing the right thing. The Order of the Garter, clearly delineated on her uniform, was proof of just how far she'd come. She had the right to take a salute from just about *everyone*.

Mitch saluted, perfectly. "Commander Mitch Campbell, reporting as ordered."

"Welcome." Admiral Onarina's accent suggested she'd been born and raised in London. "Please, take a seat. Tea or coffee?"

Mitch nodded. "Tea, please."

He sat, studying the admiral with interest. She was a striking woman—he acknowledged that, in the privacy of his own mind—but it wasn't her looks that caught his attention. It was her air of calm competence, of grim certainty she knew what she was doing...he understood, now, why so many of her former subordinates spoke so highly of her. He would have followed her anywhere too. She had the indefinable air of command that called to him. He hoped he'd be as impressive when he reached flag rank.

And the fact she reached flag rank is proof I can do it too, he thought, as he accepted a mug of tea. *She's even more of a commoner than I am.*

The admiral studied him for a long moment. Mitch wondered, silently, what she saw in him. A brave and bold commanding officer who'd saved an entire convoy from certain destruction? Or a fool who'd made a terrible mistake and lost his ship? A nervy man, a reckless idiot, or both? Mitch had read the after-action reports. Some had praised him, some had cursed him...he kept his face under tight control. It was easy for an armchair admiral to carp and criticize the men on the front lines, secure in their hindsight...and the knowledge they'd never have to make life or death decisions themselves. Admiral Onarina had been on the front lines herself. She'd know how hard it could be to determine the right thing to do.

If you can keep your head when everyone else is panicking, he reminded himself dryly, *you're halfway there already.*

"I read the reports from your last engagement," Admiral Onarina said, finally. "But I'd like you to tell me, in your own words, what actually happened."

You probably read my report as well as all the others, Mitch thought, feeling a flicker of resentment. He'd been trapped in a bed long enough to write a detailed report. *And there's nothing I can add to it.*

He put the feeling out of his mind as he leaned forward. "*Pelly*—ah, *Pelican*—was assigned to escort an evacuation convoy from Manticore to Erie," he said. "Admiral Yu believed it was only a matter of time before Manticore came under heavy attack, so he wanted to evacuate the trained workers before it was too late to do it in an orderly fashion. I agreed with his logic, particularly as my crew were overdue for shore leave anyway. We'd been on deployment for nearly a year.

"We left with seven other escorts and nineteen freighters, doing our level best to remain stealthy as we jumped from system to system. Everything went well until we ran into an enemy patrol in Dorcas. They altered course to engage us. It was only a matter of time, I thought, until they ran us down. The freighters couldn't hope to outrun the enemy warships."

The admiral nodded, curtly. Mitch felt relieved. It was hard to explain to civilians, somehow, that starships that could travel at unimaginable speeds sometimes couldn't travel fast *enough*. A freighter might move like greased lightning, compared to a hypersonic transport or maglev train, but she might as well be crawling compared to an enemy warship bent on chasing her down. The freighters couldn't even scatter if there was more than one enemy warship in the vicinity. They simply didn't have the legs to break contact long enough to go doggo and hide.

"I deployed ECM drones and altered course," Mitch recalled. "*Pelican* went at the enemy ships, all guns blazing. We tore through their formation, firing like madmen. The enemy ships were distracted long enough for the convoy to slip away into interplanetary space, the freighters pretending to be black holes while the warships pretended they were running for their lives. It worked. We bought the convoy enough time to save thousands of lives."

"At the cost of losing *Pelican*," Admiral Onarina pointed out. "And you getting severely wounded."

"It was an exploding console," Mitch said. He snorted. He was going to be a laughingstock when *that* became public knowledge. Exploding consoles were common in movies and viewscreen programs, but rare—almost unknown—in real life. "*Pelican* was hit so badly there were power surges throughout the command datanet. Ironically, it's probably what saved us. We were so badly hit they thought we were dead."

He took a breath. "One of the freighters risked everything to send shuttles to take us off the wreck," he said. "I remained in command until my surviving crew was evacuated, then handed command over to the freighter's captain."

Admiral Onarina smiled. "An interesting take on nearly fainting as soon as you were brought onboard."

"*Fainting* is perhaps too strong a word," Mitch countered. He'd been in terrible pain. His memories were broken and scattered. "But I was in no state to assume command."

He winced, inwardly. Technically, any warship commander outranked a freighter commander. Technically, Mitch should have taken command of the freighter as soon as he stepped onboard. Technically…he shook his head. He really *hadn't* been in any state to assume command. And he knew what *he'd* have said to any jumped-up officer who thought superior rank was enough to take command of *his* ship. He wouldn't have blamed the freighter's CO for finding a way to ignore regulations.

"Quite." Admiral Onarina studied him for a long moment. "Did you do the right thing?"

"If I hadn't charged the enemy fleet," Mitch pointed out, "they would have blown the convoy to atoms. There were over a hundred thousand civilians on those ships, Admiral, ranging from experienced workers to their wives and children. Losing *Pelican* was painful"—*in more ways than one*, his thoughts added—"but losing the rest of the squadron would have been worse."

He kept his face under tight control, unsure what the admiral would say. She was experienced enough to know he was right, but she might have come under heavy pressure from her superiors. The Royal Navy had held an inquest into the loss of HMS *Pelican*, but the board hadn't bothered to contact him after demanding and receiving his report. He wasn't sure if that was a good sign. They hadn't so much as asked him for clarification, let alone put him in the hot seat and shouted questions at him. He would almost have preferred to face a hostile audience than stay in the hospital room.

"I agree," Admiral Onarina said. "The board agreed as well. In an ideal world"—her lips twisted—"we would not have to worry about losing ships and crew. In the *real* world, we can only ensure our ships and crews are not risked and lost for nothing. The board found you personally blameless. Indeed, it agreed you were to be promoted to captain—effective immediately—and assigned to a new command."

Mitch sucked in his breath. He'd wanted to be a starship captain for as long as he could remember. He'd grown up on stories of Francis Drake, Horatio Nelson and Theodore Smith...although only Smith, he recalled dryly, had commanded an actual *starship*. If they promoted him to *captain*... they could never take it from him. He'd have the right to call himself *captain* for the rest of his life, even if he never commanded another starship. He tried not to grin like an idiot. He'd made it! He'd never be stricken from the rolls and forgotten...

"You'll be taking command of HMS *Unicorn*, a specialised corvette," Admiral Onarina informed him. "We believe you have the right combination of skills and experiences to handle her...*semi*-unique role. Ideally, she and her partner will be the first of a new breed of warships. We think she'll give us the edge in future engagements with the virus. I shouldn't have to tell you, *Captain*, just how important it is that we maintain and widen that edge as much as possible."

Mitch nodded, grimly. He'd seen the virus at work. It was unpredictable. There were times when it would attack like a madman—like *him*—and times when it would ignore the most flagrant provocations. He had the feeling the intelligence directing its combat operations was prepared to soak up a certain level of casualties, rather than change the plan and risk matters getting out of control. It made no sense, from his point of view, but if one regarded one's ships and crews as expendable assets, of no more importance than a fingernail, he supposed it made a certain kind of sense. Perhaps the virus had enough ships to allow it to spend them carelessly.

We still don't know how much space it really controls, he reminded himself. A handful of infected worlds had been nuked, weapons of mass destruction unleashed for the first time since the Age of Unrest, but the virus didn't seem to have been slowed down. *For all we know, we're battling a tiny fraction of its overall fleet.*

"I understand," he said. "What about my crew?"

"Fifteen of your surviving crew from *Pelican* have accepted transfer to *Unicorn*," Admiral Onarina informed him. "The remaining ten have been reassigned."

And fifteen are dead, Mitch thought. He'd had forty personnel under his command. Fifteen had died…he'd known them all, personally. They hadn't been names and faces in a file, they hadn't been statistics…they'd been real people. *I couldn't even visit their families.*

He felt his heart twist. He had no fear of death—he couldn't have done all the madcap stunts he'd done in his career if he'd been worried about dying—but he hated the thought of others dying for him. They'd known the risks, he kept telling himself, yet…he shook his head. It didn't make things any better. He hadn't wanted them—any of them—to die.

"I'm glad to hear it," he said, truthfully. "I assume there'll be new crew too?"

"Yes." Admiral Onarina frowned. "There's another concern. You'll be serving under Captain Hammond. He'll be breveted commodore for the duration."

Mitch said nothing for a long moment. Captain Hammond? The name was unfamiliar…Hammond was hardly an unusual surname. Certainly, nothing had happened to bring the name to his attention. That could be good or bad. Captain Hammond might be a competent commanding officer, well aware of the importance of being good as opposed to looking good, or he might be a reactionary stick in the mud. The war had killed a number of officers who'd been promoted for reasons other than competence, but Mitch was painfully aware they hadn't *all* been killed. He shook his head. He'd find out soon enough. A breveted commodore would hopefully know the difference between good leadership and bad.

"I understand," he said. "When do I take up my post?"

"Now, if you're ready." Admiral Onarina smiled. "Technically, you're entitled to a few days of shore leave, but..."

"I spent too long in a hospital bed," Mitch assured her. He wouldn't have minded a day or two spent visiting Sin City, or haunting a spaceport strip down on Earth, but he knew the right answer. Besides, he wanted to take command of his new ship before the Admiralty had a change of heart. "I don't need any shore leave."

"Very good," Admiral Onarina said. She picked a datachip off her desk and held it out to him. "Your orders, Captain, and details on your new command. And good luck."

"Thank you, Admiral," Mitch said. "I won't let you down."

CHAPTER THREE

"CAPTAIN?"

Thomas looked up. The shuttle was so cramped—he wasn't the only person travelling to the Hamilton Yards—that he'd been invited to sit at the back of the cockpit, even though he had a feeling the pilot would have preferred him in the rear compartment. He'd spent most of the trip studying the files on the datachip, trying to get the measure of his new command and her crew. It hadn't been easy. Too many details were left out of the files, either because they were unimportant or simply unknown. It was worse, he reflected, when dealing with a new design. The weaknesses might not become apparent until the ship was taken into combat.

"Yes?"

"We're approaching *Lion* now," the pilot said. "Would you like to come forward?"

Thomas stood and peered into space as a cluster of lights slowly came into view. The Hamilton Yards were immense, hundreds of slips, industrial nodes, defence stations and personal hubs floating near the asteroid belt. His eyes dropped to the console, picking out the IFF beacons that marked the location of dozens of starships preparing for their first deployments. HMS *Lion* floated near the edge of the facility, half-hidden behind a haze of ECM generators. Thomas suspected it was pointless—the naked eye and passive sensors could pick out quite a few details—but there was no point in questioning it. The security precautions might make it harder for a spy drone to get close to the ship without revealing its presence, or convince its controller that it had spotted something useful. The *real* secrets were inside the hull.

And I could give someone a tour without ever revealing anything important, he thought, dryly. *They'd never know they were being snowballed.*

He put the thought to one side as *Lion* took on shape and form. She was longer than he'd realised, her flattened hull suggesting she was designed to fire missiles rather than plasma bolts. It took him a moment to mentally link what he was seeing with the starship plans he'd studied to realise that *Lion* was bigger than he'd thought. The missiles were huge, by human standards, but still tiny compared to the battlecruiser. Her drive section was heavily armoured…he frowned, unsure he liked the look of it. *Lion* would definitely be in serious trouble if she took a hit to the drives. Two or three would probably be enough to leave her dead in space.

We'll just have to stay out of point-blank range, he told himself. *We don't want an enemy battleship blowing us to atoms.*

He frowned as the shuttle glided closer. He'd read the reports—he'd studied them carefully—but training and experience told him missiles were largely useless in combat. A ballistic missile was easy to avoid, a powered missile was easy to destroy. It was possible to overwhelm a starship's defences, but anyone who wanted to *try* would have to fire so many missiles that the whole exercise would rapidly become cost prohibitive. A chill ran down his spine as he remembered the *virus* deploying thousands of missiles in single engagements. The virus didn't have to care about economics, or living wages, or anything else that might detract from producing as many missiles as possible. It just didn't seem fair.

"Captain, we'll be docking at the forward hatch," the pilot said. "Do you want to surprise your crew?"

"No, thank you," Thomas said. It was unlikely he *could* surprise his crew, unless his XO was incredibly careless. Nelson Base would have sent

Lion a copy of the shuttle's troop manifest. A smart officer would at least *glance* at the list, before forwarding it to whoever was in charge of personnel assignments. "There's no point in trying."

He smiled as the battlecruiser grew larger and larger until she was practically dominating the cockpit. Up close, he could pick out point defence weapons and sensor nodes, constantly sweeping the surrounding area for threats. Men in suits and worker bees hummed around the giant ship, carrying out the final tasks before clearing *Lion* for deployment. Thomas felt a thrill of anticipation as the shuttle altered course, heading straight for the forward hatch. A low *thump* echoed through the hull as she locked on, the gravity field flickering slightly as it meshed with the battlecruiser's field. Thomas let out a breath as he turned and headed for the hatch. Hopefully, his new XO—Commander Shane Donker—hadn't arranged a meet-and-greet. Thomas knew he'd have to meet his new officers, sooner rather than later, but he'd prefer not to do it in the middle of a crowded airlock.

The outer airlock opened in front of him. Thomas felt his ears twinge as the pressure equalised, the inner airlock flowing open to allow him to board his ship. The atmosphere smelt new, as if the ship was too new to have a scent of her own. It wouldn't be long, he told himself, as he looked around. The remainder of the crew were already on their way, along with the marines and assessment officers. The ship would start to smell normal soon enough.

Commander Shane Donker stepped forward and saluted. "Captain. Welcome onboard."

Thomas returned the salute. "Thank you, Commander," he said. Donker's file had made it clear he was an engineering officer who'd switched to the command track, rather than someone who'd spent his entire career climbing up the latter to the captain's chair. A good choice, he thought, for XO of an experimental design. "It's good to be here."

"Good to have you too," Donker said. He sounded as though he actually meant it. "We've been looking forward to taking her out and seeing what she can really do."

"I've read a lot of good things in the reports," Thomas said. "How well does she handle in the *real* world?"

Donker turned and led Thomas towards the bridge. "We've powered up her drives and taken her for a spin around the shipyard," he said. "There were no major problems. A couple of components had to be replaced, when they failed upon being powered up. There was a minor hiccup in Fusion Three that turned out to be caused by a component being inserted wrongly, but the monitoring software caught the glitch before it could cause any major problems. And we've fired dummy missiles through each of the tubes."

He paused. "Naturally, we haven't taken her into *real* combat. We don't know how well she'll handle an unstructured engagement."

"We'll find out," Thomas said. He'd be discomforted to discover that *Lion* could only handle a specific form of engagement, although he'd prefer to know about it *before* he took his ship into combat. "And the crew? How are they?"

"Around ninety percent of our assigned manpower is onboard," Donker assured him. "The remainder—the gunboat pilots and the marines—will be joining us shortly. We've been running endless drills, trying to figure out what we can and cannot do before we face a real crisis. The reports are on your desk, but overall I'm pleased with progress."

Thomas nodded, feeling uncomfortably unsure of himself. The crew wouldn't know *him*. It shouldn't matter, but he knew from experience that it *would*. He promised himself he'd spend the next few days touring his ship, getting to know his officers and men before leading them into battle. He'd have to spend time in the simulators himself too, practicing everything from simple engagements to complex multi-sided battles where the line between enemy and ally was thinner than one might suppose. There was no choice.

Easy training, hard mission, he reminded himself. *Hard training, slightly easier mission.*

He dismissed the thought as the bridge hatch hissed open, revealing the nerve centre of the entire vessel. The chamber had been designed more for looks than practicality, he thought, although he had to admit it probably didn't matter. If *Lion* was hit so badly her bridge was exposed, he reflected, she and her crew were dead. He made a mental note to check the damage control simulations, to try and determine how close they were to reality. The navy believed in hard training, but there were limits. They wouldn't fire a laser warhead or heavy plasma cannon at a starship just to test the armour.

His eyes wandered the compartment. A dozen consoles—half manned—surrounded a set of command chairs and holoprojectors. *Lion* was too small to have a secondary bridge, he noted; Donker would be sitting beside him when *Lion* went into battle. Experience insisted that was a bad idea. The bridge was heavily armoured, but a lucky shot or an unexpected enemy weapon might be enough to render it non-functional. It might be better to put the XO in Engineering, when they finally engaged the enemy. The ship could be controlled from there if the bridge was taken out.

Assuming we survive whatever takes out the bridge, Thomas thought. *And that doesn't seem likely.*

He smiled as he sat on the command chair. It felt new, as new as the rest of the ship. He wondered, idly, if Donker had been using it. The officer of the watch had every right to sit in the command chair, although not all of them *did*. Thomas himself had felt a little odd about sitting in the chair, when he'd been a junior officer. He'd lost the feeling when he'd taken command of his first ship.

"Mr XO, I assume command," he said, formally. "Make a note in the log."

"Aye, sir," Donker said, with equal formality.

Thomas keyed the console, bringing up the near-space display. The yards were buzzing with activity, a grim reminder that the country was at war. There'd been rumours of slowdowns and strikes for years, ever since the pace of construction had been upped and upped again. He grimaced at the thought. He understood, all too well, just what happened if men were pushed to breaking point...but he also understood the threat. The virus would destroy everything, if it won the war. Freedom, independence, individuality...everything that made human what they were would be erased so completely no one would ever remember what they'd been. The virus wasn't a normal foe. It would crush the human race so completely humanity would cease to exist.

"You'd better give me a tour of the ship," he said, standing. "And then we can start some real work."

"Aye, Captain," Donker said. "If you don't mind, we'll start with the living quarters."

Thomas nodded, keeping his thoughts to himself. Donker's voice showed no hint of irritation at being displaced, even though it had to be annoying. Donker had been the *de facto* captain for the last three months, once *Lion* had been moved out of the slip. He would have been more than human if he hadn't hoped, against all logic and reason, that *he* would be offered the command chair. *Lion* was a new ship of a new design. Donker would have less to unlearn than a man who'd commanded destroyers and carriers. He might even have been more willing to push the limits as far as they'd go.

He listened carefully, asking questions from time to time, as they made their way through the ship. *Lion* felt undermanned, even though the reports had claimed she was so heavily automated she could be commanded and operated by a tiny handful of crew. Thomas had his doubts about *that*. The automated systems might work in theory, but—in his experience—they'd start to fail the moment enemy fire started pounding the hull. It might be better to bring additional damage control crewmen onto the ship, even if they had no other use. He made a mental note to see if he could convince the Admiralty to assign more. The manpower shortage was apparently permanent, no matter how many people were conscripted into the military.

Or we should see who we can hire from the asteroids, he mused. *It isn't as if we're not facing a common foe.*

"The original design called for the gunboats to be treated as starfighters," Donker explained, as they reached the gunboat hatches. "They'd be held internally and launched from a flight deck. Simulated versions of the design, however, suggested that it would render the entire ship useless. A jack of all trades and master of none, as they say. It would have been worse, in fact, because the flight deck would have drawn fire, allowing the enemy to shoot *into* the ship."

Thomas nodded. He'd studied some of the early designs for ships that were both fleet carriers and battleships. *Ark Royal* had served in both roles, but every successive design had proven to be unable to duplicate the feat. *Lion* would have it even worse, he thought; a direct hit to the flight deck, a nuke detonating inside the tube, would have broken the battlecruiser's back even if it hadn't blown her to atoms. The gunboats would be hellishly vulnerable, if a missile hit their berths, but it would be better to lose all the gunboats than the entire battlecruiser.

Which probably won't endear us to the pilots, he thought, as they peered into empty berths and briefing compartments. *No one likes to be reminded they're expendable.*

He glanced at Donker. "Do the gunboats live up to the hype?"

"It's hard to say," Donker said. There was something in his voice that suggested he had *opinions* on the subject. "The simulations suggest the concept is workable. Their one actual engagement, against an enemy raiding party, was a great success. We don't know, of course, if the virus had anyone watching the engagement from a distance. They may be in blissful ignorance of what's coming their way, sir, or they may be working desperately to devise countermeasures. We simply don't know."

He paused. "I've met a couple of gunboat crews," he added. "They come across as lacking polish—most of them were recruited in a non-standard manner, from what I heard—and they didn't act like naval officers, but... they were fairly sure they could do their jobs. I think time will tell if this is a good idea or not."

Thomas nodded. It wasn't a ringing endorsement, but...it would have to do. They were charged with striking a balance between naval conservatives and progressives, between officers who saw new weapons as worse than useless and officers who were so entranced with the promise of newer and better weapons that they overlooked the downsides. They'd have to test the concepts thoroughly, before they were put into mass production. He remembered the admiral's words and shuddered. The human race was thoroughly outnumbered. It couldn't hope to win a war of attrition. Their only hope was designing weapons that might give them an edge.

Or even a vaccine that might let us co-exist with the virus, he thought. Most anti-viral research was highly classified, but the rumours he'd heard suggested the researchers were no closer to a breakthrough than they'd been in the last five years. *We'd settle for something that poisoned the host, if we had no other choice.*

"We'll find out," he said. "And if it doesn't work, we'll just have to come up with something new."

"Coming up with something new isn't the problem, sir," Donker said. "There are more ideas for silver bullets than there are stars in the sky. Turning a concept into workable hardware...*that's* the problem. There's a whole bunch of ideas that are close enough to tantalise us..."

He shook his head. "And none of them are remotely practical, not yet."

"I know," Thomas said. "I've read the reports."

He frowned, inwardly, as the tour continued. The designers had done good work. They'd practically overdesigned the ship. *Lion* had enough drive nodes to give it the acceleration curve of a destroyer, something that would give the enemy a nasty fright the first time they saw her in action. They'd probably start building their own, as soon as they realised it was possible. And then...Thomas gritted his teeth. *Lion* might be able to outrun anything big enough to kill her, but she couldn't outrun missiles. The enemy would probably try to overwhelm her defences, simply by hurling hundreds of missiles at her. *Lion's* point defence might not be enough to stop them.

But the gunboats will add to our point defence fire, he told himself. *They'll provide mobile firing platforms as well as targeting data.*

Or so the simulations tell us, his thoughts countered. *We won't know how well it'll really work until we actually face the enemy.*

"I'm going to have to spend the next week getting to know the ship," he said, as they headed back to the ready room. "And meeting the crew."

He took a breath. "Please inform the senior officers that they're invited to a brief gathering this evening, at 2000," he added. "I'll meet them formally then."

"Aye, Captain," Donker said. It was rare, almost unknown, for an officer to decline an invitation from the captain. It was effectively compulsory, whatever the captain might say. "I'll let them know at once."

Thomas nodded. His terminal was blinking yellow, warning him there was a small pile of messages in his inbox demanding his attention. The XO was supposed to handle most of the paperwork and suchlike, but there were matters that could only be handled by the captain, even though the captain had only been assigned to the ship a few short hours ago. He'd have to review Donker's decisions too, he reminded himself. The XO had been the man on the spot, but it was the captain who'd pay the price if they went wrong…

"Hopefully, we'll meet our planned departure date," he said, as he took his chair. "I'll speak to you later."

"Yes, sir," Donker said. "I'll see you tonight."

CHAPTER FOUR

"YOU DON'T HAVE TO ESCORT ME TO SCHOOL," Elizabeth Gurnard whined. "You really don't."

Tobias Gurnard—he'd stopped using his first name as soon as he legally could—smirked at his younger sister. He'd sworn, six months ago, that it would be a cold day in hell before he went anywhere near his former school. It had been ten years of absolute hell, from sadistic PE teachers and a headmaster who was almost brutally incompetent to louts whose only entertainment was beating him up on a regular basis. And, despite his hard work, he'd failed to make it into university and leave the assholes behind. If the navy hadn't recruited him, he thought, he'd *still* be with the assholes. As it was, he couldn't help feeling a flicker of the old terror as he approached the school.

And yet...he smiled, despite himself, as they passed groups of boys only a year or two younger than he was. His uniform felt uncomfortable, but it was safety. Anyone who attacked a serviceman on the streets faced a life sentence in an arctic work camp, if they weren't simply put in front of a wall and shot. *That* lesson had been learnt the hard way, during the Troubles. Tobias didn't want to be beaten up in front of his sister—again—but he'd take the beating gratefully if it meant one of his former tormentors being taken off the streets. He'd never liked the idea of a military career—and he'd never expected to be recruited into the navy—yet it had its advantages. People who'd shunned him now had to salute him.

He shuddered, again, as the school came into view. It was a soulless mass of brick and concrete, more like a prison than a fitting home for young minds. A pair of teachers, both very familiar, stood outside the doors, counting heads as their students headed into school. Tobias waved goodbye as his sister hurried to the female entrance, becoming one with the crowd as she passed through the door and vanished from sight. He caught the eye of one of the teachers and winked, enjoying the surprise on the man's face. The wanker had often told Tobias he was useless, just because he couldn't kick a football. Tobias wondered, idly, which of them was laughing now.

The fates, he thought, as he turned and walked away. *They're laughing to see me in uniform.*

He felt his heart clench. It was harder to be frightened of the bullying louts after spending the last six months in the navy. They'd been trained endlessly, then flung into battle against a very real threat. The medal he wore was real. He could still be beaten up—he'd met men so strong and fit they made the louts look like.... well, *him*—but he was no longer so scared. The risk of being blown to atoms by enemy fire rather put the louts in perspective.

The streets emptied slowly as he made his way through the centre of town. Liverpool had been a dull, gray city even when he'd been a child. The houses might have been repaired or rebuilt, after the city had been flooded during the war, but there was little individuality to the buildings. He shuddered as he passed a half-empty cafe, the handful of patrons too absorbed in their coffees to pay any attention to him. Liverpool might have been where he'd lived, but it had never been *home*. He wasn't sure he'd ever find a place to call home. The navy was infinitely superior to the city, but it wasn't really home either. He would sooner have gone to university—and he'd been promised a chance to go, when he served his term—yet...would he find a home there? He'd be two years older, with a naval term under his belt. Would it be home, or would he be rejected?

Perhaps both, he thought, sourly.

He kicked a stone as he walked past the library, one of his favourite haunts when he'd been a child. He'd always held the military in contempt. Too many of the jerks and bullies he'd known had bragged openly about how they were going to join the military, get a licence to kill, and then kill *him*. It had taken him too long to realise they were bullshitting, to realise that many of the assholes he'd known would never make it in the military. They'd do their National Service and get out, perhaps taking a ticket to Britannia or another colony world where they could build a better life for themselves. It was the exodus, more than anything else, that was draining Liverpool. The young left and never came back.

The thought mocked him. He'd come back, but only for a week. His orders had made it clear he wasn't to go *too* far from the spaceport. His mother and sister had been pleased to see him, but no one else had given much of a shit. He'd never had any real friends until he'd joined the navy. Of course not. Anyone who might have befriended him had been scared off by the louts, damn them. There were times when he fantasised about taking a gunboat, flying over Liverpool and laying waste to the town. He wasn't fool enough to say that out loud. There were horror stories about what happened to boys who did.

It's hard to feel any empathy if no one shows you any, he thought, morbidly. He knew, intellectually, that the vast majority of the city's population didn't hate him. They simply didn't know he existed. But it was hard to believe, sometimes. They'd done nothing to help him and...and that hurt. *Why should I care about them?*

His heart sank as he heard music and happy laughter coming from a pub. It was barely half past nine and...and they were already drinking and laughing. He felt a pang of envy, even though he'd been warned—in no uncertain terms—not to even think about drinking, first by his mother and then by the navy. He would have liked to be popular, he would have liked to have a circle of friends who sought his company and went on wacky adventures...he would have settled for a trip to the beach or the highlands or somewhere, anywhere, other than the drab city. He could go into the pub, wearing his uniform, and someone would buy him a drink...he shook his head. He couldn't face the thought of being rejected, once again. The whole idea of just going into a pub was impossible. It was no place for him.

He turned and walked away. A pair of youths ran past him, heading to school. They'd be for the high jump when the Beast—his old headmaster—caught them. It wasn't *easy* to evade the network of surveillance systems around the school. And the Beast...Tobias snickered, even though there was little funny about the wretched man. The headmaster had bragged endlessly of his days in the military, but Tobias hadn't been able to find a single record of him on MILNET. There would be a reference, he'd been told, even if his precise history was classified. If there was no reference, there was no career history. Tobias felt his smirk grow wider. The Beast had never been in the military at all.

Which should have been obvious, the moment I met a real military officer, he thought, as he hurried home. *He was nothing like the Beast.*

His heart sank as he turned onto the street and headed down to his house...his mother's house now, he supposed. He was no longer a registered resident. The houses were practically identical, save for the handful of decorations and flags in the windows. A couple of families had lost fathers and sons to the war. He wasn't too impressed. His father had died on active service. The war had to be fought—Tobias knew enough to understand the truth—but it wasn't *easy* to lose a father. If the old man had lived...who knew what Tobias would have become?

"Tobias." His mother greeted him as he stepped into the house. "Did you have a nice walk?"

Tobias said nothing, unsure what to say. He'd hoped...in truth, he wasn't sure *what* he'd hoped for. Validation, perhaps? Respect? Or just an acknowledgement that the school was little more than a breeding ground for thugs, a place where the intellectuals were bullied until their souls were crushed and they became consumed with hatred for a world that treated them like dirt and denied them their chance to shine...he shook his head, sourly. There was no point. He'd been young and now he felt old without ever having been...been what? He wasn't sure.

"It was fine," he said. Their relationship had changed, in the past week. He'd been away for too long. She seemed torn between showing off her navy son and fear she might lose him, as she'd lost her husband. "Elizabeth got to school on time."

"Good," his mother said. "Are you still leaving this evening?"

"Yes." Tobias knew there was no more time. He had orders to report to the spaceport the following day. After that...if rumour was to be believed, the gunboats were being assigned to a carrier. "I'll be catching the last train to London and sleeping in the barracks."

"I'll cook you a nice tea," his mother said. "And pack you a lunch."

"Thanks." Tobias headed for the stairs. His room wasn't really his anymore, either. He was mildly surprised his mother hadn't cleared his stuff out, then rented it to someone in desperate need of a cheap place to live. Perhaps she just hadn't found any takers. He found it hard to believe anyone would willingly live in Liverpool. "Did anyone...?"

He shook his head and walked upstairs, leaving the question unfinished. No one was going to call for him, no one *real*. He could be someone else on the datanets, if he wished; he could claim to be anything and anyone and it wouldn't matter. But here...he sighed as he entered the room and closed the door. No one from his unit had contacted him. He supposed he shouldn't have been surprised. They'd practically been living in each other's pockets over the last few months. They all needed a break.

We'll be on our first deployment soon, he thought, as he sprawled on the bed. *And some of us might not be coming back.*

"So tell me," Patrick Miller. "Is it true the ladies *really* love a marine?"

Corporal Colin Lancaster allowed himself a grin as he drank his beer. He'd only been able to wrangle a couple of days of leave from his unit, before they left the base for their first *real* deployment, and he was determined not to waste it. The sergeant wouldn't be remotely happy if he saw Colin drinking himself senseless, but the sergeant was somewhere down south and Colin…was in Liverpool. He was disappointed that most of his old friends were scattered around the country, but…Patrick was here and a couple more had promised to meet him for a kebab and more boozing later, before he headed back to base. He'd probably regret it in the morning, yet… he snorted, rudely. There'd be no alcohol onboard ship.

"It's very true," he said. "The girls in Portsmouth? You have to beat them off with a stick."

He smiled in happy memory. The training had been intense—for the first time in his life, he'd put his head down and really *worked* at something—but it had been worthwhile. The older cadets had taken him and the others to a bar, their first day of leave, and introduced them to the girls. Dozens of girls. Some of them had been prostitutes, willing to do absolutely anything for money, but others had just wanted to spend time with a man in uniform. Colin felt his smile grow wider as he remembered one particular girl…

"Perhaps I should have tried for the marines," Patrick said. "But I thought the army would be good for me."

"It's probably a good thing you didn't try for the Paras," Colin said. "We have a sacred obligation to fight them, whenever we meet them."

"Really?" Patrick didn't sound convinced. "Even during wartime?"

Colin shrugged. Truthfully, he'd never done it himself. The old sweats had explained the rivalry was more a matter of form than anything else, a test of their skills rather than a fight to the finish. Jokes about Moe the Marine and Peter the Para battering themselves senseless over nothing were just jokes. They weren't very funny, either. The Royal Marines might wind up depending on the Parachute Regiment to pull them out of a jam—or vice versa—if things *really* went wrong. They couldn't start to think of the others as anything more than rivals.

"I don't know," he said. He took another swig of his beer. "Is Annie still around?"

"I think she's getting married next month," Patrick said. "She and Ham were pretty damn close. Rumour has it she's been knocked up."

"Ham had better be sure the kid is his," Colin said. Annie had been a very popular girl—in all senses of the word—before they'd left school. Her father had been very controlling and she'd responded by sleeping around. "What about Joelle?"

"Moved out, no forwarding address," Patrick told him. He snapped his fingers at the waitress, ordering more beer. "She did take one of the entrance exams to university, so she might have gotten in."

"Who knows?" Colin tried to remember the other girls. There'd been so many, once upon a time. "Who's left?"

"Hannah, but you know what her dad is like," Patrick said. "You even take one *look* at his daughter and he'll pound on you."

Colin laughed. "I remember," he said. The waitress returned, placing two more beers in front of him. "I guess I'm not that desperate."

He watched the waitress stroll away, his eyes lingering on her sinfully short skirt. There was one definite advantage to wearing a uniform and that was that, no matter how young you looked, the police wouldn't chase you out of the pub. He'd completed the Golden Mile wearing his uniform and no one had even thought to question his age. Not, he supposed, that anyone would mistake him for a kid. He'd been big for his age well before he'd joined the Royal Marines. And they—somehow—had forced him to grow extra muscles.

Patrick nudged him. "They say she's putty in the hands of anyone who gives her money."

Colin snorted as he drank his next beer. He wasn't sure how much he'd had to drink, but no one was counting. If he'd been alone, perhaps he would have hit on the waitress. What was the worst that could happen? A slap? He'd had worse in training. He snickered at the thought of the sergeant slapping his recruits, as a woman might slap a man who'd gone too far, the snickers becoming chuckles as he imagined the man's reaction to a suggestion he *should*. He'd be doing push-ups forever.

"What's so funny?" Patrick sounded more perplexed than annoyed. "You know her?"

"No." Colin stared down at his drink. "I'm giggling at a stupid thought. How much have we had to drink?"

"Well..." Patrick made a show of pretending to count. "One...two... three...lots?"

"Don't try to count past twenty without taking off your pants," Colin said. He put the beer aside. He didn't want to get *that* drunk, at least not until he met up with the rest of the old gang. "Is it just me, or...have things gotten quiet recently?"

"It's probably just you," Patrick said. "If you don't want that beer, pass it over here."

"That's a terrible rhyme," Colin said, pushing the glass to his friend. "Don't give up the day job."

Patrick snorted. "I'll have you know my rendition of *We'll Keep A Welcome* provoked strong feelings in the audience."

"Shock, terror, rage..." Colin laughed. "I heard a rumour someone wanted to use your soundtrack to force terrorists to talk. Unfortunately, it was deemed too cruel."

"Rats." Patrick finished the beer and belched loudly. "You'd think I'd get *some* money out of my singing."

"I think you have to be good at it first," Colin pointed out. "Bringing the house down isn't *always* a good thing."

"I should just have stuck with screaming swear words at the top of my voice while banging on the drums," Patrick said. "No one would have noticed."

Colin shrugged and stood. "Let's go," he said, as he paid for the drinks with his credit chip. "There must be something to *do* around here."

He sighed as they nodded to the waitress and left the pub. What had he *done* all day? He'd gone to school, he'd played football, he'd been in the CCF, he'd chased girls, he'd roamed the streets...he hadn't done much, had he? His world had been so *small*. He could have done more, if he'd known it was out there to do. And now...he shook his head as they started to walk. Liverpool was just too small for him now. He knew he wouldn't be coming back.

And Patrick...Patrick hadn't grown up at all. He was still the prat Colin remembered, the immature prat...it was funny how Colin hadn't seen it before. But then, Colin had been pretty damn immature himself.

"I've changed my mind," he said, as they headed down the streets. "Let's go to the maglev station. I have to get back to base."

"You're going?" Patrick belched, again. "Why?"

"It's time to go," Colin said. "Now."

CHAPTER FIVE

"WELCOME BACK, SIR," Commander Staci Templeton said. "It's like we never left."

Mitch smiled as he boarded HMS *Unicorn* for the first time. He'd spent the shuttle flight reading the files, which were as detailed as one could wish, but there was nothing like actually boarding the ship to determine how closely the reports matched reality. It was always hard to tell from the outside. Every ship had quirks of her own, issues that were never truly solved. *Unicorn* wasn't a completely non-standard design, but there were enough variances between her and a standard corvette for him to be concerned. He'd need to take her out on a shakedown cruise before he knew what his ship could *really* do.

"I have escaped from prison," he said, grandly. "The wardens kept me chained to the bed, locked in the room..."

"You were pretty badly injured," Staci pointed out. "We're lucky we didn't lose you."

"Yes, but..." Mitch shrugged. "I see you got a promotion too."

Staci tapped the stripe on her shoulder. "Vague promises were made about me getting the next corvette when she comes out of the yard," she said. "I'm supposed to learn everything I can from you in the next six months."

"Oh, dear," Mitch said. "Did they even realise you'd been my XO for the past year or so?"

"Probably not," Staci said. She grinned. "But then, you *were* in a ward for the last few months. You weren't in command of a ship."

"Don't remind me." Mitch glanced around the compartment. "Do you want to give me the tour?"

"Of course," Staci said. "If you'll follow me..."

Mitch slung his knapsack over his shoulder and followed her down the corridor. *Unicorn* followed the same basic design as *Pelican*, but there were a handful of tiny differences he made a mental note to check before he took the ship into action. He'd been so used to his previous command that he'd known her like the back of his hand. *Unicorn* was just different enough that he might injure himself if he ran through the ship without looking where he was going. It might seem the height of humour if he ran into a conduit and knocked himself out, but it would be utterly disastrous if he did it in the middle of a fight. He kept his eyes open as Staci showed him his cabin—small and cramped, but private—and then led him onto the bridge. Everything was fresh and new.

He glanced at Staci. "How's the crew?"

"A couple jumped ship, sad to say, and took transfers elsewhere," Staci said. "The remainder are in place, old and new alike. No real problems so far, save for a couple of crewmen who aren't used to life on a corvette. I've been running them through endless drills, all of which I've noted in the log. They've been getting better."

"Glad to hear it," Mitch said. A fleet carrier could afford to tolerate crewmen who slacked off, every once in a while. A corvette could not. She simply didn't have the manpower. "Anything I ought to know about?"

"Nothing too major," Staci said. "A handful of crewmen completed their additional training while you were in hospital. I've had crewmen practicing their shooting in their *copious* spare time. We should be ready to handle boarders if they risk invading the hull."

Mitch nodded, shortly. "Let's just hope we don't have to deploy boarding parties," he said. It had been dangerous enough before the war, according to the old sweats, but now it was impossible. Even hardened marines had trouble boarding infected starships. It was much safer to blow them away from a safe distance. "I assume you've been running counter-boarding drills too?"

"Yes, sir," Staci assured him. "We just don't have room to manoeuvre."

"But we do have a more coherent crew," Mitch countered. "They know what they're doing."

He sighed as he keyed his console, bringing up the system display. *Unicorn* was tiny, compared to a fleet carrier or battleship. A direct hit that wouldn't so much as scratch a battleship's paint would blow a corvette into atoms. His crew were experienced—he promised himself he'd spend time getting to know the newcomers, as well as reconnecting with the old hands—but there were limits. It was all too easy to get overwhelmed, if they had to do too many things at once. He switched to the near-space display and frowned as he saw *Lion*, holding station close to *Unicorn*. The missile-heavy battlecruiser looked as if someone had taken a corvette and scaled her up, past the boundaries of reason and sanity. *Lion* looked cool—the child in him thrilled to the sight of a ship that was neither crude nor hulking—but how well would she handle herself in combat?

I guess we'll find out, he thought. The concept seemed sound, and the scenarios he'd studied looked good, but he'd been in the navy long enough to know that nothing worked as well as the boffins claimed. The whole idea might prove worse than useless. *She does look ready for action.*

His lips quirked. Looks weren't everything, not in naval combat. Military warships simply couldn't afford the elegance of civilian designs. No one would ever call a fleet carrier *pretty*, even though they *did* have a certain charm. *Unicorn* was brutally functional, her hull designed for efficiency rather than looks. He smiled as he surveyed his ship's power curves, silently assessing her promise. She might be ugly, but there was a decent chance she was the fastest ship in space. Only a starfighter could outrun her, once she got her drives up, and a starfighter would run out of juice very quickly.

Staci kept talking, outlining everything she'd done since the transfer to *Unicorn*. Mitch listened carefully, trusting her to know what she was talking about. He was mildly surprised she'd been left under his command, particularly since *Pelican* had been scuttled. She should have been in line for promotion, if only because she *was* an experienced officer with no apparent ambition to move to larger ships. She deserved a corvette of her own.

An officer who stays with the corvettes might wind up in command well before his peers, he reminded himself. He'd once admitted, openly, that he'd gone into smaller ships because promotion tended to come quickly. There was far less competition amongst junior officers for coveted slots. *And Staci definitely deserves a command of her own.*

"And Captain Hammond has taken command of *Lion*," Staci finished. "I think he'd like you to call him as soon as reasonably possible."

"As soon as reasonably possible," Mitch repeated. "Do you think I could define *reasonably possible* as *next year*?"

Staci managed to look incredibly disapproving without quite crossing the line into open insubordination. "Are you sure it was a *prison* you escaped from?"

"I'm sure of it." Mitch grinned as he stood. "I'll make the call in my cabin, then...then we can explore the rest of the ship."

"Aye, sir," Staci said. "Good luck."

Mitch snorted and headed for the hatch. It rankled, more than he cared to admit, to be subordinate to another captain. One of the *other* reasons he'd gone into small ships was to be the sole commander, captain of his ship and master of his soul...he shook his head, telling himself not to be silly. Captain Hammond was senior to him. Protocol dictated he'd be in command of the small squadron, unless the Admiralty saw fit to put Mitch in command. It wasn't likely. Mitch didn't have the experience that would convince his superiors to put him ahead of an aristocratic officer with nearly ten years of seniority.

He scowled as he opened the hatch and stepped into his cabin. He'd spent his entire adult life in the navy, and he was proud to say his career was unblemished, but he wasn't part of the Old Boys Network and never would be. He'd had to fight for every last promotion, while watching helplessly as classmates with strong family connections were promoted over his head. It wasn't easy, sometimes, to watch...he knew it would have been a great deal harder, for him, if he'd stayed with the bigger ships. He shook his head, telling himself—again—that he loved corvettes. It was true, and he wouldn't trade *Unicorn* for *Lion*, but it was still frustrating. Too many talented officers were left behind, languishing in the ranks, because they lacked patrons in high places.

This isn't the time, he reminded himself as he sat at his desk. It was strikingly small, so tiny it felt as if it had been designed for a child. Mitch wasn't *that* big, but he was very definitely an adult. *There are more important things to worry about.*

He keyed his terminal, pressing his hand against the scanner to bring up his inbox. A hundred messages waited for him, ranging from follow-up medical appointments to missives from his last girlfriends. Mitch shook his head impatiently as he deleted them. He just wasn't ready to settle down, even though—as a naval officer—he was supposed to set a good example for the men. There might be strong social pressure to marry and have kids, but...he snorted, rudely. His career came first. Besides, he'd never met anyone he actually wanted to marry. He couldn't imagine spending the rest of his life with any of the girls he knew.

Putting the thought aside—and mentally noting a couple of messages that were actually important—he tapped a command into the console, opening a secure link to *Lion*. Captain Hammond would be notified at once, of course, but it might take some time for him to return to his ready room. Mitch would have been more concerned, he admitted privately, if Captain Hammond had answered immediately. A captain who spent all his time in his ready room was a man who wasn't on top of things. Or so he'd been told. A battleship was just too large for her commander to know *everything*.

Which is probably why battleships have the worst disciplinary issues in the fleet, he thought, with a hint of amusement. *He* knew everything about his ship...his *former* ship, at least. He'd been able to keep his finger on the crew's collective pulse, he'd been able to have a few words with officers and crew who were starting to slide off the straight and narrow...no battleship commander could hope to do it himself. *Their crews are divided into small tribes and...*

The terminal cleared. Mitch found himself looking at Captain Hammond. He looked older than Mitch had expected, his hair starting to grey. His face was all natural, without any hints of genetic engineering or cosmetic surgery. Mitch silently gave Hammond points for being comfortable in his own skin. He'd met too many aristos who had themselves shaped into living gods and goddesses, their bodies carved so perfectly they were almost parodies of themselves. Mitch had always figured it was a sign of deep-seated insecurity. It wasn't as if the aristos *needed* to be inhumanly beautiful.

"Captain Campbell," Captain Hammond said. His voice was classically aristocratic, with a hint of Sussex rather than London. "Congratulations on your promotion."

"And on your new command," Mitch said. He wondered, idly, what Captain Hammond made of him. A competent naval officer with a decent combat record or a jumped-up commoner with delusions of grandeur? Or something else? "I look forward to seeing what our ships can really do."

"As do I," Captain Hammond said. He sounded stilted, as if he wasn't quite sure what to make of Mitch and his ship. Mitch rather suspected Hammond looked down on smaller ships. Corvettes couldn't stand in the line of battle, but that didn't mean they were useless. "We'll start running drills as soon as our crews are up to speed."

Mitch nodded, feeling a flash of amusement mingled with pity. Captain Hammond had only *just* taken command of his ship. His record indicated he'd spent the last six months at the academy, trying to ensure the officer cadets learnt from his experiences. The poor man didn't *know* his ship or his crew, the chances were good he didn't know *any* of his subordinates personally. And he had to whip his ship into shape before the Admiralty started breathing down his neck and demanding results. It wasn't going to be easy.

He leaned forward. "I understand that you're in command of our joint squadron," he said, calmly. It was hard not to show a *little* resentment at the thought. "We're going to have to work hard to figure out how to operate as a team, depending on how things go."

"We'll be running simulations once *Lion* is ready to depart," Captain Hammond said. "I trust you can handle your own ship?"

"I know most of my crew," Mitch assured him. He was careful not to show his relief on his face. Some senior officers were so insecure they had no qualms about undermining the captain's authority on his own ship. It was never easy for a captain to handle an overbearing admiral. He had the legal authority to tell an admiral to mind his own business, but doing so would probably mean the end of his career. "The ones I don't know will fit in or be reassigned in the next couple of weeks."

Captain Hammond looked irked. "We have rough orders to be ready to depart in a month," he said. "But nothing too specific."

"Naturally," Mitch said. It was never easy to coordinate schedules, particularly when dealing with ships that had barely started their shakedown cruises. It was quite possible that something would go badly wrong, sending one or both of the ships back to the yard. "They don't know when we'll be truly ready to leave."

He leaned forward again. "With your permission, I'll get my ship ready for operational deployment as quickly as possible," he said. "I'd like to make sure I know what she can do before I take her into combat."

"We may not have the time," Captain Hammond warned. "I read a report suggesting the enemy will be making another thrust towards Earth in the next few months."

Mitch grimaced. Civilians talked of blocking the tramlines, of preventing enemy ships from jumping from one system to the next, but naval officers knew it was impossible. Mining the tramlines or establishing battlestations to monitor transits was a pipe dream. There was no reason the virus couldn't launch a major assault on Earth tomorrow, sneaking through the tramlines and remaining in stealth until they were within firing range. He felt his heart sink at the thought. The virus didn't seem quite so concerned about its rear areas, save for a handful of production nodes. It was quite possible the analysts were correct.

"Then we'd better be ready to meet them," he said. Earth was ringed by layer upon layer of orbital firepower—and the planet's surface was studded with ground-based defence systems—but he was all too aware it would be easy to sneak a handful of kinetic projectiles through the defences. "Or to give them a kick in the pants."

"Let us hope we can." Captain Hammond shrugged. "I'd appreciate it if you joined me for dinner in the next few days, once we know what we have to do to get our ships ready for combat."

"Of course," Mitch said. He kept his frustration off his face. "It would be my pleasure."

Captain Hammond smiled. "We'll arrange it nearer the time," he said. There was a bland note to his voice that suggested he didn't really mean it. "We both have a lot of work to do."

And you probably don't want to host the dinner, any more than I want to attend, Mitch thought. He needed to develop a working relationship with his superior, but—in his experience—formal dinner parties were never a good place to actually get to *know* someone properly. They tended to be tedious, with everyone pretending to be polite. *We should do something else if we want to get to know each other.*

"Until then," he said. "I'll keep you appraised."

"Likewise," Captain Hammond said. He raised a hand in dismissal. "Goodbye."

His image vanished. Mitch stared at the blank terminal for a long moment, trying to gather his thoughts. Captain Hammond didn't sound so bad, compared to some of the officers who'd developed dangerous habits in peacetime, but...it would take time for them to build a rapport. They were very different people, from very different backgrounds...it didn't help that they were on separate ships. Mitch considered it for a moment, then shook his head thoughtfully. It could have been worse. He'd met too many officers who didn't understand where the lines were drawn.

He stood, closing the terminal and heading for the hatch. There was no time to worry about it, not now. Reading between the lines, it sounded as if *Lion* had a long way to go before she was ready for deployment, but he knew better than to take that for granted. He wanted—he *needed—Unicorn* to be ready to go first. It would look good on his record, particularly if he had a head start. He'd look worse if he *didn't* have his ship ready to go when time finally ran out. The Admiralty would not be amused.

Hopefully, this will all work out, he thought, as he walked down the corridor. A pair of engineering techs stepped to one side to let him pass. One of them was an old hand, someone who'd transferred from *Pelican*; the other was a stranger. And *if it doesn't, it won't be through* my *lack of effort.*

CHAPTER SIX

"SO," GUNBOAT PILOT MARIGOLD HARKNESS SAID. "How was *your* vacation?"

"I think it's called shore leave," Tobias said, tiredly. He hadn't slept well. The barracks had been uncomfortable and the shuttle flight to Pitt Base had been worse. "We're in the navy now."

Marigold snorted. She'd been mildly chubby when they'd first met, back when they'd been recruited to fly gunboats, but six months of naval food and exercise had slimmed her and the other pilots down. Tobias felt a little ashamed of himself for noticing. He wasn't the sort of person who stared at girls; he wasn't the sort of person who hoped for a flash of bare skin or...he wasn't! And they'd spent the last six months in a place where privacy was a word no one seemed to understand. It hadn't been easy. He'd had issues about getting undressed in front of men, let alone women. It had to have been harder for her.

"My parents are still in denial," Marigold said. "How about yours?"

She's trying to be friendly, Tobias told himself, sharply. The gunboats were bigger than starfighters—they could hardly be smaller—but they weren't anything like big enough for him not to feel cramped. Their cabin was so small he felt as if he was in a large car, rather than a naval shuttle. *And you should be friendly too.*

"It felt as if I didn't belong there any longer," Tobias told her. "As if... it just wasn't my home."

"You've outgrown it," Marigold said. "I've been told it happens."

Tobias shrugged and peered out of the viewport. They were flying in convoy, the gunboats escorting the marine shuttles, but all he could see with the naked eye were unblinking stars burning in the darkness of space. He smiled at the thought, remembering ultra-dramatic movies and programs he'd watched as a young man. They'd had as little to do with reality as possible. The shuttles were out there—he could see them on his sensor display—but he couldn't see them with the naked eye. And the stars were barely moving, if indeed they were moving at all. The gunboat was rocketing through space at unimaginable speed, but by interplanetary standards she was barely *crawling.*

"It just felt weird," he admitted. "How about you?"

"My parents didn't have any real ambitions for me," Marigold said. "Or so they told me, right up until I joined the navy. And then they started saying I should get married and have kids like a *good* little girl."

"Ouch," Tobias said. He knew a little about what society expected—and how cruel society could be, to those who wanted to do something *else* with their lives. It was hard to believe Marigold had had it worse than him, but...he shook his head. It was cruel...it was always cruel, no matter who it happened to. "I'm sure you'd make some kid an excellent mother, but..."

Marigold gave him the finger. "Remove that foot from your mouth before we get to the ship," she said. She cleared her throat, loudly. "Did you read the mission briefing?"

"...Maybe." Tobias shrugged. "We're going on deployment..."

His heart clenched. He knew himself to be a coward. He'd been beaten up so often that it was hard to believe he could defend himself, that he could fight back, that...he swallowed, hard, as he looked at the weapons console. He'd fought, he'd killed...and yet, there was a strange disassociation between the icons on the display, the icons that vanished when he fired at them, and living people. It was hard to believe that the icons represented people with lives of their own. He'd killed hundreds, perhaps thousands, of infected people and yet he didn't believe it. Not really. It was hard to believe that he'd killed.

And yet, the prospect of his own death hurt. He stared down at the console without actually *seeing* it. He'd never done more than basic exercises, the kind of training his superiors had forced on him...he'd never so much as touched a pistol. The thought of slogging through the mud, of matching himself against the very best the enemy could provide, was alien. He'd done everything in his power to get out of PE. The idea of *willingly* exposing himself to more suffering...he shook his head. It wouldn't happen, not to him. Not to *them*. They were a good team. They wouldn't die.

"We'll be fine," he said, although he didn't believe it. "And we'll come back heroes."

"It could be worse," Marigold said. "We could be starfighter pilots."

"Yeah." Tobias had met a handful of starfighter pilots, back during basic training. He'd hated the cocky bastards with a passion until he'd looked at the statistics and realised that half the pilots he knew would probably die on their first engagement. Starfighter pilots knew, at a very basic level, that their lives could be cut short in an instant. "At least we have don't have any blind spots..."

He let his voice trail off. The gunboats could and did shoot in all directions. Their automated targeting systems could acquire a target and blow it to atoms quicker than any human could hope to react. And yet, it could not be denied that a gunboat was a bigger target than any starfighter, or that—when weighed against a capital ship—the gunboat was expendable. He'd spent weeks in the simulators. He knew the score. And yet, it was so much easier to sacrifice himself—to calmly accept he might be sacrificed—when there was nothing *truly* at risk. He wondered how Marigold took it so calmly. She had to know she might die at any second too.

"We'll be fine," Marigold said. "We go out there, we serve our term, then we go back to the academy and try to teach someone who looks *just* like us how not to get killed."

"I suppose," Tobias said. The console bleeped, warningly. They were approaching the outer edge of the yards. "You got the IFF code?"

"We'd be in deep shit if I didn't," Marigold pointed out. "Step down the sensors on my command."

Tobias nodded, feeling uncomfortably naked. The briefing officers had pointed out that the virus didn't play fair. It was quite possible for the virus to gain control of a ship and turn it against her former masters, using IFF codes—perfectly legitimate IFF codes—to get past the defences before opening fire. The ship would be targeted at once, of course, but she'd have a chance to do a great deal of damage before she was blown away. There'd be no hesitation, the officers had warned, if the gunboats so much as *looked* suspicious. The shipyard defences would blow them away before they had a chance to explain themselves.

"Ready," he said. He peered into the inky darkness. Was there something moving out there? A light that wasn't a star? It was hard to be sure. "I'm ready."

He felt his heart clench, again, as the console lit up with red icons. They were being scanned—and targeted. There were all sorts of horror stories about blue-on-blue incidents, where someone was hurt or killed by friendly fire...there was no such thing, the instructors had said, as friendly fire. A plasma bolt had no IFF, they'd warned, so watch where you fired it. Only the sheer immensity of space, even in a relatively small engagement zone, limited the risks of friendly fire.

And plasma bolts are never that accurate, he reminded himself. *Someone might not mean to fire on us, but that won't keep them from hitting us.*

The display turned green. "We're clear," he said. "Set course for *Lion*."

He leaned forward, watching intently as the battlecruiser finally came into view. He'd never really *wanted* to join the military. Survey Command had been the only section that had really interested him and Survey had been folded into the regular military for the duration. And besides...what could he have done? In hindsight, there were a lot of things he could have done to prepare for a career, but he hadn't known what he needed at the time. He'd pinned his hopes on going to university and it hadn't really materialised.

Adventure is someone else in deep shit far away, he recalled. One of his tutors had said as much, when he'd been asked about his military service. *All the books and films and whatever completely fail to convey the truth of the military life.*

"Impressive," Marigold breathed. "Isn't she?"

Tobias nodded, not trusting himself to speak. *Lion* was...striking, definitely. The console bleeped as the shuttles peeled off, heading for the lower hatches while the gunboats flew towards the gunboat ring. Tobias had his doubts about the design—the simulations had suggested the gunboat ring could be easily crippled, if the enemy realised what it was—but there was no helping it. The gunboats couldn't use a standard flight deck. Besides, they could dock the gunboats with the regular airlocks if necessary. He keyed the console, bracing himself as they glided closer. The instructors had been very patient with simulated mistakes, but he doubted Captain Hammond or Colonel Richard Bagehot—the Gunboat CAG—would be anything like so tolerant. Banging a gunboat into a starship's hull was probably not going to please her commander.

"Airlock online," he said. "Datalink established...docking in five..."

"Linking now," Marigold said. She'd argued they could automate the whole process, but the more experienced officers had overruled her. "Linking..."

A low *thud* echoed through the gunboat. The gravity field seemed to grow stronger, just for a second. Tobias felt his head spin. It was hard, sometimes, to comprehend how gravity fields curved in space. It might have been easier to operate in zero-g, but the health risks made it prohibitive. He'd seen some of the asteroid-born. They looked so thin and willowy that it was hard to believe they could survive in a low-g field, let alone on Earth. The hatch hissed open, but he ignored it. They had to power down the gunboat before they boarded the battlecruiser.

"All systems check out," he said, running his hand down the console.

"Main power going offline, secondary power drawing from mothership."

"Confirmed," Marigold said. "Datalink established, all A-OK."

Tobias stood, picked up his knapsack and headed for the hatch. The gravity field seemed to shimmer, very slightly, as he stepped into the battleship. He wasn't sure if he was imagining it. His stomach felt light, almost uneasy. It was hard not to feel as though he was completely and totally out of place. *Lion* wasn't the first starship he'd visited, but she was the first true *warship*. The low thrumming echoing through the hull was a grim reminder they were on the verge of going into war. He felt queasy. He didn't want to go.

You made your choice, he told himself, as Marigold joined him outside. *It's too late to back out now.*

They walked down the corridor and stopped in front of an airlock. The hatch hissed open, revealing a second hatch and a bioscanner. Tobias winced as he put his hand against the scanner, feeling a pinch as the sampler tested his blood. He'd been told, in no uncertain terms, that the slightest *hint* of infection would result in the outside compartments being depressurised until medics could arrive to collect him for inspection and treatment. Cold logic told him there was no choice, but he couldn't help feeling as though it was terrifyingly unfair. No one *asked* to get infected. No one *willingly* exposed themselves to the virus.

There's umpteen billion people in the human sphere, he thought, sourly. *And some of them are crazy enough to want anything.*

The inner hatch hissed open as soon as Marigold's blood was checked and confirmed free of infection. Tobias breathed a sigh of relief, then led the way into the inner compartment. It felt shiny and new, yet utterly soulless. Gunboat Country was bigger than the barracks at the academy, but… he caught himself before he started moaning. There were limits to how much space could be assigned to him and his comrades. Even the colonel had to bed down with his men.

"The washrooms are in there, if you want to freshen up," Bagehot called. He was standing by the briefing compartment, reading a datapad. "Choose your bunks or have them chosen for you."

Tobias nodded and hurried into the sleeping compartments. It was definitely larger than the barracks on the moon, but still...he shook his head and picked a bunk, dropping his knapsack on the blankets. It would be safe there, he knew. One definite advantage the navy had over school was that the rules were very definitely enforced. Someone who stole from another officer or crewman would be in very deep shit indeed. Marigold claimed the bunk next to him, then headed for the washroom. Tobias sighed and followed her.

The compartment started to fill up as he splashed water on his face, checked his appearance in the mirror and headed for the briefing compartment. He'd never really cared about his looks—or so he'd told himself—but the navy had insisted on personal grooming. So had the Beast, he supposed, but the Beast had been a...beast. Tobias had a private suspicion the key to looking good was to note what the headmaster did, then do the opposite. It made as much sense as anything else in the school.

You're out of it now, he told himself, sharply. The Beast was in the past. He needed to look to the future. *You don't need to keep dwelling on it.*

"Welcome," Bagehot said, once the entire squadron was assembled. Twenty-four young men and women, assigned to twelve gunboats. "This is, to all intents and purposes, your first cruise. Unfortunately, it is also very experimental."

Tobias nodded. The entire gunboat *concept* was experimental. It was why the navy had recruited him and his fellows as...he wasn't quite sure *what* they were. They were naval personnel and yet they weren't *quite* naval personnel. Tobias figured the navy wasn't sure what it wanted to do with them, not yet. The gunboat squadrons had been allowed a quite astonishing amount of latitude, compared to the regular navy, but that would probably change once they worked out some answers. He wondered, idly, if it would matter that much to him. Perhaps if he stayed in the navy...

"We'll be spending the next month drilling," Bagehot continued. "Your time will be divided between the simulators, live-fire exercises and your bunks. You might *just* have time to cram a ration bar or two down your throats, when you have a free moment. Hopefully, we'll work out the kinks before we have to actually take the gunboats into battle."

Tobias smiled as a handful of chuckles echoed around the chamber. Navy food wasn't bad. He didn't understand why the more experienced personnel kept complaining about it. He'd had worse at school. Sure, the food was a little bland, but there was plenty of it. Maybe he was missing something.

"Things will be different," Bagehot warned. "You're on a warship now. I strongly advise you to stay in Gunboat Country, unless you're on the gunboats or invited out of the compartment. If someone invites you, that's fine; if not, stay here. You don't want to get in someone's way. The crew outside"—he waved a hand at the bulkhead—"are working their asses off to get *Lion* ready for deployment. They don't need you running around, gawking at them."

"So I can't take a selfie of myself in the command chair?" Tammy Hedge had acquired a reputation as a joker from the moment he'd joined the squadron. His jokes were often silly, but bearable. "I promised my father I'd send him a picture..."

"No," Bagehot said, sharply. He didn't like repeating himself. "Stay in the compartment, unless you're invited out. You do *not* want to run afoul of the captain."

Tobias nodded. He was no expert on naval regulations or interstellar law, but he'd been forced to sit through a couple of classes on the basics. The captain had immense authority over his crew, with only a handful of limits on his behaviour. In theory, the crew could refuse certain orders, but in practice it wasn't clear how far that right actually went. The precedents were a little confusing. It was possible that officers who refused an illegal order would be commended, condemned or some combination of the two. The legalities baffled him. The classes had certainly discouraged him from ever going into law.

"You need to be aware that this is a full-fledged capital ship," Bagehot continued. His eyes swept the compartment. "The captain will have far less patience with you—and tolerance for you—than any of your instructors back home. The ship itself is divided into tribes—command crew, engineering, medics, marines—and while they're all meant to be pulling in the same direction, it cannot be denied that rivalry is rife. I want you to stay out of it as much as possible. The gunboat squadron is new and untested. I do not want you to ruin it by picking fights with anyone else."

"As if we would," Tobias muttered to Marigold.

Bagehot had very sharp hearing. "Glad to hear it," he said. He made a show of consulting his watch as Tobias reddened and the rest of the squadron tittered. "Now, we're heading for the simulators. Remember, you have to treat them as though they are real. Next time, it might well be."

Tobias felt sick. "Yes, sir."

CHAPTER SEVEN

"WAKE UP!"

Colin jerked awake, suddenly unsure of where he was. Five months of training, then a month on deployment had taught him to catch up on his sleep whenever he could, but...he forced himself to stand as his memory caught up. He was on a shuttle, heading to *Lion*...no, the shuttle had *reached* the battlecruiser. The old sweats wouldn't have woken him if there was nothing to do.

He glanced from side to side, noting the remainder of his fire team. Their hands reached for their weapons before they stopped themselves, a grim reminder of patrols on the wrong side of the Security Zone. Colin had no idea who'd come up with the expression "no peace beyond the line," but it suited the Security Zone perfectly. The old sweats said it had been a nightmare before the virus established itself, a haven for religious fanatics, terrorists and criminal rings that had been almost completely lawless. The handful of refugee camps had had to be heavily guarded, just to keep one or more of the factions from gaining control or targeting them for destruction. Now...the virus had turned vast swathes of the population into deadly threats, sending them crashing against the defence lines in a bid to break into the civilised zones. It had been a hellish nightmare.

A low *thump* echoed through the shuttle. He stumbled to his feet, feeling as though he hadn't slept at all. The last night on Earth had been pathetic. He wasn't sure why—he'd had no trouble finding a bedmate for the night—but he couldn't deny it. The woman had screamed at him when he'd paid her for her time...he shook his head in irritation. He wasn't sure what he'd really wanted, let alone what *she'd* wanted. Perhaps he'd simply drunk too much. His throat felt parched and dry, suggesting he hadn't drunk *enough*. He made a mental note to drink more water as soon as they were in Marine Country.

"Form up." Sergeant Ron Bowman's voice echoed through the air. "Prepare to disembark."

The hatch hissed open. Colin watched the sergeant lead the way into the battlecruiser, then followed him. The air smelt funny, reminding him of the first and only time he'd sat in a new car. A handful of his friends could drive, but the combination of heavy taxes and rationing ensured they couldn't afford new vehicles. The tanks, lorries and jeeps he'd encountered during basic training had been worse, many so badly outdated they were older than he was. The military got the good stuff, he'd been told, but most of the good stuff went to the front lines.

He felt his heart start to pound as they marched down the corridor and into Marine Country. The naval crewmen stepped aside to let them pass, studying them with a combination of interest, dispassion and scorn. Colin nodded to himself, remembering what the older and more experienced men had said. The marines weren't *always* welcome on ships, at least until they proved themselves useful. They were regarded about as kindly as the marines regarded the redcaps. The thought made him want to roll his eyes—he didn't want to be a policeman, perish the thought—but he supposed it made a certain kind of sense. They *were* the shipboard police. If the crew got out of hand, it was the marines who'd have to deal with it.

And then the captain and senior staff will be in hot water, he thought. He couldn't recall if there'd ever been a mutiny on a naval vessel, at least since the Troubles, but he doubted a captain who'd lost control to the point the marines had to be called in would be trusted with another command. *They'd probably bend over backwards to avoid things getting so badly out of hand.*

He put the thought aside as they swept into Marine Country and split up to drop their rucksacks in the barracks. The bunks were about as much as he'd expected, although better—infinitely better—than sleeping in the great outdoors or standing on guard outside a military base in the middle of nowhere. The virus had a habit of infecting large dogs and sending them against the defences, just—he thought—to be unpleasant. Thankfully, the virus didn't seem to be capable of mimicking canine behaviour. The troops had orders to shoot any animals that seemed to be acting suspiciously. Better to shoot first and ask questions later than risk being bitten and infected instead.

The fire team followed him, three men...all as green as himself. Colin wasn't sure if his promotion was a compliment or a test to see how well he handled command under fire. The Royal Marines were short on experienced manpower—the draft hadn't yielded as many willing recruits as the higher-ups had hoped—but they weren't *that* short. He'd been warned he could be busted back to private at a moment's notice, if he screwed up. It wasn't a pleasant thought. He would almost have preferred not to be promoted.

Of course, if you refuse promotion, you'll never be offered another, he thought, as he hurried into the briefing room. The entire company was assembling, senior officers speaking quietly amongst themselves as their subordinates took their seats. There was less room for formality onboard ship, he'd been told. He had a feeling that had its limits. *Woe to the marine who forgets to salute an officer.*

He allowed his eyes to roam the compartment. It was bare, the bulkhead unmarred by maps or charts or anything else he'd seen on Earth. A single holographic projector sat in front of the podium, deactivated. He guessed they didn't have a specific mission yet, for better or worse. The briefing notes hadn't been clear, and there were a lot of details that were very definitely above his pay grade, but *Lion* was an experimental design. Assignment to her was something that would make or break his career... probably. He snorted at himself a moment later. He was a corporal, only a step or two above private. He couldn't be blamed for anything unless he screwed up spectacularly.

Major Chuck Craig stepped up to the podium. The marines straightened to attention. Craig had been in a dozen major engagements over the past five years, from boarding enemy starships to establishing evacuation camps and holding the line long enough for the navy to pull the evacuees—and the marines—out of the fire. He was a short, wiry man with curly dark hair and an air of calm confidence that put Colin at ease. The Major knew what he was doing. It was more than could be said for many of the pen-pushers he'd met over the years.

And the Beast, Colin thought. He'd had mixed feelings about the headmaster, but...he'd spent enough time in the military to question the man's credentials. It wasn't something he could put his finger on, yet...the headmaster just hadn't had the right vibe. He'd never been understanding, never compassionate, never...willing to let someone go, if they weren't up to it. *Did he really know what he was doing?*

"At ease." The major's eyes swept the room. "This regiment was thrown together at very short notice. As is always the case, there was a sudden requirement for troops and the units *intended* to serve on *Lion* were assigned elsewhere. This unit, therefore, was put together from a number of other units that have never served together before. You may have noticed."

Colin nodded, wincing inwardly. Ideally, he would have been the sole FNG in a platoon or even a company. The old hands could have ridden him hard, testing his mettle until they knew what he was made of. Instead...he tried to look from side to side without making it obvious. There were a dozen unfamiliar faces within view, marines drawn from other units or released from hospital or...or something. He didn't know, but he was starting to feel he was looking at the start of a major headache. The recruiting sergeant had claimed that bootnecks were interchangeable, that a marine could move from unit to unit without any problem at all; Colin knew, from grim experience, that was nonsense. If nothing else, it would take time for the newcomer to fit in. No one would trust a newcomer unless they had no other choice.

"We will therefore be drilling extensively," Craig continued. "I know some of you are new and inexperienced, while others have only just returned to the military. I don't care. I expect you to learn to work together before the enemy starts shooting at us. We're going to be working endlessly, until we know what we're doing. And then we're going to make the country proud."

He paused. "First assignments are as follows..."

Colin nodded to himself. It wasn't going to be fun, except...it might be, once they worked out the early headaches. And then, who knew?

Time to get started, he thought, as they were dismissed. *Better to get the mistakes out of the way before someone actually starts trying to kill us.*

Thomas stood by the hatch and waited, trying not to feel impatient, as the shuttle docked on the far side. Royal Navy protocol insisted that a captain greet an equal or superior officer in person, but that a junior officer should be met by the XO and escorted to the captain's office in recognition of his junior rank. Thomas had been unsure precisely how to meet Captain Campbell, as they shared the same rank even though Thomas had seniority. He'd decided, finally, to meet the younger man in person. It wasn't as if he commanded an entire fleet as well as his starship.

The hatch hissed open. Thomas straightened as Captain Campbell disembarked, saluting the flag before saluting Thomas himself. Thomas returned the salute, then held out a hand as he studied the other man. Mitch Campbell was not classically handsome, he decided, but he had a certain charm that suggested he'd have no problem finding female company. He was tall and gangly, with floppy brown hair and brown eyes that looked as if they could turn from charm to ice within seconds. Campbell was one of the younger commanding officers in the navy, Thomas recalled, although he hadn't beaten the record. *That* had been set by someone with more patronage than common sense.

"Captain Hammond," Campbell said. If he was surprised Thomas had met him in person, he didn't show it. "Thank you for inviting me."

"Welcome onboard," Thomas said. "It's good to meet you at last."

"Likewise," Campbell said. His voice was calm, but there was an edge to it that suggested he wasn't being entirely honest. "I read your file with some interest."

Thomas nodded. "And yours," he said. It was easy to see why the admiral regarded Campbell as a fire-eater. He was brave and bold and lucky, dashing enough to be a movie star...but, sooner or later, luck ran out. "I wouldn't have risked charging into the teeth of enemy fire."

"That's why it worked," Campbell said. "The virus didn't expect it either."

"I never thought it cared that much about tactics," Thomas said. He turned and led the way up to his Ready Room. "Do you think it does?"

"It's hard to say." Campbell sounded thoughtful. "It's true enough, I think, that it prefers to study logistics over tactics. It doesn't seem to show the same flair that many human and alien naval tacticians do. And its thinking is completely alien, to the point it might be using tactics we simply don't recognise as tactics. And it's so powerful..."

He coughed. "It's so powerful, and numerous, that it might not think it *needs* tactics," he added. "It's a single entity, in a sense. It doesn't need to be clever. It just needs to bring overwhelming force to bear on us."

"It's facing us and our allies," Thomas pointed out. He opened the hatch and led the way into the Ready Room. "We might be the single greatest threat it has ever faced."

"There's no way to know," Campbell countered. "We just don't know."

Thomas motioned for Campbell to take a seat at the table. He would have preferred a proper dining compartment, but *Lion* was too small and new to have one. It was something he'd consider later, he told himself firmly. The ship wasn't designed as an admiral's flagship, charged with hosting conferences and diplomatic dinners as well as a tactical staff. That might have to change, if the navy decided to build an entire squadron of battlecruisers...he shook his head as he picked up the bottle of chilled wine. The first step was proving the concept actually worked. After that, they could worry about everything else.

"We should be ready to depart as planned," he said. "Unless we run into something that throws us back a few days."

"*Unicorn* is in excellent condition," Campbell said. "I intend to ramp up the drive tomorrow and cruise around the shipyards, before I start testing everything and running live-fire drills."

"That's good to hear," Thomas said. It was, but it was also a little irritating. "*Lion* needs more time to check and recheck everything before we're ready to start proper drills."

"It's always the case." Campbell took the glass of wine and sniffed it thoughtfully. "Every year, things cost more and take longer."

He put the glass to one side and leaned forward. "Have you given any thought to tactics yet?"

"Not enough," Thomas said. "I've studied the simulated engagements, naturally, but a lot of the tactics might not work anything like so well in real life. I think there'd be all sorts of issues. The missiles, for example, might not be as clever as the designers have claimed. Our drives and stealth units might not be as capable..."

"We ran basic power curve tests on our drives," Campbell said. "They should live up to the claims."

Thomas felt a flicker of irritation. "We need to test everything," he said. "And then we can go out looking for trouble."

"If we have time to test everything," Campbell said. "Reading between the lines, the war isn't going well."

"It looks that way," Thomas agreed. He took a sip of his wine. Expensive, but good. "We won't win the war single-handedly. We have to get used to what we've got and figure out how to use it before we go into battle."

"If we have time," Campbell repeated. "We cannot let the virus push any closer to Earth."

"And if we show the virus what we're planning, it will have time to develop countermeasures," Thomas pointed out, sharply. "We have to surprise it, once."

"And make sure we take out its flicker network," Campbell said. "Does it even *have* a flicker network?"

"It knows to take ours out, so I dare say it does," Thomas said. "I suppose an entity that depended on remaining in close communication with itself would know the importance of hindering the enemy's command and control systems, if not taking them out completely."

"It doesn't try to jam our communications as much as you might expect," Campbell said. He shrugged, expressively. "There are limits to how far you can jam signals, particularly when we're using lasers to bind the datanet together, but it could do a great deal more if it wanted. Even a little signals distortion would be enough to *really* confuse us."

"Not for long," Thomas countered. "Bare seconds, if that."

"Long enough to let the virus slip a missile through our defences," Campbell said. "We have to assume the worst."

"Yes," Thomas agreed. "But we have to give the virus a surprise, and we have to make it *count.*"

"And quickly," Campbell said. "Or it will be completely meaningless."

Thomas couldn't disagree. The admiral's words hung in his ears. Humanity and her allies were steadily losing the war. The virus was soaking up losses as it ground ever closer to Earth, sending a seemingly-endless stream of brainships, battleships, carriers and starfighters against the defences. It was only a matter of time before it punched into Sol and forced the human navies to make a grim choice between retreating to save the remainder of the human sphere—for a few short months, perhaps—or dying in defence of the homeworld. He'd heard rumours about plans to flee into unexplored space, to set up hidden colonies on the far side of distant tramlines, to work in secret until the boffins came up with a wonder weapon that would take the virus out in a single shot. He doubted the rumours were anything more than wishful thinking. The Royal Navy—and all the other navies—had to devote every last scrap of resources to keeping the virus away. There was little left for setting up a hidden colony that might—might—last long enough to rebuild and take the fight back to the virus.

"We can do it," Thomas said. It was important to project confidence, even if one didn't feel it. "Once we work the kinks out of the system."

He keyed his wristcom, summoning the steward to bring the meal. "And now we have to talk about something else," he said. He didn't have much time to get to know his new subordinate. He was damned if he was spending the entire meal talking shop. "Who do you think will win the World Cup?"

Campbell laughed. "I honestly have no idea," he said, as the steward entered. "Does it matter right now?"

"Probably not," Thomas said. They shared a smile. "Perhaps I should talk about the weather instead."

CHAPTER EIGHT

"IT'S BEEN THREE WEEKS," Lady Charlotte, his wife, said. "Can't you get even a *day* of leave?"

Thomas winced, inwardly, as he stared at the viewscreen. He'd had no trouble getting leave when he'd been at the academy, although there had been times when he'd claimed pressing business to *keep* from taking leave. He loved his wife, as much as a person of his class *could* love the woman who'd been steered towards him by both sets of parents, but he found her focus on social events more than a little tiresome. The aristocracy might claim that a constant round of garden parties, fancy balls and glittering weddings helped to boost public morale, yet Thomas considered it nothing more than a sick joke. The general public had far more pressing concerns than watching as the Lord of Somewhere married the Lady of Somewhere Else in a ceremony that cost as much as a small starship.

He studied his wife, tiredly. Lady Charlotte was still lovely, despite two teenage daughters. Her curly dark hair framed a round face with an elegant smile, the result of good breeding rather than genetic or cosmetic manipulation. She was very far from stupid—she managed the estates while he served his country—but they had less in common than he might have hoped. He couldn't talk to her about naval matters, any more than she could talk to him about High Society. Thankfully, they'd both been adults who'd known the score. They'd worked out how to live together long ago.

"I'm afraid leave is out of the question," he said, bluntly. There was no point in raising her hopes, only to dash them in the next few days. The deadline for departure was drawing ever closer. The Admiralty would ask questions if *Lion* wasn't ready to depart as planned. They might understand delays caused by a sudden glitch in the datanet, or a flaw in the design that wasn't apparent until the ship was powered up, but they'd be merciless if they thought he was neglecting his duty. "I have too much work to do."

"I can speak to my uncle, have him send you to Earth for a couple of days," Lady Charlotte insisted. "It's quite important you attend the party. Elizabeth is meeting her future husband and..."

Thomas held up a hand. "Elizabeth hasn't agreed to marry him," he pointed out. "And you really shouldn't push her into anything."

"He's a good catch," Lady Charlotte insisted. "And it's only a matter of time until someone else snaps him up."

"Elizabeth is old enough to have *opinions* on the subject," Thomas said. "And the more you promote him, the more she'll resist the thought of marrying him."

He rubbed his forehead in irritation. Lady Charlotte had turned her attention to matchmaking as her daughters reached their majorities, arranging dances for them and their peers so they could meet suitable young men under controlled circumstances. Thomas suspected she'd forgotten what it was like to be a young woman. The idea of marrying someone your parents liked...he shook his head. It had taken him years to get used to the concept of marrying for the family, rather than marrying for himself. His daughter was old enough to resent the system, without understanding why it was necessary. She didn't *have* to get married in the next year or so. Lady Charlotte just wanted to be mother of the bride for a day.

"The fact remains, there is a shortage of candidates," Lady Charlotte said. "Thomas, I understand your concern, but..."

"There is nothing more likely to sour your relationship with your daughter than throwing her at a young man she doesn't want," Thomas said.

They'd had the argument before, time and time again. He agreed it was important for his daughters to marry well, but they had different ideas of what sort of men they should marry. Titles weren't everything. For every aristocrat who served his country bravely, there were a dozen fools gracing the tabloid websites. "Let her grow up a little before you start suggesting she gets married."

"Hah." Lady Charlotte didn't sound convinced. "And how old was I when I got married?"

"Twenty-five," Thomas said. "Elizabeth has time. Plenty of time."

"Not enough," Lady Charlotte said. "What happens if her young man dies in combat?"

Thomas sighed. "It doesn't matter," he said. "She needs time to grow and develop before she takes her next step into adulthood."

"We'll see," Lady Charlotte said, in a tone that indicated the matter was far from settled. "On a different note, I hope you'll be attending the Christmas Ball..."

"I honestly don't know," Thomas said. It was his duty to host a ball, in the run-up to Christmas, but the navy came first. "It depends on where the navy sends me."

"You could always resign," Lady Charlotte pointed out. "There's a seat up for grabs in parliament. You could run for it as a *bona fide* war hero and patriot..."

"And drive you mad, moping around the hall all the time." Thomas grinned. He'd heard enough horror stories about men who'd resigned their commissions, then discovered—too late—that remaining at home wasn't always a good thing. Besides, if he ran for parliament, someone would notice he'd resigned and make an issue of it. "Charlie, I have my duty. I cannot leave at a whim."

"I know." Lady Charlotte softened, slightly. "Thomas, I don't ask for much..."

"I know," Thomas echoed. "But I can't come home whenever the fancy takes me."

"I'll give the families your regards," Lady Charlotte said. "And let them know we'll be hosting a party at short notice when you *do* come home."

Thomas winced. The aristocracy's private schedule of social events was painstakingly worked out months or years in advance. Someone hosting a party at short notice would throw the entire season out of alignment. There would be arguments and fights and petty feuds over balls being rearranged, or cancelled, or having their guests sucked away by another party…he felt a twinge of sympathy for anyone who lost out because their social superior had ruined their plans. The aristocracy was practically *dominated* by feuds that had lasted so long everyone had forgotten the original cause, if only because everyone involved was dead. He had no intention of playing the game himself. It was petty, pointless and ultimately self-destructive.

Which is something you can only say because you're so high up the tree you don't need to worry about it, he thought. *Your daughter could marry a talented commoner and no one would say boo to you.*

"It depends," he said. "I honestly don't know what'll happen."

His terminal bleeped, reminding him he had a meeting. "Charlie, I'll talk to you later," he said. "Pray for me."

Lady Charlotte looked thoroughly displeased, but nodded. "Good luck," she said, curtly. "I'll see you when you get home."

Thomas let out a breath as his wife's image vanished. He loved his wife, really he did, but she could be a little overbearing. He knew she was trying to help, yet…he shook his head in frustration. He'd tried to explain to her, time and time again, that she wasn't *really* helping, but she was too full of herself to care. If she'd directed her energy towards a naval career, or politics, she'd be commanding a fleet or running the country by now. Thomas's lips quirked at the thought. Lady Charlotte had always been more interested in subtle power, in building up a network of influence and patronage, than formal power. It was safer to be the power behind the throne than the person sitting on it.

The buzzer sounded. Thomas tapped his terminal, opening the hatch. Commander Donker and Major Chuck Craig stepped into the compartment, the hatch hissing closed behind them. They looked as tired as Thomas felt, after three weeks of intensive preparation. Thomas wasn't sure when either of them had last got more than a few hours of sleep, although logic told him they must have done. Stimulants were banned outside emergencies and, even then, regarded as the final resort. The steward entered, bringing a tray of strong coffee. Thomas motioned for his subordinates to sit down, closing the terminal to make it clear they had his full attention. They wouldn't be disturbed, unless it was a *real* emergency. Or a priority-one message from the Admiralty.

And that would mean the home system has come under attack, Thomas thought. *Lion* had her missiles now, as well as her gunboats; in theory, she could join the defenders and fight to protect the system. In practice, he wasn't so sure. They hadn't had time to carry out any live-fire tests. *We might not be able to take part in the fighting. Not yet.*

"Captain," Commander Donker said. "We just completed the formal survey of the entire starship. I am pleased and relieved to report that all stations and systems are functioning as intended. We still need to smooth off some of the rougher edges, but we can only do that when we leave the shipyard and set out on our first cruise."

Thomas nodded, feeling a flicker of relief. "Do we have any major issues of concern?"

"Not any longer," Donker assured him. "We powered up everything, from the drive nodes and fusion cores to tactical sensors and missile tubes. Our only *real* point of concern is maintaining the tactical net when warheads start popping and enemy ECM starts trying to wear us down, but simulations suggest we can handle it. We won't know for sure until we face the enemy ourselves."

"Unfortunately." Thomas had studied the reports very carefully. "We won't know how capable the system *really* is until we have to use it."

He let out a breath. The datanet was supposed to bind the battlecruiser to her gunboats, no matter how much the enemy tried to jam the system and isolate the smaller ships. In theory, the network was impossible to take down unless *Lion* herself was taken out. In practice…no one was *really* sure. It was dangerous to rely on communications lasers linking a battlecruiser to a handful of small and very fast-moving gunboats, particularly when the smaller craft would be manoeuvring randomly. A gunboat that flew in a straight line, on a predictable course, was just *asking* to be blown out of space.

"We'll test the system as much as possible, once we're underway," he said. They might have time for war games, to pit themselves against real starships and real sensor crews, but there had been a note of urgency in the last missives from Earth. It was starting to look as though they'd be going into combat sooner rather than later. "How about the crew?"

"The good news is that morale is relatively high," Donker said. "The departmental heads all agree that their departments are ready for action, thanks to the constant drills. *Lion* is no longer an unknown factor to them, which helps. They know her from bow to stern now, sir, and feel confident they understand their role within the crew."

Thomas nodded. He'd spent two of the last three weeks crawling over his ship, catching up with the departmental heads and exploring every last inch of the maintenance tubes. It had been an interesting, informative and sometimes amusing experience, particularly when the engineers had discovered a stash of chocolate bars left behind by one of the yard-dogs. They hadn't been expensive, but—thanks to rationing—they'd been rare. The poor owner had probably left his entire allotment in the niche and forgotten to reclaim it before being reassigned. Thomas was silently relieved it hadn't been porn. *That* would have been a great deal worse for all concerned.

"The bad news is that the constant drills are starting to wear down readiness," Donker added. "Frankly, sir, we've probably pushed too hard in the last few days. The emergency drills constantly leave out the emergency itself, which means we're starting to amble through them when we should be taking them seriously."

"Which isn't easy when you know there's no *real* emergency," Thomas said. "Major?"

Major Craig nodded. "The problem with crying wolf, sir, is that people eventually stop paying attention. Sure, we can vary the drills—boarders one day, missile strikes the next—but there are limits. My men have the same problem, even though we have the advantage of VR sims and suchlike. It helps we're playing against each other."

"Which isn't really possible for the tactical staff," Donker put in. "The best we've been able to do is pit ourselves against *Unicorn's* tactical staff, or run tracking and targeting exercises on the gunboats, but neither are particularly useful past a certain point. They're just too different from us."

"You'd think we could arrange a simulated exercise with another ship and crew," Thomas said, tiredly. "There has to be *someone* who'll play with us."

"The other ships in the yard aren't ready to carry out tactical exercises with anyone," Donker said. "Half of them don't even have tactical crews, not yet."

"Perhaps we can set up a direct link to the tactical staff on Nelson Base or Luna," Thomas said. "It won't be perfect, but we can work with it."

He took a sip of his coffee. The simulations served a purpose, but they tended to become predictable after a while. The computer-generated enemies simply didn't have the spontaneity of *human* opponents. It was easy enough to scale up the enemy rate of fire, or their acceleration curves, or everything else to make the training as hard as possible, but a great deal harder to account for the unpredictability of combat. An intelligent opponent might do something crazy, or something that *seemed* crazy. It was impossible to be *sure* what'd look reasonable to someone on the other side of the battlefield.

"Yes, sir," Donker said. "I'll try to arrange it, but right now I think we should be scaling back on the exercises. We're starting to pick up bad habits."

"Perhaps it's time to bring back pain suits," Major Craig joked. "If they get hurt for each and every mistake, sir, they'd be less likely to repeat them."

"The idea is to learn from their mistakes," Donker pointed out. "They have to be willing to discuss them openly, if any learning is to be done."

Thomas shrugged. "We're learning as we go along," he said. He'd already written several reports based on his observations, suggesting everything from slight changes to the starship's design to prospective tactical doctrines for her deployment. "What about the gunboat crews?"

"We've been treating them as starfighter pilots," Donker said. "That might have been a mistake. Given the way they were recruited...well, they have less polish, even now, than a cadet who's had a week or two of training. They're pretty damned sloppy, sir; they barely know how to salute, let alone how to take care of themselves in space. And there are limits to how far we can correct them."

"Ouch," Thomas said. Civilians got a great deal of leeway, if only because they simply didn't understand their environment, but the gunboat pilots were military personnel. In theory. He wasn't entirely convinced he *liked* the idea of recruiting expendable pilots, but...he shook his head. The pilots knew the risks. "How are their piloting skills?"

"Good, in simulators," Donker said. "To be fair, they did have one engagement four months ago. They performed well. But they caught the enemy by surprise. Next time, it might not be so easy. We've run simulations where the enemy doesn't know what's coming and simulations where they do. In the latter, the gunboats take heavy losses for relatively little gain."

"We can work on their deportment later, then," Thomas said. "God knows, we've been making allowances for starfighter pilots for *decades*."

"It will cause some resentment, sir," Craig warned. "The gunboat pilots have even less seasoning than a maggot."

"The crew will just have to live with it," Thomas said. "How about your department?"

"Like everyone else, we've been running endless drills and exercises," Craig said. "There have been more problems than usual, sir, as the company was thrown together at very short notice."

"*Just* like everyone else," Donker said.

"Yes." Craig frowned, heavily. "We've been smoothing out the rough edges through drilling, and simulating every possible environment, but it will take time for the entire company to learn to trust each other. Thankfully, we all share a common understanding from basic training, yet"—he shrugged—"there are officers and bootnecks who simply don't know each other very well. It'll take time."

"Keep on it," Thomas ordered. "And let me know if you need anything else."

"I'd prefer six months on Salisbury Plain, where I can operate the entire unit against an opposing force," Craig said. "Right now, we're playing our own enemies. It works fine, for platoons against platoons, but we can't take the entire company into battle. We simply don't have anyone to fight."

"How terrible," Donker said, dryly.

Thomas's wristcom bleeped. He tapped it. "Go ahead."

"Captain, this is Lieutenant Cook," a voice said. "The Admiralty just sent a formal priority-one message, your eyes only."

"Forward it to my terminal," Thomas ordered. He opened the terminal and pressed his hand against the scanner. A priority-one message was almost certainly bad news. "And then signal *Unicorn* and inform Captain Campbell that I need to speak to him."

The message opened in front of him. He scanned it quickly, feeling his heart sink. "The Admiral is coming here, personally," he said. "And we have formal movement orders. We'll be departing in a week."

Donker sucked in his breath. "A week? Sir, we're not ready."

"Then we have to *be* ready," Thomas said. He looked from one to the other. "Make sure the department heads and everyone understands that we *have* to be ready. We're going to war."

CHAPTER NINE

"YOU'VE DONE WELL, CAPTAIN," Admiral Onarina said. "*Unicorn* appears ready to go into battle."

"Indeed, Admiral," Mitch said, feeling a flicker of pleasure. The crew had spent the last month working hard to prepare for departure, ready to leave on their own if *Lion* failed to meet the deadline. He wasn't too displeased with their departure date. The crew had done well—and the newcomers had meshed smoothly with the old hands—but they wouldn't be a single unit until they'd faced the enemy. "We're ready to depart on your command."

He smiled as he sat back in his chair. They were in the mess, the largest compartment on the ship save for the bridge and the engineering section. It was awkward, to say the least, but the admiral didn't seem to mind. It spoke well of her, Mitch thought. *Unicorn* was too small to have a separate mess for officers, let alone a private dining room for her commander, but he'd known captains and admirals who'd have flatly refused to eat with the men. The thought never ceased to irritate him, whenever he thought about it. He might be a captain, master of his ship, but he still went to the toilet and put his trousers on one leg at a time, just like everyone else. Anyone who tried to pretend the commander was something other than a mortal man was asking for trouble.

"*Lion* is also ready, more or less," Admiral Onarina said. She took a sip of her tea. "Can you open the conference?"

Mitch tapped his wristcom. It felt odd to be holding a command conference in the mess, but the admiral had insisted. He wasn't sure if she'd reasoned it would take longer to inspect *Lion* than *Unicorn*, and therefore inspected the bigger ship first, or if she was sending a subtle message to her superiors. Or if it was just something she had to do. If there was one thing he'd learnt in his career, it was that there was no point in searching for a complicated motive for anything when the answers were relatively simple.

Captain Hammond's hologram materialised in the centre of the compartment, bisecting a table that was solidly fixed to the deck. It looked faintly odd, but Mitch didn't smile. A holographic conference was vastly superior to a face-to-face conference, if only because it ensured everyone would be on their ships, ready to act if the shit hit the fan. And because it imposed some distance between the participants. It was a great deal easier to respectfully disagree with one's superior if one wasn't on the same ship.

"Admiral," Captain Hammond said. If he was irked at the conference being effectively held on *Unicorn*, rather than the much larger battlecruiser, he didn't show it. "Captain Campbell."

"Welcome," Mitch said. Captain Hammond hadn't inspected *Unicorn* personally, something a hostile Board of Inquiry could turn into a dereliction of duty. Mitch had no intention of making a fuss about it. Hammond had too many problems of his own. "Admiral? The deck is yours."

The admiral smiled. "Not since I was promoted, alas," she said. "I'm just a passenger on your ship."

Mitch felt a flicker of sympathy. Admiral Onarina had been promoted to flag rank shortly after the Second Interstellar War—the Order of the Garter was a clear sign she was destined for great things—but, as far as he could recall, she'd never actually commanded a fleet in combat. She might never command a fleet again, let alone a starship. He wondered, idly, if she regretted it. High-ranking officer or not, she was still assigned to Nelson

Base instead of an independent command. It was strange to think that a captain might be more trusted than an admiral, but it was true.

And admirals have to play the political game, he reminded himself. *Captains have a degree of freedom from politics.*

Captain Hammond leaned forward. "You will be accompanying us?"

"I'm afraid not," the admiral said. "My services are required on Earth."

She took a datachip out of her pocket and inserted it into the projector. A holographic starchart appeared in front of them, a multitude of human, alien and infected star systems linked together by tramlines. Mitch's eyes narrowed. The number of infected systems seemed to have grown larger in the last few days. The naval updates had been bland. In hindsight, they'd been almost disturbingly bland.

"We've been putting together a picture of enemy movements over the last twelve months," Admiral Onarina informed them. "The virus does not appear to be very rational or sane by our standards, unlike our alien allies, but we think there *is* a logic to its actions. A number of starships have been travelling through these systems"—her finger traced a line on the display, moving from star to star—"in preparation for an attack on New Washington. We think the virus intends to launch a two-pronged offensive into the system."

Mitch frowned. He was no stranger to bold and daring stunts, and he liked the idea of doing something so crazy the enemy literally couldn't *imagine* it, but...it was the sort of idea that made perfect sense on paper and failed spectacularly when it was actually *tried*. Even with the flicker network, coordinating an assault across interstellar distances was almost impossible. There was a very real chance the two prongs would be unable to coordinate their attacks, giving the enemy an opportunity to destroy one assault force before turning its attention to the other. Was the enemy fleet so numerous the virus felt it could take the risk?

"It seems odd," Captain Hammond said. His thoughts had clearly been moving in the same direction. "Why not focus on a single prong?"

"We think—we *think*—the enemy intends to harass shipping rather than targeting the orbital defences directly," the admiral said. "Assuming they manage to take control of the outer system, they'd be able to isolate two entire sectors while opening up tramlines to five more...including a direct chain to Terra Nova and Earth. They'd also be able to rain kinetic projectiles on the planet's defences, in the certain knowledge that—sooner or later—they'd hit something important. That would give them the chance to weaken our industrial base, perhaps even opening up the orbital nodes to infection. We'd have to retake the system, whatever the cost."

"Shit," Mitch said. "How long do we have?"

"We don't know," Admiral Onarina admitted. "The last probe into the occupied system told us that the virus was setting up what looks like a forward logistics base. Given how screwed up their logistics actually *are*, we simply don't know how long it will take them to get ready and then mount the offensive. Our worst-case scenario is two months. Of course"—her lips twisted, as if she'd bitten into something sour—"that might not be pessimistic *enough*."

"They might attack tomorrow," Captain Hammond noted.

"Quite," the admiral agreed. "They may want to hold New Washington permanently. Or they might simply want to punch their way into the system and do as much damage as possible before we drive them out again. If the former, they'll need the logistics base to resupply their ships in a hurry; if the latter, it probably won't matter that much. Like you said, they might attack tomorrow."

"So we put the virus off balance," Mitch said. "We launch a spoiling attack first."

"That's the plan," the admiral said. "Right now, there's no political will for launching a major offensive from New Washington. The Americans are understandably reluctant to risk drawing down their mobile units, even though the system has heavy fixed defences. GATO agrees. *Lion* and *Unicorn*, however, represent another option. Your weapons *might* be enough to seriously weaken the enemy fleet."

Captain Hammond looked stunned. "Admiral, with all due respect, we cannot wipe out an entire fleet on our own."

"We don't have to." Mitch's mind raced, considering the possibilities. "Their fleet will include a bunch of brainships, the masterminds of the operation. We just have to take *them* out, forcing the remainder of their fleet to stand on the defensive until replacements arrive."

"Replacements could arrive tomorrow," Captain Hammond pointed out, tartly. "And the virus doesn't *need* the brainships to fight."

"No, but without the brainships it fights...robotically," Mitch countered. "We'd have the edge. The Yanks would have the edge, if the virus came knocking. An easy victory would do wonders for political will."

"It might not be *easy*," Admiral Onarina cautioned. "But yes, that's the general idea."

Mitch smiled, broadly. The plan was risky, but...it wasn't *that* risky. If it worked, the Royal Navy would throw the enemy onto the defensive and win the human race—and their allies—much needed time to rebuild its defences and develop new weapons and tactics. If it failed, if both *Lion* and *Unicorn* were blown out of space, the navy wouldn't lose *much*. Both ships were expendable, considering what was at stake. Mitch didn't like the thought of throwing his life away, but he understood the logic. Better to risk two experimental ships than an entire fleet.

"So we sneak into the system, snipe at them from a safe distance and run for our lives," he said. It wasn't a particularly honourable plan, but the virus knew nothing of honour. It had to be destroyed, or it would be the end of everything. "And if it comes chasing us, we can lead its headless ships into the American defences."

"If the brainships are taken out," Admiral Onarina said. "If not, take an alternate route as you try to break contact."

"We could always lure them onto a minefield," Mitch said. "Didn't that tactic work before?"

"Yes, once," Admiral Onarina said. "After that, the virus started being a little more careful."

"We should be able to carry out the mission," Captain Hammond said. "The only real problem is getting the missiles through the enemy point defence. We might be effectively throwing snowballs into the fire."

"The missiles are designed to be hard to hit," Mitch said. "And they're tougher than the average missile..."

"I wouldn't care to bet on a missile surviving a direct hit," Captain Hammond pointed out. There was a hint of irritation in his tone. "And it will only take one hit, if the boffins are wrong, to take out a missile."

"We won't know until we actually take them into combat," Mitch said. "Admiral, how many other ships will be assigned to the squadron?"

"None." Admiral Onarina looked grim. "You'll be travelling with a convoy until you reach New Washington, then you're on your own. We've been trying to scrape up some more ships from *somewhere*, but the blunt truth is that no one has any to spare. Everyone who has some firepower doesn't want to let go of it."

"And as long as the virus is pushing at us along multiple angles of advance," Captain Hammond said, "there's a chance that strengthening the defences in one place will weaken the defences somewhere else."

"Yes," Admiral Onarina said. "There's a handful of *possibilities* for improving our defences and freeing up more ships for aggressive operations, but none of them show more than a hint or two of promise. The formations assigned to Home Fleet are our only real strategic reserve and...well, there's hardly any political will to draw them down any further. In theory, we could cut them loose and go on the offensive; practically speaking, it would be too great a risk."

"I understand," Captain Hammond said. "We dare not lose the core worlds."

Mitch wasn't so sure. The human navies were losing. The virus was maintaining a steady pressure on the defences, wearing them down to a nub. It was only a matter of time until something broke, until the defenders had to fall back to the homeworld and abandon all hope of taking the war to the enemy. They were desperate, perhaps desperate enough to stake everything on a gamble. If he had command of the space navies, he'd certainly consider launching an all-out assault on enemy space. It might just turn the tide.

But he knew, all too well, what his superiors would say if he proposed it. Lightning strikes into the heart of enemy power worked perfectly in books and movies, but rarely in the real world. They'd risk heavy losses, both to the fleet *and* to the industrial nodes they'd be leaving undefended. They might score a tactical victory, but lose the war. His superiors would reject the idea out of hand, even though it held out the tantalising promise of total victory. They'd think they had no choice.

We can't stand on the defensive forever, he told himself. *We have to take the fight to the enemy.*

"You have orders to join the convoy in two days," Admiral Onarina said, dragging his attention back to her. "Can you make it?"

"Yes, Admiral," Mitch said. He was sure of it. His ship was ready and raring to go. "We can be on our way now, if you like."

"*Lion* should be ready to depart," Captain Hammond said. "We've already started drawing up plans to continue our training and exercise schedule while under way."

"Good," the admiral said. If she had any doubts about their ability to keep their promises, she kept them to herself. "I'm sorry your crew won't have any chance for shore leave, before you depart. We'll see what we can do when you get home."

"My crew will understand," Mitch assured her. "We know what's at stake."

Captain Hammond looked displeased, just for a second. Mitch felt a twinge of sympathy for the older man. His crew had been far more fragmented when he'd taken command, forcing him to wield them into a unit while coming to grips with a new and revolutionary starship. It couldn't have been easy...Mitch smiled, relieved *he* hadn't been given a larger ship. He'd seen once-promising commanders struggle with bigger ships, micromanaging their subordinates over tiny issues because they couldn't come to grips with the bigger ones. And Captain Hammond simply hadn't had the time for a proper shakedown cruise. The days when it could take a year for a ship to become combat-ready were a thing of the past.

"I believe my crew will have no trouble," Captain Hammond said, finally. "I'll keep them busy."

"Just make sure you keep them too busy to grumble," Admiral Onarina advised. "Speak to the Americans after you return from the mission. They'd probably let you have a few days on New Washington."

Mitch nodded. New Washington had been a colony for over a hundred years. The United States had invested billions of dollars in colony infrastructure, handing out land grants like water to ensure millions of colonists moved to the distant world. They'd done well, Mitch knew. He'd visited the system years ago, back when he'd been a lieutenant. There were parts of the planet that could almost have passed for Earth.

"We can worry about shore leave later," he said. "Right now, the mission comes first."

"Yes." Captain Hammond nodded. "We will handle it, Admiral. I'll review the files and then determine a plan of attack."

"As will I," Mitch said. He had no intention of letting Captain Hammond devise a plan without at least *some* input from him. The operation would only work if they used the capabilities of *both* ships to the full. "We'll be ready by the time we reach New Washington."

"Very good." Admiral Onarina looked from one to the other, then nodded. It was hard to guess what she was thinking. Regret, perhaps? Or a grim understanding she had to send them out to face the enemy? "I'll see you when you return. Dismissed."

Mitch took a sip of his tea as Captain Hammond's hologram flickered and vanished. The admiral seemed older for a moment, staring down at her mug without drinking. Mitch nodded. The admiral had to be under a great deal of stress, all too aware that her concepts for technical superiority might not survive their first encounter with the enemy. It was never easy to predict how the opposing force would react, or just how well the weapons would perform. The missiles might blow the entire enemy fleet into atoms, or be effortlessly picked off by point defence.

And we're about to find out the hard way, he mused. He'd run simulations that suggested there'd be a string of easy victories and simulations that suggested they'd lose the very first engagement. *There's no other choice.*

"We need to buy time," Admiral Onarina said, "but not at the cost of ultimate victory."

"Yes, Admiral," Mitch said. He was vaguely disappointed, even though he understood the logic. The admiral and her staff had to balance requirements he preferred not to consider. "Perhaps our next target should be the alien homeworld."

The admiral raised her eyebrows. "Does the virus even *have* a homeworld?"

Mitch started to answer, then stopped himself. Cold logic insisted the enemy *had* to have a homeworld, even if it was a biological weapon that had gotten out of control rather than the product of a very strange evolutionary cycle. But...did it matter? Did the virus have a homeworld it regarded with any degree of sentiment? Or had it spread so far that it no longer remembered—or cared—where it had been born? He considered the question for a moment, before putting it out of his mind. The boffins could worry about it, if they wished. He was more interested in buying them the time and safety they'd need to ask and answer their questions.

And we'll cease to exist if the virus wins the war, he told himself, as Admiral Onarina rose. *We have no choice but to fight to the last.*

CHAPTER TEN

"ALL STATIONS AND DEPARTMENTS REPORT READY, SIR," Commander Donker said. "We are ready to power up on your command."

Thomas settled back in his command chair, a low thrum echoing through his ship. The last two days had been nightmarish, to the point he'd privately determined his crew would get a rest once they were through the tramline and on their way to New Washington. They'd loaded their last supplies, checked and rechecked everything and gone through an entire list of urgent things that needed to be done before a starship left the shipyard for the first time. And, somehow, he'd found time to review the data and plan his operation. The only upside was that the admiral was smart and experienced enough to understand that the operational plan was little more than a vague set of ideas. They wouldn't be able to come up with anything *solid* until they actually probed the system itself.

He took a long breath. They'd checked everything, as far as he knew, but something could still go wrong. A power distribution node might overload and explode, a datacore might glitch, a sensor head might go blind...he knew they'd gone through everything with a fine-toothed comb, yet he wasn't reassured. His crew was exhausted. Exhausted people made mistakes. And even if they didn't, they'd never powered the ship up completely. They might discover a problem they'd honestly had no idea was even possible before they ran into it.

"Begin full power-up sequence," Thomas ordered. His mouth was dry. It had been so much easier when he'd last assumed command. "And be ready to power down if there are any problems."

A low hum ran through the ship as her systems came online. Thomas kept a wary eye on the display, wondering what would be the first thing to go wrong. There was always *something*, from a misplaced sensor node that was being jammed by a drive node to something more serious. He'd served on ships where the sensor nodes were actually *too* sensitive, to the point they'd been triggered by the drive field and reported hundreds of enemy ships impossibly close to the hull. The sensor display lit up with icons, each one representing part of the giant shipyard. A faint lattice of sensor webbing gleamed in front of him. In theory, nothing—not even the stealthiest ship in the known universe—could slip into the shipyard without being detected and engaged. In practice, no one was sure.

"Captain," Donker said. "All systems are powered up."

Thomas nodded, allowing himself a moment of relief. He'd dreaded having to explain to the admiral that *Lion* couldn't leave the shipyard. It would have been difficult, even if they hadn't been under orders to depart as quickly as possible. The admiral might have been understanding or... she might have relieved him of command for incompetence. He'd assured her they'd depart on schedule, after all. It was never easy to predict how an admiral might react to something, particularly one who'd spent the last few years flying a desk. They didn't think like shipboard officers.

She came up through the ranks herself, he thought. *She knows how easily things can go wrong.*

He sighed, inwardly, as his crew completed their checks. It wasn't uncommon for something to go wrong, something the media could blow into a total disaster. He'd read horror stories about HMS *Invincible* springing a leak, which—the reporters had suggested—had led rapidly to complete depressurisation and the death of her entire crew. It had triggered his bullshit detectors at once, if only because it was a little unlikely. Starships were *designed* to cope with hull breaches. The truth—the carrier had had an airlock malfunction, which had killed absolutely no one—had been a little more prosaic.

But the truth was a lot less dramatic, he thought, wryly. *And probably didn't sell any subscriptions.*

"Communications, inform Shipyard Command that we're moving out on our assigned vector," Thomas ordered. *Unicorn* had already left, lingering outside the defences like an over-eager puppy. "Helm, prepare to take us out."

"Aye, Captain," Lieutenant Cook said. "Shipyard Command has cleared us to depart."

Thomas braced himself. "Helm, take us out."

"Aye, Captain," Lieutenant Michael Fitzgerald said. Another quiver ran through the ship. "Taking us out...now."

The gravity field seemed to flicker, just slightly, as the ship started to move. Thomas was fairly sure he was imagining it, although no amount of logic and reason from the physicists and psychologists had been able to convince him it was *just* his imagination. The compensators were working perfectly—they had to be, or the entire crew would be dead—yet he felt as if they were moving. They *were* moving. He watched the power curves, silently counting down the seconds as more and more drive nodes came online. *Lion* was over-engineered for her size, as if the designers had more faith in her external and internal armour than they should. A direct hit was likely to take out more than one drive node, even if the ship survived the impact. He had a feeling they'd added extra drive nodes because they could.

"Captain," Fitzgerald said, formally. "We're on our way."

Thomas nodded. *Lion* was gliding through the defence network, passing battlestations and automated weapons platforms that wouldn't hesitate to turn her into plasma if they thought she was a threat. The virus *cheated*, he reflected sourly. The days when they could safely assume an enemy power couldn't operate a human starship, let alone copy and mimic human IFF codes, were long gone. The virus could turn a loyalist into a traitor very quickly, if it was allowed to infect its target unimpeded. No, *worse* than a traitor. A traitor had to make the decision to become a traitor. The virus didn't need their consent to extract their knowledge and turn them against their former friends and allies.

"Contact *Unicorn*," he said. "Order her to hold position near us."

"Aye, Captain," Cook said.

Thomas leaned back in his chair as the display continued to fill with icons. Home Fleet held position near Earth, dozens of smaller squadrons and individual ships guarding the cloudscoops or the asteroid mining facilities. It awed him to see so many ships, from so many different nations, standing ready to defend the homeworld against the enemy; it chilled him to realise they might not be enough to save the planet if the virus gathered its power and hurled its entire fleet against Earth. He'd seen the figures and projections, both the sets that were made available to the public and the ones restricted to those who had a need to know. They didn't make comforting reading. Thomas had a nasty feeling that more people understood the truth than the government was prepared to admit.

He scowled as he spotted the line of giant colonist-carriers, heading away from Earth. He'd read detailed opinion pieces proclaiming the off-world colonist program a waste of time, perhaps even a lethal diversion of resources. He could see their point, even though the colonist-carriers were cheap and nasty compared to a full-fledged warship. And yet, Earth herself was threatened. The human race would need to carry on *somewhere*...he winced as he turned his attention back to the shipyard. There might be plans to evacuate its facilities elsewhere, to give a hidden colony a chance to rebuild. But there'd be mass panic if anyone even tried.

"All systems remain nominal," Donker reported. He grinned, suddenly. "We are free and clear!"

Thomas had to smile. "Let's hope it stays that way," he said. "How long until we link up with the convoy and cross the tramline?"

"Two hours to the convoy, another hour to the tramline," Donker said. "And two weeks to reach New Washington."

"Good," Thomas said. "Order the beta, delta and gamma crews to stand down and get some rest. We'll start exercising again once we leave the system."

He checked the display, again. Civilians couldn't understand the sheer immensity of interstellar space. Starships travelled at unimaginable speeds, yet it still took weeks or months to reach the edge of explored space. It was hard to believe, even for him, that *Lion* wouldn't reach New Washington in a hurry. Who knew how the situation would change over the next few days? They might arrive at New Washington only to discover that it had been taken by the enemy. It was quite possible.

His heart clenched. He was leaving Charlotte and his daughters behind. He was leaving them, all too aware he might never come back. *Lion* was a powerful ship, but she wasn't indestructible. It would only take one moment of bad luck to cut his life short, to kill him so quickly that he didn't have any time to realise he was dead. He was too old to believe himself immortal, even if he hadn't watched too many of his friends go out and never come back. Charlotte...would she miss him, if he died? He liked to think so, even though they'd both been raised to put the family first. They might not be as close as he might have wished, but they were hardly enemies either. She would miss him. His daughters definitely would.

The seconds ticked by, each one feeling like an hour. He'd ordered the crew to make sure they recorded their final messages and checked their wills, rewriting them if necessary, to take account of any changes in their circumstances. No one really *wanted* to do it, perhaps out of fear of admitting they might die, but...he scowled. It had to be done. Half the problems facing the families of dead military personnel, killed in the line of duty, stemmed from the spacer failing to fill out a proper will. The military would back a military spouse to the hilt, but it wasn't easy if they didn't know what the dead man had actually wanted...

Not that I had much for myself, he thought, ruefully. *Three-quarters of what I own is entailed.*

He put the thought aside, firmly. There was no point in worrying about it now. He'd written his will years ago, after his first child had been born.

After that...he shook his head. He had too many other things to concern him. His fingers touched the console, bringing up the latest reports. Everything was going remarkably well, for a ship that had only left the slip a month or so ago. He'd expected *something* to go wrong.

It's probably biding its time, he thought. Every captain in the fleet knew the story of HMS *Warspite*, which had suffered a total power failure after she'd made her first jump through the tramline. *Hopefully, whatever is going to happen will happen before we run into the enemy.*

It felt weird, Tobias decided, to sit in a gunboat while the tiny craft was effectively powered down. The gunboats were designed to serve as their own simulators—he wasn't sure if that was a good idea—but they'd been told, in no uncertain terms, that they weren't to power up the craft any further until *Lion* was well underway. Tobias was fairly sure the starship's crew were worrying over nothing—the gunboats were designed to be stealthy, even when their drives were powered up—yet there was no point in arguing. Captain Hammond would probably have him flogged—or hurled out the nearest airlock—if Tobias disobeyed.

He studied the display, watching the live feed from the starship's sensors. It was hard to believe that the convoy—and the hundreds of other icons within sensor range—weren't so close together he could practically reach out and touch them. It was hard to comprehend that there were literally hundreds of thousands—if not millions—of miles between him and the shipyard, a gulf that was growing wider with every passing second. And Earth...he felt an odd little pang as he contemplated the homeworld, falling further and further behind. He'd never really considered leaving Earth...

That's not true, he told himself. *You just didn't want to leave on their terms.*

The hatch hissed as it started to open. Tobias jumped, even though he was on a starship rather than school. Old habits—the fear of being caught alone, the fear of being beaten again and again—died hard. The naval personnel he'd met had all been decent, more or less. The worst of them had grumbled about the gunboat pilots being fast-tracked, which was unarguably true. The downside was that their odds of survival weren't high. Tobias had flown through simulations that had insisted the entire squadron would be wiped out in seconds. They'd been very depressing.

Marigold stepped through the airlock. "I thought I'd find you here."

"There aren't many places to go," Tobias said. He'd once poured scorn on the idea of house arrest. Now, after being effectively confined to Gunboat Country for a month, he was starting to understand. Being trapped in a big house—as if he'd ever owned a big house—would start to grate, sooner rather than later. "Where else would I be?"

"A couple of the others have been sneaking up to the observation blister," Marigold said. She pushed the hatch shut behind her, then took her seat. "I figured you might have gone exploring, too."

"I wish." Tobias felt a surge of sudden resentment. There'd been a lot of places he would have wanted to explore, if he hadn't known it would mean a beating—or worse—if he were caught. It wasn't a danger on the ship, he supposed, but—again—old habits died hard. He'd tried to tell himself he didn't want it. He wasn't sure it had worked. "I was just trying to be alone for a bit."

"It's not easy," Marigold agreed. "You *do* know there are privacy tubes?"

Tobias felt himself redden. "I don't want to think about them," he mumbled. "Really."

Marigold blushed, too. "Yeah..."

She changed the subject, quickly enough to tell him she was also embarrassed. "Did you call your mother?"

"I spoke to my sister," Tobias said. It had been a very quick call. His mother hadn't been at home, which meant...what? She'd been offered extra hours at the laundry, but she hadn't been keen on taking them. Too much harassment, she'd said. The manager hadn't given much of a damn. "My mother...I didn't have a chance to speak to her."

"I had to write a will," Marigold said. She shook her head. "Can you imagine? I had to write a will!"

Tobias nodded. "I don't have much of anything," he said. His computer terminal, his clothes, a handful of other crap...most of it would probably be sold to a second-hand shop, if they agreed to *take* it. The clothes weren't fashionable, but anyone buying clothes from a second-hand shop probably wasn't in any position to complain. "My sister gets what little I have, if she wants it. God alone knows what'll happen to my pension."

He winced. He'd been given a bunch of documents to read about the Military Convent, about how the navy would make provision for his dependents if he died in the line of duty...but he hadn't been able to follow the legalese. The cynic in him suspected the navy wanted to make sure it could grant or revoke provision as it saw fit. Did he even *have* any dependents? He had no wife, no children...his sister was hardly *dependent* on him. He had no one who had a solid legal right to a pension, if he died.

"I looked it up," Marigold said. "Your family might be able to claim it."

"Might," Tobias said. He shook his head. "We'll see."

He winced. He wasn't so sure. The navy bureaucracy was just like school...and the benefits office. His mother had grumbled about it often enough. The people who were kind and reasonable and wanted to help were *not* the ones in charge, not the ones who could actually make decisions. The people who *were* in charge were the kind of people who resented handing out food bank vouchers, let alone actual money. They thought ill people were malingering, disabled people were fit to work...a person who had a perfect legal right to some benefits might be denied it on a technicality. The system had been breaking down even before the war had started and rationing had been introduced.

Marigold reached out and rested a hand on his shoulder. "I'm sure it'll all work out," she said. "But you know what? We're not going to die."

"I hope you're right," Tobias said. If the gunboat was hit, they'd both be killed instantly. A starfighter pilot might be able to survive, if he ejected in time to escape the explosion, but it was rare. Only a handful of pilots had survived ejection in the last two decades. The odds for gunboat pilots were even worse. "The simulations..."

"They do keep piling them on," Marigold said. She struck a mock contemplative pose. "I'm fairly sure they keep ramping up the speed and missile fire too."

Tobias had to laugh. "Yeah, but we have to take it seriously. Every time."

"It could be worse," Marigold said. She tapped the console. "We'll be jumping into the next system in an hour. And then we'll be going back to work."

"And everyone bad in my life will be on the other side of the tramline," Tobias agreed. He'd miss his mother and sister, but it didn't matter. The navy didn't care what he thought. They'd be millions of miles away even if he never left the Sol System. "Wonderful, don't you think?"

"Quite," Marigold agreed.

CHAPTER ELEVEN

WHOEVER DESIGNED OUR PERSONAL PROTECTIVE GEAR, Colin thought as the fire team carefully opened an airlock and hurled an antiviral grenade into the next compartment, *was a sadistic bastard.*

Sweat trickled down his back as the flare of blue-white light dimmed. The suit was supposed to be comfortable, without hampering his movement in any way. Colin had long since decided the designer was either an idiot or simply ignorant. The suit was fine, if one walked slowly and calmly. Anyone who actually tried to *run* overheated very quickly. He wasn't entirely sure the suit was completely airtight either. The boffins *claimed* the virus couldn't get through the filters, but they'd been wrong before. It would only take one accident for an entire platoon to be turned into zombies.

He plunged into the next compartment, rifle sweeping the section for targets. It was empty, seemingly unmarked by the antiviral grenade. The boffins claimed the flashes of light would stun the virus, weakening the biological network that united the zombies into a single hive. Colin wasn't sure of that either. The old sweats reported some pretty mixed results. Colin shivered, reminding himself that he should be grateful for the suit. They couldn't take the risk of being infected. There were enough horror stories of zombies remaining undetected long enough to do *real* damage to ensure he'd keep the suit on, at least for the duration of the exercise. They *really* couldn't take the risk.

Colin tongued his throatmike as the remainder of the fire team flowed into the chamber. "Section 77-G is clear, sir; I say again, Section 77-G is clear."

"Noted," Major Craig said. "Advance to Section 77-H."

"Aye, sir," Colin said. His team moved to the airlock. "We're going in…now."

He tensed as they tested the airlock. It was locked. Colin swore under his breath, bracing himself as his team started to manually open the airlock. It was possible the system had been locked down, to the point the automated systems were no longer active; it was also possible the enemy was on the far side, waiting for them. The biosensors should have sounded the alert…he cursed under his breath, wishing the exercise planners hadn't done such a good job. It was all very well and good to insist that hard training meant for easier missions, but he was fairly sure most of the network would remain intact. They *should* have been able to track any boarding party as it made its way into the hull.

At least they try to board our ships, instead of simply taking a nuke into the hull and detonating, Colin thought. The Royal Marines were trained for such missions, but rarely ordered into them. They were effectively suicide, only to be considered as a very last resort. *It gives us a chance to drive them back into space.*

The airlock opened, revealing a misty atmosphere. The bioscanner started screaming a warning. Colin hurled a grenade into the mist, hoping and praying it *was* the virus. Some cunning wanker had filled the air with faux-explosive gas during a training mission, then gleefully pointed out that the marines had managed to blow themselves to hell. The virus might do the same, although it struck him as unlikely. Both extreme heat and vacuum would be more dangerous to its biological network than guns, at least in the short term. He swallowed as another pulse of blue-white light flashed in front of him. The virus simply didn't play fair. He'd watched recordings of zombies taking shots to the head, then continuing their advance until their bodies were blown to bloody chunks. It was all too easy to believe the virus was unstoppable.

He plunged forward, keeping low as he looked around. They'd plunged into a storage compartment, crammed with heavy boxes...he ducked down as flickering laser light shot over his head. A marine swore behind him as he was hit, his suit locking down automatically. It might not be fatal, in a real fight, but exercise rules were absolute. Anyone who got hit was out of the fight, at least until the exercise was over. Colin knew better than to bend the rules. Devising a brilliant new tactic was one thing; flagrantly breaking the rules was quite another.

"We have contact," he reported, as he unhooked another grenade from his belt. "Two—possibly three—enemy combatants..."

He tossed the grenade. There was yet another flare of blue-white light. The zombies kept firing, popping up long enough to fire a burst of laser light before ducking back down again. Colin cursed under his breath, then signalled for the remainder of the fire team to keep the enemy pinned down while he crawled forward. There was no point in trying the antiviral grenades again, not now. The virus was safely inside the infected bodies, untouchable by UV light. Instead, he hurled a HE grenade over the boxes and ducked down. Colin thought he heard a scream as a flash of red light cast an eerie shade over the entire compartment. He snorted as he crawled around the boxes. The virus never screamed, even when the host bodies had taken enough punishment to kill a normal man. It was one of its traits he detested most.

Two men lay on the ground, pretending to be dead. Colin rolled his eyes as he checked their weapons, then walked past. They hadn't done badly, for matelots. They'd picked a good defensive position, then held their own instead of charging forward into the teeth of enemy fire. It was a shame they couldn't run a *perfect* simulation, with trained and experienced soldiers on the other side, but...he shook his head as he surveyed the compartment. The rest of the fire team was advancing...

Something slammed into his back. For a horrible moment, as the force of the impact bowled him over, he thought he'd been shot by one of his team. *That* would be embarrassing, perhaps costing him his stripe if the sergeant thought it was his fault. A weight landed on top of him, two fists beating at his helmet. He'd been ambushed...he gritted his teeth, cursing the enemy under his breath. The bastard's hands were already scrabbling at his fastenings, trying to expose him to the poisoned air. It would cost him the exercise, probably cost him his chance to make his promotion permanent. He reached back, drew a shockrod from his belt and shoved it into the figure's leg. The man convulsed, just enough to let Colin throw him off and rolled over, drawing his pistol and shooting the figure repeatedly. Under normal circumstances, it would be overkill. Against the virus, it might not be *enough* kill.

"I think you got him," Private Scott Davies said, as he came around the crate. "Really."

"I think you should have got here quicker," Colin groused. He and Davies had trained together, before Colin had earned his first stripe. It was hard to treat him as a subordinate when they'd been equals...and might be equals again, if one of them was promoted or demoted. "He nearly got me."

Major Craig's voice echoed over the communications net. "ENDEX," he said. "I say again, ENDEX. This exercise is now terminated."

Colin breathed a sigh of relief as he undid his helmet and pulled it free. The air smelled of fear and sweat, but it was cool. Blessedly cool. He helped the crewman he'd zapped to his feet, trying not to show his irritation. The cunning bastard must have hidden in one of the crates, sheltered from the grenades. Colin wondered why he hadn't simply been shot in the back. It really *would* have taken him out of the exercise. The sergeant would have been *very* sarcastic. Running past a potential hiding place for a potential ambush had been careless, to say the least. Good men had died that way.

"Sorry for shocking you," he said, rubbing sweat from his eyes. His hair felt uncomfortably wet. Perhaps it was time to shave it completely, like some of the more experienced marines. "You caught me by surprise."

"My job, son," the spacer said. "See you next time."

Colin nodded as he surveyed the remainder of the compartment. There hadn't been any real damage, *this* time. It wasn't entirely realistic—it couldn't be—but they couldn't shoot live weapons onboard ship. He turned and strode back to the airlock. Private Henry Willis lay on the deck, pretending to be dead. Colin rolled his eyes. The man wasn't lazy—no one could get through commando training by being lazy—but Willis looked as if he were taking a nap.

"Get up," Colin ordered. "The exercise is over."

"I'm dead, sir," Willis insisted. "You have to carry me back to barracks. It's realistic."

"*Realistic* would be putting your body out the nearest airlock, as you know perfectly well," Davies pointed out, snidely. "Or sticking an incendiary grenade up your arse to make sure you're actually dead."

Willis sat up. "When I'm dead, I'm donating my body for medical research," he said. "I want them to confirm I'm actually dead before they take me apart for science."

"I think we have discovered the limits of what anal probing can teach us," Davies said. "Unless we *want* to know what crawled up your arse and died."

"I think it was a ration bar," Willis said. "I thought I'd save time and..."

Colin snorted rudely as they headed back to barracks, passing a handful of crewmen on the way. The marines had been told, in no uncertain terms, that they weren't to try to tidy up after the exercise. It didn't sit well with him—they'd been taught to clean up after themselves, if only to keep the enemy from learning useful things from their rubbish—but there was no point in arguing. He understood logistics well enough to know it was important that everything went back where it belonged. The navy wouldn't thank the marines if they lost something in the supplies. Or in the files. It was where inconvenient facts went to die.

He glanced at the timer as they entered Marine Country, wondering if he had time for a shower before the briefing. He stunk. They *all* stunk. The suit felt increasingly uncomfortable. He tried to tell himself he'd been in worse places, but it wasn't particularly convincing. Even the worst of the worst felt like nothing more than a vague memory.

"Be seated," Sergeant Ron Bowman said, as he took the podium. There was no sign of Major Craig. "We did well, all things considered."

"It wasn't real, sergeant," Lieutenant Francis Coxcomb said. "We weren't firing real weapons."

Bowman shrugged. "I'm sure *that* would make for an interesting court-martial," he said, sardonically. "Do you *want* to explain how we blew away a bunch of spacer volunteers...and how they blew *us* away?"

Colin kept his thoughts to himself. It was true the combination of fake grenades and laser guns, instead of real weapons, lent the exercise an air of unreality. The fakes just didn't have the impact, literally, of their real counterparts. The marines trained with live weapons where possible. And yet...he snorted. There was nothing to be gained by using live weapons onboard ship, unless the shit *really* hit the fan. The captain would certainly not grant permission...

"We cleared the infected compartments very quickly," Bowman said. "We also stepped down the effects of the grenades, giving the enemy a potential advantage. *Don't* get complacent. We assume they're working on ways to overcome the grenades too."

Colin nodded as the sergeant talked them through a holographic recreation of the exercise. It was hard to believe the fire team had been one of many, even though he knew it to be true. They'd felt alone, isolated in a sea of troubles. Their back-up had been too far back to be anything but helpless witnesses, if things spiralled out of control. He frowned as he realised one fire team *had* been wiped out, just before the exercise had been terminated. The corporal had made a mistake, and his team had paid for it.

"We need to speed up our passage through the ship," Bowman finished. "We're just not getting to the beachheads quickly enough."

"I don't see how we can move any faster, sergeant," Lieutenant Dalton said. "We might have to rely on the navy pukes slowing them down for us."

"They can't slow them down for long, even if they survive the hull breach," Bowman pointed out, dryly. "We need to move faster."

Colin winced, inwardly. He knew, without false modesty, that he was a champion runner. He'd been quick on his feet even *before* he'd gone to commando training. In theory, they should be able to get from bow to stern very quickly. In practice, just getting through the airlocks—which automatically sealed if the ship came under heavy attack—took time, time they didn't have. The enemy boarders could make use of the time to start burning their way towards the bridge.

Or even taking a nuke as far into the hull as possible, he thought, as the discussion grew more heated. *It's only a matter of time before they do.*

"Enemy missiles at twelve o'clock," Marigold said.

"Roger," Tobias said. "What should I do until then?"

He ignored Marigold's snort as his hands danced over the console. The joke dated all the way back to the very first days of aerial combat, when magnificent men in magnificent flying machines had duelled like knights of old, with honour and glory and no ill feelings. Tobias doubted it had ever been like that—he found it hard to believe that knights in shining armour had been paragons of anything, except lust and cruelty—but it didn't matter. He'd be in real trouble if they failed to stop the missiles. The virus was already fond of hurling impossible salvos towards their targets. It would only take one or two hits to *really* ruin *Lion's* day.

The enemy missiles lanced closer, somehow accelerating even as they evaded his sensor locks. They were moving at impossible speeds, travelling faster than any missile known to exist...Tobias shivered, silently grateful for the gunboat's tactical sensors as the missiles entered their engagement envelope. They couldn't hope to take them out manually. They might as well start firing at random. Tobias cursed under his breath as a dozen missiles flashed past the gunboat, already heading out of engagement range. They'd shot forty missiles out of space, but it hadn't been enough.

"How long will it be," he asked, "before we face missiles that really *do* move so quickly?"

Marigold didn't look up from her console. "Hopefully, never," she said. "There are limits to how fast missiles can go, right?"

Tobias shrugged. "A hundred years ago, there was no such thing as artificial gravity," he said. He'd seen the first purpose-built space warships. They'd been weird gangly designs, compared to modern-day ships. "Weapons and computers and tactical sensors were useless. Now...we have better weapons and sensors and...everything else. We might wind up facing missiles that travel just below the speed of light."

"And defences will probably improve too," Marigold countered. She paused as the console bleeped. "The exercise is terminated. We lost."

"Fuck." Tobias sat back, his eyes drifting over the preliminary report without quite seeing it. "They just overwhelmed us."

"Yeah," Marigold agreed. She altered course, taking the gunboat back to the mothership. "But the real enemy won't be that bad."

Tobias let out a breath as the last of the exercise vanished from the display. The horde of enemy warships blinked out of existence, replaced by a handful of asteroid miners and freighters moving from tramline to tramline. The Terra Nova system had been calming down, before the Third Interstellar War began. Or so he'd been told. The reports had claimed that most of the interplanetary population had either left the system or gone underground, trying to hide from both the planet's new rulers and the virus. He wondered, idly, if they had any hope of remaining hidden indefinitely. A single transmission would be enough to betray them, if someone cared enough to listen.

"I hope so," he said. He grinned at her. "Next time, *I* fly the ship."

"I'm not the one who rammed an asteroid," Marigold teased. "What *were* you thinking?"

"I was desperate," Tobias said. He'd been quite disappointed to discover that one could fly an entire navy through an asteroid field without any serious risk of hitting an asteroid. Real-life asteroid fields were nowhere near as exciting as the movies made them seem. And yet, their training had included a bunch of faked asteroid fields that really *were* dangerously dense. He wasn't sure if it was a real test or someone's idea of a joke. "And you need practice with the guns."

"You mean, practice with programming the computers that control the guns," Marigold corrected. "We'll discuss it later."

Tobias laughed. They were meant to rotate slots, if only to ensure they could serve in either role. Their instructors had claimed it was to give them a chance to reshuffle the squadrons, if necessary, but Tobias didn't believe it. Anything that killed Marigold in interplanetary combat was likely to kill him as well. There was no point in arguing. The navy was still feeling its way towards viable gunboat tactics. It would probably be several years before doctrine was finalised and set in stone.

"We could have done worse," Marigold pointed out. "Statistically, the odds of them hitting *Lion* are quite low."

"It only takes one hit," Tobias countered. "And then we'll be stuck out here to die."

CHAPTER TWELVE

MITCH ALLOWED HIMSELF A TIGHT SMILE as he lay on his bunk, holding the terminal up so he could see the screen. It wasn't the most professional of appearances, and he supposed it would be slightly off-putting to a superior officer who put more credence in appearances than reality, but he found it hard to care. *Unicorn* simply didn't have a proper office for her commanding officer. He supposed he should be grateful she also produced less paperwork than a capital ship. He'd never liked paperwork, even though he understood the importance of keeping everything in line. He couldn't order replacement supplies if he didn't know what needed to be replaced.

"I must say, we're as close to combat-ready as we're likely to become," he said. "We won't know for sure until we face *real* danger, of course."

"Of course," Captain Hammond echoed. He looked displeased, somewhat to Mitch's irritation. *His* ship was probably having problems adjusting to the new reality. "Can your crew handle it?"

"Yes, sir." Mitch smiled. "Most of my officers and crew are experienced, even if they haven't served under me. The remainder are surrounded by experienced officers. They can handle anything."

And if they can't, he added silently, *we can remove them before it's too late.*

He scowled at the thought. It was never easy to tell how someone would react to *real* combat. Simulations were all very well and good, but they weren't real. It was difficult to trick someone into believing a simulation *was* real, isolating them so completely from reality that they honestly wouldn't know the difference. A person who performed well—brilliantly, even—in the simulators might freeze up when faced with actual combat. Mitch understood, but he had no time for sympathy. A person who froze might get himself and others killed before he recovered himself. Better to have that person sent to the rear, where he might make himself useful without putting the rest of the crew in danger.

"My crew is learning the ropes, now we're under way," Captain Hammond said. "We're working the kinks out, one by one."

Mitch nodded. "Are you ready for bigger and better things?"

"We're about to find out," Captain Hammond said. "And you?"

"Yes." Mitch leaned forward. "I have some ideas about how we should proceed."

He sat up, tapping his terminal to bring up the starchart and share his view with his superior. "There's very little on Farnham worth considering," he said. "Our only real concern is the enemy fleet. Right?"

"Right," Captain Hammond said. "And, at last report, it consisted of over seventy ships."

"Of which the brainships are the important targets," Mitch agreed. "There are four brainships, all of which need to be taken out quickly. I propose that we enter the system on a least-time course to Farnham itself, with *Unicorn* taking up position here"—he tapped a point on the display—"and *Lion* holding station here, just outside enemy detection range. You then fire missiles on ballistic trajectories, which go live here"—he tapped another point—"giving the enemy a very limited chance to detect them before they slam home."

"But too great a chance of running down *Lion* before she can escape," Captain Hammond pointed out. "Brainships or no brainships, they won't fail to react to an obvious threat."

"Unless they've massively improved their drives in the last few months, their capital ships won't be able to catch *Lion*," Mitch said. "And the smaller ships will be vulnerable to your fire."

He shook his head. It was the age-old equation, older than the space navies themselves. *Lion* could outrun anything powerful enough to blow her to atoms. The cold equations of naval combat admitted of little ambiguity. Given a head start, the battlecruiser might be able to reach the tramline and jump out before her enemies caught up or overwhelmed her defences with long-range missile fire. Hell, the combination of gunboats, ECM drones and point defence might be enough to render *Lion* invulnerable until the enemy closed the range. They couldn't hope to hit her with ballistic missiles.

"It's still too risky," Captain Hammond said. "We have to be more careful."

Mitch kept his face under tight control. He understood the risks—he'd been injured, nearly killed, on active service—but they were losing the war. They *had* to take risks. Taking out two or three of the brainships wouldn't be enough, certainly not enough to give the Americans a decent chance to take out the remainder of the fleet. They *had* to kill the brainships before it was too late. And that meant taking risks. Mitch hated to admit it, but *Lion* and *Unicorn* were expendable. The Royal Navy would happily sacrifice both ships if it meant buying time to build up the fleet and mount a massive counterattack.

"We need to hit them hard, catch them by surprise," he said. "If we give them a chance to see what we can do, if they have a moment to send a message further up the chain, we might run into a much heavier ambush next time."

Or worse, he thought, sourly. No one *really* understood how the virus thought—it was just too alien—but they did have a fairly good model of how it communicated. If a single brainship survived long enough to analyse what happened, the rest of the enemy fleet would know in short order. *Next time, they'll know what to expect.*

"We also don't know how well our ships will perform in combat," Captain Hammond said, coldly. "The risk is too great."

"That's what we're here to find out," Mitch insisted. "We have to push the limits as far as they will go."

"The risk is too great," Captain Hammond repeated. "We'll engage from a distance."

Mitch leaned forward. "What do you have in mind?"

"We engage from a middling point," Captain Hammond said. "*Unicorn* goes ahead to survey the system, so we have both a decent headcount of enemy ships *and* a shot at locating the flicker station. Assuming, of course, they have one."

"They should certainly have set one up," Mitch agreed. "Even if they didn't have flicker technology before the war, they'll have learnt about it from us."

He made a face. The navy took endless precautions to prevent intact datacores from falling into enemy hands, but most of those precautions could be circumvented with a zombie's willing help. It was impossible to determine what the virus did and didn't know, particularly since it had started infecting and overwhelming humanity's colony worlds. He'd read a dozen books that mentioned the flicker network, in greater or lesser detail. And knowing something was possible was half the battle.

"If we take out the station, they'll know for sure we're there," he warned. "And if we don't find the station...we won't know for sure it doesn't exist."

"We can but try." Captain Hammond shrugged. "I take it you have no objection to going in first, alone?"

"No, sir." Mitch had to smile. As if he would! "We'll just have to set up the details and plan the offensive."

"Quite." Captain Hammond looked distracted, just for a moment. "I'd like to keep running drills until we reach New Washington, then we can finalise our plans. My crew are still not at their best."

"There's nothing like battle for smoothing out the rough edges," Mitch assured him. "I'll keep working on operational plans too."

"Good." Captain Hammond nodded, curtly. "We'll speak again before too long."

Mitch nodded, stiffly, as his superior's face vanished. He'd expected better, somehow. He understood Captain Hammond's concerns—they were flying untested ships, with largely untested crews—but he didn't share them. The admiral had made it clear, time and time again, that humanity was losing the war. They *had* to buy time, whatever the cost. It might have been better, he reflected sourly, to assign a more experienced captain and command crew to *Lion*. Her captain had spent the last six months at the academy, not on a command deck. Mitch understood the importance of having experienced officers assigned to the academy—too many instructors were too inexperienced to know they were teaching the wrong lessons—but...he shook his head. There was no point in worrying about something he couldn't change. Instead, he keyed his console, bringing up the latest reports. The simulated engagements had gone better than he'd expected.

Which means we're either smoothing off the rough edges faster than I thought possible, he mused, *or we're setting ourselves up for a fall.*

He dismissed the thought as he brought up the latest reports from the survey missions. Farnham had never been considered very important, even by the Americans who'd laid claim the system. The colonists were considered harmless cranks, not the nucleus of a new civilisation. Reading between the lines, Mitch had the impression the United States thought it was just a matter of time before they took formal control of the surface. Or had, once upon a time. There was nothing left of the colony now but zombies.

Unless they did manage to go underground, he thought, as he checked the remainder of the system. Slipping in and out without being detected shouldn't be a problem. *They might be still in hiding, afraid to come out.*

He shuddered. Who could blame them? A small colony—only a couple of thousand settlers, if the records were accurate—couldn't hope to do more than slow the virus down for a few minutes. There'd been no orbital defences, nothing capable of so much as *spitting* at the enemy ships. He hoped the colonists *had* managed to hide. And that they had a way to signal the USN when it retook the system.

And they might suspect a ruse, if the navy tries to raise them, he thought. *The virus can duplicate our signals, damn it.*

The intercom bleeped. "Captain," Staci said. "We've just completed the gunnery cycle drills and passed all the markers. We're ready for action."

"Good," Mitch said. He had no illusions. *Unicorn* was not going to win the war single-handedly. *Ark Royal* was the only ship that had come *close* to winning alone and she'd had help. But he knew they could hold their own. "We'll just have to hope Hammond lets us off the leash."

"Yes, sir," Staci said.

"And meet me in my quarters at 1700," Mitch added. "We have an operation to plan."

"Aye, sir."

Thomas kept his face carefully impassive as he broke the connection, then scowled as he sat back in his chair. He understood the urge to fight, to march to the sound of the guns and open fire on the enemy ships and positions, but he also understood that his ship was nowhere near ready for combat. The design was untested, the crew were untried...sure, the various departments had been showing a marked degree of improvement since they'd left Sol, but they still had a long way to go. Thomas rubbed his eyes, wishing he had time for a proper rest. He doubted he'd feel any better until they'd faced their first real engagement.

He allowed his frown to deepen as he studied Captain Campbell's plan of attack. It was straightforward, almost brutally so. Get into position, hit the enemy and run. There was little more to it, suggesting that Campbell understood the importance of the KISS principle. And yet, Thomas had his doubts. The plan relied on everything going right. If it didn't, if *Lion* was overhauled by the enemy ships, they'd be shot to pieces. He couldn't take the risk.

Particularly when we don't have to, he mused. They could launch the missiles—on ballistic trajectories—from a safe distance. The virus would have no trouble tracking the missiles back to their point of origin, but *Lion* would have plenty of time to put entire *light-years* between itself and the enemy fleet. *They'll have no time to track us down if we retreat at once.*

He shook his head. The hell of it was that they really *didn't* know how well their missiles would perform in combat. He'd watched simulations that suggested they'd smash the enemy fleet effortlessly and simulations that insisted the entire salvo would be wiped out by enemy point defence before it entered attack range. They'd been over it again and again, before finally conceding they simply didn't know. The gunboats might make the difference between success and failure, but even *they* hadn't been tested in a *real* engagement. Their lone skirmish with the enemy had been marked by surprise on both sides. Neither had known what they were facing.

"And we still don't know if they're watching us or not," he muttered. Basic military doctrine insisted that intelligence was the second most deadly weapon in the known universe—the first being surprise—but it was impossible to determine if the virus had spy ships lurking at the edge of the Sol System. As long as they kept their drives and active sensors shut down, they might as well be invisible. "They might know we're coming."

The buzzer rang. Thomas looked up. "Come."

Commander Donker stepped through the hatch. "Captain," he said. "I have the latest set of reports from the gunboat simulations."

Thomas smiled, although it wasn't really amusing. "Should I be worried Colonel Bagehot hasn't come in person?"

"He's still working with his crews," Donker said. He held out a datachip. "The simulations, as always, were based on vastly more capable enemy starships and missiles. They still took out half of the incoming missiles, despite superior drives and ECM. We can reasonably assume the gunboats will provide a shield for us, particularly if they keep pace with the enemy missiles."

"Which they can't, in anything other than a very short engagement," Thomas pointed out, coldly. "Can we rely on their drive fields remaining stable?"

"No, sir," Donker said. His expression twisted. "We've gone through simulations, dozens of simulations. The worst case, sir, is that we lose a third of the gunboats to drive failure."

Thomas nodded. Gunboats sat oddly between missiles, starfighters and capital ships. Their drives were powerful enough to accelerate them at a clip only missiles could match, without the torrent of radiation and guaranteed compensator failure that would doom any starfighter that tried. And yet, the odds of catastrophic drive failure skyrocketed every time the drives were ramped up to full power. The gunboats might be able to keep pace with incoming missiles long enough to take them all out, at the risk of losing power and being overwhelmed by the enemy fleet. Thomas had no confidence they could mount a SAR operation before it was too late.

They're expendable, the cold part of his mind pointed out. *We're all expendable.*

He cursed himself for the thought. He'd met the gunboat pilots, *once*. They didn't have the polish of real naval personnel—it was hard to believe they *were* naval personnel—yet they were ready to put their lives at risk for their country. They'd been like starfighter pilots, but without the arrogance and complete lack of concern for rules that came with the grim knowledge they might die at any moment. Even in peacetime, the death toll amongst starfighter pilots was uncomfortably high. And it was only a matter of time until the gunboats went the same way.

We'll probably start training proper pilots, once we have the doctrine worked out, Thomas thought. He'd read the proposals Colonel Bagehot and his team had drawn out, five months ago. It remained to be seen how well the doctrine would fare in the real world. *And then the gunboat pilots will turn into starfighter pilots.*

He put the thought out of his mind. "We'll do everything in our power to avoid losing them," he said, although he knew it was a promise they'd be unable to keep. A single enemy missile would be enough to wipe a gunboat out of the skies. The virus might start turning shipkillers into anti-gunboat weapons, clearing the way for the remainder of the missiles to reach the fleet. "And to rescue them, if they lose power."

"If it can be done," Donker pointed out. He didn't sound convinced. "The virus may fire on our shuttles."

Thomas nodded. Humanity's first two alien enemies—the Tadpoles and the Foxes, both now allies—hadn't gone out of their way to commit atrocities, even though it had taken a while to establish communications. The Anglo-Indian War had been remarkably civilised, with both powers doing their level best to play by the rules. Accidents happened, everyone knew, but they could be minimised. The virus, on the other hand, didn't seem to care. It wasn't, he admitted sourly, that it shot up SAR shuttles for the sheer hell of it. It was that it didn't know the difference between a SAR shuttle and something more hostile.

Can we really call it monstrous, he asked himself, *if it doesn't have the option of* not *being monstrous?*

"We'll do what we can," he said. It was his duty. Cold logic told him the pilots were expendable, but his heart told him something else. "At the very least, we have to avoid losing pilots for nothing."

"Yes, sir," Donker said. "Speaking of which, Major Craig wanted to borrow the pilots."

Thomas blinked. "What for?"

"The marines need hostages to rescue," Donker said. "And a bunch of other missions they need to practice, like escorting the pilots through hostile territory. It *will* be a nice change for them."

"I'm sure the pilots will appreciate a change," Thomas agreed. He'd enjoyed exercising with the marines, although that had been back during the *last* interstellar war. Things had probably changed a bit since he'd been a junior midshipman. "Clear it with Colonel Bagehot before proceeding, though. He's got his own problems."

"Yes, sir," Donker said.

CHAPTER THIRTEEN

"WHO WAS IT," PRIVATE DAVIES ASKED, "who said he had that *déjà vu* feeling all over again?"

"You, just now," Private Henry Willis said, as he followed his friend down the poorly lit corridor. "A truly original expression, eminently quotable."

Colin scowled at their backs as he brought up the rear, sweat drenching his uniform. The mask and suit hadn't grown any more bearable in the last week of endless drills. He was tempted to *accidentally* lose it somewhere, despite the risk of breathing in something that would turn him into a zombie. He wanted to believe the vaccinations and booster shots they'd been given would be enough to protect him, particularly if he wore a mask. He wanted to believe...

"Get the hatch," he ordered, curtly. He unhooked a grenade from his belt, holding it at the ready. "Now."

"Aye, boss," Davies said, all business now. He knelt beside the hatch and started to work, bypassing the automated system to open the airlock manually. "Ready...now."

The hatch hissed open. Colin peered into the next compartment, silently relieved there was no place to hide. Anyone within the section would be in plain view...he inched forward, sweeping his rifle from side to side. The corridor felt cramped, even though it was wide enough for the marines to walk three abreast. The air felt uncomfortably hot as he hurried forward, reaching the second airlock before it could be opened from the other side. He had the feeling he was being watched.

We are being watched, he reminded himself, dryly. Their superiors would be watching through the sensors, no doubt coming up with a list of problems they'd have to fix during the after-action discussion. *But are we being watched by the enemy?*

Davies tapped the hatch. "The air should be clean, on the other side," he said. "Keep your mask on, though."

"Got it." Colin might joke about losing his mask, but he understood how important it was to wear. "Open the hatch."

He glanced at the other three, then tensed as the hatch inched open. The mission was supposed to be simple, but he had a feeling the exercise planners had thrown a few wrinkles into the mix. Escorting gunboat pilots from one compartment to another was the sort of mission that looked good on paper, yet tended to come with a sting in the tail. The OPFOR would be on the prowl, waiting for a chance to jump the marines and embarrass them in front of their commanding officers. And the pilots themselves were probably under orders to make life difficult for the marines too. Colin wondered, as the hatch revealed another empty compartment, if they could get away with pointing guns at the pilots. It wasn't as though they were real.

But the CO will blow a fuse anyway, he thought, dryly. *We're meant to treat exercises as reality.*

The thought made him smile as they inched forward, heading towards the next hatch. The pilots were supposed to be on the other side, trapped and helpless. Colin gritted his teeth, silently impressed by how well the SAS coped with escort and hostage rescue missions. He'd taken part in a handful of hostage rescue exercises, with all the advantages offered to his side, and they'd still lost a bunch of hostages. The SAS officer who'd coordinated the operation had detailed their mistakes in great detail, then admitted that something was always left to chance. The terrorists might manage to kill their hostages before the poor buggers could be rescued.

And here, it might be a great deal worse, he told himself. *The pilots might already have been infected.*

He gritted his teeth as they reached the hatch. The briefing hadn't been clear on *just* what the pilots had been doing, before they'd been trapped. Colin wasn't sure if that was deliberate. The CO had spoken endlessly of the fog of war, leaving Colin and his men unsure if they were saving friends and allies or clutching vipers to their bosoms. The pilots would have to be tested, as soon as they reached the safe zone. The hell of it was that the safe zones might be moved at any moment. Colin remembered earlier exercises and cursed himself for wanting something more complex. Complexity was bad. He should have remembered that before it had been too late.

The hatch felt cool to his touch. He rapped on it twice, as agreed. The hatch shuddered, then opened slowly. A handful of people sat inside the chamber, looking remarkably unworried even though they were in the middle of an exercise. Colin suspected they thought *they* would never be in any real trouble, whatever happened. They were pilots, not marines. Colin would be the one in deep shit if something went wrong.

He allowed his gaze to sweep the room. Seven people; four men, three women. They were all around the same age as himself, if he was any judge, although there was something faintly odd about their appearance. He tensed, gripping his rifle instinctively before realising it had nothing to do with the virus. The gunboat pilots looked like people who'd only *just* started intensive exercise, like people who'd been chubby and unhealthy before the navy got its hands on them. Colin felt a flicker of sympathy, mingled with contempt. Staying healthy wasn't *hard*. They could have dealt with most of their body issues in PE.

"On your feet," he snapped. He saw flashes of resentment in their eyes as they hurried to obey. "Do as you're told and we might just get out of this alive."

He checked his HUD as the pilots lined up by the door. The safe route was still safe, but...he shook his head. He doubted he could take that for granted. The enemy might be sneaking through the tubes or settling up an ambush or even plotting an assault on the safe zone itself. It wasn't *technically* on the list of things that would be considered cheating. And if he'd spotted the loophole, he was sure a more experienced officer would spot it too.

"Let us take point," he added. The gunboat pilots were practically civilians. They'd blunder around like...like civilians. He couldn't trust them with weapons. "Keep your heads down and your masks on. Don't even think about taking them off."

He gritted his teeth as he checked the rest of the room, then turned back to the hatch. The pilots should be fine, as long as they kept their masks on. Their shipsuits should provide enough protection to survive a minor hull breach, if they were lucky. Besides, it wasn't as if they had anything else. There were no EVA suits in the chamber. Even if there were, Colin would have been reluctant to use them. A lone zombie inside a suit might manage to slip through the defence lines and do a *lot* of damage.

"Follow me," he ordered. "And keep your fucking heads down."

Tobias could barely *look* at the marines—armoured and masked figures that seemed like creatures out of nightmares—as they chivvied him and the other volunteers towards the airlock. He'd been told he was going to volunteer...he cursed under his breath as he forced himself to move. The marines were blunt, crude, rude...he thought he heard a hint of Liverpool in the leader's voice, but it was hard to be sure. The mask muffled everything. It was hard to believe the figures were even *human*.

They are human, he told himself. The light flickered and flared, brightening and darkening seemingly at random. *That makes it worse.*

He managed to keep moving, shuffling out of the hatch. The air was hot, swelteringly hot. It was difficult to accept that he *knew* the corridors, that they were as familiar to him as the palm of his hand. The ever-changing lights, the faint flickers in the gravity field, the clouds of mist hanging in the air...the scene had an air of unreality that tore at his mind. He kept walking, silently relieved that Marigold had managed to escape being volunteered. It was like being forced to play team sports, only worse. His lips quirked. Here, at least, no one would give him a hard time for playing badly.

His legs wobbled. The briefing officer had told them to dawdle as much as possible, to do everything short of actual violence to slow the march down, but he didn't dare. The marines were supposed to have orders not to hurt the pilots...Tobias didn't believe it. They'd do whatever it took to keep the pilots alive, even if it included pushing them along or knocking them out and carrying them. The deck seemed to shift under his feet as they stepped through a second airlock. It was a drill—he knew it was—and yet part of him refused to believe that. It felt very real.

And what were you expecting? He remembered fire drills at school and snorted. *Rows of bored children heading for the exits? Teachers trying desperately to maintain order as their students enjoy the chance to escape classes? The headmaster waving his cane in the air as he bawls for order?*

He didn't smile as the gravity shifted again. His world had shrunk. He was aware of the pilot in front of him, and the pilot behind him, and the marines...but very little else. He kept his eyes on Jeanette's back, trying not to distract himself by looking around. Cold air blew over him, chilling him to the bone. The lights flickered and died. He heard someone cry out behind him as he stumbled to a halt, the pilot behind him crashing into his back a second later. It was easy to panic...

"Remain calm," the marine ordered, sharply. A slap echoed through the dark air. "We'll guide you. Keep inching forward."

Tobias forced himself to keep moving, somehow. The marines could see in the dark, either through night-vision gear or genetically-enhanced eyeballs, but for him...it was nothing but utter darkness. A chill ran down his spine. There'd been wankers in school who'd turned out the lights, forcing him to grope his way to the exit...the memory taunted him; mocking him, shaming him. He'd been a useless wimp. All the old doubts and fears rose to the surface. He'd been useless; a poor son, a poor student, a waste of time and space and...

Keep moving, he told himself. *Don't stop for anything...*

The deck lurched. The gravity field suddenly grew stronger. Tobias lost his balance and fell, hitting the deck hard enough to hurt. Someone—it sounded like one of the women—yelped in pain. He tried to move, but the gravity kept tugging at him. Panic yammered at the back of his mind, trying to slow him down. It was all he could do to keep crawling until the gravity field snapped back to normal.

"Get up," the marine ordered. "Hurry!"

Easy for you to say, Tobias thought. It was the sort of thing he'd never dare tell anyone. Witty remarks delivered to arseholes who couldn't count past ten without taking off their socks always ended poorly, at least for him. *He* didn't have a friendly scriptwriter putting one-liners in his mouth. *You can see in the dark.*

The light flared. Tobias stumbled, nearly falling again. They were in the corridor...he blinked, looking down as the lights grew brighter before dimming again. He'd lost track of where he was, as if he no longer knew anything...the marines shoved him forward as they opened the next airlock. He wanted to push back, or to lie down and play dead, but he couldn't. It was impossible. Instead, he just kept moving...

And then the shooting started.

Colin swore as he saw muzzle flashes from further down the corridor. "Hit the deck," he shouted. Laser pulses—invisible laser pulses—would be already coming at them. "Get down!"

He shoved the nearest pilot down, heedless of her cry of pain. The enemy had a good position, he noted sourly. They'd taken advantage of the dim light and mist to set up a barricade, studded with murder holes. He unhooked a grenade and hurled it down the corridor, more in hope than anything else. The enemy position was too good. A *real* HE grenade would probably make some room, but the dummies weren't good enough. The umpires would rule against him.

"Move the pilots back," he shouted. They couldn't go through the trap. They'd have to go around it. "We'll go down the next corridor."

He hurled another grenade as the rearguard started inching backwards. They were too far from the safe zone—and any hope of reinforcements—for his peace of mind, although he called the contact in anyway. The enemy were remaining behind their barricade...Colin half-wished they'd come out and fight. They could be cut down in short order if they exposed themselves. He snapped orders to Davies and Willis, ordering them to keep the enemy pinned down. It wasn't much, but it was all they had.

"We need a fucking antitank missile, boss," Davies shouted. "That barricade is too bloody strong!"

"Keep them pinned," Colin said. He considered using their remaining grenades, but there was no guarantee they'd work. "Get to the rear when the pilots are gone."

He glared at the pilots, who were hugging the decks like men who'd just survived their very first parachute drops. They looked terrified, even though the bullets weren't *real*. The bangs and flashes were nothing more than firecrackers...hell, firecrackers would be a lot more dangerous. But they were panicking...Colin wondered, suddenly who'd had the bright idea of sending the pilots into the fray. They weren't marines, or territorial soldiers, or even reservists seeing out their time in the Home Guard. They were...he shook his head. There'd be time to worry about it later.

"Move," he shouted. It was hard to make himself heard, over the racket. "Move!"

Tobias clung to the deck, unwilling to risk so much as raising his head.

He'd heard all the stories about combat, from teachers who'd actually served to army officers on recruitment drives. They'd talked about the military life, about testing one's self against the enemy, about the sheer joy that came with emerging victorious from yet another battle against the enemies of civilisation. They hadn't talked about the noise, or the fear, or...his thoughts ran in circles. He could barely think. He wanted to lie on the deck until it was all over.

"Move," someone shouted. "Damn it, move!"

A hand slapped his back. Tobias forced himself to obey the order, somehow. The noise was getting louder, as impossible as it seemed. The racket was deafening. He could feel his ears starting to ache as he kept moving, flashes of light following them down the corridor. Were they still on the ship? He couldn't believe it. They'd been teleported somewhere else, perhaps into hell itself. Perhaps they were dead. It felt...very much like hell.

"Move!" The marine was screaming as they turned into another corridor. "Move, you..."

The world seemed to explode. Tobias felt *something* pass over his head, so close he thought it passed through his hair. Panic overwhelmed him, just as silence fell so sharply he was half-convinced he'd gone deaf. He raised his head as far as he dared—not very far at all, really—and peered around. Everyone—pilots, marines—were lying on the deck. Were they dead?

"Well," a calm voice said. "That could have gone better."

Tobias managed to sit up. His uniform was drenched in sweat. He felt himself shaking...he hoped he hadn't pissed himself. No one would ever let him forget it, just as they'd made fun of Brian for puking up meals his mother had eaten during the nastier parts of endurance training. They'd called him the Vomit King. In hindsight, that had been more than a little unfair. They'd *all* thrown up, their first time.

"Yes, sir," the lead marine said. "We got ambushed."

Tobias barely listened as he stumbled to his feet, then helped Jeanette to hers. She looked badly shaken, eyes wide with fear. He wanted to go to whoever had had the bright idea of volunteering the pilots for the exercise and shake him, to demand to know what the fuck he'd been thinking. They were gunboat pilots, half-trained gunboat pilots. They'd be screwed beyond all hope of recovery if *they* were given rifles and told to go on the front lines.

"Go back to your bunks," the newcomer ordered. He spoke with the calm assurance Tobias had come to hate in his teenage years. "You'll be debriefed later."

Tobias nodded, not trusting himself to speak as the rest of the pilots stood. They looked as though they'd gone through hell. The marines looked more irritated than anything else. They'd all been killed…not in reality, but their superiors would give them a stern lecture anyway. Tobias had had the same treatment, once he'd mastered the gunboat. They had to treat the exercise as real.

He watched as one of the marines removed his helmet. Tobias felt his stomach clench. The marine looked thoroughly unpleasant, just the type who'd made his life miserable when he'd been a child. The wanker didn't even seem to notice him. The leader, the one with the accent, started to remove *his* helmet. Tobias walked away, then stopped—dead—as he heard a very familiar voice behind him, no longer muffled by the mask.

"We let ourselves be pinned down, sir," the voice said.

Tobias froze. *Colin*?

CHAPTER FOURTEEN

TOBIAS BARELY HEARD ANYTHING during the debriefing—more of a formality than anything else—and the meal that followed it. The voice…it couldn't be Colin. It really *couldn't* be Colin. Fear – pure, animalistic fear—ran through him as he finished his dinner, then hurried to the gunboat. It was all he could do to keep his hands from shaking. Colin had followed him. Impossibly, absurdly, he'd followed him. It was…

The memories surged up. Colin had been everything Tobias had grown to hate. He'd been a monster, a bully, a thug…he'd hit Tobias and mocked him and shoved his head down the toilet and…and everything. Tobias stared at the console, hands clutching the controls as panic yowled through his mind. It couldn't be Colin. The marine had had the voice that haunted his nightmares, but…it might not be Colin. The bastard had been shipped off for National Service, the last Tobias had heard. Tobias had hoped Colin would run into a zombie and die. The virus wouldn't infect him. Colin was too foul to be infected. And yet…he couldn't get rid of the thought. It was Colin.

He felt his hands start to shake. He'd thought the navy was *safe*. There'd be aliens trying to kill him, but…he'd thought Colin had been left behind on Earth. His thoughts ran in mad circles. Colin had followed him. He'd gotten himself assigned to *Lion* just to torment Tobias still further. And… and it was just a matter of time until he caught up with Tobias once more.

The thought was unbearable. He'd finally found his place; he'd finally found a peer group that treated him as though he mattered and…his old tormentor had followed him. It wasn't fair. It just wasn't *fair.*

Maybe it isn't him, Tobias told himself desperately. He didn't know much about the Royal Marines—he'd never bothered to research a unit he knew he'd never join—but he'd heard they recruited from everywhere. The marine he'd seen might be someone else from Liverpool. The accent was hardly rare. *Maybe it's someone who just sounds like him.*

He took a deep breath, trying to calm himself. He wasn't a child any longer. He wasn't…he scowled, realising that—in truth—he hadn't really grown up. Colin still haunted his dreams, the mere thought of the bastard reducing him to a quivering puddle of jelly. No one would help him, if Colin came after him again. Why would they? Colin had always gotten away with it in the past, gotten away with everything from name-calling to brutal bullying that had nearly gotten people killed. Tobias would have pledged himself to the worst person in the world and served him faithfully if it had meant protection from Colin. God knew the Beast hadn't been up to the task. The bastard had *liked* Colin. He couldn't expel someone who'd led the football team to victory, to a petty, pointless victory…

It might not be him, Tobias thought. He focused his mind. There was no point in panicking over nothing. He might be terrified of someone who'd never met him before now, someone who'd never heard of Tobias or Colin or *anyone*, someone who would be more than a little bemused by Tobias's reaction. *It might not be him.*

He leaned forward, keying the display. The gunboat was directly linked to the starship's datanet, including the personnel files. Tobias had played with the system often enough to know he could get into some of the files, although there was a very real risk of setting off alarms if he poked into the classified sections. The navy seemed to trust its crewmen not to play games with the files. Tobias smiled, remembering when he'd hacked into the school's network. The system had been so heavily protected that altering the files had proven impossible.

And I couldn't have gotten as far as I did without an access code, he thought, remembering how he'd watched the teacher use the computer often enough to be sure of the code. The man had grown up in a world where everyone had a computer on their desks, but he hadn't thought to protect his code. He'd probably never considered someone watching as he entered his PIN and memorising it. *It was a shame I couldn't alter the files to get Colin expelled.*

He put the thought aside as he started to skim through the files. The navy didn't seem to care if crewmen looked at the basic files, for reasons that escaped his comprehension. One of the old sweats had said something about making sure a person *did* have a navy file, even if it was classified so highly that no one was allowed to look at it without signed permission in triplicate, but Tobias hadn't paid much attention to it at the time. He wished he had as he checked his own file, then moved to the marine datacores. His heart started to race as he pulled up the list, wondering if he was already setting off alarms. The marines were on the ship, but not *of* the ship. They were meant to maintain their distance from everyone else.

And if that really is Colin, Tobias mused, *does anyone expect him to keep himself to himself?*

His eyes narrowed as a list of names flowed up in front of him, tagged with regiments and companies and other details he couldn't even begin to understand. The navy *had* given the gunboat pilots some basic training, if only to ensure they all spoke the same language, but he knew they'd only scratched the surface. The nomenclature was beyond him. He snorted in annoyance—there was probably a way to search the system quickly, but he didn't know how—then put the thought out of his mind. The names would have to suffice. He frowned as he scanned the list, wondering which of the masked men had been Burt Stanton or Roy Higgs or…

The name leapt out at him. Colin Lancaster.

Tobias's heart stopped. It was him. It had to be him. He tried to tell himself that there might be more than one Colin Lancaster—the name was hardly unique—but he didn't believe it. He forced himself to open the file, to check the handful of details it supplied. The majority of the file was locked, but there was enough. Colin Lancaster, born in the same year as Tobias... it was him. The marine had the right birthday and everything. Colin had taken great pleasure in telling Tobias, years ago, that everyone was invited to Colin's birthday party but Tobias. Tobias had taken it as something of a relief. The idea of taking the bastard a birthday present was sickening.

And yet, it had stung. He'd been left out. Again.

He slumped in his seat, unable to comprehend what he saw. Colin was a marine...he couldn't be. He really *couldn't* be. There was no way in hell an elite force would want a mindless thug on the team. Tobias had been told that mindless thugs did their National Service, then sank into the underclass...into a world of illicit drugs and sudden violent deaths. The thought of Colin and his cronies rotting away in a drug den had never failed to cheer him up after endless beatings. Tobias had wanted to make something of himself. Colin didn't have the drive to do anything of the sort. His only real skill was kicking a football around, and it was no longer possible to make a career out of it. The war had taken that, as well as everything else.

It's him. Tobias worked the console, trying to convince the files to give up something more than barebones detail. *It's him.*

The hatch clanked, then opened. Tobias started, utterly convinced that Colin had finally tracked him down. It wasn't as if it would be very hard, not when the gunboat pilots divided their time between sleeping, training and flying. Colin would probably have the entire crew eating out of his hand by now. He could be very convincing, when he wasn't being threatening. And...Tobias found himself unable to move. He wanted to run, but his legs refused to obey. There was nowhere to go. He was trapped and he'd trapped himself and...

Marigold stepped into the gunboat. "Are you alright?"

Tobias shuddered, torn between relief and shame. Marigold would mock him, if she knew the truth. She'd mock him...she certainly wouldn't look at him with anything but utter contempt. He knew it. Every other girl and boy in his life had done the same. A victim like himself had no friends, no supporters, for fear they'd be targeted too. Colin had made sure of it.

A surge of bitter helpless anger washed through him. It just wasn't *fair.*

"I..."

He shook his head, wordlessly. He couldn't tell her. He just couldn't. She couldn't do anything to help him...she probably wouldn't *want* to do anything to help him. She'd probably go straight to Colin and...Tobias's imagination revolted in horror. Girls had surrounded Colin, buzzing around him like flies buzzing around shit. Tobias just didn't understand it. Colin used and abused his girlfriends, while *he* was a nice guy who couldn't get a date...girls *laughed* at him, then mocked him. Tobias had no doubt Colin was no virgin. He'd bragged of losing his virginity long ago. Tobias wanted to believe Colin was lying, that it was just gym locker talk, but... he believed it. Colin wouldn't hesitate to take whatever he wanted in the certain knowledge no one would stop him. Tobias was sure of it.

Marigold closed the hatch behind her. "It's late," she said. "Come to bed."

Tobias couldn't help it. He giggled. Come to bed, she'd said...he found himself lost in helpless giggles. He wasn't sure what the rules were on relationships between gunboat pilots, but it didn't matter. No one would invite *him* to bed...Marigold gave him a perplexed look, then snorted as she realised what she'd said. Tobias forced himself to stop snickering. She didn't deserve it. She wasn't one of the mean girls who'd tormented him.

"It doesn't matter," he said, turning away from the console. One advantage of the gunboats was that there was plenty of space to get up and walk around, if only for a few moments. "I'm going to stay here."

"If you go to sleep on that chair, you'll wake up black and blue," Marigold pointed out, tartly. "What's bothering you?"

"I..." Tobias swallowed, hard. He didn't want to tell her anything. And yet...he *really* didn't want to tell her anything. She'd think less of him. Of *course* she would. People he'd met online had thought he was cool, until he'd let the truth slip. "I..."

"Tell me," Marigold said. "We didn't do *that* badly in the last simulation, did we?"

"That's not the problem," Tobias said. "Marigold...I..."

The words tumbled out, as if they wanted to be free. He told her about Colin, he told her about growing up with him, he told her about how he'd left Colin behind...only to be followed to *Lion*. And how he'd panicked, when he'd heard Colin's voice. Colin had been a monster and now he was on the ship...Tobias would sooner have come face to face with a zombie. No one would throw a fit if he shot a zombie.

"I see," Marigold said. "And you're sure it's the same guy?"

"The birth date matches," Tobias insisted. "It *has* to be him."

"It might be a coincidence," Marigold said. "There are only a limited number of days in the year. Statistically..."

"He has the same name, the same date of birth, the same accent..." Tobias shook his head, firmly. "It's him."

He allowed his mind to wander. "How did he even get into the *Royal Marines*?"

"Perhaps they thought he had potential," Marigold said. "Does the file say anything useful?"

"Not beyond his birthday and shit like that," Tobias said. "Everything beyond a handful of very basic details is classified."

"If he's the same age as you..." Marigold frowned. "I don't think he followed you."

Tobias glared at his hands. "Of course he did."

Marigold shook her head. "He would have had...what? About eight months to train and qualify for a shipboard posting? He'd be far too junior to pick his own assignment. I think a lot of the departments were thrown together at very short notice, save for us. There's no way he could have known you were being assigned here, let alone get himself assigned here too."

"He could have looked me up in the files," Tobias pointed out.

"Did he even know you'd been recruited?" Marigold didn't sound convinced. "Even if he did, how much of *your* file would he be able to access?"

"Colin can do anything," Tobias muttered. "He probably bribed some clerk to download a complete file..."

"I rather doubt it." Marigold spoke with a calm certainty as she ticked off points one by one. "First, he'd have to know he needed to do it. He didn't know you'd been recruited. Second, he'd have to take time away from his own training to look you up. That wouldn't have been easy for us, and commando training is supposed to be worse. Third, he'd have to convince someone he had a pressing need to read your file. That wouldn't be easy either. Data privacy is taken pretty seriously. Anyone who poked into your file without a good reason would be regarded as a voyeur. His CO would not be amused."

"His CO probably thinks the sun shines out of his arse," Tobias muttered.

Marigold laughed. "I doubt it," she said. "One of my uncles is a marine sergeant. He was never impressed with anything my brothers did. I doubt he'd be impressed by your friend either."

Tobias felt a flash of hate. "He was never my *friend*."

He stared down at his hands. It would have been so much better if Colin had died years ago, if one of his madcap stunts had ended with his death. Tobias might have enjoyed his schooling—he might even have had *friends*—if Colin hadn't been there, casting a baleful shadow over Tobias's life. And now...Tobias tried to imagine Colin being blown to pieces or wounded so badly that even modern medicine couldn't help him. He'd seen disabled men in the library, men discharged from the army after being injured so badly...he shook his head. There was no justice in the universe. Colin could walk through a hail of bullets and remain unscathed. Tobias was morbidly sure of it.

"It doesn't matter." Marigold reached out and put a hand on his knee. "He doesn't know you're here. There's no reason he *should* know. Just... ignore him."

"You make it sound easy," Tobias snapped.

Marigold gave him a sharp look. "Do you think you're the only one?"

She tapped her stomach. "You know what? I was monstrously overweight, a couple of years ago. Fat and ugly and...well, you can probably guess what I was called. You can probably imagine the jokes about how I could never go on top without crushing a guy, if any guy could bring himself to touch me. All the times you saw me online, I was so fat I couldn't bring myself to look in the mirror. And all those girls with clear complexions and perfect bodies sneered at me. They'd never believe the girl they mocked was *me*."

Tobias stared at her. "But…you're beautiful."

Marigold coloured. "I wasn't always…always like this," she said. "You've only known me for a year."

"I don't…" Tobias shook his head. "Who'd do that to you?"

"Girls can be bullies too," Marigold said, sourly. "They can be worse than the boys. Not that anyone believes it, of course. A pretty girl can get away with anything."

"Just like Colin," Tobias said. They shared a look of perfect understanding. "What now?"

"Now?" Marigold stepped back. "Now, we go back to our bunks and sleep. There's no reason to think Colin so much as knows you're in the navy, let alone that you're here. Keep your head down the next time someone tries to volunteer you for something and you'll probably be fine. And try to live well. Better that than living in the past."

"It's not that easy," Tobias said. He knew he'd be jumping at shadows for the next few weeks. The starship was supposed to be *safe*. "What would *you* do, if one of the mean girls was onboard?"

"Laugh, probably," Marigold said. "They'd never be able to cope with the bunks. Or the showers. Or the food. Or anything. I don't think any of them went to university. I'd be prepared to bet good money they're currently looking for husbands."

Tobias winced. He hadn't needed the reminder he'd probably die alone. "People will overlook anything for a pretty face."

"Quite." Marigold turned and headed for the hatch. "Come on, before someone starts asking less pleasant questions. We need our sleep."

"Coming," Tobias said. He felt cold, even as he stood and brushed down his uniform. It would be a long time before he felt safe again. Colin was out there, only a few short decks away. It just wasn't fair. Tobias had thought there were *light-years* between him and his old tormentor. "And thanks."

"You're welcome," Marigold called back. She turned and winked at him. "You can thank me by letting me fly the ship tomorrow."

Tobias laughed and followed her through the hatch.

CHAPTER FIFTEEN

THOMAS ALLOWED HIMSELF A MOMENT of relief as *Lion* and *Unicorn*—along with the rest of the convoy—crossed the tramline and entered the New Washington System. The last set of reports had insisted the besieged system remained in friendly hands, but he was uncomfortably aware that the situation at the far end of the chain could change in the wink of an eye. There were enemy ships prowling the system, launching seemingly random attacks on industrial facilities and lone starships in a bid to wear down the defenders. The virus had even launched a handful of kinetic strikes against the colony. So far, all of their projectiles had been stopped before they could strike the surface, but both sides knew it was just a matter of time before the defenders ran out of luck.

He sucked in his breath as the display filled with green, blue and yellow icons. New Washington was one of the most heavily industrialised and populated systems, with thousands of settled asteroids, hundreds of industrial facilities and millions of people scattered over the planets and asteroid habitats. The Americans had shown a rare skill at turning a colony system into a paying endeavour; there were even rumours that the United States intended to move its government to New Washington in the wake of the planned union of powers. Thomas doubted it—moving an entire government would be a political and logistical nightmare—but he could see the appeal. Emigration had stepped up rapidly as the political and military union took shape. Too many people simply didn't trust transnational political entities.

And human history tells us that mistrust is a wise response, he mused, as he studied the display. *It's very easy for a transnational force to lose all connection to the nations and people that birthed it.*

"Captain, we've just received a signal from System Command," Lieutenant Cook said, breaking into Thomas's thoughts. "They've cleared us a lane to the planet, sir, and forwarded the latest reports from the recon flights."

"Good." Thomas nodded to himself. The Yanks had come through, as requested. "Signal *Unicorn*. Send my compliments to Captain Campbell, then inform him he's cleared to leave the squadron and proceed immediately to Farnham. We'll meet up as planned at the RV point."

"Aye, sir," Cook said.

Thomas smiled. "Helm, take us along the cleared flight path," he ordered. "We'll hand the freighters over to the locals before heading to Farnham ourselves."

He sat back in his chair as *Lion* started to move, escorting the convoy towards the planet. The display was crammed with icons, so many of them that it was hard to believe that *anything* could survive long enough to threaten the planet itself. Thomas knew better. Space was vast, incomprehensibly so. A skilful commander could take an entire fleet through the defences, avoiding detection until he could bring his weapons to bear on the planet and open fire. Twelve fleet carriers, fourteen battleships and hundreds of smaller ships—the largest deployment, outside Earth itself—held station near the planet, enough firepower to take on and destroy the fleets that had fought in the First Interstellar War. Thomas was grimly aware they might not be enough to stop the virus. The allied contingents holding position nearby were a grim reminder that the massed fleets of humanity might not be enough, either. New Washington could not be allowed to fall.

His eyes lingered on the planet itself. The Americans had followed the same basic pattern as Britain and France, throwing land grants at anyone willing to set up a homestead and settle permanently. Some of the homesteads had failed, according to the reports, but the vast majority had taken root. They were scattered over the planet, hopefully spaced out enough to survive if the defenders lost control of the high orbitals. Thomas shuddered, remembering how insidious the virus truly was. If it managed to establish itself, the planet was doomed.

We might wind up moving into space permanently, he thought. He'd read a couple of articles that had advocated just that, when he'd been a cadet. The writers had pointed out the abundance of resources in space, the freedoms that could be claimed...the freedoms just *waiting* to be claimed, while leaving Earth to lie fallow and perhaps produce a second intelligent species. *It might be the only way to protect what remains of our people.*

Commander Donker caught his attention. "Captain, the gunboat CO requests permission to run a handful of practice drills against American starfighters."

Thomas frowned. The gunboat crews had come together in a way he would have thought impossible, although they had yet to face their baptism of fire. The idea of testing them against foreign starfighters was tempting. And they had time...

"Signal the Americans. Ask if they can put a drill together on short notice," Thomas ordered, curtly. It *was* very short notice. Their orders didn't allow any time for a meet-and-greet, let alone shore leave. "If not, we'll just have to cope."

"Aye, sir," Donker said.

Thomas smiled as his XO tended to his console. The Americans had deployed gunboats of their own—the gunboats had first entered service during the Second Interstellar War—but they hadn't designed a formal gunboat carrier. Not yet. He had a feeling, reading between the lines, that they were waiting to see how *Lion* performed in combat. Or simply docking the gunboats to standard airlocks and deploying them from there. It wasn't as if it would pose any major technical problems. The systems were all standard, off the shelf technology. In some ways, it was easier operating gunboats than starfighters.

They copy ideas from us, he thought, with a flicker of amusement. *And we copy ideas from them.*

He kept his expression carefully blank. The admiral had made it clear, in the briefing notes, that they no longer had *time* for international rivalries. The Great Powers—and the Lesser Powers—had to hang together or hang separately. His eyes spotted a handful of Russian starships and a Chinese carrier, holding position near the remainder of the coalition fleet. They were all sharing concepts now, building on each other's ideas to produce newer and better weapons. It was going to be one hell of a mess, he reflected sourly, if the planned political union fell into war. Militaries were always more vulnerable to a deceitful ally than a known enemy.

And if the virus kills us, he mused sourly, *it won't matter any longer.*

"Captain," Donker said. "The Yanks have agreed to a handful of practice runs."

"Then set them up," Thomas ordered. He checked the display. *Unicorn* was heading directly for the Farnham Tramline. She was barely visible, so well stealthed that *Lion* couldn't have tracked her if the battlecruiser hadn't known where to look. "We'll reverse course as soon as we've handed over the freighters."

And then go into battle for the first time, his thoughts added. *Lion's* first battle. He'd gone into battle before, but never when he'd been in command of an untested vessel. *We have to slow them down, or die trying.*

"I heard a rumour we'll be getting shore leave," Private Scott Davies said. He made a show of kissing his fingers. "Have you heard the rumours about colonial girls?"

"They've all got rifles and they know how to use them?" Colin snorted, then shook his head. "I don't think we'll be getting any leave, Scott. I think we're turning and heading into battle the moment we hand over the freighters."

"I'd like to believe we're getting leave," Davies said. "Just imagine...a beach, a girl, an ice cream..."

Colin made a rude gesture. "And I'd like to believe I'm a millionaire aristocrat with a girl on each knee," he said, sardonically. "It doesn't make it true."

"Yes, it does," Davies said. "And since you're a millionaire, you can buy the drinks."

"Go fuck yourself," Colin said, without heat. "We're not getting any shore leave."

He stared at the datapad without seeing the report. *Lion* was a huge ship, but the bulkheads had been starting to close in for weeks. There were only so many times they could stage mock battles inside the ship, or go EVA outside the ship, before it started to pall. They'd gotten better, he knew, but it was hard to measure their progress. There were just too few surprises when *everyone* knew the score. He would have appreciated a chance to match himself against an outside force. They might have managed to bring something new to the table.

"Maybe we'll board the alien flagship and do battle with the alien queen," Davies said, utterly unabashed. "And then seduce her and..."

"You're not allowed to watch *Stellar Star* any longer," Colin said. He smiled. "And I dare you to propose seducing the alien queen to the major."

"You can do it," Davies said. "He won't listen to a lowly private."

"And *I'll* be a lowly private if I dare suggest it," Colin said. "He can't bust you down because there's nowhere to bust you down *to*. He'll have to devise a whole new rank just so he can demote you to it."

"*Civilian*, perhaps," Davies said. "Or...*idiot*."

"More like that guy from the play," Colin said. "*Thick Jack Clot Sits in the Stocks and Gets Pelted with Rancid Tomatoes*."

He grinned and turned his attention back to the datapad. Major Craig and Sergeant Bowman had reviewed the latest set of exercises, then carefully picked them apart to illustrate what the marines could have done better. Things had definitely improved, Colin noted, although they still faced a bunch of limits. They couldn't take up position near the enemy beachhead because they had no idea where the beachhead would actually *be*, at least until it was too late to get there first. Colin had proposed insisting the crewmen start practicing their shooting—the crew carried sidearms at all times, now they were on the front lines—but they simply didn't have time. There was just too much else to do before they entered enemy territory.

"There's no way to speed our reaction time any further," he said, reluctantly. "Unless you're hiding a teleporter in your pants."

"I don't have room in my pants for underwear," Davies said. He struck a serious pose as he considered the question. "We *could* open the hatches, I suppose..."

Colin shook his head. Major Craig had pointed out the dangers of leaving the hatches open, even if it *would* let the marines respond to an enemy boarding party at breakneck speed. The risk to the crew was insurmountable. No one, not even the most daring of the marines, would tolerate the risk for long. Better to slam the hatches closed than risk accidentally depressurising the entire ship. They'd just have to cut down their reaction time as much as possible and hope for the best.

He put the datapad down and stood. "I think we're just going to have to wing it," he said. "And I'm probably going to lose my stripe for not thinking of anything better."

"I think that only happens if you miss the obvious," Davies said. "The major can't demote you for not thinking of something, if *he* can't think of something either."

"How...reassuring," Colin said. "How long do we have until the next drill?"

Davies shrugged. "A few hours," he said. "Unless they decide to call a drill early."

"We'll see." Colin headed for the hatch. "I need something to eat. Coming?"

He rubbed his forehead as he made his way down the corridor. Major Craig had put the marines on relaxed duty, with a grim reminder that the system might come under attack at any moment. It was the closest thing to shore leave they'd have, Colin was sure; they couldn't risk being caught on the surface if—when—the virus attacked. He smiled at a pair of crew-women as he left marine country, feeling warm inside when they smiled back. The marine uniform was good for attracting girls. It was just a shame he was too busy training to appreciate it.

Just wait until you get home for leave, he told himself. *You can chase girls to your heart's content then.*

The thought made him smile. He'd never had any trouble attracting female company at school, once he'd realised girls were more than just strange creatures from another world, but there'd been limits. His father would have beaten him to within an inch of his life if he managed to get a girl pregnant, certainly outside wedlock. The old man was forever grumbling about how he'd been entrapped by his wife. Colin had never been sure if that was true, but he'd learned a lesson regardless. An inch of prevention was better than a pound of cure.

He walked into the ship's mess and looked around with interest. The marines had often joked the navy was soft, with luxuries everywhere, but it wasn't really true. The food wasn't much better than what he'd eaten during training, although it was unquestionably better than the slop he'd eaten at school. He had no idea what the Beast was serving his students, but he had a sneaking suspicion it came from the very lowest bidder. Or the Beast had hired from the dregs of society. A lifetime spent cooking food for a school full of children struck him as a fate worse than the gallows.

"A couple of pretty girls and a boy over there," Davies muttered, as they collected a tray and piled it with food. "You want to join them?"

"Nah." Colin glanced at the stripe on his shoulder. He was meant to be the responsible one or else...he wondered, sometimes, if he had the stripe through sheer luck. He knew he'd handled himself well, but there were old sweats who'd been in the military when he'd been in diapers. He wasn't sure if he was being tested or if someone had been asleep at the switch. "We need to keep ourselves out of trouble."

Davies shot him a sharp look. "That stripe is changing you."

"I'm not going to take it off for anything," Colin said. It had taken commando training to force him to knuckle down and actually work. He'd had problems, at first, coming to terms with the simple fact that men who'd been there and done that weren't remotely impressed with his achievements. He hadn't wanted to admit there was nothing special about his victories on the playing fields of Liverpool. "I worked hard to earn it."

He tucked into his meal, feeling as if he were on holiday. The mess felt more like a school dining hall than a barracks, with different groups keeping themselves to themselves. He spotted crewmen from a dozen departments, ranging from tactical staff to engineering and gunboat pilots. The latter seemed odd, as if they didn't quite fit in. He supposed that made a certain kind of sense. The gunboat pilots had no role on the ship. They were even less useful than the marines.

A pilot raised his head and looked at Colin, then looked down. Colin stared at him for a moment, then shrugged. He'd been told there were crewmen who hated, feared or simply resented the marines, although he'd never been able to understand why. The marines might be handsome and sexy and more muscular than an army of models, but they spent half their time crawling through mud or being shot at by enemy troops. He snorted as he returned his attention to his food. The pilot probably thought the marines were homicidal maniacs, like the fictional Lieutenant Wolfcastle. Colin hadn't been a marine *that* long, but even *he* knew that anyone who acted like the star of a dozen action movies would spend the rest of his life in Colchester, if his commanding officer didn't summarily strangle him first. Senior officers were not supposed to lay hands on their subordinates, but Colin was sure the court-martial board would look the other way.

Davies coughed. "What's so funny?"

"Nothing." Colin didn't want to try to explain. "I was just thinking of a joke."

"Oh, help," Davies said. "I'm sure you're meant to have your sense of humour removed when you get your first stripe."

Private Willis joined them before Colin could think of a response. "Have you heard the latest?"

"Oh, dear," Davies said. "What's happened now?"

"We're heading straight for Farnham," Willis said. "*Unicorn's* already there."

"And we're either sitting on our butts looking stupid or fighting to save ourselves," Davies said. "What are the odds we'll be boarded?"

"What are the odds we'll be trying to board a brainship?" Willis grinned. "I heard we're going to sneak onto a brainship and take out the brain."

"I doubt it," Colin said. There'd been only one marine who'd boarded a brainship in a bid to take control and *she'd* had an unfair advantage. She hadn't survived the experience. "More likely we'll be taking a nuke onto the ship and blowing it to hell."

"Blowing us to hell, too," Willis said.

"Yeah," Davies agreed. "I like my idea better."

"Which idea?" Willis smirked. "You haven't come up with one."

"I think we should take our sick leave," Davies said. "And then run for our lives."

"So you're a coward," Willis said. "A coward and me. Do you know what that makes?"

"*Two* cowards," Davies said. "That joke's older than you are."

Colin let out a breath. "Eat while you can," he said. "We'll be back on ration bars soon enough."

A low tremor ran through the ship, the background hum growing louder. Colin shivered, even though the compartment was warm. They were altering course, heading for the tramline and the enemy system beyond. He swallowed, hard. It wouldn't be his first taste of combat, but...

"Eat up," he told his men, even though he had to force himself to do exactly that. "We're about to go to war."

CHAPTER SIXTEEN

MITCH SHIVERED as *Unicorn* glided towards the tramline. The display was clear, suggesting there were no allied or enemy starships near the invisible line of gravitational force, but he knew that was meaningless. An entire fleet could be lying doggo, watching with passive sensors and waiting for the chance to pounce. He felt alone, even though there were hundreds of friendly starships only a few light-hours away. There was no way they'd be able to intervene if *Unicorn* ran into something she couldn't handle. They wouldn't even know something had happened until it was far too late.

"Captain," Lieutenant Sam Hinkson said. The helmsman's voice was hushed. "We're ready to jump."

"Tactical, prepare to engage," Mitch ordered. "Helm, take us through the tramline."

He braced himself as *Unicorn* jumped. His stomach clenched painfully, a grim reminder that his ship was simply too small to mount proper compensators. The display blanked, then hastily rebooted. Mitch tensed, half-expecting to see missiles or angry starfighters blazing towards them. *Unicorn* was incredibly stealthy, even without her cloaking device online, but no stealth system was perfect. The cloak would have fluctuated the moment they crossed the tramline. If there'd been someone in position to see them jump, they might have had *just* long enough to establish a secure lock and open fire before time ran out. But there was no one...

The display started to fill with data. Farnham had never been considered very important. The Americans had only claimed it because the system was a single jump from New Washington. There was no gas giant to provide fuel, just a handful of rocky planets and a small cluster of asteroids drifting at the edge of the system. The population came from hardy stock, if the reports were to be believed. They'd chosen to settle Farnham to keep their distance from Washington and New Washington. They hadn't been very keen on signing up for GATO either. And now whatever was left of the colony was either in deep hiding or infected. He felt a twinge of pity. The colony would never recover.

"Captain," Lieutenant Hannah Avis said. "I'm picking up the enemy fleet."

Mitch leaned closer. They were several light hours from Farnham itself, which meant the sensor readings were several hours out of date, but it was unlikely the virus had chosen to adjust position in the last few hours. A cluster of starships—he couldn't help noticing it had increased in size, since the last recon flight—held position near the planet. The enemy fleet looked to be waiting for something. Mitch guessed it was waiting for the order to attack.

"Deploy the first sensor platforms," he ordered. "And hold us here."

He forced himself to be patient as the platforms were deployed, even though he wanted to leave the tramline and sneak closer to the enemy fleet. The ships could move at any moment, unleashing a juggernaut that would punch through the tramline and force the Americans to stand and die in defence of their world. Mitch silently tallied up the ships, fighting the coming battle time and time again in his head. Five brainships, seven battleships, nine carriers and fifty smaller ships. The Americans should have the edge, he figured, if they fought the fleet alone, but the admiral had warned there was a second prong. The Americans might defeat one fleet, only to be defeated by the next.

His eyes drifted to the second tramline. There was probably a flicker platform there, but—even if there wasn't—it was unlikely to matter. The enemy could slip a cloaked ship into New Washington and jump from there into the other occupied system, taking the shortest route between the two systems. He scowled, wondering how the tactical planners had missed *that.* They'd been so focused on the flicker network that they'd missed the simpler answer. His fingers danced over his console, updating the steady flow of observations to the jump-capable drone. If something happened to *Unicorn*, if they didn't make it home, they wouldn't die for nothing. He intended to make sure of it.

"I've zeroed in on the enemy fleet," Hannah said. She was young, so young Mitch wasn't sure how she'd been promoted so soon, but she knew her job. "There's no hint they've moved."

"There wouldn't be," Mitch said. He shared a glance with Staci, who was manning the tactical console. It wasn't common to have the XO also serve as a departmental head, let alone a bridge officer, but *Unicorn* was too small to have the roles assigned to separate people. "Tactical, your assessment?"

"We're too far out to get anything more," Staci said. "I recommend we move closer."

Mitch nodded. "Helm, take us in as planned," he ordered. "Be ready to shut down our drives or evade if we pick up even the *slightest* sniff of enemy ships within attack range."

"Aye, sir," Hinkson said.

The air on the bridge grew tense as *Unicorn* started to glide into the enemy system. The crew spoke in hushed voices, when they spoke at all. Mitch knew it was silly, as there was no way the enemy could hear them, but there was no point in commenting on it. Besides, it was better to maintain discipline than risk someone doing something that *would* alert the enemy. The latest passive sensors were supposed to be able to track something as tiny as a datanet signal pulse. Mitch had his doubts—the signal would be tiny, barely detectable—but he didn't want to take chances. The entire mission depended on the corvette getting in and out without being detected.

He kept his face under tight control as the enemy ships grew on the display. Mitch had made a career out of taunting bigger ships than *Unicorn*, yet even he couldn't help a frisson of fear as the enemy ships took shape and form. The battleships were monstrous designs, bristling with giant plasma cannons and missile tubes...each capable of obliterating *Unicorn* with a single salvo, if they so much as guessed at her presence. The brainships carried less offensive firepower, but their designers had crammed hundreds upon hundreds of point defence cannons and sensor nodes into their hulls. There were so many sensor nodes, Mitch thought, that they'd actually interfere with each other. He hoped that was the case. The more he looked at the enemy ships, the more he feared the worst.

"Deploy the second sensor platforms," he ordered, quietly. "And hold us here."

"Aye, Captain," Hannah said.

Mitch watched the sensor display as more and more data flowed into the tactical computers. It was impossible to tell when the enemy intended to move. They'd wrapped their ships in a sensor haze that would make it difficult, if not impossible, to get any closer. He'd hoped to slip a probe right through their formation, but the risk was too great. They'd have to make do with what they could see from a distance.

"As long as the ships hold position, we should have no trouble tracking them with optical sensors," Staci pointed out. "The missiles should be guided right to their targets."

"And we'll have to overwhelm their sensors," Mitch agreed. The brainships could put out more point defence firepower than anything smaller than an orbital battlestation. They could fire off so many pulses that there was a very good chance they'd take out most of the missiles even if they didn't have solid locks on their positions. "That'll be tricky."

"I think we can tailor our seeker heads to their systems," Staci said. "As long as they don't open up their formation, they should have problems coping."

Mitch nodded. "Hannah, can you pick up anything from the planet?"

"No, Captain," Hannah said. "The planet appears to be completely dead. There's no hint the enemy has a presence on the surface, let alone the original colonists."

"Crap." Mitch had hoped they'd be able to make contact, although he hadn't placed any real faith in it. The colonists had every reason to be paranoid. They'd be more likely to stay underground for the rest of time, if they could. "Did the virus just blow up whatever it could see from orbit?"

"Unknown, Captain," Hannah said. "Our current position doesn't allow for optimal observation."

Mitch frowned. It was out of character for the virus to simply drop nukes or kinetic projectiles from orbit. The virus didn't *have* to worry about spreading itself too thin. It could just infect the entire colony, turning the population into helpless slaves. It certainly didn't need to worry about leaving garrisons behind to keep the planet under control. Why bother? Once the system was infected, the concepts of freedom, independence and resistance would be gone for all time.

"Keep an eye on the planet," he said. It was unlikely the colonists would risk signalling, and he couldn't reply unless he was *sure* he was dealing with allies, but it went against the grain to just abandon the system. "Helm, hold us here, but be ready to move if there's a hint of enemy contact."

"Aye, sir," Hinkson said.

Mitch studied the display, cursing mentally as the constant sensor watch told him things he hadn't wanted to know about their weapons and defences. Their communications were odd, a strange mixture of a constant flow of information mingled with a strange quiet. A human fleet at rest would be exchanging messages all the time, from official orders and back-channel requests for information to private communications between lovers and friends. The virus didn't need to do anything of the sort, he reflected sourly. It was one entity that broke into a multitude of smaller entities and reformed into one as easily as he changed clothes. There was no individuality amongst the infected, no sense that any of them were different. The dark ships chilled him to the bone. It was all too easy to imagine the virus steadily spreading from system to system until it overwhelmed the entire galaxy and turned it into a single entity.

Imagine a boot stamping down on a human face, forever, he thought. *Now, imagine a world where there's no need to stamp down…*

"Captain, I picked up a faint signal burst from Tramline Two," Hannah said. "I think I've located the flicker station."

Mitch glanced at her. "Can you confirm?"

"No, sir," Hannah said. "Not without getting a great deal closer. But it's in the right place for a flicker station."

Mitch checked the display. They had twenty hours before *Lion* was supposed to make transit and link up with them at the RV point. He would have preferred longer, although he supposed there was little in the system that merited examination. The enemy fleet didn't seem to have a logistics element. That puzzled him, if only because the fleet *might* take New Washington only to be tossed out again by a human counterattack. The virus would have to resupply its ships…he glanced at the trackless wastes of interplanetary space and made a face. An entire fleet train could be hiding there, utterly invisible.

Or it could be on the far side of Tramline Two, so they have a buffer between New Washington and their supply base, he mused. *They could just bring them forward as soon as they start the offensive.*

He frowned. "Helm, take us towards the flicker platform," he said. It was on the other side of the system, hours away. "We'll leave the sensor platform here."

"Aye, sir," Hinkson said.

Staci glanced at Mitch. He had no trouble reading her unspoken message. The sensor platform was light-years ahead of anything the virus possessed, as far as anyone knew. If it fell into enemy hands, if they so much as got a good look at it, Mitch would be staring at a full-fledged court-martial. It would be hard to blame the brass for wanting him put in front of the nearest wall and shot, he reflected sourly. The human race's only real advantage lay in tech. Giving the enemy a chance to close the gap probably merited a fate worse than death.

We've no choice, he thought, as *Unicorn* started to move. They'd keep their distance from the alien ships as they plodded towards the tramline. *We can't be in two places at once.*

He felt the tension start to rise again as he kept his eye on the tactical console. The enemy fleet was holding position—there was still no hint they knew *Unicorn* was there—but they were steadily gliding towards a second tramline. Mitch was tempted to jump through and scan the system, even though he had strict orders not to take the risk. It might be important to know if the enemy fleet train was there, waiting to move forward. Or... he wondered, suddenly, if they'd overestimated the enemy fleet train. The virus had overwhelmed at least four alien races, judging by the zombies they'd faced since the first catastrophic encounter, but it might not be used to fighting multi-system powers. It might not have realised it was currently waging war against *three* multi-system powers.

Or perhaps that's nothing more than wishful thinking, he thought. *Why bother building a huge fleet if you didn't think there'd be anything worth fighting?*

The thought hung in his head, tantalising him. *Humanity* had built space navies before it had discovered it was not, and never had been, alone in the universe. But then, humans hadn't *needed* aliens to fight. Much of human history involved humans trying to kill other humans. The virus didn't have *that* problem, did it? It could no more fight itself than Mitch could willingly chop off his own leg. Why would it bother to build a giant fleet when it had no reason to assume it could be threatened? Who knew? It might be waging several different wars simultaneously.

He felt tired, drained, as *Unicorn* approached the tramline. The odds of something jumping through at *just* the right time to ambush them were so low they were literally incalculable, but he still felt edgy. He felt like a mouse trapped on one side of a wall, knowing the cat might be on the other side with a certainty that defied logic. There was no hint the cat was there, but...he *knew* it was there.

"Captain," Hannah said. "That's definitely a flicker platform."

"We'll mark it down for destruction when we hit the system," Mitch said. "Tactical, reprogram a shipkiller for remote operations, then deploy it. We'll send the engage command when battle is joined."

"Aye, Captain," Staci said. Her fingers flew over the console. "A shame we can't mine the tramline."

Mitch nodded. Every year, without fail, a politician would come along and insist the navy mined the tramlines. A particularly ignorant or obnoxious politician would come up with all sorts of explanations for the navy's *failure* to mine the tramlines, assigning the admirals all sorts of motives that made no sense in the cold light of day. They never seemed to grasp the sheer immensity of the tramlines. Even if the minelayers knew *precisely* where the enemy ships would materialise, it would be difficult to lay enough mines to take them out. And, even if *that* worked, the first explosions would clear the minefield, allowing the remainder of the invasion to come forth. It was a great idea, on paper. In practice, it was impossible.

"Helm, take us back to the RV point," he ordered, once the missile was deployed. "Sensors, keep a wary eye on the passive sensors. I want to know if anything so much as twitches out there."

"Aye, sir," Hannah said.

Mitch stood. "XO, I'll be in my cabin. Pass command to Commander Tucker when his shift begins, then join me."

"Aye, Captain," Staci said.

Mitch headed for the hatch, trying not to show his tiredness as he made his way to his cabin and splashed water on his face. It wasn't his first recon mission, but he would have preferred to spend longer scouting the rest of the system. Not, he admitted sourly, that there seemed to be anything worth logging. The system wasn't precisely useless—in fact, it could support a major colony—but there'd been no time to develop it before the virus had arrived, smashed the defences and infected the planet.

He shivered, suddenly unsure The virus was…insidious. He understood combat, be it hand to hand or starship to starship, but the virus was different. How did one fight an enemy inside one's body? The reports made grim reading. A marine, one of the healthiest human specimens in the world, had been infected during the very first encounter. She'd been kept alive, barely. By the time she'd died, the virus had been starting to overwhelm her again. How did one beat an enemy like that?

The hatch bleeped, then opened. Staci stepped in, looking tired. "Sir?"

"I was wondering.," Mitch said. He keyed his terminal, bringing up reports from the last few years of war. "The virus seems to have relatively few logistics ships."

Staci raised her eyebrows. "And you think it might be getting a little overstretched?"

"It's possible," Mitch said. "The war has been raging for five years. The virus has taken heavy losses."

"So have we," Stacy said.

"Yes, but it still has the firepower to overwhelm New Washington and turn our flank," Mitch said. He'd seen the enemy fleet. Two fleets of roughly the same size could take New Washington. "Why has it lingered here?"

"You might be engaging in wishful thinking," Staci said. She sounded as if she wanted to believe him, but didn't quite dare. "It's alien. For all we know, it's waiting until the stars are right."

"I know." Mitch could hardly disagree with her reasoning. "But if I'm right, we might have a chance to slow it down, perhaps even stop it."

CHAPTER SEVENTEEN

"TRANSIT COMPLETE, CAPTAIN," Lieutenant Fitzgerald said. "Welcome to Farnham."

Thomas nodded as the display rapidly started to fill with icons. The enemy fleet was still holding position—or at least it *had* been, several hours ago. His eyes tracked the ever-expanding probability spheres on the display, calculating that the enemy fleet had to be *somewhere* within a vast volume of space. There was no indication the enemy had so much as altered position in the last few hours, but there wouldn't be. He felt his heart start to race as the icons grew sharper. They were going into battle for the first time.

"Captain," Lieutenant Cook said. "I'm picking up a tight-beam laser from *Unicorn*. All command and communications protocols check out."

Which means nothing, when the virus is involved, Thomas thought, coldly. *Unicorn might have been attacked, captured and subverted the moment she crossed the tramline.*

He scowled, cursing—once again—the sheer lack of knowledge. The navy had done everything in its power to secure starship datacores, but there were limits to how far they could protect them from involuntary traitors. The xenospecialists were still arguing over how much the virus comprehended what it might have gleaned from its new hosts, yet it was undeniable it had succeeded in duplicating IFF codes long enough to get a starship into firing range. The impersonations had never lasted very long, but they'd lasted long enough to cause real trouble. And what few complex precautions the navy had been able to devise had actually hampered military efficiency.

If this goes on, we'll be utterly unable to coordinate, he mused. *We'll wind up shooting each other instead.*

He keyed the display, bringing up the datapacket. *Unicorn* had done a good job, although her commander had warned they'd been unable to get too close to the alien ships. Thomas wasn't too surprised. It was never easy to tell when and how the virus would react—it had sent entire fleets after single survey vessels and ignored entire battle squadrons trying to sneak up on it—and Captain Campbell had chosen to err on the side of prudence. Thomas had to smile. A known fire-eater would be understandably pissed at having to stand off and watch from a distance when he could be firing missiles into an enemy fleet, although it was unlikely he'd have been able to do much damage. *Unicorn* just didn't have the firepower to tip the scales one way or the other.

"My compliments to Captain Campbell," he said, "and inform him we'll proceed with Hammer-3."

"Aye, Captain," Cook said.

Thomas glanced at the helmsman's back. "Helm, take us into firing position," he ordered. "Mr. XO, inform the gunboats that they are to launch in two hours from now."

"Aye, Captain," Donker said.

And hope the crews are really up to scratch, Thomas thought, silently. He'd never been wholly sold on the program. The concept was sound, but a great many other concepts had *also* been sound...only to flop when they'd come face to face with reality. *They're about to deliberately pick a fight for the first time.*

He felt the tension start to rise as *Lion* glided further into the system. The enemy fleet hadn't moved, something that worried him more than he cared to admit to his crew. They were just sitting there. Farnham was largely useless, he supposed, but still...a human fleet would have been quartering space for unwelcome eyes or simply lurking under cloak until the time came to move to the next target. Farnham wasn't worth protecting, either. The virus could easily afford to trade space for time if the humans mounted a major counterattack. It cared as little for the infected colonists on the ground as Thomas cared about his toenail clippings.

His eyes moved from officer to officer. They'd gone through every scenario they could imagine, from the probable to the downright insane, but none of them had been real. The thought nagged at his mind, a grim reminder that *Lion* was an untested ship with an untested crew. They all had combat experience—these days, it was hard to find a front-line officer who didn't—but they hadn't fought together before, not for real. Thomas told himself that they'd drilled endlessly, until they could fight in their sleep. It wasn't reassuring. The enemy might do something unexpected and catch them by surprise.

He forced himself to scan the rest of the datapacket. The new sensors had performed well, *too* well. It was only a matter of time until the virus duplicated them, either through its own R&D program or through capturing and duplicating a sensor platform. The boffins had promised the sensor platforms were impossible to capture, that they'd self-destruct if they were discovered, but Thomas had heard such promises before. The virus had time to experiment, to learn what worked and what didn't from infected engineers and technicians. It could have found all sorts of ways to circumvent the security protocols and take possession of a piece of advanced technology...

You're woolgathering, he told himself, sternly. *There's no point in worrying about it now.*

The tension continued to rise as they approached their firing position. The crew spoke as little as possible, as if they were afraid the virus could hear them. Thomas understood, all too well. They were creeping up on an alien fleet that outgunned them twenty to one, a fleet that could run them down effortlessly if they got a sniff of *Lion's* presence and carefully prepared to give chase without emitting any betraying emissions. The virus's sensor masking was good, Thomas acknowledged sourly. It was possible its fleet could alter position, bringing the ships around to give chase. And if they did...Thomas waged the coming battle in his mind, time and time again. They'd have no choice, but to ramp up the drives and run for their lives.

"Captain," Lieutenant Commander Sibley said, quietly. The tactical officer didn't take his eyes off his console. "I have rough locks on the enemy brainships."

Thomas frowned. "Just *rough* locks?"

"Yes, sir," Sibley said. "Their drive signatures are too close to battleship signatures for me to be entirely sure, at this range. We've confirmed their locations with the records from *Unicorn*, but they could have changed positions in the last two hours."

"The gunboats will do more precise targeting," Thomas said. It would be unfortunate, ironically so, if they accidentally targeted a battleship instead. They'd have a better chance of taking the ship out—enemy battleships mounted less point defence than brainships—but they'd run the risk of leaving one of the brainships intact. "Are they ready to launch?"

"Yes, Captain," Donker said. "They're ready to depart at once."

"Begin launching missiles on ballistic trajectories," Thomas said. "And then clear the gunboats to depart."

"Aye, Captain," Sibley said.

Thomas sat back in his chair, trying to present an image of unflappable calm. The die was cast. They were about to succeed brilliantly or fail ingloriously. He keyed his console, bringing up the live feed from the gunboat hatches. The ships were coming to life, readying themselves to depart. They were supposed to be stealthy—they'd tested the stealth coating time and time again, during the long voyage from Earth—but it wouldn't take more than a single emission to betray them to watching enemy sensors. It was possible the enemy would ignore a single emission, yet...Thomas shook his head. A vague flicker might be ignored, but no human sensor officer would take the risk. Better to sound the alert and launch starfighters than dismiss the sensor contact and risk having an enemy ship slip into firing range. One couldn't go wrong by being paranoid.

And even paranoids have enemies, he reflected. *Or so they say.*

I'm going to die a virgin, Tobias thought.

He followed Marigold through the hatch, suddenly wishing he'd had the nerve to ask a girl—or a dozen girls—out when he'd gone home on leave. The navy uniform had to be good for something, right? Or he could have gone to Sin City instead. He'd heard all the stories, of everything from vanilla sex to weird fetishes that didn't sound physically possible, but he'd never dared go. An entire colony devoted to pleasure had no place for him. They'd point and laugh from the moment he stepped out of the tube 'til he turned and went back home.

The hatch banged closed behind him. The gunboat started to power up, a dull quiver running through the craft as the tiny drive nodes came online. Tobias hurried to his seat and strapped himself in, his thoughts running in circles. It wasn't the first time he'd seen combat, but...in a sense, it was. He hadn't expected to encounter *real* alien ships during the war games. There'd been no time for fear, let alone terror...his mouth was suddenly dry. He looked at Marigold and knew, beyond a shadow of a doubt, that she was scared, too. They were about to put the gunboats to their first real test.

"Hey," he started to say, then stopped himself. It was no time to ask someone out. It really wasn't. And besides, Marigold would probably say no. "Are we...are we ready to launch?"

"Just about." Marigold shot him an odd look, then turned her attention back to her console. "Make sure the missile communications links are up and running, but stay passive until we enter attack range."

Tobias started to make a sarcastic response, then stopped himself before the words left his mouth. Marigold was in command, at least for this operation. It was her duty to make sure everything was in order, although—if something wasn't—they probably wouldn't live long enough to explain themselves to Bagehot. Or Captain Hammond. Tobias had only seen the commanding officer once, but the man hadn't struck him as someone who'd forgive a minor blunder. The fact that the blunder would probably get a lot of people killed would be icing on the cake.

He won't bother with a court-martial, Tobias thought. *He'll just strangle us with his bare hands.*

"Missile links are up and running," he said, as a low *clang* echoed through the gunboat. He almost wet himself. The sound was so penetrating he was *sure* the enemy had heard it. He'd been told that, in space, no one could hear him scream...but he didn't believe it. Besides, in the movies, everyone had heard the screams. "I have control of our cluster. Back-up links are in place, ready to take over."

"Good." Marigold sounded tense as the gravity field flickered and shifted. "Here we go."

Tobias swallowed hard. A quiver ran through the gunboat. He turned his attention to the near-space display and watched, a lump in his throat, as the gunboat accelerated away from the mothership. The remainder of the gunboats were almost invisible, even though he knew where to look. He was fairly sure they wouldn't be able to locate them at all, if they weren't linked together by communications lasers. There was no way to know if the virus could track them, until they tried. The simulations had started with the assumption the gunboats were basically invisible and ended with them practically shouting their location at the top of their lungs. It hadn't escaped his notice that the latter simulations had ended with the entire squadron getting wiped out for nothing.

We're meant to be expendable, he thought. He understood the logic. The needs of the many outweighed the needs of the one and all that jazz. *But that's not so easy to take when you're the one considered expendable.*

It was hard to convince himself to touch the console as the gunboats picked up speed, steadily catching up with the missiles. The slightest mistake might reveal their presence before the missiles went active, alerting the enemy...he was tempted to step back from the console, just to make sure he didn't touch anything. Cold logic told him he was being stupid—they'd played the hunters as well as the hunted in simulations—but he simply didn't believe it. The slightest mistake...

"You know what we need?" Marigold turned to look at him. "A soundtrack. And a theme song."

Tobias couldn't help himself. He giggled. "We could always put music on the speakers," he said. He'd been told there were marines who went into battle playing rock and roll music, but it seemed a little unlikely. It wouldn't be easy to hear orders from one's superior if one was being deafened by a headache-inducing racket. "Something nicely dramatic, perhaps."

Marigold smiled. "What kind of music did you like, back then?"

"Nothing *popular*," Tobias said. The conversation distracted him from the impending violent encounter. "I never liked any of the imports."

He made a face as she laughed. There'd been a craze for rock and roll music when he'd been a teenager, despite the best efforts of parents and teachers alike. *They* seemed to believe kids should only listen to folk music and hymns, certainly nothing imported from France or the United States. Tobias had a feeling it was a cunning plot to channel rebellious children and teenagers into doing something relatively harmless, instead of something more dangerous. It was possible, but the Beast had never struck him as being that subtle. He preferred to avoid spoiling the children by not sparing the rod.

Maybe someone a bit higher up the food chain came up with it, he mused. *And the arsehole just had to follow orders.*

The display updated rapidly as they flew towards the alien fleet. He felt his stomach churn unpleasantly as the passive sensors picked out the enemy ships, telling him things—from their sensor emissions—he honestly hadn't wanted to know. The brainships sat at the near-centre of their formation, surrounded by dozens of battleships and smaller ships...it seemed impossible to slip even a single missile through their defences, let alone enough firepower to take out every last command ship. He felt sweat trickle down his back as the missile clusters updated rapidly, command links and sublinks taking shape as they picked out their targets. The enemy hadn't spotted them yet, but it was just a matter of time. A single sensor sweep locating a missile would be enough to put the entire fleet on alert.

Marigold coughed. "Missile activation in five minutes, barring detection," she said. "I say again, missile activation in five minutes."

"Understood." A timer appeared on Tobias's display, counting down the seconds. He found it hard to speak. "All targeting and counter-targeting systems in stealth mode, ready to go live.

"Understood," Marigold said.

Tobias winced, inwardly. Marigold knew the systems were in stealth mode, if only because they were still alive. Going active would have told the enemy the gunboats were out there, even if the enemy couldn't get a solid lock on their hulls. The gunboats were tiny, designed to be hard to locate and hit, but it might not matter. There were so many point defence weapons on the enemy ships that they could fill space with plasma bolts. A single hit *might* not be enough to kill a gunboat—they had some armour, unlike starfighters—but he wouldn't care to stake his life on it…

I am staking my life on it, he thought. *They hit us, we're dead.*

He had to fight to calm himself. Would anyone miss him, if he died? His mother? His sister? His mother would be able to claim she'd lost a son as well as a husband to the war…he hoped, suddenly, she'd have no trouble drawing two sets of benefits. There might be legal issues if she tried, from what he'd read. The government talked about supporting the troops and their families—God, it was hard to believe he was one of the troops—but only as long as it didn't cost money. His mother might be told she could only draw *one* set of benefits. And his sister…he hoped *she'd* miss him. Someone should miss him, just one person should miss him…

Mum will miss me too, he told himself. *Won't she?*

Each second felt like an hour. He could practically *feel* time passing, each second ticking past with a *thud* he felt in his very bones. He could barely move. It felt as if they were flying into a trap, charging madly towards certain death…he thought he understood, now, how the Light Brigade had felt when they'd charged the Russian cannons. And yet...they had to have known they were about to get themselves killed for nothing. He...he wasn't about to die for nothing. If they took out a single brainship, it would be worth the cost. Right?

"Fifty seconds," Marigold said. She might as well have said fifty *hours*. "Get ready."

Tobias nodded, not trusting himself to speak. The missiles moved to the very brink of activation, powering up everything they could without emitting anything that might betray their location. He frowned as the display picked up a hint of their presence, cursing under his breath. The emissions were too low-key to attract attention, normally, but they were in an enemy-held system. The virus *knew* it might be attacked at any moment. He keyed his console, sending the sensor records back to *Lion*. If he didn't make it back, Bagehot and the others would have a chance to learn from Tobias's experiences. The next set of pilots would know what not to do.

Sure, he reminded himself. *And you can do everything right and still lose.*

"Going active in five," Marigold said. She sounded as if she'd moved beyond fear. "Now!"

CHAPTER EIGHTEEN

"THE MISSILES HAVE GONE LIVE, SIR," Sibley reported. "I don't think the enemy saw them coming."

Thomas nodded. There was a slight time delay—the missiles and gunboats had rocketed ahead of the mothership—but not enough to matter. The display was rapidly filling up with sensor ghosts and distortions, hopefully confusing the enemy tactical sensors long enough for the missiles to get within attack range. He wondered, grimly, just how alert the enemy ships had actually been before the shit hit the fan. No military force could remain on alert forever, no matter what politicians claimed…no *human* military force. The virus was so interconnected that it might be perfectly capable of keep its host bodies on alert forever.

Which might explain why so many hosts looked emaciated in the later stages of infection, he thought, grimly. *Their bodies aren't so much taken over as hollowed out.*

He frowned as the enemy point defence weapons opened fire. The virus—or its automated servants—hadn't been on a hair trigger, then. *That* was uncommon for the virus, he thought, although it made a certain kind of sense. It couldn't *want* to run the risk of accidentally firing on its own ships. God knew the Royal Navy was paranoid about blue-on-blue incidents. The enemy fire was a little scattered, although it was getting more intense as more and more weapons came online. He cursed as he saw a handful of missiles casually blown out of space. He wanted to believe the enemy had only blasted sensor decoys—and it was possible—but he couldn't allow himself to do more than hope. He had to assume the enemy had hit *real* missiles.

Commander Donker glanced up from his console. "The gunboat command links are holding steady."

"Good." Thomas wanted to issue orders, to do *something*, but there was no point. By the time his orders reached the gunboats, it would be too late. He was nothing more than a passive observer. "Have the missile tubes been reloaded?"

"Aye, Captain," Sibley said.

"Then prepare to fire," Thomas ordered. This time, the enemy would know what was coming. The gunboats would have to establish the new command links while the virus was trying to kill them. "On my command..."

He took a breath. "Fire!"

There was no more time for fear, no more time for anything but doing his job. Tobias felt as if he'd stepped back in time, back to the days he'd spent playing *Naval Command* endlessly until he'd mastered even the hardest missions. His fingers danced across the console, adjusting the sensor decoys one moment and retargeting the missiles the next. A tidal wave of data flowed into the console as more and more enemy sensors came online, allowing him to project sensor ghosts where they'd do the most good, then pass control to the automated guidance systems. No human could handle the pace, once the distances dropped to practically point-blank range. The windows of opportunity grew so slight that they opened and closed before he even noticed they were there.

"The enemy carriers are launching starfighters," Marigold warned. "They're fanning out towards us."

Tobias barely heard her. The missiles were entering their attack sequence. The virus seemed unsure if it should be focusing all its efforts on the missiles or not, although it was starting to look as though it had made up its mind. The brainships were too important to leave unprotected, even though they were bristling with point defence weapons. He frowned as he saw a pair of missiles vanish, despite his best efforts. It felt like a game, but one that had worse consequences than embarrassment if he lost. His lips quirked at the thought. He'd joked, once, that death would be preferable to being laughed out of the league. The computer game club was the closest thing he had to a *community*. And yet, the joke didn't seem so funny now.

He watched as the missiles struck home. A handful of laser warheads exploded, stabbing beams of deadly light into alien hulls. He smiled, coldly, as one brainship was riddled with laser beams until it exploded into plasma, disrupting the enemy command and control network. Two more took lighter damage, yet lost chunks of their point defence. He steered more missiles into the newly created blind spots, directing a handful of nuclear-tipped missiles to slam into the alien hulls. The alien ships exploded violently. Tobias tried not to think about the host bodies, human and alien, that had died with the ship. The briefing officers had made it clear that the bodies were no longer human, little more than living robots who could no longer be liberated, but...he shook his head. He couldn't afford to worry about it. The host bodies—and the intelligence directing them—wouldn't hesitate to kill *him* if it got a chance.

The damage mounted up rapidly. Two missile clusters lost their targeting locks on the remaining brainships, then locked onto a carrier and blew it into atoms. Tobias scowled, even though part of him wanted to hoot and holler like a demented football fan. The carrier had been an important target, but she hadn't been one of the *real* targets. There were three brainships left and they *all* had to die. He watched an enemy destroyer place itself between a brainship and another cluster of missiles, practically evaporating when the missiles struck home. If the crew had been human, saving their ships...

"The second wave is inbound," he said. "I'm uploading the modified orders now."

He felt as if he'd moved beyond any feeling at all. The missiles had adapted rapidly, drawing on updated targeting protocols from the gunboats, but...he swallowed, hard, as the enemy rebooted their command and control networks. Their point defence was improving with every passing second. An enemy battleship casually swatted a dozen missiles out of space, picking them off with brutal efficiency. He couldn't tell if they'd hit the missiles though sheer luck, excellent sensor locks or some combination of the two. The battleship was certainly pumping out enough plasma bolts to target each and every flicker on the sensor displays. Better to waste shots than risk allowing a missile too close to the brainships.

His fingers kept moving, steering the missiles through the enemy defences and hurling them towards their targets. His clusters dropped in and out of his command net as communications links broke, then rebuilt themselves. He gambled, directing one cluster towards an alien cruiser to blow it out of the way, allowing the remaining clusters to fall on the brainship. The alerted enemy fired madly, their starfighters joining the fray instead of heading towards the gunboats. Tobias breathed a sigh of relief as the brainship exploded. The enemy hadn't made the connection between the gunboats and the missiles. Not yet. Perhaps not ever.

Don't count on it, he told himself. Another brainship exploded, leaving one. Just one. *The virus will figure it out, sooner or later...*

Marigold sucked in her breath. "They're altering course," she said. "The starfighters are coming for us."

Tobias nodded, feeling his heart sink. Starfighters were faster than gunboats and, worse, had sharper acceleration curves. They could jump to full speed practically instantly. They'd be on the gunboats before they had a chance to widen the range. He watched the last missiles explode against enemy defences, then adjusted the display to follow the enemy starfighters as they picked up speed. Marigold had been right. Hundreds of starfighters were bearing down on them.

"Point defence online," he said, as he keyed his console. "We're ready."

"A handful are altering course to circumvent us," Marigold said. "The remainder are heading right for us."

Tobias frowned. The starfighters were behaving oddly. Did they intend to rocket past the gunboats, then return in hopes of catching the human pilots in a crossfire? It would have been successful against human starfighters, but gunboats could fire in multiple directions simultaneously. Sure, he'd have problems engaging them...he smirked, knowing it wouldn't matter. A combination of a starship-grade tactical datanet and his automated servants would ensure the enemy starfighters bit off more than they could chew. Gunboats had no real blind spots. And a squadron of gunboats could put out more point defence than a destroyer.

"I'm ready," he said. He felt his smirk grow wider as more and more gunboats joined the command network. They didn't have to hide any longer. They could unleash the full potential of their systems. "Try not to let them get a bead on us."

"Teach your grandmother to suck eggs," Marigold said, without heat. "The moment you open fire, they'll know where you are."

"Yeah." Tobias glanced at the network of decoy drones keeping pace with the gunboats. The enemy might believe there were hundreds of gunboats, but that would change the moment the gunboats opened fire. Sensor ghosts couldn't pump out *real* plasma bolts. The navy had been working on ways to convince long-range sensors the ghosts were real, but so far none of the tricks had proven workable in the real world. "And they'll know where you are, too."

"Smartass," Marigold said. She frowned as more red icons appeared on the display. "Their entire fleet is starting to come after us."

"That's a little overkill," Tobias said. A computer game might have thousands of enemy dreadnaughts chasing single starfighters, but it never happened in the real world. No space navy was so large...his heart skipped a beat as he realised what was actually happening. "They're not coming after us, they're coming after *Lion*!"

Marigold said nothing for a long moment, then clicked her tongue.

"There's nothing we can do about it," she said, as the enemy starfighters closed on the gunboats. "We'll just have to look after ourselves."

Tobias shivered. *Lion* was their only way home. They'd discussed contingency plans if something happened to the mothership, but none had been very comforting. They might be picked up by *Unicorn*, they *might* be able to remain hidden until the human race launched a major counteroffensive, they might be able to land on Farnham itself...Tobias shook his head. He'd read too many horror stories about kids being dumped on planets and expected to fend for themselves. Kids like him always died first, killed by boys like Colin. And girls like Marigold got raped...

He put the thought out of his head. "Here they come," he said. "Firing...now."

"Captain," Cook said. "*Unicorn* reports that the enemy flicker station has been destroyed."

Thomas nodded, curtly. It was useful—if nothing else, the enemy would have to waste time and resources replacing the lost platform—but right now it didn't matter. The entire enemy fleet was coming after him, led by the sole surviving brainship. He had to admit it wasn't a bad tactic. The virus wanted—needed—to either capture or destroy the battlecruiser before she made her escape. And while *Lion* could outrun the heavy ships, she couldn't outrun the starfighters.

He narrowed his eyes as the enemy fleet picked up speed. They were accelerating faster than he'd thought possible, a grim reminder that the virus could innovate too. He shuddered as he remembered some of the speculative reports he'd read, the ones classified so highly he wouldn't even have known they existed if the admiral hadn't thought he needed to know. The virus seemed to get smarter in large concentrations. The thought of how much brainpower it could bring to bear on specific problems was terrifying. And it had access to everything it knew...

"Stand by point defence," he ordered. The enemy fleet was a danger—to

Lion and the system beyond—as long as the sole surviving brainship remained intact. It had to be taken out. And yet, he couldn't see how to do it. The enemy was alert, ready to shoot down his missiles. He might get lucky or he might expend his remaining missiles, shooting himself dry in a failed attempt to take it out. "Order the gunboats to move back to cover us."

A thought struck him. It would be risky. Incredibly risky. But it could be done.

His mind raced. Captain Campbell would authorise the mission in seconds. *Thomas* knew himself to be a great deal more cautious. And yet... he was short on options. They might manage to outrun the enemy fleet, staying ahead of the big guns long enough to jump through the tramline, but the enemy ships might follow them though. The Americans could handle the fleet, at the risk of weakening their defences. No, he had to stop the enemy fleet if possible. And if that meant putting his people in danger...

They're already in danger, he thought. *Better to be hanged for a sheep than a lamb.*

He keyed his console, his lips twitching at the absurdity of the joke. "Major Craig," he said, calmly. "I have a job for you."

"I want to take my sick leave, Corporal," Private Davies said. "I have this terrible pain in my back."

"Yeah," Private Willis agreed. "And when I close my eyes I can't see!"

Colin glared at them both as the assault shuttle disengaged from the battlecruiser and glided into interplanetary space. It was a tiny craft, compared to a standard shuttle—let alone a full-fledged starship—but he was all too aware they might be detected, mistaken for a weapon and blown to atoms before they knew they were under attack. There was even a possibility their *own* side would mistake them for an enemy weapon and kill them, without ever knowing what they'd done. He felt sick as he settled back into the acceleration couch, sick and utterly alone in the midst of a crowd. He'd told everyone he was brave—he knew he was—but right now he felt like a coward. The thought of being killed was one thing. The thought of being swatted out of existence was quite another.

"I'm sure the medics will have a field day with the pair of you," he said, finally. The shuttle was barely large enough to accommodate two fire teams and a pilot. He wasn't sure if it was a good thing. It would have been easier to cope, he thought, if he wasn't responsible for nine other men. "They'll have a lot of fun pouring cod liver oil down your throats."

He shuddered at the thought, forcing himself to keep one eye on the display. He wasn't in control. No one, not even the pilot, was *wholly* in control. He reminded himself, sharply, that he'd taken part in more dangerous exercises...but he'd had more control in a dinghy than on the shuttle. The mission depended on remaining quiet until the enemy ships entered attack range...he swallowed, hard, at the sheer immensity of what they were about to do. The briefing had been very quick, so quick he *knew* his superiors hadn't had time to make any *real* plans. They'd have to play it by ear.

His balls itched, threatening to crawl upwards as he looked at the backpack nukes. He knew they were safe, he knew there was no radiation leaking from the featureless devices, but he didn't believe it. Radiation was an unseen threat, something he couldn't sense until it was too late...he'd heard the horror stories from men who'd fought on radioactive battlefields, stories that had chilled him. It had been worse during meltdowns...he'd seen the video of something going wrong on Einstein Station. The experimental reactor had killed everyone on the station. The asteroid had had to be directed into the sun.

"The battlefront is about to pass over us," the pilot warned. "Get ready."

Get ready for what? Colin gritted his teeth. Pilots were renowned for bad jokes—it was said pilots had no sense of humour—but he would sooner have had terrible jokes than yet another reminder they were in the middle of a battlefield, practically naked. *Arsehole.*

He kept his eye on the display, feeling as if the world was somehow unreal. It was hard to draw a line between the icons on the screen and the real world. He'd always been aware of his surroundings on a dingy, but here...there was no hint the shuttle was so much as moving, there was no suggestion the outside world was even *real*. He closed his eyes, centring himself. It was hard to focus. The old sweats claimed one got used to it, but...

"Five seconds," the pilot said. "Get ready."

Colin opened his eyes. The display showed the enemy brainship, weapons blazing as it fired on...*something*. Colin hoped it was shooting at decoys or incoming missiles...or something, anything, other than marine shuttles. If it spotted the shuttle, it could *kill* the shuttle. The pilot had used gas jets to steer into the enemy ship's path, which were—in theory—invisible...

And half the company is probably going to miss their targets, he thought. The shuttles could catch the capital ships, at the risk of being detected and killed. No, it wasn't a *risk*. At such close range, detection was certain. *We might be the only ones who land safely.*

He heard someone praying, behind him. He didn't look. He didn't want to know.

"Contact!" The shuttle rocked, sharply, as the pilot triggered the cutters. Alerts flashed on the display as the superhot beam melted through enemy armour. Anyone unlucky enough to be on the far side would be dead before they knew what had hit them. "Go!"

Colin pulled himself free of the straps, snatched up one of the nukes and ran for the hatch.

CHAPTER NINETEEN

THE AIR INSIDE THE ALIEN SHIP FELT HOT, even though Colin was wearing a full-fledged combat suit. He told himself, sharply, he was imagining it. His HUD told him things he hadn't wanted to know about the atmosphere, starting with the grim fact it was teeming with biological matter. The virus had infected the ship so thoroughly it practically *was* the ship, bonding the host bodies and its electronic servants into a giant collective mind. He felt sweat prickling down his back as he led the way into the ship, passing through the melted remnants of corridors and compartments. The cutter had wrecked horrific damage on the enemy ship's innards. It was hard to believe it was barely a scratch.

But it is, he thought, as they poked through a gash in an inner bulkhead. The ship hadn't slowed one iota. *If they could have crippled the ship without boarding her, they would have crammed the shuttle with nukes and sent her in on automatic.*

He forced himself to keep moving as they made their way further into the ship. They had to move fast. The virus already knew they were there. It had sensed the death of so many particles...he was sure of it. The corridors were slightly larger than standard, somewhat to his surprise, illuminated by dull red lights that seemed to have been emplaced at random. The xenospecialists had suggested the virus might use corridors, rather than specialised tubes, to move munitions and supplies around the ship, but he had a feeling the virus didn't bother to standardize its host bodies. An infected human might work next to an alien whose species effectively no longer existed. He shivered as droplets of liquid condensed on his helmet. If he took off his suit, he'd be infected within seconds. He'd have to hope his squad could get him back to the ship in time for treatment or he'd wind up an alien slave...

"Down there, I think," Willis said, pointing to a sealed airlock. "The map's not very good."

Colin laughed as they hastily fixed charges to the hatch and took cover. *That* was the understatement of the century. The navy had done its best to chart out the interior of enemy ships, but even the most arrogant spooks had to admit their knowledge was limited. The virus didn't *just* infest ships. It threw their interiors together seemingly at random. What was true for one ship might not be true for the remainder of her class. The spooks had found it odd—and the starship designers considered it crazy—but Colin thought he understood. The virus knew the ship intimately. It was a single entity. It didn't *have* to worry about sticking to a single design.

The charges exploded. He threw a pair of antiviral grenades through what remained of the hatch, then hurried forward. A decaying mass of jelly greeted his eye, quivering unsteadily as it melted into a puddle. He had the uneasy sense he was staring at something completely alien as his HUD blinked a whole new set of alarms...and, worse, that the entity was looking back. The blob dissolved faster, revealing a handful of host bodies. They were so badly warped he didn't recognise the species. Humans? Tadpoles? Something he'd never even dreamed existed? He didn't know.

"Fire," he snapped.

He raised his plasma rifle and opened fire. Bursts of superhot plasma tore through the alien flesh, blowing the host bodies into bloody chunks. He felt sick, remembering—again—why plasma weapons were technically forbidden...or had been, before the war. It wasn't *just* that they could overheat and explode, although that was a very real risk. It was that they were almost always lethal. Very few people survived a direct hit, even if they were heavily armoured. Colin had been told, more than once, that the only reason the troops were issued plasma weapons was because the virus's host bodies were very hard to put down. The plasma would burn through the virus as well as the host.

The blob exploded, pieces of gunk flying everywhere. Colin tried not to think about the shit clinging to him, even as more antiviral grenades detonated. He'd need to go through a full decontamination procedure when he got back to the ship. He put the thought aside as he plunged onwards, peering further into the bowels of the infected craft. The mist was growing stronger, curling around them like something out of a bad fantasy. He'd seen mist on the Beacons, where he'd trained, but...this was worse. Far worse. He fired a plasma shot down the corridor. The spark vanished within the mist, lost without a trace.

"Hold this position," he ordered. He unslung the nuke, then pressed it against the far bulkhead. He wasn't sure if there was any point in trying to hide it within the rubble or not—he honestly didn't know if enough viral cells remained within the compartment to keep it aware of what the humans were doing—but there was no point in taking chances. "Get ready to run."

"They're coming back," Willis said. "I can sense them."

Colin glanced up. The mist was growing thicker. There were sensors mounted in their suits, but the virus seemed to be jamming them. He made a face as he turned back to the nuke, keying the authorisation code into the device and setting the timer. He'd never heard of a starship mounting onboard jamming technology to confuse boarders, but he supposed it made a certain kind of sense. A human ship that tried would jam her own systems as well as the enemy's; the virus, he conceded, didn't need to worry about it. Light flared as more antiviral grenades were hurled into the mist. It didn't seem to clear.

"The device is ready," he said. He was careful not to say anything more about the nuke, not in clear. The virus could understand, if it was hacking their communications. "Throw the final grenades, then move."

The deck quivered under his feet as the grenades detonated. The virus wouldn't be more than mildly inconvenienced, if that, but it would hopefully delay matters long enough for them to get back to the shuttle. He knew through bitter experience that mounting a counterattack wasn't easy, even though the virus had an unfair advantage. It would be in worse trouble when the shuttle departed, he was sure. The gash in the hull couldn't be sealed in a hurry. He doubted the ship would depressurise completely, but the sudden need to seal off the entire section wouldn't make things any easier for the virus. The damage they'd done to an internal hatch might vent more of the interior than he dared hope...

"Shit," Davies said, as something exploded ahead of them. "Sir..."

Colin swore as mist rushed past them, towards the shuttle...no, towards where the shuttle had *been*. Someone had blown the shuttle off the hull. A mistake? Had one of the gunboats fired on the shuttle? It didn't seem likely. The gunboats were needed elsewhere. They would have been blown out of space if they'd put that consideration aside and flown into the teeth of enemy fire. One of the *enemy* starfighters had taken out the shuttle and stranded them...

And we're on a ship that's about to explode, he thought. The virus clearly hadn't realised what they'd done. Unless...unless it thought Colin and his men weren't prepared to die for their country. He shook his head. It was stupid. They'd have to dive into space and hope for the best. *Fuck!*

"Move," he snapped. They were being drawn towards the hatch as the ship vented. The internal bulkheads would have closed, if they hadn't been closed when the marines had landed, but there was still an awful lot of atmosphere in the breached section. "Get onto the surface and jump out, then go silent!"

He checked his timer as he crawled through the hull breach. They had barely seven minutes, long enough to escape on the shuttle, but...he shook his head as he triggered his suit's jets and leapt into interplanetary space. Flickers of light shot around him, his sensors picking out enemy starships and starfighters. They didn't seem to be paying any attention to the marines, he noted. He supposed he couldn't blame the virus. It had too many other problems to worry about, starting with the urgent need to capture or destroy *Lion*.

Colin sent a single signal, risking detection to let the battlecruiser know he and his men were drifting in interstellar space, then forced himself to wait. The seconds were ticking down, steadily. He was sure the virus simply didn't have enough time to find and neutralise the nuke. The device would explode if the virus tried to throw it into space. It was as powerful as human ingenuity could devise, positioned as deep within the alien ship as they could, but there was no way to know how much damage it would actually do. Human ships had internal armour. The virus might have done the same...

The timer reached zero. The alien starship exploded. Colin breathed a sigh of relief. They'd succeeded. They'd saved the day. They'd...he felt the suit starting to spin as they drifted towards the edge of the combat zone. He knew, all too well, that they might not be rescued in time, that they might run out of air and die. He knew...he shook his head. There was nothing he could do, not now. All he could do was wait.

He smiled, despite everything. It was almost...*peaceful*.

Tobias bit down a curse as the alien starfighters closed in, firing rapidly. Half of them seemed more intent on charging *Lion*, rather than confronting the gunboats, but there were rather a lot of them. His point defence opened fire, forcing the starfighters to evade rapidly as they narrowed the range. He shuddered as it dawned on him they might intend to ram the gunboat. They'd barely scratch *Lion's* paint if they rammed the battlecruiser, but ramming the gunboat would destroy both craft.

He watched, torn between pride and fear, as the gunboats covered each other, the automated datanets weaving them into a single entity. A dozen starfighters died in the first few seconds, but the remainder kept coming. They had the edge in manoeuvrability as well as speed, he noted sourly; their evasion patterns were random enough to defeat even the most advanced predictive software. He'd expected as much, but it would have been nice if he'd been able to take his eyes off the console for a second and leave it to the automated systems...

"Their fleet is adjusting position," Marigold reported. "I think..."

She broke off as more and more information flowed into the sensors. "They just lost the last brainship!"

Tobias blinked, hardly daring to look at the main display. Brainship or no brainship, the enemy starfighters were continuing their attacks. The gunboats couldn't risk travelling in a straight line, which deprived them of the chance to put some more space between themselves and the capital ships. He had to admire the virus's grim determination to make the gunboats pay. Either they accelerated, with the starfighters snapping at their heels, or they stayed where they were long enough for the bigger ships to catch up and blow them to hell. Tobias knew they couldn't exchange fire with a capital ship and win. A lone destroyer would wipe them out effortlessly and never know it had been in a fight.

The remaining starfighters picked up speed, lancing towards the gunboats. Tobias watched as the range closed sharply, suddenly convinced they *were* going to ram. The gunboats opened fire, swatting more and more starfighters out of space...he swallowed, hard, as he saw a gunboat vanish from the display. He wasn't sure who was dead, but...he mentally slapped himself as the datanet adjusted for the missing craft. There'd be time to mourn later, when the fighting was over. Right now, they had to keep going or they'd all be dead...

"We're clear," he said, as the last of the starfighters exploded. A second gunboat had been damaged, but she was still intact. Barely. "I think we're clear."

"Not clear enough," Marigold said. She indicated the main display. "The enemy fleet's still coming."

Tobias swore. The officers had insisted that taking out the brainships would be enough to stop the virus in its tracks. They'd certainly hampered the enemy ship, but it hadn't done more than slow it down. He cursed again as he watched the enemy rebuild their datanets, readying themselves to resume the battle. A few moments of disorientation hardly seemed worth the effort. A gunboat crew was dead…for what?

We hurt them, he told himself. It was true. He just didn't really believe it. *We didn't hurt them enough.*

A low quiver ran through the gunboat as she altered course. "New orders," Marigold said, grimly. "We're to yank the marines out of space."

"What?" Tobias was astonished. They'd trained for SAR operations, as well as everything else, but the marines had been onboard *Lion*. If *she* needed SAR, the entire operation was doomed and they were all dead. "What are they doing in space?"

"Don't know." Marigold launched a handful of sensor decoys, then pushed the gunboat back into stealth. "Right now, I don't much care. Go get the airlock ready."

Tobias nodded, snapping his mask into place as he stood. The gunboat's interior wasn't very large, but it should be able to hold seven or eight armoured marines as long as they didn't mind being friendly. He tried to figure out what they'd been doing, but drew a blank. They shouldn't have been anywhere near the battle. They'd been meant to be defending the battlecruiser if she got boarded.

He checked the airlock quickly as Marigold kept up a running commentary. He didn't have anything like as many EVA hours as he would have preferred, certainly nowhere near enough to qualify for a dedicated SAR role. He made a mental note to suggest they got more as a low *clang* echoed through the ship, suggesting that something had locked onto the hull.

"We got one," Marigold called. Her voice sounded odd through the mask. "No…*four*."

Tobias opened the outer hatch, praying he wouldn't have to go outside and *catch* the marines as they drifted into interstellar space. It would be the end. There were ways to freeze someone more or less safely, at least for a short period of time, but the poor bastard might never be recovered at all. A lone man in a spacesuit was so tiny he might as well have been a grain of sand on a giant beach. And turning on his emergency beacon would draw enemy fire.

He let out a breath as a dark figure clambered into the chamber, face hidden behind a featureless mask. Three more joined him, the hatch closing behind them. Were there more? Tobias didn't know. The other gunboats might have been ordered to join the search too...he opened the inner hatch, silently grateful for the mask. The marines were covered in frozen liquid. If it was viral matter, the UV lights should take care of it, but...he shuddered. They'd be heading for decon, as soon as they got home.

"Sit down," he ordered, as the marines started to remove their helmets. "We'll get you back as quickly as possible."

"Thank you," a familiar voice said.

Tobias felt his blood run cold. *Colin...*

The gunboat was cramped—two-thirds of the craft was dominated by drives, sensors and weapons—but Colin had been in worse. There was just enough room for him and his men to sit on the deck and that was all that mattered. He had no qualms about removing his helmet, as soon as the UV light took care of what reminded of the virus. It was even more vulnerable to vacuum than humanity, he'd been told, although it was more of a scientific curiosity than anything else. There was no point in marching a zombie into a vacuum in the hope it would kill the virus. His lips twitched at the thought. *The operation was a success, but the patient died...*

He frowned as he saw the gunboat pilot staring at him. It wasn't uncommon for spacers to look down on marines, he'd been told, but...it wasn't contempt he saw in the man's eyes. It was fear. Real fear. Colin blinked in surprise as the pilot turned away, busying himself with something that was clearly make-work. His hands were shaking. Colin had heard all the jokes, but...did spacers *really* think marines would jump them at the drop of a hat? And yet...there was something about the other man that was oddly familiar, as if they'd met before. Where?

The gunboat quivered as it picked up speed. Colin sat, leaning against the bulkhead. They were effectively out of the fight. They'd go through decon as soon as they got back to *Lion*, even if the boffins were *sure* a combination of cold vacuum and UV light would kill the virus. He eyed the dead matter dripping off the suit and frowned. It looked like water, but...he knew how deadly contaminated water could be. One dose of the galloping shits had been enough to drive the lesson home. Purified water might taste funny, but at least it wasn't unhealthy.

He closed his eyes and tried to rest. His first combat mission and he'd done well. He knew he'd done well. And yet...the gunboat crewman *was* familiar. Why?

Worry about it later, he told himself, sternly. *Right now, you need your rest.*

CHAPTER TWENTY

"THE OPERATION WAS A SUCCESS," Staci reported. "The enemy fleet has lost its aggression."

Mitch nodded, stroking his chin as he studied the display. The virus's ships seemed more than a little confused, their point defence shifting back to a robotic mode of operation as *Lion* and her gunboats fled the scene. It wouldn't be long before it restored full communications links—it had to have something akin to an automated datanet, even if the virus generally handled all such matters itself rather than relying on electronic servants—but there was a window of opportunity. They had a chance to score a far more significant victory than *merely* blowing six brainships and a handful of other starships out of space.

He pulled up the sensor records and hastily reviewed them. The enemy fleet had been caught by surprise, but they'd still managed to mount a defence. His lips thinned in displeasure. The missiles had done well, but not well enough. Too many had been stopped before they could throw themselves on their targets. Mitch wasn't blind to the implications. The enemy fleet would report to its superiors, taking its sensor records with them. The next engagement might easily go the other way.

And that means the fleet has to be stopped before it reports home, he thought, grimly. The flicker station was gone. There was no reason to think there were any unseen eyes, hiding behind a cloaking field and watching the engagement from a safe distance. The virus might be left baffled, if it never found out what had happened to the fleet. *We can stop it now...*

He worked his way through the sensor records as *Unicorn* picked up speed. The enemy point defence was still fractured, each ship forced back on its own resources. It was just a matter of time until they pulled themselves back together, but until then...

"Communications, get me a direct link to *Lion*," he ordered. "I need to speak to Captain Hammond personally."

"Aye, sir," Midshipman Culver said.

Mitch waited, feeling the seconds ticking by. The window of opportunity was closing. He could *feel* it. Every instinct in his body demanded that he turn and charge the enemy fleet, launching missiles and firing plasma bolts until the enemy ships were wiped out. He would have too, if he'd thought there was even the slightest chance of survival. *Unicorn* was tough, for a ship of her size, but she'd be obliterated within seconds if she flew too close to the battleships. No, he couldn't take action on his own. He had to talk Captain *Hammond* into taking action.

He'll understand, Mitch told himself, sharply. *No starship commander can do very wrong who steers towards the enemy.*

Captain Hammond's face appeared in Mitch's display. He looked tired and worn for an officer who'd just scored a major victory. He'd proved the missile-heavy battlecruiser concept actually *worked*, even if the next engagement was going to be a little less one-sided. Mitch leaned forward, trying to communicate a sense of urgency. Captain Hammond *had* to understand. The window of opportunity wouldn't last forever. It was already starting to look as if the enemy fleet was detaching couriers to fly through the other tramline and alert its superiors.

"We've given them a nasty shock," he said, bluntly. "They're stunned, disoriented. We have to finish them now."

He pressed his case as strongly as he dared. "Hit them now, from outside their effective range. Take them out, before they can repair their datanets and fight back. End the battle with a crushing victory."

The display shifted. The enemy fleet was picking up speed. It had little hope of catching *Lion*, unless it slowed the battlecruiser somehow. He wasn't too surprised to see the enemy carriers adjusting position, clearly preparing to launch their remaining starfighters. They'd take enough of a bite out of the battlecruiser to slow her down, long enough for the battleships to catch her up and pound her into scrap. Urgency ran through him. They *had* to strike now.

"Their defences are still weak," Mitch said. "We can take them!"

Captain Hammond said nothing. Mitch felt his heart sink. They had the chance to score a crushing victory, they had the chance to smash an entire enemy fleet, and Captain Hammond was letting it go? The seconds were ticking by, one by one, as the enemy rebooted their defences and reorganised their fleets. His sensors were already picking up vast, impossibly complicated signals being exchanged between the enemy ships. Did the virus have a direct neural link between itself and its computers? Humanity had never been able to get the concept to work, but the virus was practically a sentient program in its own right. It might be halfway towards becoming a *de facto* cybernetic entity already.

"We can take them," Mitch repeated. They'd won the engagement, sure, but they hadn't won the war. He didn't care how powerful the virus was, or how many star systems and shipyards it controlled. Losing a fleet of brainships and battleships had to hurt. Even flushing their remaining missiles at the fleet would do *some* damage, surely. "Captain—Thomas—we have to act *now*."

Thomas said nothing as he studied the display. He could see Captain Campbell's point. They *had* damaged the alien datanet, perhaps weakened it beyond easy repair. The virus's reliance on brainships was an understandable weakness, but one that he had no qualms about using for his own advantage. And he knew, without false modesty, that his ship and crew had performed well. They'd given the enemy one hell of a beating. Losing the brainships would delay any planned offensive, at least long enough for them to be replaced. He was fairly sure it couldn't be done quickly.

And yet, the victory had been costly. He'd flushed two-thirds of his missiles into the enemy fleet. The tactical department was still studying the sensor records, still trying to determine how many missiles had actually hit their targets, but it was all too clear that a number of them had been shot down before they struck home. They'd have to analyse the records in more detail to determine how best to proceed, how best to coordinate their next missile launch to sneak through holes in the enemy defences. He simply didn't have time. He could close the range—again—and open fire, but at what cost? The enemy carriers were already launching their starfighters. He could turn a victory into a defeat just by lingering long enough for the enemy to strike back.

We have to quit while we're ahead, he thought, coldly. The vectors were already narrowing. The enemy starfighters would have a window of opportunity of their own. *It's time to leave.*

"No," he said. "I think we've outstayed our welcome."

Captain Campbell's face twisted, sharply. "Captain, with all due respect, opportunities like this don't come every day."

Thomas felt a hot flash of anger. "Captain, we do not have the firepower to prolong the engagement," he said. The enemy fleet's sensors were growing stronger too, ensuring he couldn't use missiles as makeshift mines. "The enemy starfighters will overwhelm us if we hang around long enough to close the range."

He gritted his teeth. He understood Captain Campbell's point. They *did* have a chance to score a victory, but it meant putting the ship—*both* ships—in serious danger. *Unicorn* was designed to be expendable, if necessary; *Lion* was not. They had to get back to New Washington, report their victory...and, if the virus insisted on following them back to the American system, let the Americans deal with it. The Royal Navy wouldn't get the credit—or at least not *all* of it—but Thomas wasn't in the business of arguing over who got credit for what. The diplomats could sort it out, after the war. All that mattered was stopping the enemy fleet and winning the war.

"But..."

Thomas pushed as much *command* into his voice as he could. "Remain in cloak and continue to monitor the enemy fleet as *Lion* proceeds to the tramline," he ordered. "Join us in New Washington once we've made it clear."

Captain Campbell looked irked. "Captain..."

"That is an order." Thomas cut him off, sharply. "A *direct* order, which you may have in writing if you wish."

The other commanding officer stared at him for a long moment. It wasn't common to ask for orders in writing, certainly not in the middle of an engagement. They tended to make it harder to calm down and sort out who'd actually been right or wrong, to say nothing of engendering bad feeling...Thomas gritted his teeth, waiting to see what his subordinate would say. If Captain Campbell demanded orders in writing, if the review board decided Captain Campbell was in the right...

"That won't be necessary," Captain Campbell said. "I'll see you on the far side."

His image vanished. Thomas took a long breath, feeling cold. The disagreement would make it harder to build—to rebuild, he supposed—a working relationship. It didn't help they were technically of the same rank, making it harder for one of them to admit the other's superiority... he cursed under his breath. The review board would study the recordings, when they returned to Earth. If they felt Captain Campbell had been in the right...he shook his head, irritated. There was no point in worrying about it now. He'd made the best call he could, based on what he knew. If the review board felt differently, if the armchair admirals produced elaborate models suggesting he could have won the engagement effortlessly, he'd worry about it later.

"XO," he said. "Have all the marines been recovered?"

"Yes, sir," Donker said. "The gunboats are returning now."

"Good." Thomas took a breath. "Order them to assume defensive positions and engage the enemy starfighters, when they come within range. Helm, take us back to the tramline. Best possible speed."

"Aye, Captain," Hinkson said.

Thomas forced himself to sit back in his chair as the battlecruiser started to pick up speed. The enemy fleet hadn't opened fire with long-range missiles, even though they *must* have a solid lock on *Lion* now. Were they too disoriented to think straight? Or did they *carry* long-range missiles? It was impossible to be sure. The economic considerations that had deterred the Royal Navy from producing missiles, at least until there was no longer any choice, simply didn't apply to the virus. It had shown no qualms about expending hundreds of missiles on a single target. And yet, it had to be aware it would be a colossal waste. The Americans might launch an offensive of their own, if they had reason to believe the enemy fleet was weakened...

"Captain," Sibley said. "The enemy starfighters will enter attack range in two minutes."

"Deploy missiles in antistarfighter mode," Thomas ordered. The enemy was still sweeping space aggressively. They'd spot even a powered-down missile on a ballistic trajectory. "Fire at will."

"Aye, sir," Sibley said.

Thomas took a breath as the range closed. They should—in theory—be able to withstand the enemy starfighters until they crossed the tramline, but the theory had never been tested. A handful of torpedoes would be enough to slow the battlecruiser, if they didn't destroy her completely. Hopefully, the enemy life support wouldn't last long enough for them to do any real damage. They were operating at extreme range, even for them. He silently blessed the designers. Naval combat tactics were going to change—again.

And we did hurt them, he thought, more to reassure himself he'd made the right call than anything else. *Whatever happens to us, we've won time for the human race.*

For a long cold moment, Mitch stared at the blank display.

He couldn't put his thoughts into words. He'd known Captain Hammond was a conservative, in every sense of the word, but he'd never considered the man a coward. He had a war record that was longer than Mitch's own, with genuine combat experience. He'd commanded starships in battle, then tried to impart lessons to officer cadets. And yet, he'd turned away from victory. A chance to really hurt the enemy and... and he'd let it go!

It was unbearable. Mitch wanted to shake the older man, to demand he showed the aggression and determination of Nelson, Rodney, Cunningham and Smith. He wanted to call the man's bluff, to demand he gave the orders in writing...to ensure the review board *knew*, in a way they couldn't ignore, what he'd done. And yet, Mitch knew Hammond would find a way to weasel out. He was an aristocrat's aristocrat. He had friends and family in high places. His career was good enough to let him coast through any controversy that might come his way. And the hell of it was that they would have a point! Hammond's record was good enough that a single mistake, particularly one that didn't get anyone hurt or killed, was not going to ruin him.

Anger burned in Mitch's gut. The perfect opportunity and Hammond had passed it up. And...Mitch had no idea what to do. Admiral Onarina would understand, he was sure, if he made a fuss...no one else would. The Admiralty would close ranks around their favoured son and...he shook his head. He had been given his orders, in a manner he couldn't ignore. He had no choice. He'd have to carry them out, then protest when he got home.

"Helm, draw us back," he ordered. "Tactical keep us in cloak."

"Aye, sir," Staci said.

Mitch watched, grimly, as the enemy fleet picked up speed. It didn't seem to care about stealth, not any longer. The fleet was emitting so many sensor pulses that a deaf man would have no trouble tracking it from a safe distance. Mitch watched the enemy ships, clearly delineated on the display, and cursed under his breath. The enemy craft would be easy to target, if

Captain Hammond had the nerve. There'd been nothing in his file to suggest any Lack of Moral Fibre. And yet...

Leave it, he told himself, sharply. *Let him explain his decision when he gets home.*

He calmed himself, with an effort, as enemy starfighters lanced towards *Lion*. The battlecruiser's gunboats spread out to meet them, forcing the enemy to fly though a hail of plasma fire. They didn't seem to be wasting time trying to take out the gunboats, something that baffled Mitch as the battlecruiser picked up speed. *Lion* was the fastest capital ship in space, unless the virus had something that could move faster, but a starfighter should have no trouble catching her. They certainly *should* have enough time to launch a torpedo attack, return to their motherships to rearm, then launch a *second* attack run before the range got too long. Maybe they were more disoriented than he'd thought. His blood ran cold as a thought struck him. The virus considered its starfighters expendable. Perhaps they were planning to ram.

"Captain," Staci said. "They're expanding their sensor sweeps. They may catch a whiff of us."

Mitch nodded, curtly. *Unicorn's* cloaking device was the best in the known universe, but it had its limits. If the enemy filled space with sensor pulses, they might pick up *something* as the cloaking device struggled to compensate. And his point defence couldn't hope to stand off an entire wing of enemy starfighters. It was definitely time to take their leave.

"Helm, pull us back," he ordered. "We'll watch from a safe distance, then jump out."

"Aye, sir."

Thomas had no time to wonder if he'd made a mistake as wave after wave of enemy starfighters bore down on *Lion*. The gunboats filled space with plasma bolts, picking off dozens of enemy craft, but the remainder punched through the defences and started attack runs. Thomas gritted his teeth as a handful of starfighters lasted long enough to launch torpedoes at the hull and break off, the point defence letting them go as it focused on taking out the torpedoes before it was too late. A low rumble ran through the starship as the missiles slammed home, alerts flashing up on the display before fading as it became clear the damage wasn't as extensive as he'd feared. His damage control teams were performing well, too. He allowed himself a moment of relief, then braced himself as the next wave of enemy starfighters started their attack run.

A shame we couldn't kill the carriers as well as the brainships, he acknowledged, in the privacy of his own mind. *Captain Campbell might have had a point.*

He frowned as the last of the enemy starfighters broke off. The enemy fleet was reversing course, clearly heading back towards the planet. He was tempted to reverse course himself and expend his remaining missiles, but there was little hope of scoring a hit. The enemy point defence was just too good. The tactical analysts would have to come up with newer and better ways to get a missile through their defences. Thomas smiled, rather coldly. He'd had a pair of ideas himself.

"Captain, we'll be crossing the tramline in twenty minutes," Fitzgerald reported.

"Good." Thomas studied the display for a long moment. "Mr. XO, recall the gunboats, but keep the crews on the craft until we cross the tramline. I don't want them in decon if we have to start fighting again."

"Aye, sir," Donker said.

Thomas smiled as *Lion* approached the tramline. Their first mission had been a success, by any reasonable standard. He had no doubt the Admiralty would agree. They'd proved the concept worked, which meant...he sighed, inwardly. The sceptics would argue that the enemy had seen the battlecruiser in action, ensuring that—next time—the virus would know what to expect. Thomas told himself not to be too pessimistic. They could come up with something new...

"Helm, jump us out as soon as we cross the tramline," he ordered. "It's time to go home."

CHAPTER TWENTY-ONE

TOBIAS SPOKE AS LITTLE AS POSSIBLE as the gunboat docked with the battlecruiser, the crew and their unwanted passengers waiting silently for permission to open the airlock and enter the decontamination chamber. He was fairly sure the marines were clean, but he didn't believe it. His skin crawled every time he thought about where they'd been...

...And Colin was there. Colin was behind him.

The thought mocked him. Tobias was *sure* Colin was right behind him, ready to slap his back and call it male bonding. Or smack the back of his head with a football or...or something. Why not? He'd done it before. Never mind that Tobias was controlling the guns, never mind that a distraction might be enough to get them all killed...he tried, hard, not to panic as the hatch finally opened. The marines got up—without waiting for orders, of course—and headed for the first decon chamber. Tobias breathed a sigh of relief, even though he knew they'd have to wait for them to pass decon before he and Marigold could leave the gunboat. At least they wouldn't be sharing decon with his worst enemy...his worst enemy, who hadn't recognised him.

Tobias shook his head in disbelief. Colin *had* to have recognised him. Tobias hadn't changed that much, had he? Marigold and some of the others had changed a lot over the last few months, but not him. He was still the same pudgy nerd he'd been in school. No uniform, naval or otherwise, could change his looks completely. Colin knew who he was. He was just biding his time, waiting for a chance to catch Tobias alone. It was just a matter of time.

The intercom bleeped. "Proceed to Decon Compartment Two."

"Aye, sir," Tobias said, although it was an automated message. "We're on the way."

He shut the gunboat down completely—the decontamination team would vent the little craft, just to make sure there was *no* trace of the virus—then headed for the hatch. Decon wasn't fun. It had been designed by a cold-blooded sadist who wanted to make damn sure that no trace of the virus got onto the ship and didn't care how many people he had to make uncomfortable in the process. Marigold didn't look remotely happy as they stepped through the hatch into the blaze of UV lights. It was hard to believe the virus could survive long enough to be dangerous. But if he was infected, the viral matter would be safe in him.

"We'd have to go through decon anyway," Marigold said, in a tone of voice that suggested she was trying to convince herself. "Right?"

Tobias shrugged as he pressed his hand against a bioscanner, feeling a little prick that—as always—made him jump. The scanner techs claimed the bioscanner would pick up even the slightest trace of the virus, but Tobias had his doubts. The virus was an intelligent being, even if its thought processes were completely alien. Perhaps it could evade the scanners, perhaps...he didn't feel reassured as he stepped into the next compartment and undressed, careful not to look at Marigold. They might have very little privacy onboard ship, but he'd give her what little he could. He doubted she was looking at him. He'd come to terms, long ago, with the simple fact neither girls nor boys found him attractive. Even a few months in the navy had done nothing to change that.

The lights seemed to grow brighter as they kept walking, passing through a chemical shower that stung his eyes. It struck him as overkill, although—again—it was hard to be sure. His blood was tested again and again, until his palm started to ache uncomfortably. He breathed a sigh of relief as they finally reached the end of the decon section, where a shower and fresh clothes were waiting. They were clean. He'd never doubted it.

Although I wouldn't be able to tell if I'd been infected, he mused. The early zombies had gotten very ill, some of them reporting themselves as unfit for duty before the virus managed to take complete control. Later zombies—or so he'd been told—hadn't suffered anything like so much before it was too late. *I'd tell everyone I was clean even if I wasn't.*

He shuddered as he showered and dressed. The uniform felt odd against his skin. His hair felt mucky, despite the shower. He wanted a hot bath and a long rest, perhaps not in that order. Was there even a single bathtub on the giant ship? He didn't know. Even the commanding officer was unlikely to have more than the bare necessities. He snorted as he checked his appearance in the mirror. If the CO had a bathtub, he was unlikely to share it with the crew.

"I need to cut my hair again," Marigold said. "It feels icky."

"Mine too," Tobias said. He glanced at the nearest display. They were back in the New Washington system, having made transit without bothering to slow down. There was no immediate risk of having to return to the gunboats and fly into battle. "Do you think they'll let us have a rest before we start training again?"

Marigold winked. "We went into battle, didn't we?"

Tobias stopped, dead. Their first engagement had been utterly unplanned, a desperate encounter with an alien squadron that had to have been as surprised to meet the gunboats as the gunboats had been to encounter it. He hadn't felt right about boasting, even though he knew he and his comrades had performed well. But this time...they'd deliberately picked a fight with the virus and won. They'd given the virus a bloody nose...cold logic told him the virus wouldn't have been that badly hurt, but he didn't want to believe it. They'd won and...he smiled, suddenly. The simple fact they'd won their first engagement was one hell of a confidence booster.

His good mood lasted until they reached the sleeping compartment.

Bagehot was kneeling by a bunk, carefully emptying the drawers into a large box. Tobias opened his mouth to remind his CO that the bunk was Jim's bunk, then stopped as he remembered Jim was dead. Jim and Sharon were dead. Ice washed through him, his legs buckling as he realised he'd never see either of them again. They'd been friends. They'd been amongst his first true friends. And they were dead.

Marigold coughed. "Sir...what'll happen to their stuff?"

Bagehot looked up. "A handful of personal items will be sent back to their next-of-kin," he said, curtly. "The remainder will be distributed amongst the squadron."

"I don't feel right about taking it," Tobias said. "Sir, I..."

"Then don't." Bagehot moved to Sharon's bunk and started to work. "They understood what would happen, just as you do. They knew better than to bring anything too personal onboard ship."

Tobias glared as Bagehot picked up a white bra and dumped it in the box. "How can you be so calm?"

Bagehot looked back at him, evenly. "I'm sorry to tell you this," he said finally, "but people die in war. Jim and Sharon knew the risks. The best thing we can do for them is honour their memory, then carry on."

Marigold turned away. "I...fuck."

"I do understand," Bagehot said, gently. "Really, I do. But there's nothing else I *can* do."

He cleared his throat as he finished emptying the drawer. "Get some rest. We'll have a formal ceremony for them later, once we know what we're doing. And we'll make sure they didn't die for nothing."

"We won," Tobias said. "Why doesn't it feel that way?"

"They say one death is a tragedy, but a million deaths are a statistic," Bagehot said. "Do you know why?"

Tobias shook his head, silently.

"It's because we cannot grasp a million lives, in all their...complexity." Bagehot's eyes were tired, tired and old. "We simply don't have the connection to understand their existence. They're just emotionless numbers. But a single human life, friend or enemy? We can understand them, we can *grasp* them. Jim liked playing computer games and had dreams of becoming a grandmaster, Sharon liked to cook and held out hope for opening her own place in the future. We *knew* them. And that's why their death hurts."

He shook his head as he stood. "Like I said, get some rest. You need it."

"Yes, sir," Tobias said. "And..."

The words froze on his tongue. He didn't know what to say. He didn't know if he wanted to thank Bagehot for his wise words or scream at him for being a cold-blooded bastard. It was hard to tell—it was *impossible* to tell—if Bagehot really gave much of a damn about Jim or Sharon. He hadn't shown them any more respect or concern than he'd shown Tobias and Marigold. He might not have let himself get too close, just as Tobias had never let himself like too many people at school. They'd leave, eventually. Better not to get too attached.

Bagehot left, closing the hatch behind him.

"Good night," Marigold said. "See you in the morning. Or afternoon. Or whenever."

Tobias shrugged as he clambered into his bunk. Jim and Sharon were dead. He'd liked them and they were dead and...he shook his head, trying to tell himself it didn't matter. But it did. They hadn't deserved to die, not like Colin. Colin deserved to die and...

He cursed under his breath. It was going to be a long time before he fell asleep.

"Overall, the operation was a success," Major Craig said. "The patient died."

Colin tried not to smile at the weak joke. Half of the deployed marines had wound up trapped in interplanetary space, condemned to drift through the enemy formation until they could power up their drives and return to the mothership. The remainder had tried to board a handful of vessels, some unsuccessfully. He knew he'd done well, but he also knew there'd been a degree of luck involved. The whole operation could have gone spectacularly wrong.

"We also know we didn't bring anything back with us," Major Craig continued. "Thoughts?"

"With all due respect," Lieutenant Pringle said, "we were in cold space. There was no real risk of bringing *anything* unfriendly back."

"People can be cryogenically frozen, then restored to life," Major Craig pointed out, calmly. "Viruses can be frozen too and"—he held up a hand—"while the boffins may claim that *the* virus is too complex to be frozen, we cannot take it for granted. An ounce of prevention is better than a pound of cure."

"Particularly when the cure involves killing a friend," someone muttered from the rear.

"Precisely," Major Craig agreed. "We don't want to wind up shooting our friends."

He paused, letting the words hang in the air. "*Lion* has orders to return to Earth. We'll spend the transit going through everything that happened, pooling our knowledge for the folks back home. There may be something of importance in the recordings, there may not be. We'll see how things go. After that...shore leave. Probably."

Davies nudged Colin. "Where do *you* want to go for leave?"

Colin shrugged. He hadn't given it any thought. Going home was damn depressing. His old man was a drunkard and his mother...Colin winced. No wonder he'd had so many problems at school. It had been a relief to leave. Maybe he'd go to Sin City or one of the spaceport strips or somewhere where the beer was cheap, the women were easy and the media was banned. Or...

"Get some rest," Major Craig ordered. "We'll be going back to work tomorrow."

"No rest for the wicked," Sergeant Bowman agreed.

Colin nodded as he stood, saluted and headed for the barracks. There'd be a shitload of work tomorrow, starting with a full debriefing. He'd have to outline everything he'd seen on the alien ship, adding what little he recalled to humanity's ever-growing body of knowledge. He wondered, idly, if they'd really seen anything new. The alien ships were just plain weird, familiar enough that the differences were disconcerting. He would almost have preferred something truly alien.

And...he frowned as he remembered the gunboat pilot. Why had he been so scared?

Worry about it later, he told himself. He felt tired, mentally rather than physically. It was funny—he'd worked himself harder during basic training—but there was no point in denying it. There were stimulants he could use, none of which were permitted unless there was desperate need. *Right now, we're in the clear. It's time to go rest.*

"We won," Willis said, slapping Colin's shoulder. "You want to go celebrate?"

"Go rest," Colin ordered. "Tomorrow is another day."

Thomas waited, watching calmly as the steward poured three mugs of tea, placed a tray of biscuits on the table and withdrew from the ready room. Commander Donker and Major Craig looked as tired as Thomas felt, although the glow of victory made it easier to deal with the aftermath of combat. *Lion* had only lost nine personnel in total; two gunboat pilots, four marines and three crewmen who'd been in the wrong place at the wrong time. It was impossible to be sure how many host bodies had died on the enemy fleet, but the total figure had to be quite high.

Not that it matters, he thought, sourly. *The virus doesn't have to worry about training its personnel.*

He took a sip of his tea, then leaned forward. "We have our orders," he said. "We're to return to Earth. Immediately."

"They must not have rushed anything like enough missiles forward to support our operations," Donker pointed out. "Without them, we're just an oversized cruiser."

"Quite." Thomas didn't like the description, but he had to admit it was justified. "We handled ourselves well, I believe. Do you have any thoughts?"

"Crew morale is through the roof," Donker agreed. "There's a general feeling we can handle anything, right now. There was some doubt over the whole concept, back when we were fitting out, but it's gone now. We've proved we can make the battlecruiser concept work."

"Good," Thomas said. Only a fool would ignore morale. The navy wasn't composed of robots. Or zombies. "I'm sure the thought of shore leave will do wonders for morale too."

Major Craig raised his eyebrows. "Are we getting shore leave?"

"I think so," Thomas said. The navy generally *tried* to give everyone a week or two of shore leave between deployments, during wartime. Longer holidays were often harder to arrange. "I would be surprised if the Admiralty ordered us back home, just to order us to turn around and go back out again."

He sipped his tea, contemplating the possibilities. Charlotte would be pleased if he managed to make it to one of her balls, particularly if he invited Captain Campbell to attend in hopes of mending bridges. A famous war hero would be a very welcome guest. And...Thomas shrugged. Captain Campbell's communications, since the two ships had linked up again, had been very formal. Thomas had no doubt the other man was still fuming.

"They might have something else in mind for us," Donker said. "We have the only battlecruiser-qualified crew in the navy."

Thomas shrugged. "We'll see," he said. "They'll tell us when they tell us."

He picked up a biscuit and ate it slowly. There was no point in speculation. The Admiralty would tell them what it wanted when they got back to Earth. For all he knew, some bright spark had calculated it would be quicker to order *Lion* to return home to resupply, rather than shipping missiles to New Washington. The staff officer might even be right. Resupplying without specialised equipment wasn't easy. He grimaced. They'd have to do something about that, if the navy decided to build an entire squadron of battlecruisers. Going all the way back to Earth would impose massive delays...

"Right now, we have to work on doctrine," he said, instead. "Does anything *major* need to be changed?"

"The gunboats performed as advertised," Donker said. "Statistically speaking, they also took fewer losses than the average starfighter squadron. The concept has now proven itself beyond reasonable doubt. I think we can safely suggest that larger ships be assigned gunboats for close-range protection as well as targeting and remote deployment."

"Quite," Thomas said.

"The tactical analysts are still working their way through the records," Donker continued. "We caught the enemy by surprise. Next time, things will be harder. But they have a few ideas. We'll just have to see how they work out in practice."

Thomas nodded. He knew that already. "Keep me informed," he said. "Major?"

"The marines performed well," Major Craig said. "There was some light ribbing over shuttles that missed their targets, leaving the poor bootnecks stranded until they could repower their drives and escape, but nothing too serious. Given how quickly we threw the mission together, relying on largely untried troops, things went better than we had any right to expect. A couple of corporals proved themselves. I think they'll get their stripes permanently."

"Good for them," Thomas said. Traditionally, promotions within the Royal Marines were handled in-house, but the starship commander's word carried weight. "I'll countersign whatever recommendations you want to make."

"Thank you, sir," Major Craig said. He tapped the datapad on the table. "It'll take us several weeks to get home. By then, we should have learnt all our lessons."

"Agreed," Donker said. He smiled, broadly. "If nothing else, we know we can fight and win."

"Quite," Thomas agreed. He finished his tea. "I'll see you both tomorrow."

"Aye, sir," Donker said, as he stood. "Good night."

CHAPTER TWENTY-TWO

"I READ YOUR REPORTS VERY CAREFULLY," Admiral Onarina said, once tea had been served and the customary greetings had been exchanged. "Do you have anything you want to add to them?"

Mitch hesitated, keeping his face carefully blank. He'd written a detailed report, pointing out there'd been a chance to weaken the enemy still further...a chance that Captain Hammond had chosen to ignore. And yet, there were limits to how far he could go. Admiral Onarina would understand, but the remainder of the Admiralty would see it as rank insubordination. Probably. The risk of losing an experimental ship had to be balanced against the prospect of crippling, if not destroying, an enemy fleet.

"I believe I included everything in my report," Captain Hammond said. "My ship—both of our ships—performed well. The missiles lived up to their promise. The gunboats and marines served well, despite the simple fact it was the first taste of combat for many of them. Overall, I think the shooter and spotter concept has more than proven itself."

The admiral's dark eyes moved to Mitch. "Do you agree, Captain?"

"Yes, Admiral," Mitch said. "The concept worked. We could have pushed things a little further, as I noted in my report, but the concept itself has been proven. We're ready to go back out."

"Once the crew has taken some leave," Captain Hammond said. "They need it."

Mitch conceded the point with a nod. "A week of being somewhere else would do wonders for my crew."

"Quite." Admiral Onarina looked from Mitch to Captain Hammond and back again. "We have a specific mission in mind, for you and your ships. We'll reconvene in a week, once all the groundwork has been laid. I trust that suits both of you?"

"Yes, Admiral," Mitch said. A week of shore leave—more accurately, three or four days—for everyone would definitely work wonders. There'd be time to visit Sin City, if nowhere else. Staci and he had already drawn up rough shore leave rosters, in hopes of making sure everyone who had a family had a chance to meet them before the ship headed back into harm's way, but they hadn't put anything in stone. "My crew will be delighted."

He smiled. *Unicorn* was too small to tolerate personality conflicts—he'd have moved a crewman on if he'd proved unable to handle his peers—but even a close-knit crew had problems from time to time. Hell, *he* had problems. It would be nice to pretend someone else had the responsibility for a few hours or so. It was just a shame he didn't have anyone he wanted to see. His last relationship hadn't survived his career.

"Very good," the admiral said. "I'll see you both later."

Mitch stood and saluted. It was clearly a dismissal. Beside him, Captain Hammond stood, motioning for Mitch to follow him. Mitch was tempted to refuse, on the grounds they were no longer on deployment, but it would be churlish. Instead, they walked out of the admiral's office and headed for the nearest empty conference room. It was clearly designed for high-ranking officers. The furnishings were of a very high quality indeed.

"I forwarded you my wife's invitation," Captain Hammond said. "Did you reply?"

Mitch blinked. The invitation had been a surprise. He'd never expected to receive a formal invitation to anything, at least outside the navy. Sure, a CO might invite him to a working lunch, but nothing else. He just wasn't the sort of person who knew how to handle himself in a formal environment. Aristocratic manners were a closed book to him. He knew how to cope with a naval dinner and that was about it.

But...he *did* have the invitation. And he had to reply.

"I do have shore leave," he said. He was reluctant to waste what little he had, but...there was no point in making enemies. Captain Hammond was a high-ranking aristocrat, and so was his wife. Hammond would understand if Mitch needed to be somewhere else, but there was no guarantee his wife would have the same understanding. He'd met enough scions of the aristocracy to doubt it. "If it's alright with my commanding officer..."

Captain Hammond snorted, dryly. "You would be welcome," he said. "I'll be shuttling down the night before, then staying two nights. I can have a room set up for you too, if you like."

"If you'll have me," Mitch said. He groaned, inwardly, at the prospect of losing most of his shore leave. "I might come and go on the same day."

"Stay one night," Captain Hammond advised. "Unless you have somewhere else to be..."

"It depends on my crew," Mitch said. He cursed under his breath. Spending two nights in a mansion was hardly *his* idea of a good time. There had to be a better excuse. "My XO needs leave too."

Captain Hammond nodded. "It could be good for your career if you attend," he said. "You're a war hero."

"So are you," Mitch said.

He sighed. Captain Hammond had a point. The chance to meet his social superiors in an informal setting, or at least as informal as possible, was not to be missed. Who knew who'd help him, if he attended? Or hinder him, if he didn't? Mitch detested the Old Boys Network with a passion, but he had to admit it had its uses. He could join, if he was willing to seek out a patron and kiss his ass...

And how good are Hammond's patrons, he asked himself, *when he's nearly fifteen years older than me and still a Captain?*

"We can make the arrangements," he said, finally. He'd still have a day or two to visit Sin City. Or a red-light district. Or *somewhere.* "Let me know and I'll work out something with my XO."

Captain Hammond nodded. "I'll see you there," he said. "Later."

He turned and left the compartment. Mitch sunk into a chair, feeling oddly as if he'd been outmanoeuvred. He didn't want to go to a ball, even if it *would* be good for his career. He'd read a bunch of stories in the tabloids...he told himself, firmly, they probably weren't true. But who knew...?

It doesn't matter, he thought, as he stood. *Right now, I have work to do.*

Colin wondered, morbidly, if he was in trouble. The summons had arrived only two minutes ago, while he'd been eating dinner. He'd crammed the remains of his meal into his mouth, jumped to his feet and headed for the hatch before his mind had quite caught up with what was happening. Major Craig had summoned him, personally. It was odd. Perhaps he was in trouble. The marines had a flatter command structure than the navy, but not *that* flat. He forced himself to calm down as he stopped outside Major Craig's office and pushed the buzzer. The hatch opened a second later, revealing a tiny compartment.

"Come in," Major Craig said. He was sitting behind a folding desk, putting a datapad to one side. "Thank you for coming so quickly."

"Sir," Colin said, as he straightened to attention. He was fairly sure he hadn't been given a choice. Requests from superiors were to be treated as orders, or so he'd been told. "You wanted to see me?"

"Stand at ease," Major Craig said. "Good news first. You and your team have been cleared for shore leave. You'll have priority access to shuttles heading to Earth."

Colin kept his face carefully blank. "And the bad news?"

"It may or may not be bad news," Major Craig said. "Your former headmaster has been following your career. He's put in a request for you to address the student body on the joys of being a Royal Marine."

"He has?" Colin blinked in surprise. "The Beast asked for me? Personally?"

"Yes," Major Craig said. "I trust that won't be a problem."

Colin knew the right answer. "No, sir."

"You'll take a shuttle to Earth tomorrow," Major Craig said. He looked...surprisingly understanding. "Take some time to study PR guidelines. Try not to get into trouble. We want to convince people to join, not scare them off."

"Yes, sir," Colin said, with the private thought that anyone who got scared off by *him* wouldn't get through training anyway. "And afterwards?"

"You'll have four days of leave, to use any way you see fit," Major Craig told him. "Just remember, if you miss the flight back, you'll be in deep shit."

"Yes, sir," Colin said. He probably wouldn't be charged with going AWOL, not as long as he made sure to alert his superiors before they started looking for him, but he'd lose his stripe and there'd be a black mark in his record. "I won't go too far from home."

"Like I said, use your leave in any way you see fit," Major Craig said. "Go to Luna, if you like, or Mars. Or even London."

"Yes, sir," Colin said. He shook his head in disbelief. "They really want to hear from me?"

"It would appear so," Major Craig said, with heavy sarcasm. "Your former headmaster asked for you specifically."

He nodded to the hatch. "Dismissed."

Colin saluted, then turned to leave. It made no sense. He'd done well on the football field, but his marks—particularly his final year marks—hadn't been anything to write home about. His parents hadn't given a shit, of course. He'd never thought the Beast gave much of a shit either. He'd overlook anything as long as a sporty student brought home the cup... he rolled his eyes. Maybe the Beast was looking for donations. *That* was absurd. Marines were paid well, but not *that* well. The cost of living was going up, month after month. He couldn't afford to send anything to the school, even if he'd wanted to...

He probably just wants me to tell the kids about all the hard work and knuckling under I did when I was a boy, he thought. He laughed, humourlessly. He hadn't known what hard work was until he'd joined the marines. *A shame I can't tell them the truth.*

His datapad pinged as he headed down the corridor. He checked it, noting the orders and the attached travel vouchers. A day on detached duty—he wondered, absently, if he'd be paid—and then four days of leave. Four days…a reward, a punishment or a test? It would be quite easy to fall back into bad habits, now he didn't have instructors breathing down his neck. He could meet his friends, he could…he shook his head. He had too much to lose. He couldn't risk letting himself go.

And I can go anywhere, within reason, he thought. There was no reason he *had* to stay in Liverpool. Quite the opposite, actually. *That should be fun.*

Davies waved to him as he entered the barracks. "You got a bollocking for something?"

"No." Colin had to smile. "Worse than that. I'm being held up as a good example."

"Really?" Davies struck a shocked pose. "We're doomed. I tell you, we're doomed!"

"Hah," Colin said. He explained, quickly. "They want me to tell the kids to behave themselves."

"Doomed," Davies repeated. "Why don't you just tell them the truth?"

Colin rolled his eyes, remembering some of the guest speakers while he'd been a student. Some of them had been more interesting than others, but they'd all followed the government line. It was little comfort to know they probably hadn't wanted to speak to the students. The students hadn't wanted to hear them, either. Colin wondered, suddenly, if that had been deliberate. Nothing killed a kid's interest in doing something quicker than being told they *had* to do it.

He looked at his friend, putting the thought aside for later contemplation. "A speaker tells the truth? Now you really *are* being perverse."

"Really?" Davies grinned. "Are you telling me I wasted all my time trying to invent a new sex position?"

Colin made a rude gesture. "I think you've ruined sex for me. Forever."

"Don't worry about it," Davies said. "Just go there, tell a few lies right out of the latest movie about us and depart before someone starts asking smart questions."

"It's not that sort of school," Colin said.

"You might be surprised," Davies said. He sounded thoughtful, rather than teasing. "My class had a kid who had a general for a father. The poor kid grew up reading his father's books. And whenever we had a speaker who was a little too big for his boots, the kid would tear the war stories apart."

"I wish I'd thought of that," Colin said. "He must have got into a *lot* of trouble."

"Not really," Davies said. "He exposed a Walt or two. Just don't tell any lies and you'll be fine."

"Hah," Colin said.

Tobias lay on his bunk, staring up at the ceiling. The last round of exercises and drills had ended poorly, with the entire squadron wiped out by simulated enemy fire. Bagehot had been quite sarcastic about the whole thing, even though the gunboat pilots had been sleeping when the alarms had gone off and they'd been ordered into their craft. The virus wouldn't send advance notice of a planned attack, would it? They had to be ready to fight at all times.

He rubbed his forehead. They'd returned to Sol. They'd been promised leave, although the gunboat pilots had no idea when they would be allowed to depart. There was a small collection of emails and vmails from his mother and sister in his inbox, stored within the navy servers until *Lion* had returned to Earth, but he hadn't been able to force himself to open them. He wasn't sure he wanted to go back to Liverpool, to revisit old haunts... he snorted to himself. He really *didn't* want to see Liverpool again.

The hatch opened. Marigold stepped into the compartment. "You heard the news?"

"What news?" Tobias turned his head to look at her. "Good news?"

"In a manner of speaking," Marigold said. "You want to go visit Armstrong City?"

Tobias sat up. "You and me?"

"We both have leave, apparently," Marigold said. She held up her datapad. "Starting from tomorrow, you and I and the rest are free to do whatever we like for three days. And there's a shuttle heading for Armstrong. We can go there for a couple of days."

"That would be nice." Tobias checked his inbox. The shore leave rota had finally arrived. "And afterwards?"

"Pick a place," Marigold said. "There's lots of things to see on the moon."

Tobias nodded as he reread the email. He was tempted to suggest Sin City, but...he knew he didn't have the nerve. And Marigold probably wouldn't be any more comfortable there than he was. God alone knew what she'd make of it if he asked. He checked the shuttle schedule again, then started to key through the list of possible hotels. Armstrong City was a big tourist destination. There'd be no shortage of places to stay. The prices were high, even with the military discount. He hesitated, then shrugged. It wasn't as if he had anything else to do with his money. The navy paid all his expenses as long as he served.

"There's a bunch of places I'd like to see," he said. "Heinlein Crater, Asimov City, Selene..."

"Anywhere," Marigold said. "I just want to see something new."

Tobias nodded. Tourism was for the wealthy, on Earth. The days when Britons headed to France or Spain in vast numbers had died decades ago. He'd liked to imagine travelling, but...it had been a pipe dream. But, in space, the rules were different. He could go wherever he liked, within reason. The navy wouldn't be very pleased if he tried to visit a secure zone without permission.

"We only have three days," Tobias said. He frowned. Three days was hardly long enough to see *everything.* The moon was littered with sites of historic interest. "But if we stay in Armstrong, we can take day trips to everywhere else."

"Good idea," Marigold said. "I'll book the hotel. You book travel."

Tobias hesitated. Would they be sharing a room? Would they...he wanted to ask, but he didn't dare. They'd shared a barracks, and a decon chamber, yet...that was different. He couldn't imagine sharing a room with her outside the navy. He knew what Colin would say, if he knew they'd shared a room...his blood ran cold. Colin. Would Colin be coming after them? His hand shook. Armstrong City was popular. Colin might go, too...

No, he told himself. *Colin will be going to Sin City and...*

Marigold poked him. "You've gone quiet."

"Just thinking," Tobias said. Colin wouldn't go to Armstrong City. He'd never been interested in history, even stories of brutal battles and raiders pillaging, raping and burning their way across the continent. "Sorry."

"Don't worry about it," Marigold said. "Just think of it as a chance to broaden your mind."

Tobias nodded. He'd see where Neil Armstrong had taken the first steps on the moon. He'd see...there was an entire list of places he'd like to see, from the very first mining colonies to giant telescopes and independent settlements. He wondered if they'd have a chance to visit Roddenberry City. He'd been told it was welcoming to people like him, although the entry requirements were very strict. God knew he hadn't considered it a possible destination back when he'd been looking for a place to go, after he left university...

I might be able to go now, even if I never went to university, he told himself. *They might take me.*

He stood. "We'll make the arrangements," he said, silently promising her a good time. "And we'll come back happy."

"Yep." Marigold grinned. "And then the CO will *know* we're planning something."

CHAPTER TWENTY-THREE

"JUST REMEMBER TO CIRCLE THE BALLROOM," Charlotte said. "And make sure you talk to everyone."

Thomas tried to hide his dismay. What had been meant to be a relatively small gathering had mushroomed into a giant party, with aristocrats rubbing shoulders with famous reporters, military officers and celebrities. He'd hoped to spend time with his wife, not...he sighed, inwardly. He'd known his wife wanted to host a party, but still...

"I'll do my best," he promised, as the music grew louder. The band was local, hired from the nearest village. His wife had said something about supporting the local economy. Thomas hadn't paid much attention at the time. "You have fun. Really."

He pasted a polite expression on his face as he started to circle the room. It was easy to spot the patronage networks, clients, cronies and lickspittles surrounding their patrons like planets orbiting stars. The unconnected looked isolated, licking their lips nervously as they tried to work up the nerve to intrude. Normally, as host, Thomas would have done his level best to make sure they felt included. It helped to bring good publicity, but right now he felt too tired to care. The day had been long and it was far from over.

This is meant to be shore leave, he thought, as he spotted a trio of aristocratic women heading into the garden. *Not...work.*

He smiled as he spotted Captain Campbell, who was chatting to two younger girls in the corner. The girls were probably considering Campbell's prospects, if Thomas was any judge. It was traditional to bring talent into the aristocracy, a tradition that no one—not even Thomas—could defy. And Captain Campbell was talented...Thomas was tempted to amuse himself by pushing the trio together, but decided against it. Charlotte would kill him, probably literally. She'd worked hard to make the party happen. She'd probably put a great many noses out of joint.

"Captain," a voice said. "I trust I'll be seeing you in the house?"

Thomas turned to see Duncan, Lord Shields. The older man was a high-ranking politician who'd taken advantage of his brother's career to boost his own into orbit. Thomas disliked him, yet he had to admit Lord Shields was pretty good at manipulating the system to suit himself. Not the sort of person he'd invite to a private party, he supposed, but definitely someone worth knowing. There'd been suggestions Lord Shields would be Prime Minister one day. He had the clout, the connections and the experience to do a good job.

"It depends on my orders," Thomas said. Technically, he had a seat in the House of Lords; practically, Charlotte had held his proxy since their marriage. "I may be leaving the system again in a week or so."

"Or so we're told," Lord Shields said. "The navy has something in mind, doesn't it?"

Thomas shrugged. He'd be very surprised if Lord Shields didn't know *precisely* what the navy had in mind. It wasn't as if the First Lord of the Admiralty was a law unto himself, beholden to no one. The War Cabinet had probably authorised the operation weeks ago, long before *Lion* had returned to Sol. Thomas kept his face under tight control. Lord Shields was digging. But digging for what?

"There's talk of putting together a whole new offensive fleet," Lord Shields said. "What would you say to that?"

"I'd say it was about time," Thomas said. He'd seen the reports. The human race was on the defensive, which was tantamount to accepting inevitable defeat. "However, it would depend on how many ships we could free up without weakening the defences."

Lord Shields lifted an eyebrow. "And do you have any feel for how many ships we *could* redeploy?"

Thomas frowned. The conversation had wandered into dangerous waters. "I'm not familiar with the overall state of the fleet," he said. It was true, although he could make a pretty good guess from what he'd heard over the last two days. "The decision would have to be made by someone a little higher up the chain of command than me."

"And organising a multi-species fleet isn't easy," Lord Shields said, as if Thomas hadn't spoken. "What's your take on *that*?"

"We must hang together or hang separately," Thomas said. "I think the certainty of total destruction if we fail will concentrate a few minds."

He sighed, inwardly. Everyone—human and alien alike—had good reason to cooperate, but there would be problems. Of *course* there would be problems. Humans and aliens thought differently, ensuring that something one race would consider a minor matter would be a deal-breaker for another. The Tadpoles and Foxes found human politics to be as incomprehensible as humans found theirs. It was hard, sometimes, to even get a fleet going in the same direction. If it wasn't for the virus, he had a feeling the known races would have continued to maintain a polite distance from each other. Better that than another round of interstellar war.

Lord Shields shrugged. "And the planned union?"

Thomas gave him a sharp look. "Is there a reason you ask, My Lord?"

"We are caught on the horns of a dilemma," Lord Shields said. "Do we risk forming a union that may grow into a *de facto* world government? Or do we risk forming an alliance that does not, that cannot, force everyone to work together?"

"I thought it was a done deal," Thomas said. "It's been five years!"

"Fifty years might not be enough," Lord Shields told him. "I think..."

The dinner bell rang. "I think you'd better have this discussion with my wife," Thomas said, as the guests started making their way towards the dining hall. "She's the political mastermind of the family."

He bowed, then headed towards the dining hall himself. Lord Shields had worried him. There were political implications to his words Thomas couldn't pretend to understand. Was the older man trying to lure him into… into what? Thomas shook his head. It wasn't as if there was any *need* for underhanded dealings. Everyone knew everyone did it. If Lord Shields wanted to form a political alliance, he could do it openly. And there'd be no hint of anything untoward about it.

And instead he chose to talk to me privately, Thomas thought. The older man had placed him in an awkward position. He might wind up clashing with people who outranked him. *What is going on?*

Charlotte nodded to him as he took his seat at the high table. The hall was crammed with tables, with guests carefully assigned to promote good feeling and conversation. Or at least conversation…Thomas smiled as he noted a pair of society reporters, women who could be relied upon to produce a fawning account of the evening. He'd never understood why some people followed the aristocracy as if they were animals in the zoo, particularly people who would never have the breeding or connections of born aristocrats…he rolled his eyes. The nobility was deluding itself if it thought the majority of the population cared. They had too many other problems.

"We need to talk, later," he said. "Lord Shields had some odd questions for me."

"Later," Charlotte agreed. The servants were already bringing great plates of meat and vegetables out of the side doors, placing them on the tables for the guests to pick at as they pleased. "Right now, keep smiling."

"Yes, My Lady," Thomas said.

"I mean it." Charlotte's voice hardened. "I went to a lot of trouble to get the right people here."

Thomas nodded, concealing his irritation behind a blank mask. "Yes, *My Lady*."

Mitch hadn't been quite sure what to expect, when he'd accompanied Captain Hammond to his family seat. A big house, naturally, but what else? Someone—he couldn't remember who—had once remarked that the only real difference between the very rich and everyone else was that they had more money, but...stepping into the hall was like stepping into a very different world. There was a butler, a dignified older man who could have stepped out of a period drama, and a small army of manservants and maids who appeared to have been chosen for their looks as well as their competence. The hall was like a giant hotel, complete with swimming pool, massage services, a library and just about everything else. Truthfully, he found it a little overwhelming. The modern world co-existed oddly with a past that had never really existed.

He shook his head in disbelief as the dinner was served. The aristocracy was a world unto itself. He could have gotten laid a dozen times, he thought, from the way some of the younger girls had been flirting with him. Mitch was no stranger to women—he'd never had any trouble finding female company—but there'd been something about the girls that had bothered him. He wasn't sure how to put it into words. It was...it was as if they had completely different ideas of how the world worked.

His gaze wandered the room. There was enough food on the tables to make them groan under the weight. The fine wines were so expensive he *knew* he couldn't have purchased a single bottle on his salary, if they'd been for sale. He had a feeling they couldn't be obtained for love or money, unless one had the right connections. And the guests...he couldn't help feeling as though they were nothing more than peacocks. The men wore suits, the women wore dresses...both so expensive that, again, he could never have afforded them on his salary. He breathed a sigh of relief that he was expected to wear his dress uniform. As uncomfortable as it was, at least he didn't have to pay for it.

The dinner was cooked to perfection, of course. Roast meat—beef, lamb, chicken, venison—mingled with piles of potatoes, vegetables and puddings.

He ate slowly, savouring every bite even as he tried to look unimpressed. The aristocracy...he felt a dull flash of envy for anyone who grew up in such an environment. They were the lords and masters of everything they surveyed...he understood, suddenly, just *why* the girls had been so forward. They didn't think anything could go wrong, not for them. If they ran into trouble, they just had to throw money at the problem until it went away.

And the virus is not going to be impressed, he mused, as the evening wore on. *You can't bribe it to go away.*

He smirked at the thought, then sobered. The maids had given him a tour of the hall. They'd shown him Captain Hammond's railway set—apparently, he'd built it when he'd been a child—and a dozen other diversions for kids who rarely saw their parents. Mitch had been too stunned to say much of anything. The whole hall was like a VR game, one where the player could afford anything, anything at all. He was reminded of the BBC's shows about lottery winners, most of whom spent their way back into bankruptcy within months, but here...the money never ran out. Captain Hammond and his family were so rich they could practically buy their own battleship. His lips thinned at the thought. It would be a more productive use of their money.

Captain Hammond's wife tapped her glass for silence, then introduced a government minster Mitch didn't recognise. The guests listened politely as the minster spoke about government and naval policy, somehow managing to make it sound boring. It was lucky, Mitch decided, that the poor bugger had a captive audience. He'd once attended a wedding where the bride's stepfather had decided to lecture everyone about a great opportunity to make money, only to watch in dismay as the guests walked out. The poor bride had never lived it down.

He forced himself to pay attention as a handful of other speakers held the floor for a few brief moments each. They didn't say anything of importance, certainly nothing Mitch couldn't have gleaned from a few moments with a newspaper or two. He'd half-hoped some of them would touch on something *interesting*, but there was nothing. It was an endless combination of vague remarks about policy, fawning over the host's beautiful house and two beautiful daughters...really, Mitch found the latter more than a little creepy. The poor girls were both victims and victimisers. It was...odd.

And it's a good thing I'm not one of them, he mused, as the speeches finally came to an end. The guests clapped politely. The maids started distributing brandy, cigars and mint chocolates. *Anyone who grows up in a place like this must wind up warped.*

He felt an odd little pang as he joined the throng, unsure where to go. Captain Hammond had vanished, as had most of the senior aristocracy. The younger guests were dancing in the hall, looking as carefree as any other bunch of teenagers...some of whom, he was fairly sure, were in their mid-twenties. He snorted, then turned and left the hall. It was no place for him, not really. He walked down a long corridor, passing endless rows of portraits that gazed disapprovingly at him, and out onto a balcony. The garden below was shrouded in darkness, broken only by a handful of lanterns. He could see couples as they moved in and out of the light, seeking a place to kiss and cuddle and...he rolled his eyes. The mansion was a whole other world.

"It looks better in daylight," a voice said.

Mitch jumped. He hadn't heard anyone coming up behind him. He cursed under his breath as he spun around, one hand dropping to his belt. If that had happened back home, he'd be in real trouble. And he wasn't wearing a pistol...he caught himself as he saw Lady Charlotte, her eyes looking past him. She seemed more concerned with putting on a good show than anything else. Mitch's eyes narrowed. Where had *that* thought come from?

"I'm sure it does, My Lady," he said, putting his glass to one side. He'd really drunk more than he should. He wouldn't be too surprised to discover there was extra alcohol in some of the drinks too. He'd seen aristocrats swigging fine wines as if they were cheap beers. "What can I do for you?"

"Just call me Charlotte," Lady Charlotte said. She stepped past him until she was standing by the balcony. "I'm sorry I haven't had time to get to know you better."

Mitch frowned. There was something in her tone...he studied her, thoughtfully. She was in her late forties, at the very least, but there was something about her that called to him. Curly dark hair, a curvy body...her dress hinted at her curves without revealing anything below the neckline. Her smile was almost sad, almost winsome. Mitch felt a stir and looked away, hastily. He shouldn't be even *thinking* about her.

"It's quite alright," he said, honestly. "I understand you weren't expecting me."

"I invited you," Lady Charlotte said. "What did you make of the party?"

Mitch hesitated, unsure if he should answer honestly. He'd met officers who appreciated honesty, even if they were hearing things they didn't want to hear, and officers who blew a gasket whenever someone dared to offer an honest opinion. Lady Charlotte was an aristocrat, distantly related to the monarch herself. She'd probably never heard a word of criticism in her life...

"You can answer honestly," Lady Charlotte said, as if she'd read his thoughts. "How else would I run the family estates?"

Mitch blinked, then reminded himself—sharply—that Lady Charlotte was probably old enough to know how to read someone. And she would have handled her husband's affairs, as well as her own, while he'd been on active service. Hell, for all he knew, it was Captain Hammond who'd married into money. The older aristocrats made a habit of marrying for money, rather than status. They had all the status they could possibly desire.

"I think it's nothing more than a distraction," he said, finally. "How many of the people who attended are really important?"

"More than you might think." Lady Charlotte didn't seem offended at his remark. "Some hold powerful positions, in the government or the military or big business. Others will hold positions, one day, or marry those who do. The whole party is a chance to meet informally, without the pressure of a formal meeting; a chance to chat about important matters without letting anything get in the way. You might be surprised to know how much government policy comes out of parties like this."

"Ah," Mitch said. "No wonder the country is such a mess."

Lady Charlotte laughed. "You're not the first person to make such a joke."

"It wasn't a joke," Mitch said. He waved a hand at the darkened lawn below. "How much money is being wasted on this...this *party*, while people starve?"

"People don't starve," Lady Charlotte said. "And this party...it cost far less than a battleship. Or what we pay in tax."

Mitch glanced at her. "And everyone here is born to wealth and power," he said. It was technically true that no one starved, but government-provided ration bars looked like cardboard and tasted worse. "They don't know what it's like to live out there."

"Which is why we need people like you, to tell us how it is," Lady Charlotte said. "That's why you were invited."

"Really?" Mitch wasn't sure he believed her. "And how many of you listen?"

"Enough," Lady Charlotte said. She gave him a thin smile. "I listen to you."

Mitch shrugged. "Why?"

"Because you're a war hero," Lady Charlotte said. "You have credibility. That gives your words weight. And I listen."

CHAPTER TWENTY-FOUR

COLIN STOOD OUTSIDE THE MAIN ENTRANCE of the school and stared at the concrete building. The district had never struck him as particularly pretty—dehumanising and ugly were the words he'd usually heard used to describe the poorer parts of Liverpool—but the school was easily the ugliest place in the city. It was a solid concrete block, looking more like a prison than the actual prison they'd toured a few years ago in hopes of convincing them not to commit crimes that would either get them banged up for years or a short walk to the gallows and the hangman's noose. The main entrance was only for teachers, he'd been told; students, male and female alike, used the side doors. His stomach churned, unpleasantly, as he forced himself to walk through the gate, past a statue of some geezer forgotten long ago, and up to the door. It opened, revealing a young boy and girl wearing school uniforms and blazers. Colin felt his stomach clench, again. They were so *young*, so unscarred by life...

The girl stepped forward. "Captain Lancaster?"

"*Corporal* Lancaster," Colin corrected. The thought of making *captain* a bare eight months after joining the marines was absurd. He'd had to work his arse off to make corporal and he was all too aware he could lose the stripe at any moment. He wondered, suddenly, if the Beast had summoned the wrong man. *Lancaster* was hardly an unusual name. "I hope I've come to the right place."

The girl giggled. "Yes, sir," she said. "The headmaster is waiting to see you."

Colin nodded, feeling a growing sense of unreality as the prefects led him through corridors that looked to have been cleaned for his visit. He was no longer a student, no longer a forced inmate...he no longer belonged in the school. It was no longer his place. He felt his stomach churn as they stopped outside the headmaster's office and knocked. The last time he'd been here, he'd been told he'd never amount to anything. Now...he wondered, suddenly, if the Beast even remembered him. There'd been over a hundred students in his year. To the Beast, Colin would have been just one face in a crowd.

The Beast stepped out of his office, wearing his gown and mortar board. Colin blinked in surprise. His memories had made the headmaster out to be a monster, but now he was a very small man indeed. Colin had expected...he wasn't sure what. The Beast had been a monster and now he was...he was something else. Colin told himself, as he straightened to attention, that he'd grown up. The tyrant of his childhood and teenage years was no longer a threat.

"Welcome back," the Beast said. His face looked ratty, very ratty. His voice brought back memories, none of them pleasant. "I trust you have prepared a speech?"

"Yes, sir," Colin said. There was no point in antagonising the Beast. God! He'd forgotten the man's real name. Did he even *have* one? It was a silly question, but it hadn't been so silly when he'd been a child. "I hope everyone is ready to listen?"

"I've called a special assembly," the Beast assured him, once he'd put his coat and bag in a locker. "Everyone will attend or I'll know the reason why."

Colin turned away, feeling a sudden surge of disgust. The Beast *would* have summoned everyone. Of *course* he would have summoned everyone. He wouldn't have wanted a guest to go away with the impression the school hated him, naturally. Colin was tempted to point out how counterproductive it was, then shrugged. If the Beast paid no attention to scribbling on toilet walls, he wouldn't pay any attention to a very junior marine. Maybe if Major Craig had had a quiet word with him...

He put the thought out of his mind as the Beast led him down to the assembly hall. The scent of cooked cabbage hung in the air, a mocking reminder of school dinners that tasted worse than ration bars. It would have been better, he was sure, if they'd simply handed out a bar or two at lunchtime, if the students couldn't go home for something nice. Not, he supposed, that most of the kids had had that choice. Their parents were often working two jobs just to put food on the table.

"We're very proud of you," the Beast assured him. "You're an inspiration to the rest of us."

Colin resisted the urge to snort. Did the Beast expect him to *believe* that? Did the Beast believe it himself? Colin wondered, idly, which would be worse. There was no way the Beast would have given a damn about him if he hadn't accomplished something, yet...he couldn't be the only former student to make something of himself. He silently cursed the PR genius who'd convinced Major Craig to order him home. He would sooner have shined his CO's boots than gone back to school.

The sense of unreality grew stronger as the Beast led him through a door and onto a stage. The audience—students, ranging from twelve to eighteen—stared at him. Colin shivered, remembering the days when he'd sat in a crowd and tried not to be too obviously bored as an honoured guest lied his arse off. Now...he felt a pang of guilt. The girls and boys in front of him hadn't wanted to be there. Some of them might see the assembly as a welcome break from lessons, but others...he hid a smile as he saw a young boy wearing a pair of modified glasses. If Colin didn't miss his guess, he was watching something else...

Clever, Colin thought. *Who was it in my year who found an ingenious way to skive?*

He kept the thought to himself as the Beast introduced him with a long and flowery speech that managed to get almost *everything* wrong. Colin *hadn't* had good marks, Colin *hadn't* had his pick of universities and Colin *hadn't* won the Headmaster's Prize for Good Conduct. He hadn't won anything that meant something, even the Miss Joyful Prize for Raffia Work. The only thing the Beast had given him was six of the best!

"And now, I give you Corporal Lancaster," the Beast said, once he'd finished poisoning the well. "Please welcome him."

Colin hid his amusement at the handful of claps. Anyone would think the students weren't happy to see him. He stepped forward, clasping his hands behind his back. He'd been given a list of material to cover—the PR officers hadn't trusted him to speak without detailed instructions—but he intended to say something himself first. And to hell with the Beast. He couldn't complain to Colin's superiors without looking remarkably petty.

"It has been an eternity since I stepped within these walls," he said, pitching his voice so he could be heard right across the hall. "But I do remember that not *everyone* wanted to attend these little talks. If any of you want to leave, or read, or go to sleep, feel free. I don't care. Really."

He smiled at the Beast, daring him to say something. The headmaster looked murderous, but had the wit to keep his mouth shut. Colin grinned, feeling as if the old man no longer had any power over him. Or anyone, really. The worst he could do was bitch and moan to Major Craig—or, more accurately, to the PR officers. Colin thought he could talk his way out of trouble. And even if it cost him his stripe...it was worth it.

"I didn't do *half* of what the headmaster credited to me," Colin continued. He saw a handful of quickly hidden smiles amongst the childish faces. It was hard to believe he'd ever been that young. "I really haven't been out of training that long. I do have some war stories to tell you, but you know what? There are people in the military who were in the thick of it while I was in my mother's tummy."

There were a handful of snickers, quickly suppressed. Colin grinned and launched into the speech he'd been given, with a handful of slight revisions. He had no idea where the PR officers had been educated, but he was fairly sure it wasn't a council school. In fact, he was fairly sure they'd never been young in the first place. Boys who wanted to join the marines wanted to go to war, to test themselves against the best the enemy had to offer. Colin wasn't foolish enough to think the other roles weren't important, but they weren't that exciting either. No one wanted to hear about endless training, garrison duty or disaster relief. They wanted excitement, not boredom.

He finished, just as the bell rang. The students jumped to their feet and hurried to the doors without being dismissed. Colin smiled inwardly as he glanced at the Beast. The headmaster looked *pissed,* pissed and making a half-assed attempt to hide it. It was too late to stop the deserters. The teachers weren't making any attempt to slow the exodus down. They were probably bored too. Those who could, did. Those who couldn't, taught. He felt his smile grow wider as he turned away. Anyone who said that to an army instructor was likely to regret it. The poor bugger would be doing push-ups for hours.

"You didn't have to tell them that," the Beast said, once the hall was empty. He sounded weak, weak and unsure of himself. "It's important that take these assemblies seriously."

"Really, sir?" Colin wondered, sourly, why he'd ever taken the Beast seriously in the first place. "Then why do you make them compulsory?"

The Beast let out a rude noise as he led the way back to his office. Colin looked around with new insight. The wall of trophies—practically an 'I love me' wall—looked neat, but the Beast hadn't earned any of them. There were no medals, no commendations...not even a teaching certificate. He was tempted to ask if the Beast even *had* a teaching certificate. The council was so desperate for teachers that it might not have looked too closely... he shook his head at the thought. They couldn't have been that lax, surely.

"I think it would be better if you were to leave," the Beast said, stiffly. "I'll be speaking to your commanding officer about this."

"My commanding officer will be singularly unimpressed," Colin said. He'd once dreamed of knocking the headmaster out with a single punch, but now...the old man was just pathetic. "And I do wonder at your claims of military glory."

The Beast turned an interesting colour. "Get out."

Colin saluted, perfectly, then headed for the door. The prefects were waiting outside...as if they were MPs, called to deal with a rowdy soldier. Colin had no idea when they'd been summoned, if indeed they'd been summoned at all. The Beast was egoistic enough to keep the prefects dancing attendance on him...Colin shrugged. It wasn't his problem any longer.

"Sir," the boy said, as they collected Colin's coat. "Is what you said true?"

"Most of it," Colin told him. "It's great to be a marine, but you have to work hard."

He donned his coat, then frowned as a thought struck him. "Can you take me past the Remembrance Display?"

"Of course, sir," the girl said. "Right this way."

Colin followed her, feeling a flicker of sympathy. He could have found his way himself, easily, but the Beast was in a beastly mood. The prefects would be in trouble if they didn't stick to Colin like glue, at least until they showed him to the gates and bid him farewell. The Beast would be looking for someone to bear the brunt of his anger and humiliation...

He frowned as they entered the long corridor. A handful of photographs—former students who'd died in the war—greeted him. He looked past them, towards the final set of class photographs. It was easy to pick out himself, standing next to Susan Dryden. He'd had his hand on her ass, if he recalled correctly...and he did. She'd put out for him and...he wondered, suddenly, what had happened to her. She hadn't had any ambitions, as far as he could remember. She'd certainly never discussed anything with him. He was tempted to give her a call.

His eyes wandered over the photograph. They'd all been somewhere between seventeen and eighteen, but they looked young. Too young. The photograph told a lie. He looked from face to face, picking out boys and girls he'd known...

Colin swore as a face jumped out at him. A very familiar face.

"Impossible," he breathed. It was the gunboat crewman. It had to be. And yet...Colin rubbed his forehead. The face was younger and softer, but it was the same person. "I..."

"Sir?"

Colin remembered the prefects and glanced at them. "I...I just saw a face from the past," he said. He pointed to his picture. "That's me, there?"

"But you look so handsome," the male prefect said. "That can't be you."

His partner elbowed him. Colin had to smile.

"I was younger then," he said. He hadn't been *that* much younger, but military training changed a man. It had clearly changed the gunboat pilot too. Colin hadn't recognised him and he had the awful feeling he should have done. He checked the notes and found a name. Richard Tobias Gurnard. "You'd better show me out before you get in trouble for missing class."

"It's quite all right," the girl assured him. "We get extra credit for showing guests around the school."

"Which will be meaningless, once you're out of the school," Colin told her, bluntly. His mind was elsewhere. "Unless you think you can get a job here."

The prefects looked at each other in horror. Colin grinned as they turned and led him down the stairs, back to the entrance hall. He hadn't lied to them. Sure, they might get extra credit for showing him around, but it would be worthless when they left the school. They'd probably be around sixteen to seventeen, he guessed. Maybe they could afford to miss a handful of classes, but not many. The Beast wouldn't go to bat for them if they got marked down for non-attendance. Probably.

He bid them farewell, then hurried out of the school and down to the pub. The manager noted his uniform and saluted, pouring him a free drink. Colin took it and looked around. Patrick was sitting at a table, drinking. It looked as though he'd spent the morning drinking. Colin felt a flicker of disgust. He hadn't *had* to invite Patrick to join him. What was he doing these days? He should be on National Service, not...drinking.

"Hey, mate." Patrick giggled as he tossed back the remnants of his beer. "How did your return to school go?"

"I embarrassed the Beast," Colin said. He might get in trouble for it, but he didn't much care. Not any longer. "Patrick...do you remember Richard Gurnard?"

Patrick giggled. "Little faggot, thought his shit didn't stink. The dickhead. You don't remember him?"

Colin stared at his hands. "I..."

"You used to yank down his pants whenever you had a chance," Patrick said. "He deserved it too. Wanker."

He giggled, again. Colin shivered. He hadn't been that bad, had he? And yet, the fear in the gunboat pilot's eyes had shocked him. A boy called Richard...it had been easy, too easy, to shorten his name to Dick. And then make fun of him, endlessly. He felt shame curdling in his gut. He'd been awful to Richard, awful and...just awful.

"He was the one who asked out Lizzie," Patrick said. "You remember her? I dated her, for a bit. I think she turned into a lesbian..."

"I don't blame her," Colin said, sharply.

"Here," Patrick said. He waved his hand, drunkenly. "You watch your mouth. I was too much of a man for her..."

Colin stared at his friend, seeing him in a new light. Patrick...had wasted his life. Whatever he was doing with himself, it wasn't National Service. He'd be surprised if it was *anything*. Patrick was stupid and shallow and violent and...useless. He'd spend the rest of his life in the underworld, loitering on the edge of society until he overdosed or wound up in a work camp or *somewhere*. Colin's stomach churned as he stood and stumbled back. Patrick was a black hole, dragging him down. And coming back to Liverpool again had been a mistake.

"Where are you going?" Patrick started to stand, but his legs failed. "We'll go find some sexy ladies in need of some good loving..."

"You're too drunk," Colin said. A hundred sharp remarks ran through his mind, but he knew none would make any impact on the drunkard. He'd turned his life around. Patrick...hadn't. And never would. "Goodbye."

He turned and strode out the door. A glass flew past, bounced off the wall and hit the ground without breaking. Colin felt a sudden mad urge to turn and beat his friend—his former friend—into a pulp, but chose to ignore it. There was no point. Patrick wouldn't learn anything from the experience and...the landlord was already coming around the counter, shockrod in hand. Patrick would wake up in the drunk tank, begging for a drink. Who knew? A period of enforced sobriety might be good for him.

Fuck, Colin thought, as he kept walking. The memories mocked him. He'd forgotten Richard Gurnard until...until they'd met again, as adults. *What the fuck do I do now?*

CHAPTER TWENTY-FIVE

TOBIAS HAD NEVER CARED *THAT* MUCH ABOUT HISTORY. The history classes he'd taken in school had alternated between insisting that everything had worked out for the best and stripping the life from history until reading about great heroes became about as exciting as watching paint dry. The handful of semi-illegal history modules he'd downloaded from the darker corners of the datanet hadn't been much of an improvement, bashing Britain where the official records had praised Britain. One side thought Britain could do no wrong, while the other had argued Britain could do no right. But looking at Apollo 11, he couldn't help feeling a thrill. There was *real* history wrapped up in the tiny lander.

He held Marigold's hand as they walked around the railing, staring at where Neil Armstrong had first set foot on the moon. The Americans had turned the entire scene into a tourist attraction, but they'd been careful to preserve everything they could. No tourists were allowed to get any closer to the lander, let alone put their footprints beside the first on the moon. It didn't matter. He felt history peering down at him as they read the plaque near the lander, then returned to the tunnel that led back to the city. It felt as though he was finally free.

"Perhaps I'll move here," he said, as they passed through a pair of airlocks. "It's so much better than home."

Marigold grinned and squeezed his hand. He wasn't sure when they'd joined hands, but he sure as hell wasn't going to let go. Armstrong City was bright and open, even though half was buried beneath the lunar surface. There was a sense of boundless optimism in the natives that was so lacking back home. And it wasn't even the freest city on the moon, perhaps not even the best place to live. He smiled, promising himself he'd to find a place to live when he was discharged. He'd have his spacer's badge by then. It should be easy to immigrate. Luna was always looking for new settlers.

They passed the flying dome, with tourists donning wings and flapping around like birds, as they headed back to the hotel. Tobias was tempted to try it himself, something he never would have dared on Earth. Colin...he shook his head, banishing the bully from his mind. It was the first time he'd been on a proper date with a girl and he was damned if he was letting Colin, even a memory of Colin, ruin it.

"We could try that tomorrow," Marigold said. "The tourist bus to the crater might have been cancelled."

Tobias frowned. "Did they say why?"

"No," Marigold said. "But it probably has something to do with the war."

Tobias said nothing as they reached the hotel, passed through the automated gates and entered their room. It was more of a small apartment than a room, designed to allow them to cater for themselves if they didn't feel like going out and finding somewhere to eat. The preserved food tasted better than he'd expected, certainly better than the ration bars handed out on Earth. It was hard to believe the beef burger wasn't real beef, even though meat was still expensive on the moon. Vat-grown meat was cheaper, but not by much.

He shook his head. He hadn't really wanted the reminder about the war. It was easy to forget, in Armstrong City, that there was a war on. The tourists still thronged the streets, the locals still laughed and sang and... and all of that would come to an end, if the virus attacked the colony. The Tadpoles had bombarded the moon, back during the *first* war. The virus would hardly be any kinder. It might decide there was no point in preserving the colony and simply smash it from orbit.

"It's definitely been cancelled," Marigold said. She sat on the bigger of the two beds, studying the viewscreen. "We'll have to find something else to do tomorrow."

Tobias sat next to her. "Go flying?"

"If it's open," Marigold said. She started to flick between channels. "What do you want to watch?"

"Anything," Tobias said. They had similar tastes. He knew that much. "Pick anything."

Marigold put on a light comedy and leaned against him. Tobias allowed himself a moment of relief, mingled with fear. What if he did the wrong thing? What if he went too far? What if...he was torn between the urge to press against her and the fear she'd slap him—or worse—if he tried. He hesitated, then lifted his hand and put his arm around her shoulders. She snuggled against him, turning her head to his. It was suddenly very easy to kiss her. Their lips met.

Tobias felt a surge of excitement as she pressed against him. Her hands stroked his back as they kissed, again and again. He started to reach for her breasts, giving her a chance to say no and draw back if she changed her mind. He'd had all the lectures on consent, on letting the girl set the pace, but they'd never meant much to him. No girl had so much as given him the time of day, until now. She quivered against him as his fingers brushed against her shirt, then crawled under her clothes. It was hard, surprisingly hard, to undress without tearing anything...

Afterwards, he lay against her, oddly unsure of himself. He was a virgin. He was...no, he'd *been* a virgin. He stared at her, drinking in her naked body. He'd seen porn—he'd seen a *lot* of porn—but none of it came close to a living, breathing girl. He wondered if it had been good for her, if she'd liked what he'd done with his hands and mouth and...he wondered, suddenly, if it had been her first time. He simply didn't have enough experience to know. The boys had bragged for hours in the changing rooms, but he was *sure* they'd been lying. They had to have been lying.

Marigold shifted against him. He swallowed, then asked. "Was it good for you?"

She giggled. "Yeah," she said. "And you?"

Tobias didn't answer. Instead, he kissed her again.

"You're back early," Sergeant Bowman said, as Colin peered into his office. "Should I be concerned?"

"No, Sergeant," Colin said. It had been a day since he'd given his little speech. If the Beast had wanted to lodge a complaint, he'd have done it by now. "I...I wanted to ask your advice."

"Oh, dear," Bowman said. He waved a hand at the folding chairs, positioned against the far bulkhead. "Take a chair, and a deep breath, and tell me about it."

Colin hesitated, unsure what to say. The sergeant was his superior, even though he wasn't an officer. Bowman outranked him. And Bowman had far more experience than he did. It was true a sergeant was meant to be a father-figure to the men, but...Colin really wasn't sure what to say. What would Bowman think of him? What would *anyone* think of him?

"I need your advice," he said. "Can we talk privately?"

"So you said," Bowman reminded him. "For the record, I do have an obligation to report certain things to the CO."

"I...I understand." Colin frowned. "I don't know what to say."

"If she's pregnant, get a medical certificate before you do anything stupid," Bowman said, dryly. "If she's dumped you, get over it. If *he's* dumped you, get over it. If she never even knew you existed, and married someone who *also* never knew you existed, grow the fuck up before you do something stupid. Does that advice help?"

"No, Sergeant," Colin said. "What...what *do* you have to report to the CO?"

"Use your common sense," Bowman said. "What do you *think*?"

Colin decided not to worry about it. "Sergeant, when I was in school..."

He broke off. "I...Sergeant, when I was in school..."

"I'm sure you were taught to be concise," Bowman said. "Are you going to get to the point before I die of old age?"

"No, sir," Colin said. He wasn't sure how old Bowman actually *was*. "I...when I was in school, I was...I was awful to someone."

"Indeed?" Bowman cocked an eyebrow. "In what way?"

Colin felt a hot flash of anger. "I was a bullying bastard, Sergeant," he said. "I was a right little monster."

"I hope you've grown up," Bowman said. "You wouldn't be the first person to come to us with a chequered record."

"He's onboard ship," Colin said. "I...didn't even recognise him, not at first. I didn't even remember him. But he remembered me."

"I'm not surprised, if you were a bullying bastard." Bowman studied Colin for a long, cold moment. "How do you feel about it now?"

"I was a fucking arse, Sergeant," Colin said. It crossed his mind he shouldn't use such language in front of the older man, but it was already too late. "I...I...I don't even know why I was such an arse to him. And I was..."

"I see," Bowman said. "And did he do anything to provoke you?"

Colin shrugged. The hell of it was that he simply didn't know. He'd honestly forgotten the poor bastard until he'd seen the photograph. The memories were faint. Richard Gurnard—he was apparently going by *Tobias* now, according to the records he'd checked—had just been part of his life, one of the world's eternal victims. He burned with shame at just how awful he'd been. Provocation? What sort of provocation deserved a life sentence of endless bullying? He understood, now, too late.

"I don't know," he said. "I don't think so."

"You don't think so." Bowman's eyes bored into him. "And if you don't think so, do you have any kind of excuse?"

Colin said nothing. He'd had a rough upbringing, but so what? He'd had trouble at school...so what? Richard—Tobias—had been crap at sports... so what? Treating him like dirt had impressed the girls...or had it? He'd heard a little something about mob psychology during training, when they'd been cautioned they might have to cope with civil unrest. A thug could convince everyone to support him, for fear of what he'd do if they didn't. Better someone else got the beating...he stared down at his hands. He'd been a bastard and now...he didn't know what to do.

"Well?" Bowman leaned forward. "Do you have any kind of excuse?"

"No, Sergeant," Colin said. "I don't."

"I'm glad you admit it," Bowman said. "And what do you intend to do about it?"

"I don't know," Colin said. "What *can* I do?"

"My, it's a tough one." Bowman's voice hardened. "Can you go back in time and kick the shit out of your younger self?"

"I'm not sure it would have helped," Colin said. "I was a right..."

"So you said." Bowman cut him off, effortlessly. "What can you do about it?"

"I don't know," Colin repeated. "What *can* I do about it?"

"If you were in his place," Bowman asked, "what would *you* want done about it?"

Colin shrugged. He'd *never* been in such a place. In school, he'd fought to establish himself as a big man. In the marines, he'd knuckled down and worked until he'd earned some respect—and his first stripe. The idea of someone battering him down so completely he couldn't raise a hand to defend himself was...unthinkable. Even the dreaded Conduct After Capture course, which had approached borderline torture, hadn't beaten him down. He'd heard the warnings, he'd been cautioned that *real* enemy interrogators might do worse than his training officers, but... it was hard to believe. The virus didn't *need* to torture captives. It just infected them.

"Think about it," Bowman advised. "What would you want? What would you *fear*?"

Me, Colin thought.

He scowled. "Can I just apologise?"

"Perhaps you should," Bowman said. "But would you be apologising because you want to...or because you think you should?"

"Sergeant?"

Bowman leaned forward. "You're not the first person to have royally fucked up, when you were a kid. Believe me, you're hardly the worst I've seen. At least you realise it, which is more than some of the others ever did. And you got some of the attitude knocked out of you during commando training..."

"Yes, Sergeant," Colin said. He tried to imagine what his instructors would have said, if he'd tried to bully them. He would have been safer boarding an infected starship stark naked. "I was...I tried to grow up a little."

"A little," Bowman said. "Let me tell you your story. You grew up an angry young man in a rough area. You were deprived of any good examples, because your father never taught you the right lessons. You learnt, probably without really being aware of it, that you had to assert yourself to survive. You did this, like everyone else in your position, by making examples of people who couldn't really push back. You found yourself a pack of fair-weather friends and a small harem of girls who didn't really like you, but feared what you'd do if they rejected you."

Colin stiffened. "It wasn't really like that..."

"Quiet," Bowman said. It was very definitely an order. "You picked up a bunch of bad habits. You never thought to question them because they were keeping you at the top of the pecking order. You never thought to wonder what harm they were doing to you, and everyone else, in the long run. And then you left school and went straight into commando training. You finally had someone teaching you better lessons, teaching you how to control and direct your anger. You grew up.

"Problem is, you still have to deal with the past. Don't you?"

"Yes, Sergeant," Colin said, sullenly. "I...I never forced any girl to..."

"I'm glad to hear it," Bowman said. "Are you sure?"

"I...I think so," Colin said. He remembered all the girls he'd kissed. Had they wanted to kiss him? Or...he shuddered. He didn't want to think about it. "I never forced anyone."

"I'm glad to hear it," Bowman said. "And here's something you will *not* be glad to hear."

Colin said nothing. He just waited.

"You haven't told me anything new," Bowman said. "You haven't found a new way to screw up. You're just acting out a script that was old when the human race was young. No one called you out for it, not until now."

"Why not?" Colin asked. "Why?"

Bowman smiled. "If you take a swing at me, what do you think will happen?"

"You'd kick my ass," Colin said. He'd seen the sergeant fight. "It wouldn't be a contest."

"No," Bowman agreed. "If you'd taken a swing at one of your teachers, or one of your fair-weather friends, you might have escaped punishment. You *might*. And...even if you weren't inclined to punch anyone who questioned you, who would? Teenagers are wired to resent their friends acting like parents. A grown man like me can call you out for being an ass, which I will. Believe me, I will. One of your comrades? I very much doubt it... and if they did, you'd be pissed."

Colin swallowed. "Fuck."

Bowman met his eyes. "What do you intend to do?"

"I don't know," Colin said, in frustration. "I really don't know."

"So you keep saying," Bowman said. "Here are your options. You can do nothing. You can seek him out and apologise. And you can...well? Is there anything else you can do?"

"...No," Colin said. "Unless I ask for a transfer."

"You'd better come up with a damn good reason," Bowman said. "You are *nowhere* near important enough to request a transfer, not yet."

Colin smiled. "My sergeant thinks I'm a lout?"

"Hah," Bowman said. "That'll get you a lecture from the CO, not a transfer. You want my advice?"

"Yes," Colin said. "I came to *ask* for advice."

"Send him an email. Apologise to him. Have as little as possible to do with him afterwards. You're in different departments. You don't need any interaction outside actual combat, where I expect you to handle yourself like a mature professional. You didn't ask to meet him onboard ship and I'm sure he didn't ask to meet you either. One of you will be transferred off, soon enough. And then let the matter rest."

"Yes, Sergeant," Colin said. "But...what if he refuses to accept my apology?"

Bowman raised his bushy eyebrows. "And you think you have the right to *force* him to accept your apology?"

"No, Sergeant." Colin felt his cheeks heat. "I just want to put it behind me."

"I'm sure he feels the same way too," Bowman said. "Make your apology, then let it go."

"I should try to find a way to make it up to him," Colin said. "I can't just let it go."

Bowman snorted. "Are you going to beat yourself up? Maybe give yourself a black eye? Or pound on the bulkhead until you smash every bone in your hand? Or...or what? If you were a total wanker to him, do you honestly think there's any chance to make it up to him? Do you honestly think there's any way you *can*?"

He shrugged. "And seeing you came back early, you can help me with the paperwork," he said. There was a wry sparkle in his eye. "It should quench any dreams you have of becoming a sergeant."

"Yes, sergeant," Colin said. "Is this a cunning plan to keep me from trying to get your job?"

"Oh, bugger, you've found me out," Bowman teased. "You're officer material for sure."

"Thanks," Colin said, sardonically.

CHAPTER TWENTY-SIX

THOMAS DIDN'T FEEL *MUCH* RESTED as he was escorted through the security screening and into the admiral's office. The two days after the party had been marred by discussions with his wife that had turned into arguments, mostly over trivial matters. Lady Charlotte had expected him to stay longer, even though he was no longer the master of his own fate. The days when he could take a day or two away from his duties at short notice were gone. They'd died when he'd assumed command of *Lion*.

And if I kept pretending I could leave whenever I liked, he thought, *I'd return home to find the airlock hatch closed.*

He smiled humourlessly as he looked around the office. Admiral Onarina sat at a table, flanked by another admiral and a civilian Thomas didn't recognise. Captain Campbell sat facing her...Thomas felt a sudden stab of paranoia, wondering if Campbell had been summoned ahead of time. *That* boded ill...he told himself, firmly, that he was being ridiculous. He'd been in the navy long enough to know that passing through the endless security checks could take longer than anyone intended. Captain Campbell might just have arrived a little earlier than he had. Admiral Onarina nodded to him, then waved to an empty seat. It seemed that informality was the order of the day.

Thomas sat, schooling his face into a bland mask. Captain Campbell was lowest-ranking person at the table, unless one counted the civilian, yet he seemed unfazed by being the low man on the totem pole. Thomas almost envied him. *He* was all too aware that saying the wrong thing to the wrong person could come back to bite him, often so much later that it was hard to draw the line between the act and the consequences. Admiral Onarina tapped a switch on a datapad—the hatch locked, loudly enough to startle Thomas—then smiled at the junior officers. Thomas had the uneasy impression of a shark making its way towards an unwary swimmer.

"Thank you for coming," Admiral Onarina said. She activated the holographic projector, displaying an image of a blue-green world. "Brasilia."

"I take it we're paying it a visit," Captain Campbell said.

Thomas wanted to bite his head off for speaking out of turn. Admiral Onarina seemed unfazed.

"Quite." Admiral Onarina adjusted the display, pulling back until the entire system was clearly visible. "Brasilia was discovered roughly thirty years ago and claimed by Brazil, which embarked upon a full-scale terraforming and settlement project. The wars slowed colonisation down a little, which caused a multitude of minor problems, but matters were proceeding apace until *this* war began. The virus invaded and infected the system shortly after it began its push into human space and...well, as far as we know, there's no one left uninfected. Recon sweeps through the system revealed no hint of surviving uninfected colonists."

"They could be lying doggo," Captain Campbell said.

"Yes," Admiral Onarina agreed. "But, as far as we know, there are no uninfected people on the surface. Worse"—her eyes narrowed—"the planet's atmosphere is uniquely *good* for the virus, a threat we didn't anticipate until it was too late. If anyone survived the first landings and infections, they'd have to be pretty much permanently in environmental suits if they wanted to remain uninfected."

Thomas shivered. He'd grown up in a world where there was very little privacy, unless one wanted to go completely off the grid, but this was an order of magnitude worse. The idea that one could be infected, in a single moment of carelessness, and turned into a soulless monster was terrifying. Anyone left on the planet would have to remain underground and hope for the best, knowing it would never come. Given time, the virus could grind down resistance and eventually obliterate it.

"There's a possibility the virus might be studying the terraforming stations," the other admiral said. "It may be trying to figure out how to alter *Earth's* atmosphere."

"Shit," Thomas said, quietly. "If it tries...can we stop it?"

"We don't know." Admiral Onarina looked pensive. "We've built up quite a body of expertise in terraforming and weather modification, but... no one's ever tried to terraform a planet like Earth. Small modifications—the introduction of human-compatible plants and animals—are as far as we've ever gone. Full-fledged tectonic adjustments and suchlike were formally banned, after we started to exploit the tramlines. Thankfully"—her lips thinned until they were almost invisible—"the virus would practically have to *win* the war before it could start heating the atmosphere, melting the icecaps and whatever else it would have to do to alter the atmosphere."

"Thank God for that," Captain Campbell muttered.

Admiral Onarina smiled. "The interesting fact about this system is that it is actually somewhat isolated from the remainder of pre-war space. The neighbouring systems are practically useless, at least to the Great Powers. The virus doesn't seem to have shown much interest in any of them, beyond blasting a handful of colonies and driving others underground. Given the system's location, we think the virus has decided the planet is unimportant and only deployed a handful of ships to the orbitals."

Captain Campbell smiled. "A perfect target."

"But meaningless, if the system is truly unimportant," Thomas countered. "The virus could have downloaded everything from the terraforming stations by now."

"Perhaps," Admiral Onarina said. "The planet's...oddities may actually work *for* us, as well as against us. Admiral Mason?"

The other admiral cleared his throat. "What I'm about to tell you is classified at the very highest levels," he said. He looked around the same age as Admiral Onarina, with brown hair slowly turning to a darker hue. "If you breathe a word of it, before the mission is declassified, you will spend the rest of your lives in Colchester. Understand?"

"Yes, sir," Thomas said.

Admiral Mason nodded. "We've been studying the virus from the moment *Invincible* made First Contact," he said. "It's a complex entity, easily the most complex...*thing*.... we've encountered. It actually seems to work a little like a distributed computer network, with subunits merging and separating without any issues at all...at least, as far as we've been able to determine. Worse...it doesn't so much take over a host as it simply...builds its own control networks within the host's body. It's a little like attaching additional rockets to a starship and pushing it in the wrong direction."

Captain Campbell leaned forward. "But it's capable of...accessing information within the host's brain."

"Sometimes," Admiral Mason agreed. "We've watched the process carefully. Sometimes it works, sometimes it doesn't. We've been trying to put together a biological defence, but—so far—we don't have anything that will stop the infection without killing the host. Indeed...accidentally poisoning the host and killing him make it *easier* for the virus to take over the body."

Admiral Onarina smiled. It didn't touch her eyes. "You remember those cartoons about little people inside the human body, pulling on ropes and pushing buttons to make the muscles work? It's a little like that."

Thomas frowned. "You've been testing this on living people?"

"Some of them were infected when they were moved to Alpha Black," Admiral Mason said, bluntly. "Others...were prisoners, who were on their way to the gallows when we offered them a chance to serve their country instead. They were going to die anyway."

"That's horrific." Thomas felt sick. "I thought human experimentation was banned."

"They were going to die anyway," Admiral Mason repeated. "Would you like to see the files? Would you like to know what they did? I forced myself to view the files, all the evidence collected by the police before they were put in front of a jury, found guilty and sentenced to death. There was no doubt about their guilt."

Thomas winced. "But…"

"But what?" Admiral Mason looked displeased. "Do you think we'd have done it if we'd had any other choice?"

"The decision was made by the War Cabinet," Admiral Onarina said, sternly. "The remainder of GATO made similar choices. Continue."

Admiral Mason took a moment to compose himself. "Like I said, we've been studying the process. Our attempts to create an effective vaccine have largely failed because the virus isn't *really* a virus, not in any true sense. The old fear of us catching an alien version of the common cold and dropping dead, or vice versa, hasn't *really* been realised. There's little hope of producing proper antibodies because the virus doesn't attack the human body directly. Instead, it builds its own control structures and takes over."

"I'm sure that makes sense on some level," Admiral Onarina said, dryly.

"It's never easy to explain," Admiral Mason said. "The point is, the virus isn't *quite* part of the host body. It's something that just happens to co-exist with it."

"Like putting marines on a starship," Captain Campbell said. "The marines are *on* the ship, but not part of the crew."

"Close enough for government work." Admiral Mason grinned at them. "Point is, in theory we can break the virus down without killing the host bodies. In theory…which we're going to try to put into practice."

Thomas felt a frisson of excitement, mingled with fear. "What do you have in mind?"

"We've been experimenting with the virus itself," Admiral Mason said. "It took us some time, to be honest, to accept that we were dealing with a biological warfare problem on an unprecedented scale. The tailored viruses that got loose a century ago are *nothing* compared to *the* virus. It's not only extremely aggressive, it's adaptable and more interested in taking control—in turning itself into a parasite—than even the nastiest biological weapon. The most virulent biological weapons don't spread far because they make their hosts ill very quickly, which reveals their presence. They burn themselves out. This one doesn't.

His eyes hardened. "And it's very nature may prove to be its weakness.

"We've been producing a modified version of the virus, a virus that preys on *the* virus. It spreads the same way as its unmodified cousin, but attacks the command and control structures the virus builds to control its hosts. As long as it has a steady supply of food, it keeps going; when it runs out of food, it starts to die. And the only thing it can eat is unmodified viral matter."

"You made a virus intended to kill the virus," Campbell said. "Sir... does it work?"

"We've tested it in the lab," Admiral Mason told him. "It works."

Thomas swallowed, hard. "And what happens to the host bodies?"

Admiral Mason looked grim. "It depends," he said. "Based on our experiments, some return to themselves."

"And some die," Thomas said. Dull horror washed though him. "How many people are we going to condemn to death?"

"They're going to die already," Admiral Onarina said. "Do you think that anyone, anyone at all, would agree to risk committing genocide if they thought there was any other choice?"

Thomas stared at his hands. Biological weapons were an obscenity. He'd seen the records of the plagues that had washed over Africa and the Middle East, threatening to break through the defences and infect the civilised world. He hadn't known—he hadn't wanted to know—that Britain was experimenting with biological weapons. In hindsight, he'd honestly never thought about it. It should have been obvious. The only way to defend against biological weapons was to study them.

He looked up. "How many people are living on Brasilia?"

"Before the infection, there were over five hundred thousand registered settlers," Admiral Onarina said, quietly. "Perhaps more. The records were never very good. Now...each and every one of them has been condemned to a living death. They'll regard death as a mercy."

"If we demonstrate the ability to hurt it, to *really* hurt it, perhaps we can force it to come to the table," Captain Campbell said. "It *must* be able to talk to us. It simply doesn't *want* to."

"Wishful thinking," Admiral Mason said. "We've never been able to open communications."

Thomas shook his head. "What's to stop it just copying *our* anti-infection protocols? There's no way we can hide the infection, the counter-infection, from the virus. It would know what we'd done."

"Nothing." Admiral Mason smiled. "But it would have to practically shut down the biological datanet, if it wanted to keep the infection from spreading. Either way, we'd come out ahead."

"Until it devises a counter," Thomas said. "I'm not comfortable with committing genocide."

"No one is," Admiral Onarina said. "But, right now, we are faced with the uncomfortable choice between being the perpetrators or the victims of genocide. There is no way we can negotiate, there is no way we can surrender...defeat means the end of the universe. It will be the end."

And if I refuse to carry out my orders, they'll find someone else who will, Thomas thought, sourly. He knew the admiral was right. He just didn't want to believe it. *We must destroy the virus, or be destroyed in turn.*

He cleared his throat. "What do you want us to do?"

Admiral Onarina smiled. "Operation Thunderchild," she said, as she touched her datapad. A handful of lines appeared on the starchart. "*Lion, Unicorn* and a handful of other ships will proceed through the tramlines to Brasilia. You'll engage the enemy ships and take control of the high orbitals, then land marines. They'll deploy the BioBombs and secure a handful of tactical positions on the surface, including the terraforming facilities. Ideally, the bombs will work and liberate the planet's population."

"And leave them in a state of shock, at best," Thomas pointed out. "The virus has had four years, more or less, to burrow into their minds."

"We know." Admiral Onarina looked grim. "There's nothing we can do to save them."

"Fuck," Thomas said. "Have we really fallen that far?"

"Yes." It was the civilian who spoke. "The virus is maintaining its pressure on the defence lines. It's only a matter of time until it breaks through and smashes its way to Earth. We've being doing what we can to ensure the war will go on, if Earth falls, but it isn't enough. We just don't have the resources to expand our industrial base while meeting the military's demands. We are coming to the end of the line."

"And so are our allies," Admiral Mason said.

"Yes." Admiral Onarina nodded. "The decision to deploy the BioBombs was not taken lightly, Captain. We see no other choice."

Thomas said nothing for a long moment. He wasn't blind to the implications. The biosphere that made the planet attractive to the virus would also make it attractive to the BioBombs, ensuring it would spread widely. It might not expand so far, or so fast, on Earth. And testing the BioBombs somewhere hundreds of light years away would safeguard the homeworld, if it turned out the BioBombs were as great a threat as the virus itself. And... he felt his stomach churn. The idea of condemning hundreds of thousands of people to death didn't sit well with him. It was no consolation to tell himself that they were already trapped in a living hell and would welcome death.

"I understand," he said, finally. He felt as if he'd betrayed himself. Or he'd been betrayed. "When do we leave?"

"Five days," Admiral Onarina said. "I'd prefer to assign more ships, Captain, but we're desperately short of deployable units. And...there's a decent possibility the virus will ignore you, if it spots you in transit, because you'll have only a small number of ships under your command."

"Or we might be grasping at straws," Admiral Mason said. "You might have to fight your way through an enemy blockade."

"We can get there without being detected," Captain Campbell said. He shrugged, dismissively. Getting there wouldn't be hard, as long as they were careful. The enemy couldn't watch every last inch of the tramlines. "Would it not be easier to bombard the planet with ice projectiles?"

"It's unlikely that either the virus or the counter-virus would survive the trip through the atmosphere," Admiral Mason said. "We're working on other ways to deploy the counter-virus, but none of them are particularly good. Not yet. We need a certain density of viral matter to have any effect at all."

Admiral Onarina leaned back. "I appreciate that this isn't going to be pleasant," she said, in a tone that suggested disagreement was pointless. It probably was, if the War Cabinet had signed off on the operation. He couldn't stop it by saying *no*. "But it has to be done."

"We understand, Admiral," Captain Campbell said. "It will be done."

Thomas nodded. "We'll make sure of it, Admiral."

He kept his thoughts to himself. The virus infected *brains*, as well as bodies. He couldn't believe its sudden destruction would liberate the host-body, not when the virus had been carving the poor bastard's brain into mush. Thomas had heard all the jokes about brainless bureaucrats and civil servants, but...he shook his head as they were dismissed. Brain injuries were not funny. Even the slightest damage could prove fatal. And he couldn't imagine the former hosts shaking off the virus and getting back to work. It simply wasn't going to happen.

"See you on the far side," Captain Campbell said. He sounded disgustingly cheerful. "If this works..."

"If this works, we will have condemned hundreds of thousands of people to death," Thomas said, sharply. "There's no way to avoid it. The best we can hope for is shock and trauma on a massive scale, an entire planet's worth of people who have literally been enslaved suddenly finding themselves free...that's absurd, so optimistic that..."

He shook his head. "We're going to commit genocide. Doesn't it bother you? Just a little?"

CHAPTER TWENTY-SEVEN

DOESN'T IT BOTHER YOU? JUST A LITTLE?

Mitch scowled as he made his way back to the shuttle. Captain Hammond's question hung in his mind, but not for the reasons the older man might think. Mitch was perfectly aware that the BioBombs were likely to devastate the human population—he hadn't needed Captain Hammond to point it out—yet he understood they didn't have the luxury of time. The older man was an aristocrat, a man with a safety net that could keep him from losing everything...unless he did something *really* stupid or criminal. Mitch had grown up in a rough area, all too aware that the slightest mistake could cost him everything. The idea of everyone living in genteel harmony was nothing more than a joke.

For me, at least, he reflected sourly. *I never had the luxury of knowing I could get out of anything by mentioning the family name.*

He felt his scowl deepen as he considered the briefing. The blunt truth was that there was nothing they could do to save the infected population. He'd studied the reports, read them carefully. Only a handful of people had ever been saved from infection and *none* had come away unscarred. Their bodies had been permanently altered, to the point where no one could say—with complete certainty—that their thoughts were truly their own. And saving them had required so much medical intervention that there was no hope of saving more than a few thousand people. Captain Hammond could have his moral qualms, if he wished, but Mitch couldn't allow himself the luxury. The poor bastards on the planet were trapped in a living death. They'd welcome *real* death.

Dull hatred burned in his thoughts as the shuttle undocked and headed for *Unicorn*. He had no fear of death, no fear of squaring off against an enemy bigger and stronger than himself, but the virus was something else. Invisible to the naked eye, floating in the air...just waiting for him to take a breath and suck it into his bloodstream. It could infect him, it could start turning him into a soulless monster, and he'd never know. He could infect countless others before the symptoms became obvious, without ever being aware of what he was doing. The virus just didn't play fair. There could be no compromise. It had to be destroyed.

He plugged the datachips into his datapad and scanned the files, one by one. Admiral Onarina had put together a good plan, although it was a little basic for Mitch's tastes. She'd been a starship officer herself, he recalled. She probably knew to give basic orders, then leave more detailed planning and execution to the people actually charged with carrying them out. Mitch felt a wash of appreciation, tempered by the grim knowledge they'd be in deep shit if the virus reacted quickly. They'd be going beyond the flicker network, going so far out of contact that there'd be no hope of summoning help before it was too late. There was a very good chance the Royal Navy would never know what had happened to them, if things went spectacularly wrong. He smiled, unfazed by the thought. The flicker network was, like most innovations, good and bad. It was useful to have a direct link home, sometimes, but it also meant senior officers looking over one's shoulder. It could a pain in the arse.

The shuttle shuddered as it docked. Mitch stood and headed for the hatch, which opened as he approached. He stepped into the airlock, pressed his hand against the bioscanner and waited for it to clear him. The virus didn't seem to be able to take root without permanently altering the host's blood, or so he'd been told. Mitch had his doubts about it. The virus might not be remotely human, but it was intelligent. It had to be constantly looking for ways to evade the bioscanners.

"Captain." Staci greeted him as he stepped onto the bridge. "Did you have a good leave?"

"In a manner of speaking," Mitch said. He'd been glad to leave Captain Hammond's estate, the day after the party. It was just a shame he hadn't had time to do *much* with his leave. "Yourself?"

"Found a couple of girls and had fun," Staci said, with a shrug. "Do we have new orders?"

"Yes," Mitch said. He filled her in, quickly. "Are we ready to depart?"

"Pretty much, once the rest of the crew gets back," Staci said. "It wasn't as though we expended most of our weapons."

Mitch frowned as he took his command chair and studied the reports. Their first mission had been interesting, but...he couldn't help feeling as though he'd done nothing while *Lion* did all the work. And then...he shook his head. He'd made his feelings clear, when he'd written his report. Admiral Onarina hadn't raised the issue, as far as he knew. She probably felt it wasn't worth the effort. Captain Hammond would have to do something dire to get in real trouble.

"Good," he said. "Inform the crew I want them all back in three days. We'll have time to settle in before we depart. Again."

"Aye, sir," Staci said. "There'll be some grumbling, of course."

"Of course," Mitch echoed. "We'll cope with it."

Staci grinned. "If this works, it could shorten the war."

"Yes." Mitch nodded. If the counter-virus worked, it was time to start dusting every infected world. The virus would be rocked back on its heels, then obliterated. "All that remains is the proper application of overwhelming force."

Tobias tried hard to look professional as the shuttle glided towards the docking port, but it was impossible. The urge to grin was overwhelming.

They'd spent three days in bed and...he smiled, remembering just how close they'd come to missing the shuttle. It had been a learning experience—in hindsight, he probably shouldn't have watched so much porn—and it had taken them time to get the hang of it...

He squeezed Marigold's hand. He couldn't believe she liked him. They had a lot in common, he supposed, but...he just couldn't believe it. He was tempted to pinch himself, time and time again. Who'd have thought anyone would like *him*? He remembered all the crap he'd heard in the locker room, all the rude talk about girls and sex and girls and...he shook his head. It had been nothing more than bullshit. He knew that now, beyond a shadow of a doubt. Anyone who *really* liked a girl, who did stuff with a girl, would keep his mouth firmly shut. The girl wouldn't be happy if the boy bragged.

I bet Colin was lying his arse off, Tobias thought. He was in such a good mood that he regarded his nemesis with contempt, rather than fear. *No girl in her right mind would do all the horrid things he said she did.*

He sobered as the shuttle docked, the hatch hissing open. They were still holding hands. It wasn't easy to step back and let go, despite everything. He wanted the entire world to know...he frowned. Maybe there was something to the bragging after all. Maybe. He winked at her as they headed for the hatch, pressing their hands against the bioscanners as they passed. The system didn't bleep an alarm. They were clean. He wondered, suddenly, how they were going to make love onboard ship. The sleeping compartment was hardly *private.*

"Briefing in twenty minutes," Bagehot said, as they entered Pilot Country. "I'll see you both there."

"Aye, sir," Tobias said.

He splashed some water on his face, checked his appearance in the mirror, then nodded to himself. His lips looked normal. Marigold, thankfully, didn't use lipstick. The rest of the gunboat pilots wouldn't be remotely professional if they saw red lipstick on his face, he was sure. Marigold washed herself, gave him a quick hug and headed for the hatch. Tobias grinned and followed her. He tried not to look at her too openly. The others would notice and then...

This isn't school, he told himself. *Everyone will be a little more professional.*

"First order of business," Bagehot said. "Emily and Quentin have been reassigned to the academy. They'll be teaching the next generation of gunboat pilots so they learn from our experiences—and our mistakes. I was hoping to avoid losing them so quickly, but the Admiralty was very insistent the program is pushed forward."

"Poor them," someone said, from the rear. "What did they do to deserve it?"

Bagehot snorted. "We have four new pilots assigned to the squadron," he continued, indicating the newcomers. "You'll have a chance to meet them formally later, and you'll be in simulators with them from tomorrow until we meet the enemy, but I expect you to welcome them."

Jim and Sharon's replacements, as well as Emily and Quentin's, Tobias thought. He felt...odd. Jim and Sharon had been friends. The brief memorial service hadn't been enough, not really. The newcomers were trying to take their place...he knew, intellectually, that the newcomers didn't mean to take *anyone's* place, but he couldn't help feeling a little resentment. He told himself not to be stupid. *It isn't their fault.*

"Second, we'll be departing in five days, unless the schedule is put back again," Bagehot continued. "Same as before, take the time to record last messages and rewrite your wills if you wish before we actually depart. You should understand, now, that death can strike at any time. Don't leave something you want to say unsaid."

Tobias bit his lip. He'd thought about visiting his mother and sister, but...he shook his head. He wouldn't have given up his time with Marigold for anything. And yet...he knew he'd feel guilty for not calling them, let alone visiting. He told himself, sharply, that he could record a message at any time. He might even be able to call them directly. They weren't *that* far from Earth.

Bagehot continued, outlining a handful of details and duty rosters. He didn't say much about the mission, somewhat to Tobias's surprise. They'd probably get the details once they were on their way to…to wherever they were going. Not, Tobias supposed, that it mattered. He doubted Captain Hammond wanted, or cared, about his opinion. The gunboat pilots were pretty low on the totem pole.

"Tobias, Marigold, stay behind," Bagehot concluded. "The rest of you, dismissed."

Tobias blinked as the other pilots hurried for the hatch. He was being held back…no, *they* were being held back. He forced himself to remain calm, even though he was suddenly very unsure of himself. He and Marigold… were they going to be rewarded? Or punished? In his experience, being asked to remain behind was never good news.

Bagehot leaned forward. "I trust you enjoyed your leave?"

Tobias blushed. "Yes, sir."

"And that you enjoyed each other too?" Bagehot's face was carefully blank. "Right?"

Marigold's voice sounded remarkably even. "I don't know what you mean, sir."

"You're orienting on each other," Bagehot said, dryly. "Your relationship went to the next level, did it not?"

Tobias felt his blush grow deeper. "Sir, I…"

Bagehot held up a hand. "Two things," he said. "First, I don't give a damn what you do on your time off. Starfighter pilots have always had a great deal of latitude and it looks as though gunboat pilots are going to have the same. Live fast, die young, leave a cloud of free-floating atoms in space. There are privacy tubes, for privacy. Use them.

"Second, I expect you to behave professionally when you're on duty. No hugging, no kissing, no screwing in the gunboats…no attempts to repeat the experiment to determine how many young idiots you can fit in a starfighter. If you break up, I expect you to stay professional even if you come to hate each other. Behave professionally and we won't have to have another chat. Act like idiots and you'll wind up in hot water."

"Yes, sir," Marigold said.

"Good." Bagehot's eyes moved from Tobias to Marigold and back again. "You're not fooling anyone. The rest of the squadron will know soon, if they don't know already. Just...keep it professional when you're on duty."

"Yes, sir." Tobias wanted to die of embarrassment. He'd known couples who'd been caught behind the bike sheds and wondered, at the time, why they'd made a fuss. They'd been kissing...at least they'd had someone to kiss! He understood now. "We'll be professional."

"Good," Bagehot said. "I appreciate your careers are unconventional. I also appreciate that you and your fellows are unlikely to spend the rest of your working lives in the navy...assuming you survive. However, I expect a degree of common sense. I have neither the time nor the patience to handle a teenage scream act and, believe me, nor does the captain. If you do something that brings you to his attention, it will be too late for NJP."

Tobias swallowed. "Yes, sir."

Bagehot nodded. "Out," he ordered. He pointed a finger at the hatch. "I'll see you in the simulators tomorrow."

"Yes, sir," they said.

Marigold said nothing else until they were heading back to the sleeping compartment. "We'd better be very careful," she said. "The captain can order us spaced."

"Yeah." Tobias considered it for a moment. It had been only a few short hours since they'd been in bed together and his body was insisting, despite everything, that it had been too long. "Do you think the privacy tubes are free now?"

"I have no idea," Marigold said. She winked at him, then made a show of looking up and down the corridor before kissing him quickly on the lips. "And right now, I think we need to sleep."

"That's the last of the reports, sir," Donker said. "We have a full complement of missiles again."

Thomas nodded, barely hearing his XO. The reports had been clear and comprehensive. *Lion* was ready for action again. The tactical staff had communed with their fellows on Nelson Base and updated their doctrine, ensuring that—next time—they'd be able to hurt the enemy. Thomas's lips thinned. Enough enemy ships had survived the previous encounter to report back to higher authority, ensuring the virus knew what had happened to its brainships. At the very least, it would make sure to deploy more point defence units to its fleets. It might even deploy armed shuttles or gunboats of its own.

There's certainly no reason why it can't, Thomas thought. *We know it likes long-range missiles. Twinning them with gunboat targeting systems will hardly pose a real challenge.*

He scowled at the datapad, then looked up. "And the squadron?"

Donker frowned. "Calling it a *squadron* is perhaps pushing things, sir."

Thomas nodded. He'd wondered why someone higher-ranked hadn't been assigned to the mission, perhaps with a dedicated staff of his own, but he hadn't needed more than a glance at the squadron list to figure out the answer. There were eight ships assigned to the squadron, only three of which were *real* warships. The remainder consisted of a troop carrier, an escort carrier and three missile-heavy freighters. In theory, the latter could fire missiles as effectively as *Lion* herself. Thomas had his doubts. It was far more likely they'd be doing nothing more than hauling missiles for the battlecruiser.

Which is better than being nothing more than sitting ducks, he mused. *At least they can shoot back if they spot raiders coming at them.*

He let out a breath. "We have what we have," he said. "Are they ready to depart?"

"They say so," Donker said. He didn't sound as though he believed himself. The crews were merchantmen, conscripted into the navy. They'd know their jobs—space was unforgiving to the ignorant or stupid—but they lacked polish. They might also push the limits of the possible as far as they'd go. "However, we've had no time to train as a unit."

"I think we'll have to do that on the way," Thomas said. He rubbed his forehead in exasperation. The squadron was unlikely to survive a direct confrontation with the enemy fleet. He might be better off ordering the freighters—and the escort carrier—to remain in stealth while the warships did the hard work. Better that than watching helplessly as they were blown into atoms. "If not...we'll just have to leave the older ships out of the line of battle."

"Yes, sir," Donker said. "I'd be happier with more training, though. It feels as though we've picked up the dregs of the service."

"We probably have," Thomas agreed. The Admiralty hadn't assigned front-line warships to the squadron for the very simple reason it didn't have them to spare. He'd checked, during the flight from Nelson Base. There just weren't enough ships to go around. "We'll make do with what we have."

He scowled, again. He'd been busying himself fiddling with tiny details to keep from thinking about what they were going to do when they reached their destination. There was no way to avoid it, no way to get out of the mess. He'd gone through the files time and time again, trying to find... something. He wasn't sure what he'd been looking for, but...he hadn't found it. They were going to kill hundreds of thousands of people. And there was no way to avoid it.

I could protest, he thought, sourly. He was a war hero. His word carried weight. But not enough to stop the mission. *And they'd be more than happy to accept my resignation and give the mission to someone else.*

CHAPTER TWENTY-EIGHT

COLIN HADN'T HAD MUCH TIME to mull over the sergeant's words during the frantic preparations for departure. Sergeant Bowman had been as good as his word, ensuring that Colin had a chance to see just how much staff work went into even a relatively small military deployment. Colin had never thought his superior officers were lazy—the Royal Marines worked hard to ensure that officers had combat experience—but he'd never really seen them at work either. He was so busy that it was almost a relief to be reassigned to normal duties, when the squadron finally left orbit and jumped through the tramline. They had to be ready to hit the dirt when they reached their target.

And yet, he found his thoughts returning to Richard Tobias Gurnard time and time again. It was the same person. He no longer doubted it. Richard might go by Tobias now, but...it was the same person. Colin found himself unsure what to do. He wanted to fix the situation, if only to keep from leaving an enemy at his back, yet he had no idea how to proceed. He'd tried to write an email, but he'd never been much of a writer. Everything he'd managed to write had looked insincere, at best. It was funny, he reflected sourly, how he'd been taught how to write reports, but not how to put his feelings on the page.

I should probably have paid more attention at school, he thought, although he'd known better than to write anything that might wind up being used against him. The school psychologist had been about as helpful as...as a very unhelpful thing indeed. Tell the stupid bitch the wrong thing, the older lads had said, and you'd be in a borstal before you had a chance to explain it was a joke. *What am I supposed to say?*

He keyed his datapad and brought up the shipboard surveillance systems. It was easy to track someone, as long as they wore their wristcom or carried their personal datapad. Tobias—Colin told himself, sharply, to keep thinking of Richard as *Tobias*—spent much of his free time with another pilot. He didn't seem to have much free time, little more than Colin himself. Colin supposed that shouldn't be a surprise. The gunboat pilots needed to train too. He frowned as he studied the records. He couldn't enter Pilot Country, not without a valid excuse. But Tobias didn't seem inclined to leave either.

I can't meet him alone, and yet I have to meet him alone, Colin thought. A vague idea shot through his head. The pilots hadn't been volunteered—this time—to serve as pretend hostages, but...he could send an order for Tobias to report to an unused compartment. It would be odd, yet...would he think to question it? Colin had no idea, but he couldn't think of anything better. He wanted to lay the issue to rest before it was too late. *If I send the order...*

He hesitated. He could get in real trouble if Tobias reported him. Hell, he could get in real trouble if Tobias *didn't* report him. The datanet might note the unusual order and query it. Sergeant Bowman would be unamused...no, it would be something a little higher up the chain of command. Colin hesitated—he was risking more than NJP—and then sent the order through the network. He owed it to himself to take some risks.

Standing, he checked his datapad—again—and then headed down to the disused compartment. Tobias hadn't shown any interest in exploring the ship, according to the records, which didn't really surprise him. Tobias knew *he* was there, somewhere outside Pilot Country. Colin felt guilt tearing at him...he wondered, not for the first time, if Tobias would even *listen* to him. He opened the hatch and stepped into the compartment, silently relieved he'd gotten there first. Tobias wouldn't feel trapped. He could get back through the hatch in a moment, if he wished...

Colin braced himself as he heard footsteps coming towards him. Tobias. It had to be Tobias. And yet...for a moment, he honestly thought he'd made a terrible mistake. It was hard to reconcile the person in front of him with the vague memories from school. Tobias had grown up a little, just like Colin. Military life and discipline had been good for him. And yet... the fear in his eyes, the fear and the shock, was very real. Tobias was too scared even to run.

"We need to talk," Colin said. He unholstered his pistol and held it out, butt first. It would earn him a bollocking if the sergeant saw him, but it was the only way he could think to prove his sincerity. "That's a loaded gun."

He wondered, suddenly, if Tobias even knew how to *use* a gun. He'd never been in the CCF or the shooting club or...or anything. His family probably didn't own a gun. The navy should have given him basic lessons, but he might not have kept up with them. Colin certainly hadn't seen Tobias at the shooting range. Giving a gun to someone who didn't know how to use it, even if that someone didn't want him dead, was probably a mistake. The idea of being shot by *accident*...

Colin calmed himself as Tobias took the gun and held it, gingerly. He owed it to himself, he reminded himself, to take some risks. And it was the only way...

"You gave me a loaded gun," Tobias said. "Is it really loaded?"

"Yes," Colin said, flatly.

Tobias stared at him. "Why...?"

"I was terrible to you at school," Colin said, evenly. The hell of it was that he hadn't even *remembered*, until he'd had his memory jogged. "And I want to apologise."

Tobias's hand shook. "You want to apologise? You?"

"Yes." Colin took a breath. "I never...I...I was having a rough time and..."

"Tell me something," Tobias said. It was almost a snarl. "What can you say, what excuse could you *possibly* give, that could make up for everything you did to me?"

His voice rose. "I had no friends, because of you. I couldn't walk home from school safely, because of you. I barely dared leave my house, because of you. I…I had to lie to my mother about the bumps and bruises, because of you. Because of you!"

Colin nodded. "Yes."

"Yes?" Tobias's finger curled around the trigger. "Is that all you have to say?"

"No," Colin said. Sweat prickled down his back. The gun could go off at any moment. "I was wrong. I…I treated you terribly. And you're right. There was no excuse."

"No," Tobias said. "What do you want from me?"

"I…I don't want anything from you," Colin said. "I just want to apologise."

Tobias wondered, morbidly, what would happen if he kept tightening his grip on the trigger. Was the gun loaded? Was it even a *real* gun? Tobias didn't know. He'd had a few lessons in handling firearms, and that was that. No one had been particularly interested in teaching gunboat pilots to shoot. If they were forced to fight onboard ship, as opposed to off it, they were screwed already. He wouldn't put it past Colin to give him a fake. He'd already been lured to the compartment under false pretences.

His fingers felt as if they were made of ice. If he pulled the trigger and it was a real gun, Colin would be dead. If it wasn't a real gun, Colin would know Tobias had tried to kill him. Literally kill him. Tobias wanted to test the weapon, yet he didn't quite dare. His thoughts ran in circles. Colin wanted to apologise? How the hell could he apologise? For everything he'd done…it would take years to list everything he'd done, then apologise. Tobias didn't *have* years. He was pretty sure Colin had practically forgotten him. God knew he certainly hadn't said his name when they'd first seen each other clearly.

"You want to apologise," he said. The words felt heavy in his mouth. He'd never dared talk back to Colin before, even when the bastard had mocked him, his family and his dead father. Saying something would just make it worse. "You *really* want to apologise."

"Yes," Colin said, patiently. The conversation was going in circles, but he didn't seem to mind. "I do. I want to make it up for you."

Tobias fought down the urge to giggle. It was never safe to laugh at people like Colin. They beat you up for laughing at them…or even if they *thought* you were laughing at them. A wave of pure hate shot through him, staggering in its intensity. He had left his home and planet and yet Colin had followed him. Marigold had insisted that Colin could hardly have followed him, not for real, but Tobias didn't believe her. Colin…was he ever going to be rid of Colin? His finger tightened on the trigger. Perhaps he could try to shoot the bastard. If it failed, he could run before the arsehole caught him.

He found his voice, somehow. "The only thing you could do to make it up for me is to die," he said. "And, if you wanted to do that properly, you'd have to do it before I ever met you."

His heart clenched. Colin had always been part of his life. Tobias couldn't remember a time before Colin. They'd known each other in nursery, let alone primary and secondary school. He couldn't remember Colin from their shared childhood, but he'd been there. Tobias was sure of it. There was no getting away from him.

"I understand," Colin said. "I…just *listen*…"

He leaned forward. Tobias took a step back, holding the gun as through it were a protective talisman. He'd always dreamed of having Colin at gunpoint, of forcing him to humiliate himself as Tobias himself had been humiliated, but…he'd never dared try. There was no easy way to get hold of a weapon, not for him. And now…he wanted to pull the trigger and he didn't want to pull the trigger and it was a terrible, fucking mess…

"I was a bastard," Colin said, evenly. "And…and I recently had my nose rubbed in just how bad a bastard I was. I can't make it up to you, but I can apologise and…"

"And what?" Tobias took another step back. "Do you think there's *anything* you can say to me to convince me? What do you want?"

"I don't know," Colin said. His face twisted. "Forgiveness, perhaps."

Tobias couldn't help himself. He laughed. "Are you fucking crazy?"

He realised what he'd said, a second too late. But Colin didn't move.

"I didn't expect to see you here," Colin said. "I didn't know. But we're on the same ship, on the same side..."

"Really?" Tobias tightened his grip on the gun. His palm felt uncomfortably sweaty. "What a shame you didn't realise that sixteen years ago."

"Yes," Colin said, bluntly. "Barry is dead. Peter is dead. Blair is dead. Patrick...seems to have wasted his life."

Tobias blinked. Colin's cronies had never been as bad as their leader, but they'd been pretty damn bad. "They're dead?"

"Bought it along the security zone," Colin said. "I looked it up, when I went back home. They're dead and gone..."

"I'm sure they left a pair of illegitimate brats behind," Tobias snarled. "What do you *want*, Colin?"

"To put the past behind me," Colin said. "To let it go."

Tobias let out a long breath. He wanted to pull the trigger. And yet, it would ruin everything. If it was a real gun, he'd be arrested for murder. No one would believe Colin deserved to die. If it was a fake gun, Colin would know...

"You can't," he snapped. "*I* can't."

His thoughts went wild. Was Colin planning to court Marigold? To take her from him? God knew he'd had plenty of success convincing other girls, supposedly intelligent girls, to open their legs for him. Marigold was clever, but...Tobias didn't want to think about it. Or was he in some kind of trouble? Tobias found it hard to believe that Colin could be in *any* trouble. He was violent, sadistic, mindless and everything else the army found attractive. Everything he'd done at school would probably earn him a pat on the back and a licence to kill.

That isn't true, he told himself. He hadn't known many military officers, except the Beast, and he had his doubts about him. *The military's not like that.*

"You want to put it behind you?" It was hard to think straight. "You want to let it go? Very well. Leave me alone. Leave me and my friends alone. Stick to your life and stay away from mine. And...*don't* lure me here again."

Colin nodded. "If that is what you want."

Tobias scowled. "What happened to you?"

Colin hesitated, unsure how to answer the question. He'd tried to imagine how the conversation might go, but it was clear that his imagination had been *way* off the mark. Tobias had no reason to like him, no reason to make it easy for him...Colin's thoughts churned, a mixture of outraged entitlement mingling with a grim understanding that he had *no* right to demand anything from Tobias. They'd done too much to each other...no, *Colin* had done too much to Tobias. They couldn't hope to be friends.

"I grew up," Colin said, finally.

Tobias looked sullen and angry and desperate and...fearful. "And you think I haven't?"

"I don't know," Colin said. He fought down a surge of exasperation. "If you want me to stay away from you, I'll do my level best to do just that. If you"—he shook his head—"I understand. You don't want to know me and I don't blame you. And if you want me to do something to make it up to you..."

"Jump out an airlock," Tobias said, flatly.

"Within reason," Colin said. He held up his hands. "Let me know if—when—you want something. I'll do it for you. Until then...I'll stay away from you."

He indicated the hatch. "Put the gun down when you leave, then go," he said. "I won't follow."

Tobias stared at him for a long moment, then shrugged. "I hate you," he said. "That won't change."

He backed out of the compartment, put the gun on the deck and hurried down the corridor. Colin stepped forward, picked up the gun gingerly and checked it. If Tobias had pulled the trigger, Colin would be injured or dead. Even firing the gun randomly within the compartment might have killed one or both of them. The bulkheads were solid metal. He returned the gun to the holster, then stepped out of the compartment. Sergeant Bowman stood in the corridor.

"Sergeant!" Colin hastily straightened to attention. "I...how long have you been there?"

"Long enough," Bowman said. "Quite an interesting conversation, don't you think?"

"Yes." Colin kicked himself, mentally. How long had the sergeant been there? How much had he heard? Tobias hadn't seen Bowman, but that was meaningless. Bowman was good at sneaking around. He shouldn't have been able to hear anything...Colin knew he couldn't ask. "I had to talk to him."

"Quite," Sergeant Bowman said. "And I suggest"—his tone made it clear it was an order—"that you leave him alone from this moment on. He'll get in touch if he wants to."

"Yes, Sergeant," Colin said.

"And you can come help me too," Sergeant Bowman added. "Think of it as a reward *and* a punishment."

Colin nodded. "Yes, Sergeant."

Tobias's heart didn't stop pounding until he was back in the gunboat, staring at blank displays. Colin had...it was impossible to believe Colin was sincere. He was the same person who haunted Tobias's nightmares, the same monster who'd beaten him and mocked him and...Tobias wished, suddenly, he'd thought to keep the gun. He could have taken it to the shooting range and tested it, just to find out if it was real. If Colin had given him a real gun...

He swallowed, hard. Tobias had no illusions about his lack of physical strength. Colin could take a punch in the groin from him, without any ill effects. And yet, he wasn't invulnerable. A bullet through the head would stop him. Hell, a bullet through the chest or heart might prove fatal even if he was rushed straight into surgery. Tobias had heard something about bullets being designed to inflict massive damage, just to stop the zombies in their tracks. Colin could have died, if Tobias had pulled the trigger.

And yet, he would have had the last laugh, Tobias thought. The realisation tasted like ashes in his mouth. *I would have gone to jail if I didn't go out the airlock.*

His thoughts ran in circles. What did Colin want? Forgiveness? Really? The thought was laughable. Tobias couldn't forgive the bastard, even if he wanted to. Was it part of a plot? Or...or what? What did Colin want? Marigold? One of the other female pilots? Or was he overthinking it? Colin didn't need Tobias's forgiveness to chase women...

It doesn't matter, Tobias told himself. Marigold was an adult. She could take care of herself. He didn't own her. And he'd already told her about Colin. *As long as he stays away from me...that's all that matters.*

His wristcom bleeped. It was time to go back to work.

CHAPTER TWENTY-NINE

THOMAS PACED HIS COMMAND DECK, feeling uneasy.

The squadron was, to all intents and purposes, alone in the universe. They'd left friendly space a week ago. There was no hope of rescue, if they ran into something they couldn't outrun or outfight. Indeed, the official mission orders suggested that Brasilia's distance from the main shipping lines worked in their favour. The squadron might manage to get in, launch the operation and get out again, leaving the virus with a disturbing mystery. Thomas didn't take *that* for granted. The virus was a sentient *virus*. It *had* to have considered the possibility of running into other such entities, just as humans had imagined humanoid aliens. And...

He frowned as he studied the empty display. He'd had too much time to brood on what they'd been ordered to do. They were, at best, going to kill hundreds of thousands of humans. He'd read the files very carefully, noting the questions that had been glossed over or simply left unasked. The researchers *claimed* the victims would return to themselves, but Thomas couldn't believe it. They'd ensured the poor bastards had all the medical treatment the navy could provide. There was no way *Lion* and her squadron could offer the same to the infected colonists. They couldn't even *begin* to do it.

And that means we're sentencing the colonists to death, he thought. *And yet, they were dead the moment they became infected.*

He shuddered. He was all too aware the universe was not fair. One could do everything right, and morally, and still lose. There were limits to the practical, limits to what could be done…there was no way they could provide even a fraction of the medical care an infected colony would need. Sometimes, there was no good answer. And yet, it felt as if he were rationalising genocide. The great naval heroes of past generations would roll over in their graves. Britain had gone to war to *stop* genocides. Now… they were going to commit…mass murder, if not genocide. The difference really didn't matter.

The logic was clear. He'd gone over it again and again. There was no choice. But he couldn't begin to accept it.

He forced himself to sit and study the reports. They'd spent the last three weeks working on endless simulations, drilling and exercising their way through a hundred different variants on what might happen when they reached their destination. Thomas had forced them to go through everything from complete success to utter failure, torn between the grim understanding they needed to succeed and unexpressed hope they might fail. He didn't want to kill so many people, no matter how it was rationalised…he cursed himself as he pushed the reports aside. He was still brooding. He'd be brooding until he knew for sure what he'd done.

"Captain." Sibley spoke with low urgency. "Long-range sensors are picking up a starship on attack vector."

Thomas tensed as a red icon flickered into existence. "ID?"

"None as yet," Sibley reported. "But she really *shouldn't* be out here."

"Not if she was friendly," Thomas agreed. The reports stated there'd been no recon missions up the chain for the last six months. If the incoming ship was human, she would have either tried to contact them or simply maintained her distance. "Red alert."

He leaned forward, silently calculating the vectors as the enemy ship glided towards them. She'd caught a sniff of something, but what? She didn't look heavy enough to take on a battlecruiser, let alone the rest of the squadron. His eyes narrowed as he surveyed the vast deserts of interplanetary space between the tramlines. The virus could have concealed a sensor platform somewhere near the tramline, a platform that had picked up their transit and sent an alert further up the chain. Or the squadron might simply have gotten very unlucky. He didn't have enough ships to waste time looking for a platform that might not even exist.

She's not going to come close enough to let us blow her away, he thought, grimly. *And if we launch the gunboats to take her down, we'd be signalling our presence to anyone lurking under cloak.*

"Signal *Unicorn*," he ordered. "She's to sneak around the enemy and engage when she breaks off."

"Aye, Captain," Cook said.

Thomas leaned back in his chair, forcing himself to wait. The enemy ship was an unknown quantity, but he was fairly sure her sensors couldn't be any better than his own. Assuming so, she'd get close enough to see *Lion* clearly in twenty minutes—he considered, then dismissed, the idea of altering course—and then break off, if her commander had the sense God gave a snail. He scowled as it occurred to him the virus might not give much of a damn about the ship. She might try to ram the battlecruiser instead.

"Tactical, establish and maintain passive sensor locks," he ordered, curtly. "If she ramps up her drives and comes at us, fire at will."

"Aye, Captain," Sibley said.

Thomas felt sweat prickling down his back as the enemy ship drew closer. They'd been seen, but did they *know* they'd been seen? And were there other ships following in her wake? His eyes tracked *Unicorn's* presumed position as the scout circled around the rear of the enemy ship, ready to engage her when—if—she backed off. Thomas would almost have preferred to run into a full-sized battle squadron, even if he'd had no choice but to retreat. At least he would have known what he was facing.

And they clearly got a sniff of us at some point, he thought. *How much did they see?*

"They're reducing speed," Sibley reported. "I think they're trying to sneak right up to us."

"We'll engage them just before they enter sprint-mode range," Thomas said. The enemy ship was behaving rationally. It made him suspicious. "We need to take her out with the first salvo."

Sibley sounded doubtful. "Aye, sir."

Thomas nodded in sour understanding. They'd have to fire enough missiles to be sure of overwhelming the enemy's point defence, a difficult task when they had no idea just how much point defence the enemy craft actually mounted. The analysts had thrown up a set of possible answers, but there was no way to know which one was accurate. They could be completely wrong and he wouldn't know until the alien craft opened fire. The only upside, as far as he could tell, was that the enemy ship couldn't carry enough missiles to do serious harm to *Lion*. She'd have to ram the battlecruiser if she wanted to take her out.

Which she might, Thomas reminded himself. The range steadily closed. *They'd come out ahead if they succeeded.*

"Captain, I think they're coming about," Sibley said. The vectors changed, again. "They're preparing to sneak out again."

Thomas nodded, tartly. It wasn't completely bad. The enemy ship was presumably too far from other enemy ships to signal them through lasers, rather than radio. If the enemy ships were closer, the scout could have kept them informed without risking detection. Instead...he forced himself to think. *Unicorn* was supposed to be in position to snare the scout, but there was no way to be sure Captain Campbell could take the alien ship. Thomas knew *Lion could*, if he was prepared to expend the missiles. It was doable, yet it would be far too revealing. The virus might not understand how many ships were coming their way. Thomas didn't want to let it know.

"Stand ready to assist *Unicorn*," he ordered. He briefly considered trying to capture the alien ship, then dismissed the idea. It wasn't worth the risk. "And continue to monitor the enemy ship's position."

His eyes moved to the long-range sensor display. The system was a barren wasteland. The primary star was orbited by a handful of comets and little else. If there were any humans within the system, they were keeping their heads firmly down. Thomas didn't blame them. The only people who'd settle such a system willingly were people who wanted to stay away from *other* people. They'd be trying to stay off the sensors even before the virus started a whole new war.

And hope Campbell can stop her before she makes her report, Thomas thought. *We really don't want to let them know we're coming.*

Mitch allowed himself a cold smile as *Unicorn* slowly crept up on the enemy ship. It felt wrong to get so close without being detected—and he knew it was quite possible that they *had* been, that the alien ship was playing an elaborate game of bluff and counter-bluff—but the enemy ship had other problems. By his rough calculations, judging by the approach vector, she'd picked up *Lion*...and possibly *Lion* alone. She'd be somewhere else if she'd picked up the entire squadron.

And probably trying to scream for help, he added, silently. The enemy ship wasn't beaming messages in all directions, as far as his sensors could determine, but that might be meaningless. The absence of leakage didn't prove anything. She *could* be signalling her comrades through lasers, if she wasn't using tight-beam transmitters. *She doesn't know what she's found.*

"Captain," Staci said. "She's starting to back away from *Lion*."

"She must have gotten a clear look at her," Mitch said. He'd done his fair share of investigating sensor contacts, back when he'd been on *Pelican*. Sometimes, the emissions were nothing more than random energy fluctuations. Sometimes, they were an entire fleet of enemy ships bearing down. The enemy CO—assuming the virus even had a CO—must have had the fright of his life. "Helm, hold us here. Tactical, prepare to engage."

"Aye, sir," Staci said.

"And fire at once if they scan us," Mitch added. *Unicorn* was doing her best to pretend to be a hole in space—she was fully cloaked, with her emissions dialled down as far as they'd go—but the range was narrowing sharply. The risk of being accidentally rammed was still pretty low—both starships were tiny on an interplanetary scale—yet the risk of detection was continuing to rise. "Don't wait for orders."

He braced himself, silently counting down the seconds. They had to hit the enemy ship when it entered the red zone, when the missiles could reach the enemy ship before she could bring up her point defence or return fire. He shivered, feeling alive for the first time in weeks. If the enemy ship reacted quickly, or if she knew *Unicorn* was there, she might be able to get her retaliation in first. Her point defence might already be on alert. She'd be deprived of her active sensors, at least until she brought them up, but it wouldn't matter. They'd have no trouble tracking the missiles as they roared towards their target.

We should have dropped a mine behind us, he thought, ruefully. *If we'd known which course she intended to follow...*

"Fire when she reaches Point Alpha," he said. "And stand by to repel attack."

"Aye, Captain," Staci said. "Firing in ten...nine..."

The display flashed red. "They see us," she snapped. "Firing...*now*!"

Unicorn shuddered as she emptied her external pods towards the enemy. Mitch leaned forward, watching with grim approval as his crew performed admirably. They'd drilled so extensively they could practically perform their duties in their sleep. The point defence snapped to alert, ready to take out any missiles before they could reach attack range. It was risky—they might be detected by any other prowling enemy ships—but, if they were lucky, the enemy would think *Unicorn* was alone. They wouldn't know about the remainder of the squadron.

As long as the first ship doesn't manage to get off a signal, he thought, as the missiles started to slam home. The enemy ship hadn't fired a single shot. *She has time to scream for help...*

He smiled, feeling a flash of cold pleasure as the enemy ship staggered under his fire. Laser warheads stabbed deep into her hull, tearing the ship apart. Contact nukes detonated within the hull, completing her destruction. Mitch breathed a sigh of relief as the enemy ship exploded, the final missiles flying into the ball of expanding plasma and vaporising. He smiled, despite himself. Some jobsworth back home was going to get on his case about wasting missiles, he just knew it. Hopefully, Captain Hammond would back him up. They couldn't afford to take chances.

His eyes moved to Staci. "Did she get a message off?"

"Unknown, sir," Staci said. "But we didn't pick up any omnidirectional signals."

Mitch nodded, briefly. The odds were in their favour, but not as much as he would have wished. *And* anyone watching from a distance would have seen the brief one-sided engagement. He stared at the display, wondering if there was *anything* out there. The Royal Navy wanted to picket each and every known system, but it simply didn't have the ships and crews to spare. The virus might have the same problem.

Sure, his thoughts mocked. *And they might have so many ships they can afford to picket every system between their core systems and ours.*

"Signal *Lion*," he ordered. "Copy our sensor records"—*Lion* would have her own, but it was good to compare notes—"and request orders."

"Aye, sir," Midshipman Culver said.

Mitch nodded as he settled back in his chair. There was no point in trying to pick up survivors or pieces of enemy tech. There just wasn't enough left of the alien ship to make it worth the effort. And that meant they had to get back underway as quickly as possible. The virus might not have enough ships to picket everywhere, but it sure as hell would want to picket the border systems. A fleet on its way to Brasilia might keep going until it stabbed deep into the virus's core worlds. The virus would do whatever it took to stop it. No interstellar power could possibly survive losing its heartlands.

But we nuked Alien-One five years ago, he reminded himself. He'd seen the records. They'd been part of every mission briefing during the first two years of the war. *And the virus kept coming anyway.*

He put the thought out of his head. "And pass a message to the crew," he added. He knew better than to claim *all* the credit for himself. Every great naval hero had had a well-trained fleet and crew behind him. "Well done."

Thomas wasn't blind to the implications of running into an alien starship here, between New Washington and Brasilia. The tramline chain might be inefficient, compared to a least-time course from New Washington to Alien-One, but it was an easy way to sneak through enemy defences and hit their homeworlds. The virus wouldn't have relied on just *one* ship to monitor the approaches, which meant...what? He glared at the display, as if glaring would be enough to reveal cloaked ships or stealthed sensor platforms. How much had the enemy ship *seen*? How much had she managed to forward to her comrades before she'd been blown away? Thomas had no way to know.

There were no signals detected before she was destroyed, he told himself. None of the ships had detected any enemy emissions, which implied they'd killed the alien ship before she could raise the alarm. *And that means any watching eyes won't know* precisely *what killed her.*

His mind raced, all too aware he was looking for excuses to call off the operation. He felt a surge of self-disgust, mingled with an emotion he didn't want to face. Perhaps he was a coward, morally if not physically. Perhaps...he told himself, firmly, that it was unlikely the enemy ship had had a chance to report back. Any watching eyes would have seen *Unicorn*, but nothing else. If, of course, there *were* any.

"Helm, alter course," he ordered. He drew out a line on the display. It would add an extra three days to their transit time, if his calculations were correct, but reduce the odds of being detected if the enemy deployed additional ships to the system. "Tactical, deploy additional passive sensor platforms."

"Aye, Captain."

"And send my congratulations to *Unicorn*," Thomas added. Captain Campbell had done well. He deserved more than *just* congratulations, but right now they were all Thomas could offer. "Order them to rejoin the formation."

"Aye, Captain," Cook said.

Thomas forced himself to sit back in his chair and *think*. If there were other enemy ships in the system, the alert was probably already on its way back to the enemy high command. There was nothing he could do about it. What would they do? Deploy additional ships to the system? Or decide there was no point in searching for the human ships in a worthless system and go elsewhere? They'd be much better off if they deployed ships to defend Brasilia. A handful of additional starships would be more than enough to make the mission impossible.

Although we could still try to deploy the BioBombs, he thought. The orders had been more than a little vague on *precisely* what he was supposed to do if he couldn't take the high orbitals, although—reading between the lines—he was sure he was to do everything in his power to test the weapons on an enemy population. *If nothing else, at least we'd know if we had an effective weapon.*

He frowned as a dull vibration echoed through the hull. They'd won the brief encounter, they'd won so completely the enemy hadn't even managed to get a single shot off...so why did it feel like they'd lost?

Because you don't want to carry out your orders, he told himself, sourly. *And yet, you have no choice.*

CHAPTER THIRTY

"TRANSIT COMPLETE, CAPTAIN," Staci reported. "No enemy ships within detection range."

Mitch nodded. The remainder of the flight to Brasilia had been uneventful, which hadn't stopped Captain Hammond from fretting every time they jumped through the tramlines into a new system. Mitch understood just how badly things would go wrong if the enemy detected them—again—but the odds of being detected were quite low. Altering course a couple of times, more or less at random, would throw off anyone who'd managed to get close enough to the squadron to secure a solid lock on the hulls.

"Helm, take us towards the planet," he ordered. The remaining facilities within the system were inconsequential, if the briefing notes were accurate. "Tactical, maintain a full passive sensor watch at all times."

"Aye, Captain," Staci said.

Mitch leaned back in his chair and watched as the display started to fill with icons. There were five starships, all destroyers, orbiting the planet itself. The orbital stations, established twenty years ago, were gone. Mitch hoped that meant they'd been set to self-destruct and abandoned, not that the enemy had blown them away when they'd invaded the system. The stations had been large enough for falling debris to represent a serious threat to the surface, assuming they hadn't been blown up properly. Not, he suspected, that the colonists really cared. Right now, they were trapped in a permanent living death.

He shuddered, wondering—not for the first time—just what it was like to be infected. No one had been truly saved, not after a few months of total infection. Were the zombies still aware, screaming inside their own minds at what their bodies were being made to do? Or did they simply go to sleep and never wake up? Mitch found the idea to be utterly horrific. He would sooner die, blowing his body to bits, rather than allow himself to be turned against his comrades. But the virus was apparently good at preventing suicide...

No one wants to admit they might die, Mitch reminded himself. There'd been cases of spacers not taking their poison pills after a disaster, even though they'd been beyond all hope of rescue. *And that they might be infected and on the verge of becoming a brain-dead slave.*

He dismissed the thought as *Unicorn* slipped towards the planet. Brasilia looked normal, although the combination of limited natural resources and sheer distance from the remainder of explored space had dampened the planet's appeal. It was still hard to believe that the planet was infected... his skin crawled at the thought of going down to the surface without an armoured combat suit. The virus found Brasilia to be very welcoming indeed. No wonder it had been chosen as the test site for the BioBombs. There was little hope of liberating the world and cleansing the infestation without them. And what would they do—what *could* they do—if they couldn't liberate the world?

We might have to destroy the planet in order to save it, Mitch thought. *And that would leave us with a destroyed and useless planet.*

"Captain, we've completed our first sensor sweep," Staci reported. "If there are any other starships within the system, they're outside sensor range."

"Or cloaked," Mitch said. He studied the display for a long moment. "Copy the sensor logs to the drone, then launch it. Captain Hammond will need to see the raw data."

"Aye, Captain," Staci said.

Mitch nodded, studying the sensor readings himself. Brasilia was almost...dead. The planet wasn't radiating any electronic emissions, as far as his people could tell. Brasilia had been developing an agricultural economy first, to ensure the population could feed itself if something went wrong, but there'd been *some* industry on the planet's surface. Now...he wondered, not for the first time, just how much had been lost in the brief engagement before the virus had secured control of the high orbitals. The threat had been understood when the system had fallen. The colonists might have destroyed their industrial base, such as it was, to keep it from falling into enemy hands. The virus was the ultimate parasite. It had no qualms about pressing human—and alien—equipment into service. And he had to admit it gave the virus an edge no other race could match.

"Drone away, Captain," Staci reported.

"Helm, take us to Tramline Two," Mitch ordered. It would be several hours, at least, before *Lion* was in position. "If there's a flicker station here, I want to find it."

He scowled as his ship carefully altered course. There hadn't been a flicker station in the system before the war. Brasilia just didn't have the funding to emplace one and plans to establish a multinational system had floundered, before the war had made the whole issue academic. There'd been little enthusiasm for spending money on the FTL network outside the Great Powers and their colonies...he shook his head. The virus didn't care about human economics. If it wanted to establish a flicker station, it could have done so.

And if it has, we'll find it, he told himself. *And take it out before it becomes a threat.*

Thomas breathed a sigh of relief as the squadron made transit into empty space. Cold logic—and decades of naval service—told him it was unlikely they'd jump right into an ambush, but the virus was dangerously unpredictable. Just because they hadn't spotted any watching eyes didn't mean they weren't out there, shadowing the squadron and signalling ahead to make sure their superiors prepared a proper reception. He was all too aware they might be sailing into a trap, that they might be about to run into something they couldn't handle. The only upside, he acknowledged silently, was that the virus would have to divert fleets from the battle fronts to deal with them. It might give the hard-pressed defenders a chance to repair the damage, rearm their ships and—perhaps—retake the offensive.

He stroked his chin as they started the long plod towards the planet itself. Brasilia's defences were too weak to stop the squadron, although—if they managed to get into point-blank range—they could do some damage before they were blown out of space. There was no point in *letting* them get close, not when he didn't have to. He smiled as he checked and rechecked the projections, making absolutely sure of his next step. It was time to put the gunboats to work. Again.

"We'll launch ballistic missiles at Point Rodney," he said, as he designated points on the display. "The gunboats can follow them up, while the squadron reveals itself at Point Drake."

"Aye, Captain," Donker said. "They won't have time to evade before the missiles slam home."

Thomas nodded, curtly. The enemy ships were in a loose formation, something that suggested they expected attack…he told himself, sharply, that he was overthinking it. There was no need to hold ships in orbit, ready to drop KEWs on human targets. The virus didn't have to worry about an insurgency, about any kind of resistance on the ground. If there were any free humans left, they'd been effectively neutralised and confined to hidden bunkers. A single breath would be enough to infect them, reducing them to slaves…or worse. His stomach churned at the thought. Maybe the BioBombs were the only answer, even if the cost was high. The remainder of the human race was at risk.

Which is precisely the argument the admiral used, he thought. *And you wanted to reject it.*

He keyed his console, following developments as his crew hurried to their combat stations. They'd simulated everything, time and time again, but this was *real.* He reminded himself, again, that they'd face a degree of randomness now, that the enemy might do something that seemed inherently crazy and thus unpredictable. The crew was ready, yet...he shook his head. They'd done everything they could. *He'd* done everything he could. And now, all he could do was wait.

"Captain," Donker said. "We are coming up on Point Rodney."

"Begin launching missiles," Thomas ordered. "And then deploy the gunboats."

Tobias hadn't had much time to himself, ever since *Lion* had left orbit and headed for Brasilia. There'd just been too much to do, from taking part in endless simulations and training exercises to spending time in the privacy tubes with Marigold. They weren't the only gunboat pilots—or naval personnel—that had paired up, he'd noticed. He'd forced himself to read regulations he'd never thought would apply to him, just to be sure they weren't breaking any rules. Bagehot might be understanding, but there was no guarantee he would remain in command. Or that the CO wouldn't override him.

He hadn't had much time to *think* either, not until the gunboats had been launched on ballistic trajectories. Colin had...left him alone, the one thing Tobias would never have expected. The bully had seemed incapable of leaving Tobias—or anyone—alone, but he had. Tobias wondered, time and time again, if Colin had given him a real gun. Everyone said that bullies were cowards, that they'd break if you hit them hard enough, but Tobias had to admit—sourly—that Colin was no coward. He might just have given Tobias a real gun.

Which would have been one hell of a gamble, Tobias thought. He kicked himself, mentally, for not bothering to keep up with his shooting practice. It had never seemed necessary. In hindsight, that had been a mistake. He might have been able to tell if it was a *real* gun or not if he was more familiar with firearms. *I'll have to fix that when I get home.*

"The enemy ships don't seem to have spotted us," Marigold said. She was all business when they were on duty, somewhat to his relief. "They're not moving at all."

Tobias frowned. The engagement plan struck him as inherently risky. They were relying on the enemy not spotting them until they reached engagement range. The missiles could outrun any starship—perversely, the best antimissile tactic was to steer *into* the salvo—but they were flying on ballistic trajectories. The enemy would have time to alter course and bring up their point defence, if they saw the missiles coming before they powered up. Tobias thought the enemy would still be in trouble, but it was hard to be sure. The simulations suggested the enemy ships would have a good chance of either escaping or screaming for help before they were blown away.

"The missiles have locked on," he said. "I'll cycle the targeting systems if the enemy ships start to move."

"Good," Marigold said. "We go live in ten minutes."

Tobias nodded, his thoughts returning to Colin. What *was* the bully doing? Tobias found it hard to believe Colin *really* wanted to apologise... what *else* had he done? Tobias didn't know. The marines had been exercising constantly, just like the rest of the crew. Colin hadn't had time to start chasing girls...Tobias snickered. *He'd* found time to make love to Marigold.

Marigold glanced at him. "What's so funny?"

"I'll tell you later," Tobias said. He'd told her about Colin luring him to a meeting, and putting a gun in his hand, but...he didn't think she'd like the joke. Or see it as particularly funny. "When we get back home."

"Wherever home is, these days," Marigold said, wistfully. They hadn't talked much about the future, but there'd been an unspoken agreement they'd face it together. "You still want to move to Luna?"

Tobias nodded. He'd spent a few hours looking up immigration requirements. There were some colonies that were closed to outsiders, and others that were little better than Earth, but the remainder looked welcoming. He thought he qualified for immigration if he made an application before he was discharged. If nothing else, he could apply for residency in Clarke or Wells. The British colonies would probably accept him, although it would be little different from living on Earth.

Fewer idiots, he reminded himself. Space was lethal, if someone took it lightly. He'd had that drilled into him, back during basic training. The slightest mistake could get someone injured or killed. *The moon is a harsh mistress and all that.*

The console bleeped. Marigold frowned. "I think they may have spotted us," she said. "We just picked up a low-power sensor sweep."

Tobias frowned as he studied his display. The closer they got before the missiles went active, the greater the chance of wiping out the enemy ships before they could escape or open fire on the gunboats. But, as long as they remained on ballistic trajectories, their flight paths would be easy to predict. The enemy could track them on passive sensors, waiting—very patiently—for the gunboats to fly close enough to pick them all off with a single salvo. It would be easy...

The display flashed red. "They got us," Marigold said, as alarms started to howl. "We were just scanned by a high-power sweep."

"Power up the drives," Tobias said. His hands danced across his console, inputting commands he'd practiced so often he thought he could have issued them in his sleep. "Missiles going live...now."

He braced himself as the missile icons flashed from blue to green, their drives coming online and thrusting them towards the enemy destroyers. The enemy ships were powering up their own drives, their point defence starting to spit poison towards the missiles. Tobias took direct control, steering the missiles through a series of evasive patterns that were as close to random as possible. He swore as a handful of missiles vanished, picked off by enemy fire. The destroyers were pumping out so many plasma bolts that they were bound to hit *something*.

"Missiles entering terminal attack range now," he said. The missiles picked up speed, hurling themselves forward. He braced himself as more flickered and died. Their courses were now all too predictable. "Impact in ten, nine, eight..."

The gunboat lurched. "That was a little too close," Marigold said. "They're trying to hit us instead of the missiles."

Tobias nodded as the lead missile struck home, followed by three more. The enemy destroyer seemed to waver, then blew apart into a sheet of overheated plasma. The remaining four destroyers were picked off quickly, the last one launching a pair of drones before meeting its end. Tobias muttered a curse as the drones shot into interplanetary space, heading directly towards the tramline. There was no hope of catching them, even if they redlined the drives. He supposed it was a good sign. The enemy wouldn't have needed drones if they had a flicker station somewhere within the system.

"All targets destroyed," he said. His console bleeped as new orders arrived. "They want us to scan the planet."

"I'll try not to go too low," Marigold said. In theory, the gunboats could make it through the atmosphere and land safely...for a given value of safe. In practice, it was very much a last resort. Landing safely would be a challenge even if the atmosphere wasn't deadly. "You keep an eye on the sensors. Those ships might not have been alone."

"Will do." Tobias studied the active sensors as they came online. There was no point in trying to hide any longer. Local space looked clear, but he knew that could change at any moment. There could be an entire enemy fleet heading towards them with blood in its eye. "The planet looks nice, doesn't it?"

He frowned as he glanced at the ever-growing orb. It was easy to forget that planets were *big*. The simulators suggested they were little bigger than the starships, when—in reality—the largest colonist-carrier mankind had constructed would vanish without trace against the sheer immensity of a colony world. He swallowed, hard, as he remembered the briefing. Landing without protective gear would be lethal. They'd breathe in viral particles and become infected. Death would be preferable.

"I think I'd prefer to go back to my childhood home," Marigold said, tartly. "There's nothing for us down there."

Tobias nodded as more and more data flowed into the display. A city sitting on a river...a bunch of towns and villages, all seemingly deserted. There were no radio signals, as far as he could tell. His visual sensors spotted people in the fields, but...what were they doing? They looked like a giant swarming mass, covering the land. He wondered, suddenly, if the infected even needed to *eat*. It seemed impossible they could survive without food, but...the impossible became possible on a daily basis. The virus might have no qualms about animating walking corpses.

"I'm not picking up any ground-based defences," he said, dragging his attention back to his work. The sensors couldn't pick up passive sensors, or handheld antiaircraft weapons, but there were no fixed defences. Given the planet's atmosphere, he rather suspected the virus wanted them to land. "There doesn't *look* like anything standing in our way."

"Good," Marigold said. "Inform *Lion*."

Tobias nodded, feeling a twinge of...something. Guilt? Or satisfaction? Colin was going to go down there and, if there was the slightest hitch with his mask, Colin would be infected. The nasty part of his mind insisted it would be a great improvement. The virus wasn't pointlessly sadistic. The virus didn't take pleasure in hurting people. It was monstrous, but...it wasn't evil. Not like Colin. To be truly evil, one must have the option of *not* being evil.

"Signal sent," he said. Colin wasn't his problem, as long as they kept their distance from each other. "And now we wait."

CHAPTER THIRTY-ONE

"I NEED A PISS," Private Davies said. "Stop the bus!"

"You should have gone before we left," Private Willis called back. "Go in the bag."

"Shut up, the pair of you," Colin growled. The shuttle was starting to shake as it dropped into the planet's atmosphere. "We'll be hitting dirt in a few minutes."

He felt his skin start to itch as the shaking got worse, even though he *knew* the shuttle was a sealed unit. The virus hadn't managed to get inside, not yet. The briefing had made it very clear that removing his mask, even for an instant, might be enough to get him infected and sentenced to—at best—a very uncomfortable spell in sickbay. Major Craig had gone over the problem in extensive, perhaps excessive, detail. There would be unpleasant injections, radiation treatments and endless tests. And a person who was pronounced clean might not be allowed to return to duty.

The shuttle rocked, again. No alerts flashed in front of him, but he still felt cold. The craft was dropping so rapidly he felt as if he'd left his stomach behind in orbit, banging and clattering as turbulence shook them to their bones. He'd never *liked* parachuting, but this was worse. He wanted to get down on the ground before it was too late. They had their orders, very clear orders. They had to snatch the terraforming station before the virus rallied its troops and counterattacked.

"We'll be down in two minutes," the pilot called. Another gust of wind shook the craft. It felt as if God Himself had reached down and slapped the shuttle with the back of his hand. The lack of pilot humour only made it worse. "Get ready to move."

Colin braced himself, trying to ignore the yawning gulf in his stomach as he looked from marine to marine. He was no coward—he knew how to handle himself—but he was all too aware that a single missile hit would be enough to blow the shuttle out of the sky. If, of course, there were MANPADs on the ground. The records *claimed* the planet's settlers didn't have anything nastier than rifles, the sort of outdated gear that was normally shipped to colony worlds, but Colin knew better than to take that for granted. Smugglers were quite happy to sell weapons to colonists, even if the virus hadn't shipped in a small arsenal itself or reprogrammed what remained of the planet's industry to produce weapons. God knew there had been rumours of colonists plotting wars of independence for years.

The shuttle shook again, then crashed down. Colin stumbled to his feet as the hatch slammed open, revealing something akin to a gravel quarry. He looked from side to side as the fire team followed him out, noting just how close they were to the terraforming station. They had to secure it, quickly. He checked that everyone was out, then led the way towards the station. It wasn't designed for defence—the structure looked rather odd, like an old-style factory bleeding smoke into the air—but it didn't matter. If the virus had armed men nearby, it could put up a vicious defence. Colin couldn't afford to risk destroying the structure if there was any way to avoid it.

He felt warm, despite the armour's cooling units. Alerts flashed up in his helmet, cautioning him about droplets of viral matter in the air. Ice ran down his back. The planet had only been occupied for four years, yet it was already practically uninhabitable. The virus was *everywhere*. He stared at a deer-like creature, grazing near the complex. It raised its head and looked at him. Colin shivered, helplessly. The virus had infected dogs and cats. Why couldn't it infect an alien creature?

The creature leapt at him. Colin shot it, his bullets tearing the body apart. Chunks of blood and gore landed everywhere. Colin felt sick. The bullets had been illegal, five years ago. They inflicted so much damage that shooting someone in the leg could easily prove fatal, if the victim didn't receive medical attention quickly. Now. . .no one thought twice about using them. The zombies had to be taken down before they could tear him and his men apart with their bare hands. Ripping their bodies apart was the only way to guarantee a kill.

"Jesus," Willis said. "You killed Bambi."

Colin swallowed the response that came to mind as he hurled a grenade at the door, blowing it off its hinges. The station looked unmanned, but he knew better. The virus was drifting through the air, perhaps even linked to the station's command and control system. He threw a pair of antiviral grenades into the corridors, then charged through. Two figures hurled themselves at him, only to be blown away before they could get close. Colin felt sick. He had no qualms about killing terrorists, or enemy spacers, but the people in front of him had been innocent. The virus had turned them into slaves.

They swept the rest of the complex quickly, moving from room to room. He couldn't help noticing how little concern the virus showed for its hosts. Some of them were unclothed, some were injured. . .one of them, he thought, would have died if the virus hadn't infected his body. It looked very much as though the virus had done more than just take control of his nervous system. It had literally rebuilt enough of the bone structure to keep the body functioning. Colin refused to admit it could be breathing.

More alerts flashed up in his HUD as they entered the control centre. It was very decidedly civilian, right down to a complete lack of security. Colin wondered why the virus hadn't improved on the system, then snorted at himself for not thinking straight. The virus didn't *need* to install elaborate security systems. There was no such thing as independent thought within its society. It could no more betray itself than Colin could deliberately lose an exercise.

He attached the datanet node to the console, then keyed the switch. The WebHeads had wanted to drop with the marines, but Major Craig had overruled them. The risk of being captured and infected was just too high. Even now, there were horror stories of men who'd made the mistake of removing their masks...Colin thought he would never do anything so stupid, but he had to admit it was possible. It wasn't *easy* to be aware of one's surroundings in a helmet. He'd take off the helmet in a heartbeat if it was *safe*.

"Link established," a female voice said. The WebHead, probably. Colin had never met her, or any of the other analysts. Her voice was brisk, utterly businesslike. "Download starting...now."

Colin smiled to himself. The WebHead might be all business now, but who knew what she was like off duty? Perhaps he could ask her out, during the long flight home. She might be the kind of person to be impressed by a marine. Or simply desperate for some company...he shook his head as the download continued, the WebHead steadily hacking her way through the system. It was a pleasant fantasy, but nothing more. For all he knew, the WebHead might be more interested in women than men.

He put the thought to one side as he checked the live feed from the sensor drones. The majority of the marines and ground combat units had landed to the south, taking up positions near the city. There was no hint of a major enemy response, but it was just a matter of time. The entire planet was infected. The virus had to feel their presence, like a needle jammed into human flesh. Or a splinter, perhaps. He knew from experience that splinters were painful, but normally harmless. The virus might believe the landing party would fall victim to it eventually. It was in for a nasty fright.

The remainder of the station was completely empty, save for the ever-present viral matter. The beds seemed untouched, as if they'd been left to decay for the past few years. Colin felt an odd sense of unreality as he peeked into empty food cabinets, noting how the virus had made no attempt to replace the food. It was supposed to be able to consume anything, he recalled. If human likes and dislikes were no longer an issue, he supposed it could simply strip the bark from the trees and eat *that*. There'd be almost no nutritional value, but...it might not care.

He frowned as three more shuttles landed, unloading the reinforcements. Colin didn't salute as the CO hurried towards him—salutes were forbidden in combat zones, although no one knew if the virus cared enough to watch—but nodded tersely. There was no point in taking chances. Besides, the very air itself was turned against them. He checked the live feed as the CO surveyed the terraforming station. The BioBombs were being deployed. He half-expected to see flashes of light, to feel the ground shaking under his feet as the weapons went off, even though it was silly. The counter-virus was nothing more than a...a virus.

"Good work," the CO said, curtly. "Is your fire team ready for redeployment?"

"Yes, sir," Colin said. He wasn't sure quite how the chain of command functioned, with so many different units trying to operate in the same general area, but he was very definitely outranked. "We can rejoin the remainder of the marines or..."

"I want you to check out the nearest village," the CO said. "The BioBombs should have hit it by now."

Colin nodded, gathered his men and set off. The road was pathetic—it reminded him of some of the older roads he'd seen, so badly used it was practically on the verge of breaking up—although it was relatively new. He wondered if it was deliberate. The settlers had needed the roads, but they'd also needed a lot of *other* things. And the virus had probably not cared enough to keep maintaining the network. He eyed the trees warily as they closed in, all too aware that *anything* could be lurking within the shadows. Infected monkeys carrying grenades and IEDs had proven a deadly threat in the past.

He felt sweat trickling down his back as the road suddenly widened to reveal a farming village. Or what he *thought* was a village. The neat fields were so heavily overgrown that he couldn't help feeling it had been abandoned years ago. He was no farming expert, but even *he* knew crops had to be rotated to keep the crops fresh or something. The barn in the distance looked empty. Up close, there was a gaping hole in the wooden roof. The farmhouse itself was a ruin.

"Shit," Davies whispered. "What the fuck happened here?"

"I guess the virus couldn't be arsed growing food," Colin said, although he wasn't sure it was true. If the virus could eat anything, it didn't have to worry about crop rotation and shit like that. "We'd better check the farmhouse."

He called in as they reached the house and inched inside. It had been nice, once. Now, it was a ruin. Everything had rusted. A faded painting of a dark-skinned couple hung from the wall. Mould grew everywhere. He drew his bioscanner from his belt and pressed it against the nearest patch, unsurprised to pick up viral traces. The virus was truly everywhere. He wondered, suddenly, if the host bodies would eventually die. The virus had managed to maintain a civilisation, but...was that an illusion? He didn't want to think about it.

"Got movement outside, Corporal," Willis said.

"Call it in," Colin snapped. A flash of excitement ran through him as he crawled to the window and peered out. Dozens of infected people stood there, watching the farmhouse through terrifyingly blank eyes. They were flanked by cows and lambs and goats and horses and...he shuddered, helplessly. "We need to move."

He forced himself to think as they hurried to the rear of the building. The farmhouse was probably impossible to defend, not if the enemy had any real weapons. Colin wouldn't bet good money on the walls, already weakened by years of neglect, standing up to a lone bullet. There were no exits at the rear, but they could make one. He unhooked a shaped HE charge from his belt and slapped it against the wall as Willis and Davies joined him in the room and took up defensive positions. Colin let out a breath, then triggered the charge. The wall exploded outwards. He lifted his rifle and ran through the hole. Outside, he saw the zombies start to move. The marines would be run down before they reached the dubious safety of the trees.

"Take them," he snapped.

He dropped to his knee, switched his rifle to automatic and opened fire. It was far too close to 'spray and pray' for his peace of mind, but there was no time to select targets. The lead zombies practically disintegrated under their fire, the bullets tearing through their bodies and flying on to kill the next row and the next. Colin felt his stomach churn, remembering jokes he'd made in school about joining the military to earn a licence to kill. They weren't so funny now...no, they'd never been funny at all. No wonder Tobias hated him.

The zombies kept coming, pressing into his fire. Colin saw a small boy gunned down, his body still moving towards the marines until a second bullet ripped him apart from head to toe. Others—men, women, animals—fell and died, only to be replaced within seconds by more and more. Colin couldn't believe it. Were they *trying* to make the marines waste bullets? It made a certain kind of grim sense. If one regarded host bodies as expendable, one could throw them away for a greater cause.

He keyed his communicator as he slapped a new magazine into his rifle. "We need fire support now," he snapped, then babbled out the coordinates. They didn't dare turn and run, not when the zombies would catch up within seconds. "Now..."

Two combat shuttles roared across the sky, scattering antipersonnel weapons onto the enemy horde. Colin hit the ground as the bomblets exploded, one by one, then picked himself up again and ran. The zombies seemed to have been stunned, just for a moment. Colin shouted orders to the rest of the fire team, hoping they could get back up the road before the zombies collected themselves. Had the virus lost control? The BioBombs should have hit them by now. No one, no one at all, had been able to suggest how long it would be before the weapons took effect...

If indeed they ever did, Colin thought. He reached the trees and stopped, turning to look at the burning remains of the farmhouse. *I wonder...*

His eyes narrowed. A bunch of zombies were roaming around like madmen, howling at the blue skies overhead. Others were lying on the ground, dead or stunned or...he didn't know what they were doing. Had they been freed? Or had they been killed? Or...

"We need to move," Davies said. "They'll be coming after us again."

"Yeah." Colin took one last look, then motioned for the remainder of the fire team to follow him back to the terraforming station. "I think we've done all we can here."

Doctor Sarnia Carson was scared out of her mind, although she was determined not to admit it. The marines didn't scare her—it wasn't her first combat drop, nor the first time she'd been pressed into service beside the marine medics—but she knew, all too well, that the slightest breath could prove fatal. Evacuating someone wounded in combat could prove impossible, she'd been warned. They'd done their level best to come up with procedures that would keep the virus from infecting the medical staff, while saving the wounded, but even the best protocols might not be enough. Sarnia hatred to admit it, but someone who got wounded on the planet might be lost forever.

She frowned as the marines pushed a figure towards her. The infected colonist was naked, his body covered in viral patches...she shuddered as he struggled against his bonds, flakes of viral matter spilling in all directions. The metal ties looked strong enough to hold anyone, but she knew the infected sometimes demonstrated remarkable strength. Him breaking free wasn't the real danger, she reminded herself. It was the viral matter surrounding him that might pose the real threat...

"The bioscanners are having trouble calibrating themselves," she said, more to herself than to the marines. She'd been told what to watch for, but no one had tried deploying the BioBombs against an infected *planet.* Sarnia had been studying the virus ever since the war had begun and she still had problems grasping the sheer scale of the threat. "But it looks as if the counter-virus is having some effect."

She frowned as she took a blood sample, then scanned the twitching body. "The viral structures are under attack," she said. "But it isn't spreading as quickly as we'd hoped."

"The atmosphere doesn't seem to have been affected," a marine agreed. "How long will it take?"

"I don't know," Sarnia admitted. The virus had—yet another—unfair advantage. They were trying to fight it on its own ground. She had the nasty feeling they'd barely scratched the surface of its adaptability. "It'll take as long as it takes."

She shuddered. "It's working," she said. The data flowing into her sensors would fuel further research. Alpha Black would devise newer and better BioBombs, given time. "We just need a little more time."

CHAPTER THIRTY-TWO

THOMAS SAT IN HIS READY ROOM, DRINKING TEA.

"The latest reports are clear," he said. "The BioBombs are working. They're just working slower than we might have preferred."

He grimaced. The doctors were still studying the results, as the counter-virus spread through the planet's atmosphere, but they'd reluctantly conceded that the virus was effectively fighting back. The BioBombs had reduced the concentrations of viral matter within the atmosphere, yet they hadn't significantly weakened the enemy forces. They kept insisting it was only a matter of time, but Thomas had his doubts. They were fighting on a planetary scale. By the time the counter-virus spread over the entire world, the virus might have devised an entire series of countermeasures.

"It's having some effect," Captain Campbell said. The younger man's image seemed to lean forward. "They have yet to mount any major offensive against our positions."

Thomas nodded, curtly. The virus hadn't challenged the marines, save for a handful of minor skirmishes. He wasn't sure if the virus was choosing not to fight or if it felt it had too many other problems. There was no hint the host-bodies had enough weapons to do more than irritate the marines. Human wave assaults might unnerve the uninfected, but orbital fire support would stop them dead in their tracks. Thomas hated to think of the slaughter, yet he knew he had no choice. The landing force *had* to be protected.

"And they may not have gotten word out, not yet," Captain Campbell added. "We cannot declare the mission a failure *yet*."

"I have no intention of retreating," Thomas said, stiffly. He knew the squadron was exposed, too far from friendly territory to expect help if the shit hit the fan, but they were safe for the moment. The virus might not even know the squadron was there. There was no hint the virus had managed to get a message out before the squadron had destroyed its ships. "However, we must be sure the BioBombs have actually proven effective."

"I think it's just a matter of refining the technique," Captain Campbell said. "And finding something that consumes viral matter so quickly there's no time for the virus to realise its under attack."

"And while I'm wishing, I'd like a pony," Thomas said, dryly. "It may be years before we can put together a silver bullet."

He scowled. He'd read the briefing notes, then accessed files and government records that were barred to the general public. The Great Powers hadn't banned genetic engineering, but they'd ensured that all research was conducted under strict safeguards. Some of the independent asteroids hadn't been so prudent, although it was hard to sort out the truth from the lies, misconceptions and outright enemy propaganda. Genetically-engineered superhumans who could leap tall buildings in a single bound? Unbelievable. Enhanced individuals who could use pheromones to influence unmodified humans? A little *more* believable. He suspected the Great Powers would have to do something about unrestricted genetic engineering sooner or later, although it wouldn't be easy. The reports had hinted that many prominent politicians and businessmen had made use of genetic engineering techniques in one way or another. If a child was born with a severe disability, who could fault a parent for doing whatever it took to save them?

Not me, Thomas thought. His daughters had been normal, but he knew one family with a mentally disabled son. *What would I have done, if my daughters…?*

He left the thought unfinished as he studied the latest reports. The entire planet seemed to be waiting. There was no trace of enemy activity, outside the settled zones. And yet, the virus *had* to know the landing force had taken up position. The shuttles were hardly *quiet*. The host-bodies could have *heard* them landing. Thomas shook his head. He had a feeling he should be glad of the quiet. The virus would mount a counter-offensive soon enough. Unlike *him*, the virus knew when reinforcements would arrive.

"A silver bullet would be nice," Captain Campbell said. "When can we expect one?"

Thomas gave the younger man a sharp look. He'd been in the navy long enough to know that newer wasn't always better, even in wartime. New weapons systems, or experimental starships like *Lion* and *Unicorn*, rarely lived up to their promise. It took time to work the kinks out, time which would give the *enemy* time to work out defences and countermeasures. The boffins swore blind the BioBombs were unstoppable, that the counter-virus would burn its way through *the* virus until it ran out of sustenance, but it didn't seem to be working out that way. Thomas wished he was surprised.

"It will come when it comes," he said, finally. "Until then…"

"I can probe the nearby systems," Captain Campbell said. "And see if I can spot death coming our way."

"I think it would be a waste of time," Thomas said. The nearest systems to Brasilia were largely barren, as well as being off the shipping routes between Earth and Alien-One. It was unlikely the virus had bothered to do more than survey them briefly, as it burnt its way towards Earth. And besides, there was no way to predict which route the reinforcements would take. "You'd be better off covering us here."

He ignored the flicker of irritation in Campbell's eyes. Thomas understood Campbell's annoyance—independent command was a dream come true, a dream he wouldn't enjoy as long as *Unicorn* flew with *Lion*—but there was no time to worry about it. They were sitting on the edge of a branch, with the virus moving heaven and earth to saw it off behind them. It was just a matter of time until *something* happened, from the counter-virus being victorious to a major enemy fleet arriving with murder on its mind. The peace of the high orbitals was an illusion. The true test was yet to come.

"Yes, sir," Captain Campbell said, finally. "We'll continue our patrol route as ordered."

Which will give you some independence, Thomas thought, *although not as much as you might wish.*

He snorted, inwardly. They'd seeded local space with passive sensor platforms—and kept their active sensors online—but he was all too aware the enemy might manage to sneak up on them. He'd kept a wary eye on the tramlines, yet...they were just too far from the gravitational lines to have any hope of spotting a fleet as it made transit. They just didn't have enough starships and sensor platforms to do anything more than lull themselves into a false sense of security. Better to keep reminding themselves they couldn't watch all the approaches than accidentally convince themselves they *could*.

"And we'll keep track of developments on the ground," he said. "If we're lucky, the BioBombs will actually work."

"Yeah," Captain Campbell agreed. "The virus might be frightened."

Thomas leaned forward. "How do you mean?"

"Humans react badly to the unknown," Captain Campbell pointed out. "And also to invisible killers, like radiation and poison gas and the virus itself. They frighten us, even though the risks can be handled. There were millions upon millions of Luddite idiots who marched against nuclear power a couple of centuries ago, just because they thought the risks were unbearable. The virus might feel the same way."

"It's never shown fear before," Thomas reminded him.

"It should be *capable* of feeling fear," Captain Campbell said. "We just needed to find something that could scare it."

Thomas considered it for a thoughtful moment. Captain Campbell might be right. The virus could shrug off thousands of dead host-bodies, and hundreds of destroyed ships, because it knew it would continue. The virus wasn't quite a hive mind, but it was as close to it as any intelligent species could become. And yet...the BioBombs threatened it with total destruction. Brasilia would become extremely unwelcoming to infection, at least until the counter-virus died out. The virus *might* blanch at the thought of something that couldn't be countered. It would be a very *personal* threat indeed.

"We'll just have to hope," he said, finally. He would have liked to believe it, but blind optimism had never been part of his nature. The virus might be far more capable of reacting to a viral threat than any merely *human* immune system. If nothing else, it was fighting on the same level. "Until then..."

Captain Campbell raised a hand in jaunty salute. "See you on the flip side," he said. "Bye."

His image vanished. Thomas stared at the blank display thoughtfully. It wasn't easy for either of them, as the first engagement gave way to a long period of boredom. He'd expected fighting on the surface, or an enemy fleet to arrive within the first few days, but instead...nothing happened. It wasn't very reassuring. He feared the worst. The virus might be scared, it might be terrified of the counter-virus, but it could handle it. The counter-virus needed direct contact to spread. It could no more survive in vacuum than an unprotected human.

He keyed his terminal, bringing up the projections even as he damned himself for risking a false sense of security. The projections were only as good as the data he—and his tactical staff—fed into them and he knew the data was little more than guesswork. He wouldn't have been very sure of it if he'd faced a purely human enemy, let alone the virus. There was no way to be *sure* what assets the virus had nearby, ready to deploy. It could have nothing, or an entire battle fleet, or anything in between. And there was no way to determine how it would react either. It might just write the entire system off as worthless. It might not bother to so much as scan the system to see what had happened to the colony, let alone dispatch a fleet to liberate it. There was just no way to know.

Thomas felt his stomach churn. He *knew* something was going to happen, but he had no idea what or *when*. It would be so much easier to take if he knew the worst, even if it *was* a hundred battleships bearing down on him. He'd certainly know to turn and retreat if he knew such a large fleet was on its way…

He shook his head. There was nothing he could do, but wait and see.

Colin knew, without false modesty, that he was *good* at sneaking around. He might be a big man, by human standards, but he was tiny compared to the battlefield. An entire squad of marines could go unnoticed, particularly if something was happening to distract the enemy. He lay on his belly and crawled forward, heedless of the mud soaking his uniform as he sneaked up on the ridge. He'd been in worse places. Probably. The viral matter in the air—weakened, the boffins claimed—might beg to differ.

He braced himself as he reached the ridge and peered down at the small town. It looked surprisingly well laid-out for a colony town, a handful of prefabricated buildings flanked by wooden huts and stone houses. The colonists had been urged to use local materials wherever possible, if only to cut down on shipping costs. Colin was no expert, but it stood to reason that the price of anything shipped from Earth—or even New Washington—would be astronomical. Better to use wood and stone than anything from Earth.

A shiver ran down his spine as his eyes passed over the buildings. There was something…decayed about the town, even though there was little actual decomposition. The townspeople looked…odd, like creatures out of a horror movie. They moved in odd patterns that seemed completely random, their skins covered in viral patches that looked like rotting mould. A handful lay dead on the ground, ignored by the rest. Colin touched his mask, checking the seals for what felt like the thousandth time. There was so much viral matter in the air that the slightest breath would be enough to damn him.

"They look as if they're in shock," Davies said. He'd come up behind Colin, while the remainder of the fire team hung back. "Look at them."

Colin said nothing as he surveyed the scene. It was deeply disconcerting in a manner he knew he couldn't articulate. There was enough familiar, enough *human*, about it for the rest to be fundamentally wrong. The townspeople were zombies. The virus ruled now, turning their bodies into extensions of itself. And yet, some of the host-bodies had dropped dead. He didn't know why, or how long it had been since they'd died. The bodies didn't seem to have decayed, but...it was meaningless. The virus had changed them on a very basic level. He didn't have a baseline to estimate how long it had been since their death.

Since the death of the virus within them, he mused, as he took photographs and forwarded them to higher authority. The boffins hadn't been allowed to go any closer to the once-human settlements. *They might not be able to recover.*

He shuddered, considering the implications. The briefing had skipped over the details, but he was no fool. If someone was infected so completely they lost all control of themselves, perhaps even the awareness of ever having been aware in the first place, what would happen when the control was gone? He was familiar with how oddly hostages could behave when they were kidnapped and held prisoner, but the infected were at least an order of magnitude worse. Would they recover? *Could* they recover? No one had been cured, once the infection passed a certain point. Colin was all too aware that he might have to shoot someone—a friend, perhaps—to save them from a fate worse than death. A living death...

"There's nothing here for us," Davies said. "They should burn this whole place to the ground."

"They probably will," Colin said, although he wasn't sure there'd be any point. The prefabricated buildings were designed to last, but the remainder wouldn't last long without proper maintenance. A couple of years without human occupation would be enough to return the settlement to the jungle. "I think..."

He broke off as he heard crying. Not a child, not an adult...he frowned as he started to crawl down the ridge towards the source of the sound. It sounded like someone pushed to the breaking point and beyond, someone like...guilt stabbed into his heart as he remembered making Richard—*Tobias*—cry. He'd hurt him...no, he'd done worse. Boys didn't cry and, if they did, they were ruthlessly mocked. Colin gritted his teeth, putting the memory out of his head as he checked his weapons. The crier was unlikely to be friendly. Anyone who'd been on the planet since the invasion had almost certainly been infected.

"Stay back," he muttered to Davies. Better one of them was in danger than both of them. Davies might be required to perform a mercy kill if Colin got infected. He'd heard of infected marines who'd killed themselves, when they knew it was hopeless, but he didn't know if he could do it himself. "Call it in, then cover me."

The sound grew louder as he peered into a gully. It had once carried water down to the town. Now...a young figure lay on the ground, sobbing helplessly. Colin shuddered as he saw the viral blotches on the figure's visible skin, warping the figure so badly he couldn't tell if it had been male or female. It looked like a young teenager, but...he couldn't tell. The form was so emaciated that it could have been older...he felt sick, recalling some of the horrors he'd seen in refugee camps. The refugees had been starving. Here...the virus had made things worse. Much worse.

"Careful," Davies said, after he'd finished speaking to the operations officer. "Please."

Colin nodded as he advanced closer. The figure was shaking helplessly, sobbing so deeply that he couldn't help feeling sorry for it. He reached forward with a gloved hand and turned the figure over. A blotchy face looked up at him, one eye missing behind a viral growth that looked utterly *wrong*. Colin staggered back, feeling the urge to retch. The sight was disgusting, disgusting beyond words. It was inhuman...He had to swallow, hard, to keep from throwing up. Vomiting in the mask would be a good way to get himself killed—or worse.

The...person...shuddered one final time, then lay still. Colin eyed it warily, unwilling to risk going any closer. Dead? Or shamming? He didn't know. The viral detector bleeped an alert, warning him that there were high concentrations of both viral and counter-viral matter in the air. He guessed the virus, or what remained of it, was trying to escape. It could abandon a body as easily as a human could abandon a starship or a shuttle.

His earpiece bleeped. "Corporal, we have a recovery team on the way," the operations officer said. He sounded astonishingly dispassionate. Colin hated him with a sudden passion, even though he knew the officer hadn't seen the body. Davies's description hadn't done it justice. "Stay on guard. Don't let them take the body."

"Yes, sir," Colin said. The figure hadn't moved. It was still impossible to tell if it was male or female. There were no visible bulges that might have suggested one or the other. "Tell them to come in full armour."

He stepped back, his stomach churning. He was going to have nightmares. He just knew it.

Davies stood beside him. "Is that the fate that awaits us all?"

"Probably, if the virus wins," Colin said. The counter-virus might have killed the virus, but...the host hadn't been able to survive. "I just don't know."

"Fuck," Davies said. "Just...*fuck*."

CHAPTER THIRTY-THREE

MITCH KNEW HE DID NOT COPE WITH BOREDOM very well. He was the kind of person who always had to be doing *something*, from chasing women to picking fights with alien ships. Inaction had never sat well with him, even if logic insisted he *had* to wait. The idea of patrolling the outer edge of the formation, in hopes of either picking up an incoming fleet or luring it to him, simply wasn't enough to keep him engaged. He would have preferred to scout the connecting star systems, just to ensure he was doing something.

He scowled at the empty display as *Unicorn* patrolled the system. The helmsman was having fun, following a semi-random course that was designed to tempt any cloaked watchers with a chance to sneak closer to the fleet that didn't exist, but everyone else was just as bored as their commanding officer. Mitch had ordered a handful of drills, just to ensure everyone kept their skills sharp, yet there were limits to what they could do in a combat zone. The risk of someone not taking a *real* emergency seriously was just too high. He forced himself to settle back in his chair, trying to set a good example. It was probably too late. No one volunteered for corvettes if they wanted a quiet life.

And we should be deploying the BioBombs everywhere, he thought. The latest reports from the surface had made it clear the BioBombs were working, although slower than he would have preferred. *And* that the host-bodies were largely beyond recovery. *There's nothing left to salvage.*

He felt his scowl deepen. The Troubles had taught the Great Powers that giving in to terrorism was the worst of a set of bad choices. Mitch wouldn't deliberately kill civilians who'd been taken hostage, but he wouldn't let the risk of accidentally killing them paralyse him either. Better to teach the terrorists that their tactics brought them nothing but pain than give in and deal with worse problems in the future. And now...they couldn't let fear for the virus's victims stop them from deploying the sole effective weapon they'd found. He'd seen the images from the surface, too. The virus promised nothing but perpetual living death.

It's them or us, Mitch thought. Captain Hammond had qualms, moral qualms...Captain Hammond had never been in a position where the slightest mistake could cost him everything. Mitch understood morality, but he also understood the dangers in letting morality dictate tactics. The entire human race was staring down the barrel of a gun, facing complete extinction. *We have to destroy the virus, or be destroyed by it.*

It wasn't a pleasant thought. Humans and Tadpoles had managed to figure out a way to co-exist. Humans, Foxes and Cows had managed to work out how to live together. Humans and Vesy...the Vesy were primitive, simply unable to pose a threat. But the virus...the universe simply wasn't big enough for the virus and anyone else. It was the soulless alien menace the human race had feared, ever since it reached the point of being able to comprehend the possibility of non-human races. How could they share a universe? They couldn't even *talk* to the virus. It didn't even bother to demand surrender!

"Captain," Staci said. Her voice was carefully controlled, but he could hear a hint of excitement. "Long-range sensors are picking up hints of turbulence."

Mitch leaned forward, all boredom gone as hazy icons appeared on the display. It might be nothing—it probably *was* nothing—but the contacts needed to be investigated. They were further away than he'd expected, yet...he made a mental note to commend the boffins for the latest passive sensor platforms. They'd picked up *something...*

Of course, it might be nothing, he told himself. *But at least it'll be a change.*

"Helm, alter course to intercept," he ordered. "Communications, alert the flag."

He studied the display, silently running through the possibilities. The enemy—if there *was* one- was moving under power, rather than pretending to be a hole in space. He wasn't too surprised. In theory, a starship could move on a ballistic trajectory; in practice, it wasn't so easy to build up a decent velocity without setting off alarms across the system. And using drive fields would give the intruder a chance to evade, if—when—it realised it had been detected. A skilful intruder could break contact and escape, leaving him unsure if there'd ever been an intruder at all. He'd done it himself, more than once. There was something very satisfying in sneaking up to an enemy fleet, acquiring all the data his superiors could possibly want, and then slipping back into the darkness.

Staci glanced at him. "Captain, they'll know we're coming."

"Yeah." Mitch considered it for a moment. There was no point in trying to hide, not even if they powered down and went completely passive. The enemy would have a rough idea of where they were for quite some time. And yet...he could take advantage of the situation instead. "Ramp up *all* the sensors. I don't want a single piece of space dust to remain unexamined."

"Aye, Captain," Staci said.

Mitch leaned back in his chair, waiting. The enemy would know *precisely* where they were. The enemy could target their weapons without needing active sensors of their own. But, at the same time, they wouldn't find it easy to hide. The more their cloaking device was challenged, the harder it would be to pretend to be a hole in space. And Mitch had dozens of passive sensor platforms monitoring local space. The enemy might hide from *Unicorn*, but not from the ever-watching platforms. It didn't even know the platforms were there.

Although it might deduce their presence, he reminded himself. *The virus has certainly had every opportunity to read our tactical manuals.*

His eyes narrowed as the range steadily closed. The hints of turbulence grew stronger and stronger, although the enemy cloaking fields remained intact. There was definitely *something* there. Mitch issued orders, readying his ship for charging the enemy position or swinging around and running as fast as they could. If they were unlucky, the range would narrow to the point they'd *have* to charge the enemy and hope for the best. They simply wouldn't be able to change course and run before it was too late. Mitch disliked the idea of suicidal tactics, but their options were steadily narrowing along with the range...

"Contact," Staci snapped. The hazy icons sharpened, suddenly, as the cloaking fields collapsed. "Nine starships...six cruisers, three unknown."

Mitch nodded calmly, despite a flicker of excitement. The enemy ships had messed up the timing. If they'd remained cloaked for a few seconds longer, *Unicorn* would have been trapped between the devil and the deep blue sea, unable to retreat *or* close the range to the point she could do real damage. As it was, he had an excellent chance to get back to the squadron and coordinate a counterattack. The cruisers were tough, perhaps tough enough to give *Lion* a very hard time, but a combination of missiles, gunboats and starfighters should be enough to blow them to hell.

"Helm, bring us about," he ordered. "Tactical, continue to feed live data to *Lion*."

"Aye, Captain," Staci said. "They're bringing their own active sensors and ECM online."

"Good," Mitch said. The enemy didn't need to hide any longer either. "That'll make it harder to miss."

He smiled, coldly. The enemy tactics were brutally simple. They were advancing on the planet, forcing Captain Hammond to choose between retreating at once—perhaps firing a handful of shots for the honour of the flag—and risk being crushed against the planet. Neither side would be particularly concerned about stray missiles striking the planet itself, but... they'd both prefer clear space, if they were to have a full-scale engagement.

And the humans would have the advantage. Captain Hammond might be cautious to a fault, but even *he* wouldn't miss the opportunity. They could give the virus a bloody nose even if they lost the planet.

"Take us back to the squadron," he ordered. The virus didn't seem interested in trying to swamp his defences, but there was no point in letting the enemy brain-blobs decide it was worth the effort. "And stand by to repel attack."

Thomas knew, all too well, that his military service had been largely sterile. He'd never had any passion for blood sports, never felt any inclination to join the army instead of the navy...he'd watched enemy ships die, but he'd never shot someone personally. He'd certainly never been spattered with blood and gore...he wondered, suddenly, if he should have spent more time chasing foxes over the countryside. It was barbaric and pointless, but it might have prepared him for the gruesome sight in front of him. The seemingly dead body was rotting in front of him.

"Explain it to me in layman's terms," he ordered. He sat in his ready room, feeling alone. "What's happening to her?"

"The virus's control structures effectively disintegrated," Doctor Sarnia Carson said. She was surprisingly young, for a top expert in her field. "In layman's terms, you could say most of her bones and muscles turned to jelly. The body collapsed under its own weight."

"But it wouldn't have," Thomas said, slowly. "The host body itself should have remained unaffected, right?"

"The virus apparently pervaded most of the body," Sarnia said. Her voice betrayed no disgust, none of the horror she *must* be feeling. "It replaced muscle mass, which was rendered useless; it dug into the brain, accessing memories and damaging her mind. I believe she was effectively dead a long time before the counter-virus got into her system."

"And so we killed her," Thomas said. Someone had said, once, that a single death was a tragedy while a million deaths were a statistic. Stalin?

He wasn't sure. But it was true. The dying—effectively dead—woman on the display had been a living person, with a family and friends and everything of her own. Her death touched him in a way the obliteration of an entire colony would not. Could not. He just could not comprehend a million individual lives. "Are they all going to die?"

"Yes, Captain," Sarnia said. "I think there just isn't enough brain matter left for them to survive, even if they were given the best medical care in the known universe and..."

The alarm rang. "Captain to the bridge," Donker said. "I say again, Captain to the bridge."

Thomas stood. "We're going to have to table the discussion, Doctor," he said. "We may have incoming."

He deactivated the terminal, then hurried onto the bridge. The display glowed with nine red icons, enough firepower to do serious harm if it got close to the planet. Thomas took his command chair, checking the status reports as his ship prepared for war. The crew had responded well, very well. His lips twitched. Two successful missions—and months of intensive training—had done wonders. It had been weeks since the department heads had reported any problems.

"Captain," Donker said. "The enemy will be entering engagement range in forty minutes."

"Assuming we hold position," Thomas said. He didn't want to let the enemy ships any closer to the planet than strictly necessary. The risk of them taking a pot-shot at the colony was too high. It might be too late to save the human settlers—the host bodies, he reminded himself sharply—but a handful of nuclear strikes would wipe out the marines. "Helm, lay in an intercept course."

"Aye, sir."

Thomas nodded to himself. "Take us out."

"Aye, sir."

"XO, prepare to deploy gunboats," Thomas ordered. His fingers danced across the console as the intercept vectors sharpened. "We'll launch in ten minutes."

"Aye, Captain," Donker said.

Thomas allowed himself a smile. Nine starships, six of them cruisers... the remaining three might pose a threat, but they weren't any bigger than the cruisers. It was hard to believe the enemy fleet could seriously threaten the squadron. Unless they packed some weapon he'd never dreamed possible, the virus's ships were completely outgunned. They were picking up speed, probably in hopes of closing the range to the point the odds would start to tip in their favour...it would have worked, he acknowledged wryly, if they'd faced a conventional enemy. *Lion* could pick them off at a safe distance and, if they survived, beat a hasty retreat without ever letting them get into engagement range. It might not be fair, or brave, but he didn't care. The virus was too dangerous to take lightly.

He settled into his chair and watched the seconds tick down to zero. The virus's fleet was filling space with sensor pulses, as if they thought Thomas had a battleship squadron in his back pocket. They didn't know they were wasting their time...he wondered, suddenly, just when and where the virus had determined the system had been invaded and occupied. Had his sweep of the system missed something? A cloaked picket or a flicker station? Or had the ship they'd destroyed *en route* had a friend who'd evaded discovery and managed to report to its superiors?

There's no brainships, he mused. *They can't be thinking very clearly.*

"Captain," Donker said. "The gunboats are ready to launch."

"Good," Thomas said. He didn't need them, not when the enemy was obligingly revealing their own positions, but it was well to be careful. The craft would do no good if they were locked to his hull. "Launch."

Tobias cursed under his breath as he scrambled into his flightsuit, then headed for the hatch. Marigold followed, hastily buttoning up her suit. They'd been in one of the privacy tubes when the alarm had sounded, thankfully before they'd proceeded past the cuddling stage. His face burned with embarrassment as he wondered how many of their fellows knew what had happened, imagining the jokes they'd make...he shuddered. There'd been boys and girls caught behind the bike sheds at school, publicly humiliated even if they didn't face any formal punishment. He didn't want to imagine what people might say...

He put the thought out of his head as he hurried into the gunboat, took his seat and brought up the targeting systems. Marigold slammed the hatch closed, then sat and powered up the drives. The timer was already ticking down, a grim reminder that they'd been caught—quite literally—with their pants down. He snorted, ruefully. It was the sort of thing that would have been funny if it had happened to someone else. He hated to think what Colin would have said. Tobias was pretty sure it wouldn't have been anything pleasant.

A low shudder ran through the gunboat as the craft disconnected from the battlecruiser and headed out into interplanetary space. The remainder of the squadron spread out around them, picking up speed as they flew towards the alien ships. Yellow icons pulsed on the display as the battlecruiser launched her first salvo of missiles, command and control links hastily establishing themselves as the missiles moved past the gunboats. Tobias scowled, reminding himself it was quite possible to accidentally steer *into* a missile's path. It had happened during simulations. He was reasonably sure that the odds of it happening had been scaled up a little, but he didn't know how badly...

"We'll enter enemy point defence range in five minutes," Marigold said. "Pick your targets."

Tobias nodded as he took control of his missile cluster and steered it towards one of the mystery ships. An escort carrier? A troopship? He didn't know. The ship didn't *look* large enough to take more than a couple of hits without exploding, although there was no way to be sure. He'd been told the virus couldn't innovate, but he didn't believe it. The virus had absorbed millions of human and alien minds. It must have learnt from them.

"I'm having some problems getting a precise lock," he said. "They're pumping out a *lot* of ECM."

"Go for the sources, if you can't get a lock on the hulls," Marigold advised. She swung the gunboat from side to side, although the virus didn't seem to be trying to get a sensor lock on the craft's hull. The range was so short it probably didn't need a precise lock to score a hit. "It'll be easier to target them than the ships themselves."

"Understood." Tobias frowned as he worked his console. The sensor haze was getting stronger, but—perversely—it was actually making it easier to locate the sensors themselves. It was almost as if the virus *wanted* the sensors destroyed. His eyes narrowed. It made no sense. There was no brainship, but that didn't mean the virus was stupid. "I think..."

He widened the sensor focus as the missiles closed on their targets. If the enemy weren't being stupid, it meant they were up to something and...

"Impact in one minute," Marigold said. "I'm altering course."

"Hold us for a moment," Tobias said. The enemy *had* to be up to something. "I think..."

He broke off as the missiles started to strike home, wiping out the enemy sensor sources. The display seemed to blank, just for a second, then cleared. Tobias sucked in his breath as he realised, too late, what the virus had been doing. They'd been tricked. No wonder the virus had kept its active sensors online. It had distracted the human sensors, blinding them to the real threat.

"Shit," he breathed. Red icons appeared on the display. Seven, perhaps eight, enemy ships. Big ships. "We've been suckered."

CHAPTER THIRTY-FOUR

"CAPTAIN," SIBLEY SAID. "I'm picking up one brainship, three battleships, one carrier and three heavy cruisers."

Thomas sucked in his breath. They'd been tricked. The enemy had used the light ships to mask the heavier ships...*clever,* he noted sourly. He'd been lured into an engagement that was likely to go poorly, even if he broke off at once. *Lion* could outrun the enemy fleet, at the cost of leaving the remaining ships exposed. It was not going to end well.

"Tactical, fire a full salvo at the brainship," he ordered. "Helm, bring us about and prepare to retreat to the first waypoint."

"Aye, Captain," Sibley said.

Thomas forced himself to think. The gunboats had done well, wiping out seven of the nine lighter ships. But they were now exposed, forced to take command of the missiles while the enemy fleet bore down on them. They'd be better off withdrawing, except he needed them to direct missiles towards their targets. And...he told himself, sharply, that the gunboats were expendable. He'd spend them wisely, but he would spend them.

"Continue firing," he added. "XO, order the squadron to retreat."

"Aye, Captain," Donker said.

"Communications, signal the planet," Thomas added. "Inform the marines that they have to go dark."

"Aye, sir," Cook said.

Thomas scowled. He'd just abandoned the marines, at least until a friendly fleet managed to regain the high orbitals and liberate the planet. Again. The counter-virus would continue its work, he was sure, but would it be enough to stop the virus before the marines had to take off their masks? They'd never planned for a long occupation. In hindsight...he mentally kicked himself for not considering the possibility. They'd assumed they'd get in, deploy the BioBombs and then watch the results from a safe distance. He'd never considered being caught so badly out of place.

The virus might hammer them from orbit, if it gets a sniff of their presence, he thought. *Or it might just destroy the entire planet to make sure the counter-virus doesn't spread.*

He looked at Cook's back. "Communications, signal *Prestwick*. She is to leave the formation and proceed directly to the nearest forwards base, taking with her copies of our records and sensor logs. We'll keep her appraised until she passes through the tramline."

"Aye, sir," Cook said.

Thomas nodded as he returned his attention to the display. *Prestwick* was a lone destroyer. Her firepower wouldn't make much, if any, difference once the range closed to the point the virus could open fire, but she was able to take a message home. Earth had to know what had happened when the BioBombs were deployed. And what had happened to *Lion* and the remainder of the Thunderchild Squadron.

The display sparkled with red light. "The enemy have opened fire," Sibley said. "They appear to be fairly standard long-range missiles."

"Activate point defence, then deploy decoy platforms," Thomas ordered. "Helm, move us to cover the other ships."

He frowned, then leaned forward. "And deploy drones as well," he added. "The freighters are to cloak and alter course as soon as the drones are active. Let them head to the waypoint alone."

And hope to hell the enemy doesn't see them in time to blow them to hell, he thought, as the enemy missiles closed on his ships. The navy had plans to build a fleet of fast tenders to support the fleet train, but production had been delayed by the urgent demand for actual warships. *They have to rely on stealth to survive.*

Lion shuddered, again, as she unleashed another spread of missiles. Thomas gritted his teeth as the enemy missiles came closer, zeroing in on his ship. They'd fired enough to be *sure* one or two would get through the point defence, despite everything. And then...Thomas checked the live feed from the damage control teams. They were about to face their first real test.

"The enemy brainship is taking damage," Sibley reported. "However, I don't believe we've crippled her."

"Designate the carrier as secondary target," Thomas ordered. The enemy carrier hadn't entered the fray, but it was just a matter of time. "Fire at will."

He braced himself as the enemy missiles entered his point defence envelope. Dozens—hundreds—fell to his point defence, or wasted themselves on harmless decoys, but the remainder survived long enough to strike home. Two hammer-blows struck *Lion* in quick succession, each barely fended off by the armour. Thomas had no time for relief before a laser warhead exploded far too close to his armour, driving a stabbing needle of energy deep into *Lion's* hull. His ship shuddered, red alerts flashing up on the display. The damage control teams raced to the wound, while the remainder of the section was evacuated. Thomas told himself, grimly, that it could have been worse.

"We lost two of the gunboat ports," Donker said. Behind him, the displays constantly updated as the damage was cleared. "A third is effectively gone."

"Noted." Thomas had no time to worry about it. They could dock the gunboats at a standard airlock, if anyone survived long enough to do it. Right now, the damaged or destroyed point defence weapons were a considerably greater concern. "Rotate the ship, then keep us moving. We have to clear the range."

He studied the display. The enemy capital ships didn't have the legs to catch the battlecruiser, once she started to run. He issued orders, directing the battlecruiser to increase speed as soon as the freighters were clear. Maybe they could fire missiles, but...they had no place in the line of battle. If they engaged, the enemy would just blow them away and that would be that. Better to get them out if there was no other choice.

And hope they see the planet as more important than we are, he thought. They could escape, but they needed time to repair the ship, reload their missile tubes and plan their next step. The marines couldn't be abandoned, not if there was the slightest chance he could get them out before they were infected or killed. *We need a diversion.*

"I've got a solid lock on the fleet carrier," Tobias said, as a cluster of missiles shot past the gunboat. "Missiles inbound...now!"

He watched, grimly, as the fleet carrier started to *finally* launch its starfighters. He wasn't sure why the virus had waited, unless the brainship had felt it would be better to keep the starfighters protected within their carrier than throw them into a maelstrom. It was going to regret that, Tobias was sure. The starfighters were nimble in space, but helplessly vulnerable if something happened to their carrier. He smiled, coldly, as three missiles survived long enough to strike the carrier's launch tubes and explode. The carrier hadn't been destroyed, but it would be a long time before she could launch and recover her starfighters again. The impact *had* to have set off a chain of explosions that threatened to rip the entire ship apart.

"Good shot," Marigold commented. She yanked the gunboat to one side as an enemy missile roared past. It detonated a second later, too late to catch them in the blast. "Shit!"

"Waste of a good missile," Tobias commented. The gunboats weren't as fast as starfighters, but they'd been outside the blast radius before the missile had even detonated. "I think we have incoming..."

He took direct control as the enemy starfighters closed on the gunboats. They were remarkably quick—he reminded himself, again, to watch for suicidal tactics—and very capable, but they couldn't fire in all directions. The gunboats closed up, covering each other as the enemy starfighters swooped closer. Tobias felt sweat prickling down his back as his guns fired, time and time again. Thankfully, the enemy seemed unwilling to throw themselves away. Plasma bursts bored through space, but they didn't close to point-blank range. It was definitely a relief.

His console bleeped. "Return to base," Bagehot said. "I say again, return to base."

Tobias blinked. It wasn't that bad, was it? They'd damaged both the brainship and the carrier...the other ships had taken their knocks as well. But...he swore under his breath as he assessed the situation. The enemy fleet hadn't slowed. It would enter orbit in less than twenty minutes. And it might just overrun the battlecruiser. The gunboats were supposed to be designed to enter planetary atmospheres, but Tobias had no intention of trying. Colin was down there somewhere.

And so is the virus, he thought. He felt a stab of sympathy, although he wasn't sure who he was truly sorry for. Colin? Or the virus? *Poor bastards*."

"Aye, sir," Marigold said. She altered course, heading back to the battlecruiser. "We're on our way."

Tobias winced. The enemy fleet was still firing, hurling salvo after salvo of missiles towards the human ships. The gunboats fired on the missiles whenever they came into range, but there were a *lot* of missiles. He shuddered, remembering the days when he'd played games intended to simulate *real* warfare. The enemy seemed to have used cheat codes, superheating its economy in ways no human could match. There was no way the Royal Navy could produce and deploy so many missiles for a relatively minor engagement.

"We'll be back within five minutes," Marigold said. "And then..."

"Yeah," Tobias agreed. The battle was far from over. "We'll be back."

"Captain, the gunboats are returning," Donker reported.

"Order them to assume escort position," Thomas said. Docking the gunboats now would be worse than useless. "And continue firing until we clear the range."

"Aye, sir," Donker said.

Thomas nodded, projecting an image of calm as the range started to widen. Stern chases were inevitably long ones, even when the ships were evenly matched. The admiral had assured him that *Lion* could outrun anything that could outfight her, although he would have preferred to test the claim under less dangerous circumstances. His ship hadn't lost any of her drive nodes, thankfully, but losing even one—right now—would be fatal. They *had* to put some distance between themselves and the enemy fleet.

"Captain, they're reducing speed," Sibley reported. "I think they're more interested in the planet."

Or they think we can't harm them, Thomas thought. It didn't take a genius to calculate, roughly, how many missiles *Lion* carried. Even if her entire hull was crammed with missiles, there would be limits. *They may assume we shot ourselves dry.*

He frowned as the enemy ships slowly fell behind them. The virus had every reason to investigate the planet quickly, but…Captain Campbell could be right. The virus might be genuinely afraid, for the first time in five years of war. It might be terrified of the counter-virus, yet aware it needed to analyse the viral matter and devise countermeasures. Thomas had faced his own fears, years ago. The virus could do the same.

It isn't human, he reminded himself, sharply. He'd taken part in debate classes, when he'd studied at Hanover Towers. Two people could arrive at the same conclusion, unaware that they'd started in very different positions and taken very different routes to reach the same destination. *It doesn't think like us.*

"Communications, order *Unicorn* to remain near the planet and maintain a watch on the enemy fleet," Thomas ordered. "We'll proceed to the first waypoint and rearm."

"Aye, sir," Cook said.

Thomas told himself he was right, even though he feared otherwise.

The logic was sound. The planet was unimportant, in the grand scheme of things. The virus wouldn't leave an entire battle fleet orbiting Brasilia when it needed them elsewhere. If it had enough ships to do that, the war would be over and humanity would have lost. No, there had to be limits. There would be a chance to rescue the marines, if he waited. If nothing else, he was far enough from Earth that it would be weeks before he received any orders to fall back and abandon them.

At least we proved the BioBombs worked, he thought, although he still had his qualms about the whole concept. God alone knew how many colonists were dying on the green and pleasant world on the display. *The mission wasn't a total failure.*

But he knew, deep inside, that they hadn't succeeded either.

"Hold position," Mitch ordered. "Tactical, keep us under cloak."

He glared at the display as if it had personally offended him. He did not enjoy embarrassment. He'd been tricked and, worse, it had happened in front of his immediate superior. Captain Hammond would report the matter to Earth and...Mitch clenched his fists as his ship started to coast. Earth would not be impressed, even though no one else had seen disaster looming either. It would not look good in his file.

Assuming we get home in time for it to matter, he thought. The enemy fleet was heading directly towards the planet, but it might change course at any moment. *Lion* and her consorts were still clearly visible on the display. *The enemy might start planning something soon enough.*

He pulled up the starchart and considered the possibilities. When had the enemy been alerted to their incursion? When they'd destroyed the scout? Or when they'd invaded Brasilia itself? If the former, the enemy had had eight days to get the alert, organise a fleet and get it to Brasilia; if the latter, the enemy had done it in four. And that meant...he frowned as the possibilities started to narrow. The virus wouldn't have been *sure* of the human squadron's destination until the squadron had hit Brasilia itself.

Mitch scowled. The timing was all too revealing. They'd missed either a starship or a flicker station, probably the latter. That wouldn't look good in his file either.

Unless they started probing up the tramline and just happened to run into us here, he told himself. It was possible, but unlikely. *We could just have unknowingly passed each other in the night.*

He pushed the thought aside as he returned his attention to the near-space display. The enemy fleet hadn't started bombarding the planet, not yet, but it didn't matter. He'd read the reports. The marines were doomed, even if the enemy never engaged them directly. They had to be recovered and fast, before their life support started to fail. They couldn't risk sticking with the shuttles and they couldn't risk trying to cannibalise colonial gear, assuming they could find any. Mitch started to contemplate possibilities, tossing ideas around in his mind. There had to be something…

"Captain, they're launching shuttles," Staci warned. "Half of them appear to be on recon patrol; the remainder are dropping into the planet's atmosphere."

"Keep our distance from the patrollers," Mitch ordered. Shuttles were easy targets, no bigger than gunboats, but that didn't make them harmless. "And establish passive locks if they come too close."

"Aye, Captain."

Mitch nodded as he returned his attention to the console. There had to be something they could do, but…but what?

"We're clear," Marigold said. "And we have permission to dock."

"Thank God," Tobias said. They'd been in the gunboat for hours. He was ruefully aware he stunk. The entire craft would probably have to be fumigated. He had no idea how starfighter pilots coped. Perhaps they just turned a blind eye. Or had their noses surgically removed. He'd heard so many stories about starfighter pilots doing stupid things that it was hard to know what to take seriously. "Take us in."

He breathed a sigh of relief as the gunboat mated with the battlecruiser's hatch. They were safe...for a given value of *safe*. It felt rather more like they'd merely postponed their death a few more hours. The battlecruiser had been hit...not badly, according to the reports, but enough to worry him. The next hit might take the entire starship out of action, or simply blow it to atoms. If they were deployed at the time...he shook his head. Right now, it didn't matter. They needed a shower and rest, perhaps not in that order.

"We'd better move," Marigold said. She sounded as tired as Tobias felt. "I need coffee."

"Just put in a tube and inject it into my veins," Tobias agreed. He had no idea how some crewmen managed to remain on duty for two or more days without sleeping. They probably used stimulants. Bagehot had told them it was possible, but strongly discouraged. "I need sleep."

Marigold smiled. "You must be tired," she said. Her face looked worn, as if she had been pushed to the limits of her endurance and beyond. "You didn't make the obvious joke."

"No," Tobias agreed. He stumbled to his feet, somehow. The deck seemed to be vibrating slightly, as if they were caught in a storm. An impossible storm. "I think we'd better go before we collapse."

The hatch opened. Bagehot stood there, looking grim. "Get to your bunks," he said, curtly. "The crews will shut down the gunboat."

Tobias wanted to argue. They'd been told, time and time again, that they had to take care of their gunboat. It was like owning a car, they'd said, although Tobias had never owned a car in his life. He couldn't have afforded it. Now...Bagehot would have hit the roof, normally, if Tobias had shirked his duty. It had to be bad...

"Yes, sir," Tobias said. He could feel his mind wandering. It was only a matter of time until he collapsed. "What's...what's going to happen?"

"Leave it to the CO," Bagehot said. He helped Tobias out of the hatch, then did the same for Marigold. The crew hurried past, into the gunboat. "You two get some rest. You'll be back out there, soon enough."

Tobias was too tired to salute. "Yes, sir."

CHAPTER THIRTY-FIVE

"YOU THINK THEY'LL NUKE US?"

Colin glared as they finished securing the camouflage netting over the shuttle. In theory, now the craft was powered down and covered, it should be invisible from orbit. In practice, there was no way to know. The enemy sensors might pick out something—anything—that would point them at the shuttle. Or they might track the marines through the trees as they assumed combat position. The virus might easily decide the planet couldn't be saved and drop nukes on each and every moving target. There was simply no way to know.

"No," he growled. He felt his skin crawl as they hurried away from the shuttle. The viral matter in the air was supposed to be dying, but he refused to take it for granted. It would be a long time before he felt comfortable removing his mask, even though it was bulky and unpleasant. The slightest speck of microscopic viral matter might be enough to turn him into a brainless drone. "I don't know what they'll do."

He glanced up as they kept moving, heading back to the planned defence line. The marines were spread out, partly in fear of a nuclear or KEW strike, but there was no point in trying to go underground and hide. The clock was ticking, even if they didn't want to admit it. They simply didn't have the resources to survive on the planet, not until the counter-virus had finished its work. Colin felt trapped, even though the enemy was nowhere to be seen. All the virus had to do to win was absolutely nothing.

The sense of being watched gnawed at him. He glanced up again, seeing nothing. He didn't really expect to see anything. He'd been in exercises where surprise attacks had been foiled by drones drifting so high above the ground that they'd been invisible to the naked eye, their operators quietly tracking the assault force and moving the defenders into position to catch and kill the intruders. There was no escaping the unblinking eyes, once they had a solid lock. It almost made him feel sorry for people who tried to run the border defences. They simply couldn't escape being caught and unceremoniously tossed back across the line.

A sonic boom split the air as they rejoined the rest of the company. Major Craig had taken command and deployed his troops to wear down any enemy offensive, something that would have been solid tactics against almost anyone else. Colin glanced up again, wondering when the bolt from the skies would fall. The virus had deployed nukes against planetary targets before, showing a disturbing lack of concern for the host-bodies…he wondered, sourly, if the virus would show any *less* concern for the planet's population. They'd been infected with the counter-virus. The virus might be planning to scorch the entire world, just to make sure the counter-virus didn't spread.

Not that it matters, he told himself. *We know it works, at least to some degree. It won't be long before we start dropping the counter-virus everywhere.*

Sergeant Bowman nodded to them. "Success?"

"We concealed the shuttle," Colin said. It looked as if the fire team would be going into the personnel pool, rather than being assigned to the defence line. "It shouldn't be visible from orbit."

"Good," Sergeant Bowman said. "The enemy appear to be landing shuttles around the settlement. Collect two MANPADs, then get as close to the landing zone as you can and hit them."

Colin nodded. The orders weren't very precise, but the marines were making the operation up as they went along. It was too much to hope that losing a shuttle or two would be enough to stop the enemy, yet it might buy time. Might. The fire team was expendable, if push came to shove.

He took a breath. "Understood."

The day seemed to grow warmer as they collected their weapons, then started the long walk down to the nearest settlement. The population had been hit hard by the counter-virus, he'd been told, but he was careful to stay on alert as they neared the town. Dozens of shuttles landed in the distance, seemingly coming down over the ocean and dropping within the city itself. Colin nodded, recognising the tactic. It was safer to fly over the ocean. Someone with a MANPAD could really ruin a shuttle's day.

"The population is dying," Davies said. "Fuck."

Colin followed his gaze as they peered into the town. There were bodies everywhere, dead or dying. He forced himself to look, though it made his stomach churn. He saw a middle-aged man pawing the air, hands twitching uselessly as viral matter flowed from his pores; he saw a bunch of children, lying in a heap on the ground. The virus had turned them into drones, infected them so thoroughly the host-bodies could no longer survive without the virus. He turned away, cursing under his breath. Nuking the entire town was starting to look like a very good idea. It could no longer be reclaimed. Burning it to ashes was perhaps the only realistic option.

"I'm picking up a bunch of signals coming our way," Willis said. "I think they're deploying drones."

"Shit." Colin motioned for the team to get under cover. "How many?"

"I'm not sure," Willis said. "At least three sources..."

Colin thought fast. He had two MANPADs. He could take down two drones, but the third would either return fire or provide targeting data to orbiting starships or ground-based artillery. Colin was prepared to take the risk—and shooting down the drones would delay the enemy, at least until they deployed new drones—yet he wanted bigger targets. The enemy would start using their shuttles to leapfrog up to confront the marines, sooner or later. It was a fairly standard tactic. The virus would have learnt from its human hosts if it hadn't figured it out already.

"Hold us here," he said. "We'll leave the drones unless they shoot at us."

Davies gave him a sidelong glance, but nodded. Colin understood. The drones would make it harder to break contact, when—if—the enemy sent a pursuit force after them. And they might drop a bomb on their heads. A starship could afford to let the enemy fire first, in the certain knowledge she would see the missile coming in time to return fire, but troops on the ground couldn't take the risk. They'd barely have a moment to realise they had incoming before the bomb blew them to hell. His lips quirked. The drone could probably kill them at any second, if it got a sniff of their presence.

Sweat trickled down his back as they waited, hearing distant explosions to the south. Colin wasn't sure what the virus was shooting at—as far as he knew, there were no troops on the far side of the city—but it didn't matter. If the virus was shooting at nothing, he wasn't going to try to stop it. He wondered, grimly, if the virus was shooting host-bodies that had been infected with the counter-virus. It made a certain kind of sense. Infected refugees had been shot on Earth, when they'd tried to cross the line. He tried not to think about the possibility that some of the refugees *hadn't* been infected.

And the longer we fight an utterly inhuman foe, he reflected, *the more inhuman we become.*

"I've got something coming our way," Davies announced. "Shuttle emissions, two of them."

Colin took the MANPAD off his back and clicked on the passive sensor. The display lit up, revealing a handful of possible targets. He frowned as he spotted the drones, then carefully selected the incoming shuttle instead. Beside him, Willis targeted the other shuttle. Colin glanced from side to side, making sure they had a clear line of retreat, then switched the MANPAD to active mode as soon as the shuttles came into view. They looked astonishingly crude to his eye, even for military craft that prized functionality over form. He couldn't help thinking the virus hadn't bothered to put anything beyond the basics into its craft. The hull looked tarnished, as if it hadn't even been painted.

Maybe it isn't the first combat drop the shuttle made, he thought. The MANPAD bleeped, reporting a solid lock. *It could have landed on a dozen worlds by now.*

Colin squeezed the trigger. The missile lanced into the air, striking the shuttle and blowing it into a giant fireball. Willis fired a second later, his missile taking down the second shuttle. There was no time to cheer. Colin threw the launcher to one side, then turned and ran as though all the demons of hell were after him. Davies was already beating feet into the jungle, running for his life. Colin sensed, more than heard, something fall behind them. The shockwave picked him up and hurled him forward, sending him crashing to the muddy ground. Panic—pure panic—ran through him. If he'd lost his mask...

He breathed a sigh of relief as he realised the mask was solidly in place. It didn't *look* damaged...he told himself it was fine, that he hadn't been infected. He'd have to check his blood when he got back to the defence lines, just in case...he pushed the thought aside as he rolled over and looked back at the firing position. There was a giant smoking crater where he'd been standing, only a few short seconds ago. The virus had reacted with astonishing speed. And yet, something felt odd about the whole scene. It could have dropped something heavier on them. It could have scattered bomblets all over the area, catching the marines before they got into cover.

"I've got more shuttles inbound, coming in low," Davies said. "You want to make a run for it?"

"I want to know what they're doing," Colin said. The virus was up to something. He could feel it. "Willis, stay back. Davies, you're with me."

He felt his heart skip a beat as three more enemy shuttles flew overhead and landed in the settlement. The hatches slammed open a moment later, infected troopers deploying with commendable skill. They were humanoid, but it was impossible to tell if they were human or another infected race. The environmental suits they wore looked...wrong. He frowned as the alien soldiers deployed, unsure what he was seeing. It was uncommon to see the host-bodies in protective suits. Even boarding parties wore relatively little protection.

They're trying to protect themselves against the counter-virus, he thought, as the alien troopers started to hurl grenades into the abandoned houses. He'd thought the settlement needed to be burned to the ground, but he hadn't expected the virus to actually *do* it. The fire spread rapidly, flames licking from house to house. *Do they think that can actually stop it?*

"We've got trouble," Davies said. "They're coming our way."

Colin followed his gaze and swore. A bunch of alien troopers were heading directly towards them, moving so openly that he *knew* substantial forces were following a little more stealthily or positioning themselves to catch the humans when the beaters drove them into their arms. It was an old tactic, older than space travel and even firearms...he rolled over, putting the thought out of his mind as they hurried back to Willis. They needed to move, now. The virus was coming after them.

"They might have gotten ahead of us," Davies said, as they hurried into the jungle. "When did they even see us?"

"The drones, perhaps," Colin said. He was surprised the drones hadn't simply blown them away, if they'd caught a sniff of the marines. They weren't important enough to capture...were they? He was the senior amongst the fire team and he was a mere corporal...it wasn't as if the virus was trying to chase down Major Craig or Sergeant Bowman or someone else who gave orders. "Or..."

He looked at the trees. Were they infected? He could hear insects buzzing through the air, disturbed by their passing. He'd been told the virus couldn't infect anything smaller than a rodent, but...hell, there could be infected rats within the trees, watching them and reporting back to their superiors. There wasn't so much viral matter in the air now, and the infected animals should be dead, yet...he couldn't afford to take anything for granted. They might have been made the moment they headed down to the settlement. The marine defence lines might have been made too.

And if they know where we are, he mused, *why haven't they nuked us?*

The question puzzled him as he kept moving. Visibility was poor, at least for him, but the virus might be able to see through the trees. If it really *had* infected them...he remembered exercises where they'd had to avoid sensors so tiny they literally couldn't be seen with the naked eye. They hadn't had time to *look* for them either, not with the sort of gear they'd need to actually find them. It had been impossible to be sure they were being watched...he glanced back, hearing something crashing through the trees. The virus's troopers were coming, making no attempt to be quiet. It only confirmed his fears that there might be an ambush up ahead.

His mind raced. Letting the enemy drive them *into* an ambush was a good way to get killed—or, worse, infected. Standard counter-tactics were to head sideways or turn in hopes of ambushing the beaters, as the beaters tried to drive them onwards. But if they were being watched, there was no way they could break contact and escape, let alone turn on the beaters. They'd see the ambush as it took shape, then...do whatever they saw fit. He felt a flicker of envy. The virus didn't have to worry about the fog of war.

"On my mark, throw antivirals in all directions," he ordered, curtly. He cursed under his breath. Was the virus listening to him? It would make it harder to give orders if the virus was listening too. He could make a hundred pop culture references that would be meaningless to any normal alien foe, but the virus? Would it understand a reference? He simply didn't know. "As soon as they start to flash, follow me."

He waited for their nod, then drew a pair of antiviral grenades from his belt and held them up. "Mark!"

Blue-white light flashed. Colin had no way to know how effective it had been, but it should have given the enemy pause. Their environmental suits might have protected them from the antivirals—he rather feared that was the case—but the grenades would have killed any viral matter in the air and, hopefully, turned the enemy force into a collection of individuals. They'd rebuild their network, he was sure, yet...he turned and ran west, hoping to cut across the road. If they were lucky, they'd manage to put enough distance between themselves and the enemy force to get back to the defence lines without further contact...

The ground heaved. Colin found himself flying through the air again, slamming into a tree hard enough to hurt. He heard a series of crashing sounds as he hit the ground, his arm twanging painfully as he rolled over. His ears hurt...it took him a moment to realise the enemy had called down KEWs on them. The strikes hadn't been particularly well targeted, but it hardly mattered. They'd devastated the forest, knocking down trees and tearing up the ground. And...

"Shit," Willis said. "Colin, you have to move. Now!"

Colin stared at him in numb horror. Willis's mask was gone. His leg looked so crooked Colin *knew* it was broken. Willis had breathed in the virus and now...Colin swallowed, unsure what to do. The antivirals had been effective, but...had they been effective *enough*? He wanted to pick up his friend and carry him back to the defence lines, yet...horror swelled through him. It was just a matter of time until Willis became another host body. The marines simply didn't have the resources to treat the infection.

He heard the enemy troopers rushing towards them, crashing through the remnants of the trees, and swore, inwardly, as he realised the truth. The virus hadn't killed them because it wanted them alive. It wanted—it *needed*—to understand what the human race had done. The counter-virus needed to be countered...Colin almost laughed, despite everything. He didn't know anything about the counter-virus, beyond the mere fact of its existence. None of them knew anything. The virus was wasting its time. And yet, it had caught Willis. It would catch the rest of them, given time...

Willis met his eyes. "Go!"

Colin drew his pistol. He couldn't abandon his friend to a fate worse than death. Willis was doomed. The enemy would rush him off the battlefield and keep him somewhere safe, at least until the virus took full control. Colin knew there was nothing he could do, but grant his friend a merciful death. And yet, he felt as if he was crossing a line.

"Do it," Willis said. "Hurry!"

Colin pointed the gun at Willis's head, bracing himself. The brain had to be destroyed, quickly. Willis didn't know much, but some of what he knew could be disastrous if it fell into the wrong hands. And it would... Colin had never doubted Willis's loyalty, but the virus made a mockery of everything. Willis couldn't keep secrets, once he became a zombie. His brain would be drained and everything he knew would be used against his former comrades and...

"I'm sorry," Colin muttered.

He turned his head, then pulled the trigger.

CHAPTER THIRTY-SIX

"FOURTEEN DEAD," COMMANDER DONKER SAID, quietly. "Seventeen more badly injured."

Thomas said nothing as they sat in his ready room. It had only been a day—less than a day, really—since they'd been driven away from Brasilia, but it felt longer. It wasn't the first time he'd lost crewmen in combat, yet... it never failed to hurt. He knew he'd have to say something at the memorial service, and write to their families, but...right now, he couldn't think of anything. He felt as if he'd failed.

We let ourselves get tricked, he thought. He wanted to blame Captain Campbell, but—in truth—he knew he'd failed, too. They'd both failed. *We didn't see the virus as a serious threat and that blinded us to the truth.*

He grimaced. "And the ship herself?"

"The damage control teams have patched the hull," Donker reported. "We've reloaded our missile tubes, replaced the destroyed point defence weapons and suchlike. We had to dock two of the gunboats at the standard airlocks, as we can't repair the gunboat docking ring without returning to the shipyard, but everywhere else...? We've done as much as we can."

Thomas glanced at the report without quite seeing it, then lifted his eyes to look at the in-system display. The enemy fleet still held position near the planet, shuttles moving to and from the surface in a steady stream...

he wondered, not for the first time, just how the virus had managed to put a reaction force together so quickly. It helped, he supposed, that the virus didn't need specialised troops. Its host bodies could be missile techs one day and ground-combat experts the next. It made little sense in human terms, but it seemed to work for the virus.

He shook his head, tiredly. The marine report had made it clear that the virus was trying to take captives. It would be good news against almost any other foe. Against the virus, it was a very mixed blessing. On one hand, he supposed, the marines weren't going to be blasted off the face of the planet. On the other, anyone who fell into enemy hands was going to be infected, interrogated and sent back to cause havoc. He gritted his teeth, cursing his mistake. There hadn't been enough time to recall the marines when the enemy fleet made its appearance, but they could have either started to prepare an evacuation or dropped supplies to ensure the marines could hold out indefinitely.

We need to get them off the planet, quickly, he thought. *They can't survive forever.*

He frowned. Major Craig had sounded confident, in a manner that suggested he really *wasn't*. Thomas understood the importance of sounding as if you knew what you were doing, but there were limits. If the marines couldn't accomplish the mission, it was better to point it out before they actually tried to do it. His hands clenched as a surge of bitter helplessness threatened to overcome him. The marines could get into space if they secured their shuttles and blasted off, but they'd be sitting ducks. The enemy would blow them to atoms before they even reached orbit.

Donker cleared his throat. "With your permission, sir, I'd like to return to my duties."

Thomas nodded. "Do so," he said. "And make sure you get some rest, too."

He rubbed his forehead as his XO retreated. *He* hadn't managed to get any rest either, not really. A brief nap on his sofa had left him feeling worse than ever. He stared at the display, his head starting to ache. They could fall back, but that would mean leaving the marines to their fate. Thomas knew the needs of the many outweighed the needs of the few, yet...he was damned if he was just showing his heels and running. He couldn't leave the marines behind. And yet, he couldn't see any way to retake the high orbitals long enough for the marines to escape.

And we can't even call for reinforcements, he thought. *By the time they get here, it will all be over.*

His intercom bleeped. "Captain," Cook said. "Captain Campbell is requesting a private conference."

Thomas scowled. *Unicorn* was supposed to be holding position near the planet, keeping an eye on the alien fleet. And yet, what could she do if the virus decided to nuke the entire planet? Nothing but bear witness. The virus wouldn't even care...Thomas put the matter out of his head. It was hard not to blame Captain Campbell for the disaster, even though Thomas knew there was more than enough blame to go around. He told himself to grow up. He might as well see what Captain Campbell had to say.

"Captain," he said, as the younger man's image appeared in front of him. "Has the alien fleet changed position?"

"No," Captain Campbell said. "However, I believe it is only a matter of time before the marines on the ground are overwhelmed. We need to act fast."

Thomas bit down a sharp remark about the dangers of teaching one's grandmother to suck eggs. He knew the problem as well as Captain Campbell, perhaps better. Major Craig had been a friend...no, he *was* a friend. There was no way Thomas could leave him to his fate, yet...there was no way to get them off the planet either. Or...he leaned forward. Captain Campbell wouldn't have called him to belabour the obvious. He might just have a plan.

"Agreed," he said, curtly. He'd forgive the younger man a great deal if he got the marines out of the lobster pot. "So far, I haven't been able to come up with a plan. Have you?"

Captain Campbell smiled, as if he'd scored a point. "Yes," he said.

"And I believe it represents our best chance to get them back before they're overwhelmed and killed."

Thomas kept his face under tight control. "Explain."

Mitch allowed himself a smile as he started to outline his plan. It was risky, perhaps riskier than the older man would have preferred, but it *would* give them a chance to get the marines out and run before it was too late. And, if it failed, they wouldn't be committed. They could back off and try to think of something else. He supposed that would appeal to the older man. They wouldn't be staking everything on one throw of the dice.

Although we might as well be, if we return home now, he thought, grimly. *The Admiralty will not be amused when we admit we've left a bunch of marines to die.*

He spoke rapidly, trying to ignore the gnawing sense of guilt. It had been his failure that had allowed the virus to catch them with their pants down. Sure, Captain Hammond hadn't spotted it either...but *Lion* had been considerably further from the alien fleet than *Unicorn*. The Board of Inquiry was going to have fun going through the records, the armchair admirals and generals pointing out little clues that—with the benefit of hindsight—had been missed at the time. He ground his teeth in frustration. Anyone with actual naval experience would know the people on the bridge often could and did make mistakes, if only because they were grappling with several problems at the same time, but armchair admirals tended to think they knew better. They never realised the people on the spot didn't have the advantage of hindsight. They were too busy battling the fog of war.

"Risky," Captain Hammond observed, when he'd finished. "And dangerous, if you get the timing wrong."

"We can break off, if things go too badly wrong," Mitch said. He had no intention of giving up as long as there was the slightest hope of success, if not outright victory, but he understood the need for an escape route. "We simply don't have the time to try anything else."

His eyes narrowed. "Unless you think we can just charge the alien formation and blow them away?"

Captain Hammond looked irked. He was a competent officer, even if he lacked the flair Mitch had seen in some of his earlier commanders. He knew as well as Mitch himself that they were short on options, that doing nothing was effectively condemning the marines to certain death—or worse. And yet, the plan might go disastrously wrong. Mitch had thought he'd covered all the bases, but the virus was dangerously unpredictable. It was quite possible it wouldn't take the bait.

"No, I don't think we can do that," Captain Hammond said. Charging the enemy might work against a conventional foe, if only because they'd have the advantage of surprise, but the virus would simply blow the squadron to atoms. "The plan should work."

He let out a breath. "How long do you need to get ready?"

"Five hours, assuming you let me borrow the manpower," Mitch said. He'd calculated the requirements, then asked Staci to run the calculations herself. "There's some leeway built into the planning, but—realistically—the marines don't have enough time for us to make sure of *everything*."

He let out a breath. The latest reports were grim. The marines were under heavy pressure. And, if the virus decided it didn't want to take captives any longer, the marines could be effortlessly wiped out. Mitch's gut burned with grim determination. They *had* to get in and get the marines before the virus ran out of patience. He cursed under his breath. In hindsight, sending *all* the marines to the surface had been a mistake. They could have tried to board the enemy brainship and shut it down.

"Quite," Captain Hammond said. "Rejoin the fleet, then start preparing. We'll move in"—he glanced at the chronometer—"seven hours."

Mitch wanted to argue, but he knew it would be pointless. Captain Hammond was being smart. The timetable could be moved up, if they managed to get ready ahead of time, but it was well to leave some leeway. They weren't doing something *entirely* new, he supposed, yet...he shook his head. Better to do everything in their power to ensure success. The crews would need some rest too. He'd sent half his crew to their bunks, but...he'd be surprised if any of them had managed to sleep. He hadn't managed to sleep either.

"Understood," he said. "We'll meet up with you in thirty minutes."

He tapped his console, breaking the link. It was hard not to feel nervous. He'd staked everything on one last throw of the dice, from the marines on the surface to his career and perhaps even his life. *Unicorn* would be taking the most dangerous risk, particularly if the enemy saw what was coming and declined to take the bait. He owed it to himself, he supposed, to try. The marines could not be left to die.

And if we fail, some arsehole will say we threw good money after bad, he thought, as he stood and headed for the hatch. *And that I wanted to wash away my failures with blood.*

He snorted in disgust. History—and entire *regiments* of armchair admirals—would judge him. And Captain Hammond. And everyone else involved in planning the mission, from the tactical staff on *Lion* to Admiral Onarina herself. Mitch rather suspected he knew what they'd write. They'd question everything, they'd accuse him—and everyone else—of being incompetent or treacherous or both, particularly if the operation failed. He dismissed the thought with a flicker of irritation. History could make up its mind, once the operation was concluded. Right now, he had more important problems.

"Captain?" Staci looked up as Mitch stepped onto the bridge. "What did he say?"

Mitch took his seat. "We have clearance to proceed," he said. "Once we've loaded the missile pods and decoys, we can give the enemy a nasty surprise."

He studied the display for a long moment. "Is there any sign the enemy carrier is being repaired?"

"Unclear, Captain," Staci said. "They haven't launched any starfighters since the first engagement. Post-battle analysis suggests she might have lost her starfighter complement as well as her launch tubes, but it's impossible to be sure."

Mitch nodded. The carrier wasn't entirely useless—she was big enough to carry heavy plasma cannons as well as missile tubes—but she had no place in the line of battle. Her starfighters were her main weapons and if they were unusable, her striking power would be much reduced. *Ark Royal* had served as a battleship as well as a carrier, but she'd been unique. The virus should have sent the damaged carrier back home for repairs. Mitch scowled as he studied the latest sensor readings. The carrier might be less damaged than the analysts thought. It was easy to fall into the trap of believing something if you wanted it to be true.

A low quiver ran through the hull as *Unicorn* glided away from the planet. Mitch sighed, pushing the matter to the back of his mind. They'd assume the carrier was fully capable, even though she was clearly damaged. It was the safest course of action...he smiled, suddenly, as his ship picked up speed. The carrier and the enemy battleships packed enough firepower to exterminate the entire squadron. The safest course of action was to turn tail and run.

But that would mean leaving the marines behind, he thought. *I'm not going to do that. Not yet.*

"Check the sensor platforms, then open a link to the marines," he ordered. "They'll have to be ready to move when the shit hits the fan."

"Yes, sir," Staci said.

Marigold was in her seat, flying the gunboat. Marigold was in his lap, kissing him. Tobias knew, at some level, that she couldn't be doing both, but it was hard to think clearly. She was dressed. No, she was undressed... her breasts were pressing into his naked chest. He kissed and sucked her nipples as she knelt between his legs, her mouth warm and welcoming as she took him inside her...

...It was suddenly very warm. He looked down. Marigold was burning, flames licking her body as she pulled him closer. He wanted to push her away and run, but he couldn't move. She was burning. He was burning. The gunboat was burning and the flames were consuming everything and…

Tobias woke up. The dream—the nightmare—had been so intense he'd thought it was real. He sat up, nearly cracking his head against the overhead bunk. The compartment was dark, so dark he could barely make out Marigold's head on her pillow…he breathed a sigh of relief, feeling a strange combination of fear and horniness. He wanted her and yet…he was scared to wake her, to discover—perhaps—that he was still dreaming. The dream mocked him. He'd thought she was dying in front of him.

He wiped sweat from his brow. He knew they could both die at any second. He shuddered helplessly. If the gunboat was hit, if she died, they would die together. Bagehot and the other instructors had claimed there was an excellent chance of survival, but none of the gunboat pilots believed them. They'd be flying into the teeth of missiles and plasma cannons designed to engage starships. There was no way in hell gunboat armour would stand up to them for more than a microsecond or two. The odds of survival were not great.

He wanted to go back to sleep, but he couldn't. The nightmare overshadowed his mind. Instead, he swung his legs over the side of the bunk and stood. The deck felt wobbly, as if the ship was being buffeted by gusts of wind. He knew it was an illusion, but it was hard to believe it. He stumbled into the washroom, undressed quickly and climbed into the shower. If there was one advantage to being a pilot, it was that regular water restrictions didn't apply. And, with the rest of the squadron fast asleep, he could stay in the shower as long as he liked.

And you can't stay in the shower forever, his thoughts mocked him. *You have to get out eventually.*

He gritted his teeth as he stepped out and dried himself. He didn't want to go back to sleep or…or do anything, really. No, that wasn't true. He wanted to wake Marigold and take her to the privacy tubes, but he knew better. She needed her sleep, just like he did. He changed into a new uniform and shipsuit, then headed for the hatch. He could get some coffee, review the briefing notes and wait for orders. Who knew? Maybe they'd have come up with a grand plan to save the marines on the ground.

Colin is down there, he thought. He was torn between delight at the thought and fear for the rest of the marines. They didn't deserve to die, not like that. *Fuck*.

Bagehot was seated in the common room, drinking coffee. He looked up as Tobias entered. "Can't sleep?"

"No, sir," Tobias said. "Bad dreams."

"They happen," Bagehot said. "Did you have the dream about bursting into flame? Or the one about being turned into an egg?"

Tobias frowned. "The egg dream, sir?"

"Old joke," Bagehot said. He waved a hand, dismissively. "Don't worry about it. Just pour yourself some coffee and sit down."

"Aye, sir," Tobias said. He wasn't going to share all the details, but… he had to ask. "Is it normal? I mean, to have dreams…"

"Of death?" Bagehot shrugged. "We all get them. Every pilot I know has dreamed of his own death. They say it means you're still human."

"Great," Tobias said. "And to think I was starting to doubt it."

Bagehot laughed. "That's nothing some coffee won't fix."

CHAPTER THIRTY-SEVEN

"WE JUST RECEIVED WORD from the marines, sir," Staci said, as *Unicorn* prepared for action. "They're ready to evacuate on command."

Mitch nodded. They'd spent the last six hours frantically preparing to mount an operation that would go down in the history books, either as a textbook-perfect piece of misdirection or as a grim example of what *not* to do. He'd gone through the plan time and time again, teasing out all the weak points and doing his level best to compensate for them, but he was all too aware that elements of the plan depended on the enemy doing the right thing. Captain Hammond had pointed out, rather sarcastically, that relying on the enemy to act in a certain way was asking for trouble. Mitch hadn't tried to deny it.

And there would be no point in trying, he thought. *He's right.*

He surveyed the display, checking the escort carrier and the drones holding position near the ship. They'd go live on his command, taking a page out of the enemy's tactical handbook and turning it against them. Hopefully, the brainship would misunderstand what it was seeing. The escort carrier would make it easier to convince the enemy that *Unicorn* was the real threat. There was no way—not yet—to fake starfighter emissions.

"Activate the command datanet," he ordered. "And then prepare to take us out."

"Aye, sir," Staci said. The display updated rapidly. "We're ready to move."

Mitch nodded, feeling an odd calmness come over him. The die was about to be cast. "Take us out," he said. "We'll activate the drones at Point Enterprise."

He sucked in his breath as a dull rumble echoed through the hull. The enemy should have no idea of their location...hell, the enemy might think the entire squadron was halfway to New Washington by now. It was quite possible, given how little the virus cared for its host bodies. It might assume Mitch and Captain Hammond had simply abandoned the marines to their fate. Or...he glowered at the display. The virus had learnt a great deal from infected humans over the last few years. It might be expecting some kind of recovery mission. And it might even know time was short, no longer on humanity's side.

Unless the counter-virus really did spread through the planet's atmosphere, Mitch thought. *If it did, it might be safe for the marines to breathe without masks.*

His eyes tracked the enemy fleet. It hadn't moved ever since it had entered high orbit. Mitch hoped that meant it was just waiting for orders, rather than holding position until the marines were infected or wiped out. Captain Hammond had been right, when they'd been thrashing out the details of the plan. *Lion* could do a great deal of damage, if the enemy fleet refused to take the bait, but she couldn't recover the high orbitals. There was no guarantee, either, that she could take out the brainship. And no guarantee, of course, that taking out the brainship would be enough to shatter the enemy fleet. The battleships were easily large enough to carry a critical mass of viral matter and base cells.

He kept his eyes on the display, feeling the tension growing as the ships crawled towards Point Enterprise. There was no reason to believe the enemy could track them—there was no reason to think the enemy had so much as seeded space with recon platforms—but it was easy to feel paranoid. They'd been caught by surprise once, after all. The virus had been more imaginative than anyone wanted to admit. God alone knew what it would do next.

And what would we do, he asked himself, *if we were a single mind bound and directed by a single will?*

He kept the thought to himself. He'd read some of the more alarming projections from the analysts and he hadn't been able to escape the feeling they simply weren't alarming *enough.* The virus didn't have humanity's weaknesses, all the petty follies and prejudices and stupid short-term thinking that had nearly condemned humanity to death; it didn't share the joys and sorrows of being human. It could easily decide to dismantle a planet, then bring together the resources to make it happen...Mitch had seen the proposals to blow up Mercury for raw materials, but he doubted it would happen. Space was filled with raw materials, ready for the taking. Why bother blowing up an entire world?

"Captain," Staci said. "We will reach Point Enterprise in two minutes."

Mitch nodded. "Good. Is *Lion* in position?"

"Yes, sir," Staci said. "She's ready to move."

We'll have only a few short moments to pull it off, when we create the window of opportunity, Mitch thought, grimly. *And if the virus realises what we're planning, all it has to do is nothing.*

His lips twitched, humourlessly. The idea of someone winning by doing absolutely nothing struck him as absurd, yet...it could happen. Victory was sometimes a matter of doing nothing more than keeping cool, refusing to respond to provocation and simply waiting for the enemy to give up and go away. Mitch disliked the thought of doing nothing, and of the enemy doing nothing, but...he shook his head. They had to appear as threatening as possible to convince the virus to take them seriously. The virus had to believe it *had* to do something.

"Activate the drones," he ordered. "And launch the probes."

He let out a breath as the drones went live. The virus would see the entire squadron advancing on the planet, the missile-heavy battlecruiser readying itself to strike. What would it do? If Mitch was any judge, it would leave orbit and close the range as much as possible, both to allow itself some manoeuvring room and to give its missiles a better chance of scoring hits. He'd devised the tactic as carefully as possible, trying to steer the virus towards a specific course of action. And the only way to convince it to take the bait was to let it have a chance to win.

"Communications, signal *Haddock*," he added. "They are cleared to launch starfighters."

"Aye, Captain."

Mitch leaned forward. The range was already narrowing rapidly. The time-delay was minimal. The virus already knew they were coming. What would it do? The starfighters should allay whatever doubts it might have, ensuring it took the bait. Unless it thought the starfighters were nothing more than sensor ghosts. It was possible.

It knows we've been experimenting with improved ECM, he thought. *For all it knows, we have cracked that particular problem.*

"I have targeting locks," Staci said. "The brainship is the priority target."

Mitch nodded. They *still* weren't sure if the enemy carrier could launch starfighters. If it could, it had to be taken out; if not, it could be safely ignored until the battleships were gone. He doubted it carried enough heavy weapons to make a difference in a long-range engagement.

"Hold the locks on the brainship," he ordered. The virus would do everything in its power to protect the brainship, but if it could be taken out..."Fire on my command."

He waited, feeling the seconds tick away. Would the virus take the bait? Or would it wait for the ghost squadron to come closer? Mitch had endlessly simulated the mission, but the outcome had depended on factors outside his control. If the virus didn't move...

"Captain," Staci said. "The enemy fleet is breaking orbit. It's heading towards us."

Mitch let out a sigh of relief. Millions of tonnes of firepower were heading towards them, which wasn't the sort of thing he'd normally regard as *good* news, but at least the plan had worked. The window of opportunity was starting to open. And it was just a matter of time before he took advantage of it...

"Copy our records to *Lion*," he ordered. The probes weren't signalling the battlecruiser directly. The laser beams were supposed to be undetectable, but it would only take a minor accident for the enemy to realise something was wrong. "And deploy the missile pods."

"Aye, sir."

"Incoming!"

Colin ducked into the trench as a mortar shell crashed down on the position. The ground shook, mud flying everywhere. He forced himself to stand, peering down towards the enemy position as another human wave attack began. The survivors, the infected settlers who hadn't been killed by the counter-virus, were being thrown into the fire. The virus seemed intent on getting rid of as many of them as possible, using their bodies to soak up bullets. Colin thought it made a kind of sense, if one didn't give a damn about the dying host bodies. The marines couldn't replenish their ammunition in a hurry.

Or at all, he thought, as he fired at a cluster of host bodies. Two of them disintegrated, as if whatever was holding them together had vanished; the remaining bodies kept coming until they were shot to pieces. It was like being in a horror movie or a nightmare, one where the enemy troops kept coming until you were ripped to pieces. *We're going to run out of ammunition soon.*

He cursed as a pair of shuttles flew overhead. One was blown out of the sky by a MANPAD, the debris crashing somewhere to the east; the other landed roughly amidst a marine position and deployed its troops. They were gunned down quickly, but not quickly enough. Colin swallowed, hard, as he realised the lower trench lines were on the verge of breaking. The zombies just kept coming.

His earpiece bleeped. "The enemy fleet is leaving orbit," someone said. It sounded female, but otherwise...she was unfamiliar. "Prepare to retreat to the evacuation shuttles."

"Swell." Colin cursed as another row of zombies, little more than rotting corpses, threw themselves towards the defenders. They were practically dead already. He shuddered as they disintegrated under human fire. "When do we…?"

He heard a roar and looked down. A trio of tanks—alien tanks—were making their way towards the trenches. Behind them, he could see aliens in protective suits. Troops, he guessed. They moved with an odd jerkiness that reminded him of untrained men pretending to be soldiers, but the weapons in their hands were very real. He guessed the virus had expended the settlers purely to wear down the defenders, as well as making use of the host bodies before they died. And now the marines were in no state to hold off the tanks…

"Call down fire," he snapped, harshly. He wasn't sure who was in command of the trench any longer. The line was dissolving, piece by piece. He could see zombies cracking the lines, seemingly undeterred by antipersonnel mines that had been banned for years before being authorised for this war. "Hit those bastards."

He swallowed, hard. The trench was no longer tenable. They had no antitank weapons, no MANPADs that could be pressed into the antitank role. He glanced at Davies and the rest of the unit, then signalled the retreat. He'd be in real trouble if he *wasn't* the senior officer—he snorted; a corporal wasn't *really* an officer—but he saw no choice. If they stayed where they were, they'd die.

A zombie landed in front of him, the rotting corpse so worn-down Colin couldn't tell if it was male or female or even *human*. He'd never seen a body so shattered, not outside his worst nightmares. He kicked the corpse as it lashed out at him, sending it crashing to the ground; he stamped on its arms and legs, then ran past it as mortar shells started to explode around the tanks. The virus had had to have shipped them in, unless it had managed to bring more of the local industry back online. Hopefully, it had only a very limited supply. Perhaps, just perhaps, they could be taken out before it was too late.

"Fall back to Point Adam," Major Craig ordered, over the intercom. "And keep your heads down."

Colin nodded. The shuttles were waiting, but...he shuddered. They'd shot down enemy shuttles. The enemy would try to do the same to them. And if the spacers couldn't clear the way, the shuttles would be hopelessly vulnerable when the enemy starships returned. The virus would probably give up hope of taking the marines prisoner if it saw the marines running for their lives. A lone destroyer would be more than enough to take out all the shuttles.

He forced himself to keep running. They'd done everything they could to make the evacuation work. And the rest of it was in the hands of the gods.

Mitch studied the enemy fleet, silently calculating and recalculating vectors. The range was steadily closing and, soon enough, the virus would open fire. Mitch had a feeling the only reason the virus hadn't opened fire already was that it was probably short of long-range missiles, although he knew it couldn't be taken for granted. Perhaps the brainship, assuming the ghost squadron was actually real, had calculated it couldn't reasonably hope to overwhelm its point defence. It would be right, if the ghost fleet was real...

"Captain," Staci said. "They're targeting us."

Mitch hesitated. The timing wasn't perfect. The greater the distance between the enemy fleet and the planet, the better. But...the more the enemy fleet probed the sensor drones, the greater the chance it would realise it was being suckered. He'd done everything he could to ensure the virus would ignore the first few doubts, but...they just didn't have enough ships to play shell games indefinitely. If the virus cracked one of the illusions, it would pretty quickly crack them all.

"Fire on my command," he ordered. The missiles should banish the nagging doubts, at least for a few moments longer. The virus would assume that sensor ghosts couldn't fire missiles. Technically, it would be entirely correct. "Fire!"

"Aye, sir."

Mitch leaned forward as the missile pods opened fire. The missile targeting wouldn't be anything like as precise—they'd left the gunboats on *Lion*—but the seeker warheads *should* be able to draw information from the probes and sensor platforms. Mitch felt a hot flash of irritation as the missiles picked up speed, confirming—seemingly confirming—that the ghost fleet was real. In hindsight, they shouldn't have had to jury-rig an interface between the sensor platforms and the missiles. It was the sort of oversight they should have identified and fixed during the planning stage.

We'll have to do something about that, when we get home, he thought. *Next time, we might not be so lucky.*

The display sparkled with red icons. "Captain, they've returned fire," Staci said. "It looks as though they're trying to swamp the drones."

Mitch nodded. *Unicorn* and *Haddock* had been targeted as an afterthought, if they'd been targeted at all. It didn't matter. They'd be wiped out in an instant if the virus realised the truth and acted fast. And they'd done everything they could...

"Bring up the drones, then alter course," he ordered. Hopefully, they could keep the enemy confused for a few moments longer. "And cloak us as soon as *Haddock* has recovered her starfighters."

He felt his heart start to race as the display updated, time and time again. There were so many missiles heading towards the ghost fleet that the icons were blurring together, the projectors struggling to handle a wall of death that would vaporise an entire battleship effortlessly. They'd unloaded all of the freighters and towed the missile pods into firing position, but... it felt as if they'd merely spat into a hurricane. His eyes followed the missile clusters as they stabbed towards the brainship. Hundreds died, picked off effortlessly; a dozen made it through, laser beams stabbing into the armoured hull. If nothing else, he told himself, the virus would be hurt...

The brainship exploded. Mitch breathed a sigh of relief as the remaining missiles threw themselves at the battleships. The brainship was gone, which meant...he hoped, prayed, it would take the virus some time to recover. The battleships would need to sort out a new pecking order. But how long would it take?

"Sir, *Haddock* has recovered her starfighters," Staci said. She shot him a grim smile, then returned her attention to her console. "She's ready to run."

"Take us into cloak," Mitch ordered. It didn't matter which way the escort carrier went, as long as it was away from the enemy fleet. She knew what to do if *Unicorn*—or *Lion*—didn't make it. "Helm, get us out of here."

"Aye, sir," Hinkson said, loudly. He sounded nervous, even though they'd been in worse scrapes. "Getting the hell out of here!"

Mitch watched the torrent of missiles as they slammed into the ghost fleet. No point defence weapons tried to stop them. He smiled, allowing himself a moment of relief. The virus had to know it had been tricked, but it was too late. There was nothing it could do, now, to keep itself from expending hundreds of missiles. It had fired off so many Mitch didn't have an accurate count, all of which had been wasted. He felt his smile grow wider as the ghost ships vanished, the remaining enemy missiles detonating uselessly in interplanetary space. Even if the virus started looking, it would have real problems tracking *Unicorn* and blowing her to hell.

And the virus has other problems, he thought. *It shouldn't have time to worry about us.*

"Signal *Lion*," he ordered. He smirked. His counterpart wouldn't be amused by a flippant message, but it was what he was going to get. "The window of opportunity has been broken open. It's time to snatch and run."

CHAPTER THIRTY-EIGHT

"CAPTAIN," SIBLEY SAID. "The enemy fleet has taken the bait."

Thomas had to fight not to let out a sigh of relief. The plan had been too rough for his peace of mind, with too many things that could go wrong. *Lion* was under cloak, but the virus was filling space with sensor pulses. The battlecruiser could have been detected at any second, forcing her to turn and run. As it was, the window of opportunity was shorter than he'd hoped. The enemy would presumably reverse course the moment the virus realised the battlecruiser was recovering the marines.

And using a battlecruiser to pick up the troops is unprecedented, too, he thought, as the seconds ticked away. *Unicorn* and her ghost fleet could give the virus a bloody nose, but only once. The enemy fleet would survive, long enough to decide if it wanted to return to the planet or try to run *Unicorn* down before she could make her escape. *Their window of opportunity for stopping us is narrower than they might hope.*

"Helm, take us into high orbit," he ordered. "XO, prepare to launch the gunboats."

"Aye, Captain," Donker said. "Gunboats ready to launch on your command."

"And signal the marines," Thomas added. "I want updated targeting information, and I want it yesterday."

"Aye, Captain."

Thomas sucked in his breath. *Lion* wasn't designed for planetary bombardment. She could drop KEWs, just like anything capable of flying under her own power, but she lacked the sheer firepower of a monitor or assault carrier. Her targeting sensors were good, yet they simply didn't have the time to isolate the enemy positions and build a proper targeting matrix. They'd have to rely on the marines to provide targeting data, even if it *was* danger close. The last reports had made it clear the marines were being pressed hard, that human positions were increasingly intermingled with alien troops. It was quite possible the KEWs would hit the wrong targets.

They know the risks, he told himself. Any marine who called down fire on his own position, or close enough to run the risk of a blue-on-blue, had to be desperate. *They'll be careful.*

"Captain," Sibley said. "The ghost fleet has opened fire."

"Good," Thomas said. The sheer volume of missiles roaring towards the alien fleet would be very convincing. Perhaps a little *too* convincing. He'd actually considered suggesting that they reduced the first barrage, just to avoid tipping their hand too soon by firing more missiles than *Lion* could launch in a single salvo. "Do we have updated targeting information?"

"Yes, sir," Sibley said. "Primary and secondary targets are locked. Ready to deploy on your command."

Thomas nodded. "Decloak," he ordered. "Launch gunboats. Start the bombardment."

He watched, grimly, as the first volley of projectiles fell into the planet's atmosphere. The tubes were already reloading, preparing themselves to fire a second barrage. They'd wipe out what remained of the colony, putting the dying host bodies out of their misery. The beancounters would probably whine about the expenditure, but KEWs were nothing more than compressed rocks. They could be replaced effortlessly. And besides, they were no use in ship-to-ship combat. If *Lion* had to shoot her way back to friendly space, the KEWs would make no difference.

"Impact in ten seconds," Sibley reported. He broke off as the display started to update rapidly. "Captain, the alien fleet is reversing course."

Thomas nodded, unsurprised. The virus knew what they were doing. Trapping *Lion* against the planet was its only real hope for salvaging something from the disaster. He remembered the reports from the ground and shuddered. The virus might well have captured and infected someone who knew *something* about the counter-virus, although all the medics and researchers were accounted for. The captives were dead—or they would be, when the KEWs struck the surface. Whatever the virus had learnt would never leave the planet.

But it'll figure out what we did, sooner or later, he thought, numbly. *And it will try to devise countermeasures.*

He put the thought out of his head. "Tactical, deploy missiles when the enemy fleet comes into range," he ordered. "Slow it down as much as possible."

"Aye, Captain," Sibley said.

Thomas forced himself to remain calm. The alien fleet had lost its brainship. It would take time for it to work out how to work together again, although...he narrowed his eyes as the alien fleet picked up speed. It might have already sorted out the new pecking order. A standard human datanet was designed to designate a new command ship immediately, if something happened to the old one. There was no reason the virus couldn't do the same. Hell, it might have copied the more decentralised structures beloved of spacers. The net couldn't be shattered with a single blow if there was more than one command ship.

And it doesn't have to worry about any personality conflicts either, Thomas thought, sardonically. *It's a single entity in billions of bodies.*

"Captain," Donker said. "The marines are ready to begin the evacuation."

"Proceed as planned," Thomas ordered. "Helm, prepare to reverse course."

He watched the display as the battlecruiser opened fire. The enemy fleet didn't look deterred. It was steering into the teeth of his fire, aware it packed enough point defence to thin out the missile clusters before they reached their targets. Thomas felt a stab of envy, mingled with fear for the future. It was only a matter of time before the virus started churning out missile-heavy battlecruisers of its own, if it didn't simply update the battleships it already had. And who knew what would happen then?

We'll have to devise something new, he told himself. *In that, at least, we have the edge.*

He took a breath. One way or the other, it would all be over soon.

"Incoming," someone screamed. "Danger close! I say again, danger close!"

Colin hit the dirt, an instant before the hammer of God Himself struck the planet. The ground shook so violently he thought it was an earthquake, the force of the impact strong enough to send pieces of debris flying in all directions. He had no time to spare a thought for anyone but himself as the shaking went on and on, waves of pressure rushing over his back and vanishing into the distance. The infected zombies had been in the open. They'd have been utterly flattened by the KEW strike.

Silence fell, so abruptly he thought he'd gone deaf. His ears had been extensively modified during basic training, and his earpieces should have given him additional protection, but he'd never been so close to a KEW strike before. He swallowed, hard, as he forced himself to stumble to his knees. He'd never had fire called down so close to his position before, not even during training exercises. It was very much a last resort. The risk of actually hitting his own positions was just too high.

His earpiece crackled. "Group One, withdraw to the shuttles," the coordinator said. "Group Two, hold the line."

Sure, Colin thought. He felt punch-drunk, as if he'd been beaten so badly he'd gone beyond pain. *That* had never happened before. *Hold the line against what?*

He stared towards the remains of the city. The forest was gone. The trees had been reduced to sawdust and smoking craters. In the distance, he could see flames rising from the settlements...the former settlements.

The air was hot, but still. If there were any zombies left, he couldn't see them. They were dead and gone, literally atomised. He heard a whining noise behind him and turned to see the first shuttles, stabbing their way towards space. It looked, very much, as though the battle was over.

"They're hitting the city," Davies said, quietly. "Look."

Colin followed his pointing finger. Streaks of light were falling from orbit, seeming to move slowly even though he *knew* they were picking up speed with every passing second. They touched the ground...he looked away as brilliant flashes of light rent the horizon, the sound bursting over them seconds later. He'd seen KEWs before, back on Earth, but never so many. The days when mass orbital bombardment was the order of the day for dealing with rogue states and terrorists were over. These days, the military rarely needed more than one or two KEWs to make its point.

He couldn't move, even though he *knew* they stood in the open. Snipers had picked off targets from five kilometres or more, but...it was hard to believe there was *anyone* left alive, apart from the marines themselves. The planet's population had been trapped in living death before the counter-virus and the KEWs had struck, granting them a merciful release. He wiped sweat from his brow. If there were any infected host-bodies left, they were doomed. They certainly didn't have time to organise a counterattack.

"Group Two, fall back to the shuttles," the coordinator ordered. "Hurry!"

Colin turned and forced himself to jog up to the remains of the terraforming station. The shockwaves hadn't been kind to the structure, knocking it to rubble. He hoped the spooks had gotten what they wanted, before the station had been abandoned. The marines simply didn't have time to sift through the piles of rubble, not any longer. The briefing had made it clear. Once they got into orbit, they were going to be running for their lives.

He who fights and runs away, lives to run away another day, he thought, as they ran towards the shuttles. The craft were already powering up, a dull whine echoing through the air as they prepared to leap into orbit. *We'll be back.*

Sergeant Bowman checked them off as they reached the hatch. "Where's Willis?"

"Dead," Colin said. His heart clenched, suddenly. Willis was dead. Colin had shot him. He knew he'd had no choice—Willis had died the second he'd been infected—but it still tore at him. If they'd had proper medical gear, if they'd been able to get their friend to sickbay in time…he told himself, again and again, that he'd had no choice. "I'll…I'll report later."

He scrambled into the shuttle. The marine units had been jumbled up, unsurprisingly. He sat next to a stranger and buckled in, bracing himself as the drives grew louder. The shuttle shook, time and time again. More KEWs? Or…he wasn't sure he wanted to know. They were sitting ducks, if an enemy MANPAD team had survived long enough to get into firing position. Or if the enemy fleet returned before it was too late. He told himself, firmly, to stop thinking. His mind refused to obey.

You get out of this, you'll have one hell of a story to tell, he thought. He'd heard a *lot* of stories from the old sweats, from detailed accounts that had the ring of truth to tall tales he'd flatly refused to believe. *And no one will believe you either.*

The shuttle shook one final time, then jumped skywards. Colin heard someone praying in a language he didn't recognise, save for a handful of words. Latin? Or something else. He didn't blame the stranger. They'd been taught that God helped those who helped themselves, but they could no longer do anything. It was in the pilot's hands now.

He smiled, suddenly, as a memory surfaced. The Beast had been very insistent on everyone attending assembly, where they'd sung hymns and listened to Bible readings. Colin hadn't been impressed for all sorts of reasons. The stories of Muscular Christians being Extremely Muscular all over the planet would have been more interesting if they hadn't been interspersed with tedious little morality tales about the importance of Virtue, Clean Living, Obedience to Authority and Avoiding Vice. It was certainly hard to imagine the *Beast* believing in God. He'd never had any qualms about insisting that sparing the rod spoilt the child.

And if I get home, I'll really look into his military career, Colin promised himself. *I wonder how the School Board would react if they discovered he was a Walt?*

He felt his smile grow wider. The School Board would *not* be amused. And who knew what they'd do?

"Captain, the second wave of marine shuttles has left the planet," Sibley said. The display updated again, showing thirty shuttles breaking atmosphere and heading towards the battlecruiser. "However, the enemy fleet is redlining its drives."

They must be desperate to score some kind of victory, Thomas thought. It was a little out of character for the virus—it had never shown any real hint of anything resembling human feeling—but it was possible it was panicking. The counter-virus had to seem like an Outside Context Problem, rather like radiation or the virus itself. *Or maybe they want to deter us from trying it again.*

He shrugged. *That* wasn't going to happen. Admiral Onarina was hardly going to stop, even if the entire squadron vanished without trace. And *that* wasn't going to happen either. The remainder of the squadron was going to make its own way home and report to its superiors. They'd know the counter-virus had worked and start looking for ways to make it even more effective. Thomas's stomach churned at the thought. Like it or not, they were on the verge of committing mass murder on a planetary scale. Again. And even the certain knowledge the host-bodies were dead anyway didn't help.

"Helm, increase speed," he ordered. "But don't leave the shuttles behind."

"Aye, Captain," Fitzgerald said.

Thomas nodded, grimly. The equation had just become brutally simple. The shuttles had legs—and an acceleration curve anything larger than a starfighter or gunboat might envy—but they had very short range. Their power cells had probably already been drained. The marines hadn't had time to recharge, let alone anything else. Thomas's plan was relatively simple—the shuttles could latch onto the hulls like limpets, their passengers waiting until the battlecruiser was clear before they boarded *Lion*—but it relied upon the shuttles reaching the battlecruiser first. And that meant there was a very real chance of the enemy hammering *Lion* before she could open the range again.

We can take it, he told himself, although he knew it wasn't entirely true. *They won't have us in range for very long.*

"XO, inform the gunboats that they are to continue harassing the alien ships," he ordered. "Tactical, fire to cover the shuttles."

"Aye, Captain," Sibley said.

"The enemy battleships are tough," Tobias said. It was frustrating, but true. "That brute just took four nukes and she's still coming."

He cursed as a streak of plasma shot past the gunboat. The enemy point defence was concentrating on protecting the capital ships, but they had enough firepower to divert a handful of plasma cannons to try to engage the gunboats. Tobias knew they were a very small target, yet significant enough to be worth the effort. The virus might disrupt the missile targeting if it took out the gunboats.

"Try to take out her drives," Marigold advised. She swung the gunboat into another series of evasive manoeuvres. "Just punch out a drive node or two."

Tobias scowled as he assumed command of another missile cluster. The range was steadily closing. The enemy was already pumping missiles towards *Lion*, the odds of a direct hit growing steadily higher with every passing second. *Lion* was firing as rapidly as she could, running the risk of shooting herself dry. There just weren't enough laser warheads to make a real impression…

His fingers danced over the console, directing five laser warheads against the nearest battleship. Three were blown out of space before they could detonate, while the remaining two sent ravening beams of energy digging into the enemy ship's hull. She shuddered, spewing streams of superheated plasma from the wound as her drive field started to disintegrate. Tobias watched, hoping they'd punched out enough of the nodes to slow her down. She would be harmless if she couldn't bring her weapons to bear on *Lion*.

"I think you hurt her," Marigold said. Another battleship fell out of formation as their comrades landed a handful of blows. She exploded a second later, scattering debris in all directions. "How much of her do we get to paint on the hull?"

Tobias laughed, then sobered as his display lit up. The enemy fleet carrier appeared to be breaking up, shedding debris even though she'd been largely ignored. None of the gunboats had so much as shot a single missile at her, let alone tried to take her out. She just wasn't important. And yet...his eyes narrowed. Had she been hit? It didn't seem likely. His sensors hadn't tracked any missiles striking her hull...

Red icons appeared on the display. "Oh, hell!"

"Enemy starfighters," Bagehot said. He was safely on *Lion*, for a given value of *safe*. If the battlecruiser came under heavy fire, he'd be blown away with the rest of the ship. "I say again, enemy starfighters!"

"I saw," Tobias said. He cursed under his breath. The enemy launch tubes had been destroyed, but not the starfighters themselves. The carrier's crew had literally burnt through their own hull to launch the starfighters. They'd put nearly three whole squadrons into space. "We need some cover..."

His eyes narrowed as the enemy starfighters zoomed into attack position, then roared *past* the gunboats without even *trying* to engage. They didn't even snap off a handful of shots as they passed. The gunboats did, killing a pair of enemy craft before the range opened again. Tobias stared, unsure what he was seeing. The enemy starfighters were behaving oddly. Surely, they considered the gunboats priority targets...right?

Oh no, they don't, he thought. His heart sank as he realised the truth. *They're not going for us. They're going for the shuttles!*

CHAPTER THIRTY-NINE

"CAPTAIN," SIBLEY SAID. "The enemy carrier has force-launched its starfighters."

Thomas nodded, sharply. He'd served on carriers. He'd *commanded* carriers. Hacking through the hull—and layers upon layers of ablative armour—wasn't something to be done lightly. Hell...he kicked himself, mentally. He'd been blinded by his own service. If one of his carriers had taken so much damage, she would have lost the starfighters as well as the launch tubes. The virus must have buried its hangar decks deeper in the hull. It wasn't something any other race would have done, but he supposed it made a certain kind of sense. There was a greater need to protect the starfighters than the pilots if the latter were considered expendable...

He dismissed the thought. "XO, recall the gunboats," he ordered. Thirty-odd starfighters were bearing down on the shuttles. They'd be like wolves amongst sheep if they were permitted to proceed unmolested. "They're to cover the shuttles until they reach our point defence envelope."

"Aye, Captain," Donker said.

Thomas felt a hot flash of anger as he calculated the vectors. The virus had timed it well, even though the brainship was gone. He couldn't slow *Lion* to cover the shuttles without giving the enemy fleet a chance to catch up and shoot him to pieces. And yet, *not* slowing the battlecruiser would make it harder for the shuttles to evade their tormentors. He silently gave the virus credit for presenting him with a sadistic choice, one that would cost him no matter what he did. He had to save the marines, but he couldn't risk the battlecruiser any further…

And recalling the gunboats limits my ability to hit them, he thought. *Or does it?*

"Communications, establish links to *Unicorn*," he ordered. "If she can coordinate our missile strikes, she is to do so."

"Aye, sir," Cook said.

Thomas scowled. It wouldn't be perfect. *Unicorn* was out of position, too far from the enemy fleet to react to tiny gaps in their defences. The time delay alone would make her efforts less useful than anyone might have hoped, even if they weren't—*quite*—worse than useless. But it would have to do.

He gritted his teeth. They could make it out. They *would* make it out. But it wasn't going to be cheap.

"Incoming enemy fighters," the pilot warned. "If you know any good prayers, say them."

Colin swallowed, hard. He'd forgotten every prayer he'd been taught. There might be no atheists in foxholes, an expression he'd never understood until he'd wound up in a foxhole himself, but they tended to have no time to pray. He felt awkwardly exposed, utterly helpless…unable to do anything to so much as save himself. He was just a passenger, his fate determined by the pilot and the enemy gunners and…

This must be how Tobias felt, all the fucking time, he thought. Self-disgust shaded his thoughts. *Poor bastard.*

He closed his eyes. One way or the other, it would all be over soon.

Tobias found himself with mixed feelings as the gunboats rocketed towards the shuttles and enemy starfighters. The shuttles didn't seem to be evading, certainly not well enough to save themselves from round after round of plasma fire. Two shuttles died as he watched, picked off by enemy starfighters. The marines were too stupid to evade...no, he realised dully; they literally didn't have the *power* to evade. They were cutting their flight very fine indeed. If their power cells died while they were in transit, there was little hope of rescue before they suffocated.

Colin's on one of those craft, Tobias thought. He refused to believe the bully was dead. People like Colin never died. They had the luck of the devil himself, surviving things that would break or kill ordinary mortals. *I wonder...*

He accessed the datanet as the range closed, wondering if there was a troop manifest. The marines had thrown the evacuation plan together at great speed, improvising everything, but it was just possible...Colin's name leapt out at him, a helpless passenger on a nameless shuttle. The enemy starfighters were already moving to attack. Tobias stared, transfixed. It would be so easy to do nothing, to let the starfighters take their shot. Colin couldn't hope to escape an alien starfighter. His shuttle wasn't even trying to evade.

"I'm closing the range," Marigold said. She didn't know what he was thinking. How could she? "Hit them as soon as you can. Make them jump and scatter."

Tobias nodded, his thoughts elsewhere as he opened fire. It would be so easy to aim to miss. Hitting a starfighter was never easy. The craft were tiny, even when they weren't dancing from side to side randomly to make their course impossible to predict. It would be so easy...a cold glee ran through him as he realised he could fire the fatal shot himself. He was already shooting burst after burst of plasma fire towards the starfighters, forcing them to abandon their attack formations and scatter. They were in the middle of a dogfight. It would look like an accident...a terrible accident, to be sure, but an accident. He could snap off a shot that hit the shuttle and blew Colin to atoms...

Time seemed to slow as he stared at the targeting console. Temptation howled through his mind. He could do it. Colin wouldn't stand a chance.

No one would ever know. Others would be killed, but...they'd accepted Colin as one of them. They didn't deserve to live. Thugs and bullies...he could kill them too. His thoughts ran in circles. Colin's life was in his hand. *This* time, he knew he had a weapon. It would look like an accident. All he had to do was fire. The entire world would cheer.

And yet, his thoughts mocked, *you're not a child any longer.*

He drew back from the brink, then opened fire on the alien starfighters. Colin would never know it, perhaps, but Tobias would know—would always know—that he'd had the chance to kill Colin without consequences, and he'd let it go. He could have shot Colin in the back and...he'd made the choice, the very deliberate choice, to let it go. He'd always wonder if he'd made a mistake, he admitted as he scattered the remaining enemy starfighters, but at least he knew himself a little better now. He wasn't a murderer.

And, perhaps, someone would have figured it out, he thought. He had a life now, a girlfriend and a career and a future that—perhaps—was bright. He didn't want to throw it away for a worthless piece of shit like Colin. *Who knows what would have happened if I killed him and someone studied the battle extensively enough to realise what I'd done?*

He put the thought out of his head. Colin scared him—Colin would *always* scare him—but it was no longer the sheer terror the bully had once evoked. Now...Tobias knew he could have killed Colin, if he'd been willing to risk going down, too. He'd never be so scared again.

His lips quirked as the last of the enemy starfighters died under their fire. Colin had survived. In a sense, he even owed his *life* to Tobias. Tobias was tempted to tell him that, if nothing else. What would Colin make of a world where Tobias could have killed him, or simply sat back and watched him die? There'd been times, hundreds of times, when he'd fantasised about having the chance to kill Colin, either by killing him deliberately or simply turning his back and walking away. And now...

"We're being recalled," Marigold said. "We're to hold station with *Lion* until she gets out of enemy range."

Tobias nodded, resetting the targeting console as the gunboats escorted the shuttles to the battlecruiser. Had he done the right thing? He didn't know. And he feared, deep inside, that he never would.

"The shuttles are latching on now," Donker reported. "The gunboats are holding station behind us."

"Ramp up the drives as far as they'll go," Thomas ordered. He studied the enemy fleet for a long cold moment. It had taken a beating, one hell of a beating, but it was still formidable—and dangerous. He'd completed the mission; he'd sneaked in, recovered the marines and given the enemy a bloody nose into the bargain. "I think we've outstayed our welcome."

He leaned forward, studying the displays as the battlecruiser started to open the range. The enemy fleet was still firing, but they were growing increasingly short of missiles. They just weren't firing enough to wear down his defences, let alone get past the gunboats. He was almost tempted to circle around and try to kill the remaining ships, but they'd pushed their luck too far. Besides, they might need their remaining missiles to fight their way back to New Washington.

"Captain," Cook said. "Captain Campbell is requesting a conference."

Thomas's eyes narrowed. Captain Campbell was supposed to break contact, slip back into cloak, evade the enemy fleet and link up with *Lion* once both ships had jumped through the tramline. He wasn't supposed to be anywhere near the battlecruiser, certainly not close enough to request a realtime conference. Thomas frowned, then keyed his console. He had a feeling he knew what Captain Campbell was going to say.

"Captain," he said. "You're meant to be a lot further away."

"I thought it would be wise to shadow the enemy from a distance," Captain Campbell said, curtly. "Captain, we can take them. We can finish the job."

Thomas would have smiled, if the situation hadn't been so serious. He'd been right. Captain Campbell *did* want to press the offensive…Thomas considered it, again, but he knew they'd taken the engagement as far as they reasonably could. They might be withdrawing under fire, yet the range was growing wider with every passing second. It was just a matter of time until the enemy fleet gave up or *Lion* managed to break contact, recall her gunboats and slip into cloak herself. And then they could sneak back to New Washington at leisure.

"No," he said, bluntly. He had a sense of *déjà vu*. "We've completed our mission. We've proven the BioBombs work, if not as well as we might have hoped. We recovered the marines and hammered their fleet. There's nothing to be gained by continuing the attack."

He smiled. "Haven't we had this discussion before?"

Captain Campbell looked thoroughly displeased. "There are three enemy battleships and one carrier within weapons range," he said. "We could take them out, now."

Thomas kept his voice calm. It wasn't easy. "We have nearly shot ourselves dry," he said. "We stripped every last missile out of the freighters, just to take out the brainship. We simply do not have the firepower to win, while giving the enemy a chance to take us out instead. In short, we are going to quit while we're ahead."

He understood. He'd admit that much, at least in the privacy of his own mind. It took upwards of eighteen months to churn out a battleship, even if the shipyard crews cut every corner they could. Taking out the remainder of the enemy fleet *would* make life harder for the virus, although they had no way to know how *much* harder. The fleet chasing them might represent ten percent of the virus's deployable forces, or one percent, or even less... he shook his head. It was academic. His ship was in no state to continue the engagement.

"Break off, as ordered, and link up with us at the RV point," he said, coldly. He was tempted to offer to issue the orders in writing, even though that would put them on the record for the rest of their careers. "I'll see you there."

"Yes, sir." Captain Campbell's tone was also cold, barely one step short of insubordination. "Be seeing you."

The connection broke. Thomas stared at the empty screen for a long moment, then turned his attention back to the display. He understood the urge to win, but not at all costs. There was no hope of winning the engagement, not without risking everything. And they'd won. The virus had been forced on the defensive for the first time since the war had begun.

Next time, we'll hit a major world, he thought. *And the counter-virus might spread onto the enemy fleet.*

Mitch scowled at the display. Captain Hammond just didn't have what it took. It was blatantly obvious, from the steady reduction in enemy fire, that the enemy fleet was shooting itself dry. *Lion* had been *designed* to hammer enemy ships from beyond their own range, certainly beyond *energy* weapons range. The combination of speed, agility and gunboats would be more than enough to tip the odds in her favour, particularly if the enemy couldn't shoot back. Mitch had no qualms about blasting an enemy ship to atoms from a safe distance. Experience had taught him the virus would happily do the same to him.

He felt his mood worsen as the range continued to increase. Three battleships and a carrier, the latter so badly damaged she was effectively a sitting duck. They'd thought that before, he conceded, but if the carrier had been able to launch more starfighters she would have done so when her craft were engaging the shuttles. No, she was no longer combat-effective...

Mitch forced himself to think. If *he'd* been in command, he would have held the range open and shot the enemy fleet to pieces. At best, total victory; at worst, he could have retreated once he'd run out of missiles. Captain Hammond might fret about encountering something nasty between Brasilia and New Washington, but they'd *already* encountered something nasty behind them. His thoughts ran in bitter circles. Captain Hammond simply didn't have the aggression to handle his ship properly.

He studied the display, looking for options. The enemy fleet was too alert for tiny *Unicorn* to do any real damage. He considered a ballistic missile strike, but...the odds of slipping even one missile through the defences were very low. *Unicorn* didn't mount a shipkiller plasma cannon, either... he conceded, angrily, that there was no hope of prolonging the engagement any further. Captain Hammond wanted to quit while they were ahead.

And we'll see those ships again, shooting at us, he reflected. *Damn it.*

"Helm, take us out on an evasive course," he ordered. They'd be flying alone for a few hours, but...it was unlikely they'd run into anything they couldn't handle. The remainder of the squadron was already on the far side of the tramline, waiting for the warships to join them. "Tactical, continue to monitor the sensor platforms as long as they remain within range."

"Aye, Captain," Staci said.

Mitch settled back into his chair, trying to resist the urge to brood. They *had* done well. They'd proven the battlecruiser-corvette combo—and the BioBombs—worked. And they'd given the enemy a punch in the jaw. Mitch remembered the brainship exploding and smirked, despite his frustration and rage. The virus would have to rethink its tactics in a hurry, now the brainships were vulnerable. It was just a shame they hadn't been able to take out the entire fleet.

Next time, he promised himself. If he played his cards right, he could wind up in command of *Lion's* sister ship. He'd show Captain Hammond *precisely* how to use his firepower to best advantage. *Next time, things will be different.*

"Transit complete, Captain," Fitzgerald reported.

"Local space appears clear," Sibley added. "We appear to have broken contact."

Thomas allowed himself a moment of relief. The enemy fleet had broken off, eventually, but there'd been no guarantee the virus hadn't been deploying cloaked ships to shadow *Lion* or simply signalled ahead. The question of *precisely* how the virus had managed to deploy a fleet in time to catch them had yet to be answered and probably never *would*, unless the spooks found a way to hack the virus's records. It wasn't likely to happen. The best the analysts had been able to suggest—that they'd missed a flicker station, somewhere along the tramline chain—wasn't very helpful. He put the thought out of his mind. Right now, he had too many other things to worry about.

"Helm, take us to the RV point," he ordered. "XO, have the marines evacuated the shuttles?"

"Yes, Captain," Donker said. He glanced at his console. "We can handle the life support demands, for the moment. We'll be pushing it if we have to keep the marines for more than a week or two."

"Then we'll keep moving," Thomas said. Adding seven hundred marines to the crew would strain the life support to the limit, to say nothing of blocking corridors and generally making it harder to get from compartment to compartment, but they could handle it for a few days. The crew would cope. "I think we've outstayed our welcome."

He leaned back in his chair. They'd link up with the remainder of the squadron, jump to the next system and pause long enough to transfer the marines to the troopship, then head straight back to New Washington. They could make their report from there—he sighed as he remembered he'd have to write a detailed report himself—and then wait for orders. If they were lucky, they'd be ordered to travel straight to Earth. His lips quirked. Charlotte would be happy. Her last message had threatened him with another party.

And we won, he thought. He couldn't help feeling tired, but happy. *We gave the virus a nasty fright and...*

His mood soured. *And now we've proved the counter-virus works, we'll be using it again. And again. And how many people, humans and aliens, are we going to kill?*

CHAPTER FORTY

"YOU PROBABLY SAVED MY LIFE," Colin said.

Tobias said nothing. The trip back to Earth had been uneventful, uneventful enough for him to spend days and weeks second-guessing himself. Had he done the right thing? He'd spent entire nights lying in his bunk, wondering if he should have blown the shuttle out of space...or given the enemy an opening to do it instead. By the time they'd reached the homeworld, he was utterly unsure of himself. And then Colin had asked for a meeting, inviting him to the observation blister for a chat. Tobias had come very close to refusing to go.

"Thanks," he said, finally. He made a decision. Colin would never know how close he'd come to death. "What was it like, down there?"

"On the planet?" Colin's eyes darkened. "It was a nightmare."

Tobias nodded. "I can believe it."

"I never realised just how bad it could be," Colin said. "It wasn't my first encounter with the zombies, but...back then, it was nothing like as bad."

"I'm sure," Tobias said. He supposed the shock had done Colin some good. *He'd* never had the luxury of thinking himself the apex predator, not when Colin and his cronies had constantly reminded him he was right at the bottom of the pecking order. "What did you want to say?"

"I wanted to say thanks," Colin said. "And…I would like a chance to make things up to you."

Tobias looked him in the eye. "What can you offer that would make up for nearly two decades of mistreatment?"

Colin looked back at him. "What would you like?"

"I thought I'd already answered that," Tobias said. "But you can't give me what I want."

He sighed. "I could have killed you."

"I put the gun in your hand," Colin said. "All you had to do was pull the trigger."

Tobias frowned. He hadn't meant *that.* "You gave me a real gun?"

"A real gun, loaded and with the safety off," Colin said. "I thought you knew how to shoot."

"I just had a few lessons," Tobias said. He smiled, suddenly. He'd feared Colin would trick him, assuming he wouldn't know how to tell if the gun was loaded or not, but…Colin had assumed he *would* know. "They just told us to point one end at the enemy and pull the trigger. I kept missing my targets."

Colin smiled. "Would you like me to teach you? Properly, I mean?"

Tobias hesitated. "We might be assigned to different ships," he said. "We have a week's leave and then…and then what?"

"We might," Colin agreed. "The sergeant seems to think we—the marines, I mean—will stay together, rather than get broken up again. He might be wrong, but…I don't know. If we're on the same ship, though, would you like me to teach you?"

"I…" Tobias stared at the deck. He didn't know. Part of him wanted to say no, to have as little to do with Colin as possible; part of him was tempted to take lessons. He was a military spacer. He had an automatic right to carry a gun if he passed the basic firearms qualifications test. "If you're still here, then yes."

Colin nodded. "I'll drop you a note when I get back," he said. "I'm on my way to Liverpool."

"Ouch," Tobias said. "What did you do to deserve that?"

"I have people to see, things to do, you know how it is," Colin told him. He raised a hand. "I'll see you later."

Tobias nodded. "Have fun."

He turned and left the compartment, passing a pair of repair technicians as they surveyed the ship. Marigold and he were supposed to leave later in the day, heading for a few days on Luna before returning to Earth to meet the parents. Both parents...he felt his stomach twist at the thought of meeting Marigold's father. What would he make of Tobias?

It could be worse, he told himself, as he stepped into the sleeping compartment. *She could have brought home Colin.*

Marigold looked up at him. "Why the smile?"

"I just had a stupid thought," Tobias said. "Are you ready to go?"

"More or less," Marigold said. "And you?"

"I just have to shove everything in my bag," Tobias said. He felt oddly free, now Colin and he had come to an...understanding. He guessed it was part of growing up. "Do you think your father is going to like me?"

"He'll love you," Marigold said. "Take my word for it."

Tobias grinned. Things were definitely looking up.

"You performed well, both of you," Admiral Onarina said. She sat behind her desk, studying the mission logs. "Do you have any insights into the operation that *didn't* make their way into the reports?"

Thomas frowned. "Very few, Admiral," he said, finally. "My concerns about the BioBombs were not unfounded, I believe. They are, effectively, a genocidal weapon. There's no way we can hope to save even a fraction of the infected population, not even if the best medical care was available from the get-go. We condemned everyone on Brasilia to death."

"They were dead anyway," Captain Campbell pointed out. It wasn't the first time they'd had the argument. "They were trapped in a permanent state of living death. There was no way we could have saved them."

"No," the admiral agreed. "The virus does immense damage to its host, even if the host seeks immediate medical attention. Past a certain point, it is simply impossible to liberate the host or repair the damage. The bodily damage is bad enough, but the brain damage is worse. There's no way to save the host without killing the poor bastard in the process."

"The BioBombs were not *immediately* effective," Captain Campbell added. "The virus was able to realise the problem and take precautions, even though they weren't enough to save the settlement. It was canny enough to deploy suited hosts...something that probably impeded its operations as much as the counter-virus itself. I think it will be looking for a more... useful solution too. A counter-counter-virus, if you like."

"We'll be studying the records closely and trying to figure out ways to improve the counter-virus," Admiral Onarina said. "I think"—her eyes narrowed in contemplation—"there are a handful of possible options, now we've secured hard data from an infected world. It will give us time to regain our footing, produce newer and better ships and take the offensive."

"It will also encourage the virus to retaliate in kind," Thomas pointed out. "It may start looking for new ways to infect us."

Captain Campbell snorted. "What can it do," he asked, "that's worse than what it's *already* doing?"

Thomas smiled, humourlessly. "Do you want to find out the hard way?"

Admiral Onarina cleared her throat, loudly. "Those matters will be discussed in the War Cabinet and GATO," she said. "They'll make the final call. Until then"—she leaned forward—"I believe that both *Lion* and *Unicorn* performed well. Do you agree with that assessment?"

"Yes, Admiral," Thomas said. "I believe the design and concept has proved its value."

"Agreed," Captain Campbell said. "We need to work out how to handle the design more aggressively, but overall I think both ships have proved their value."

"Very good," the admiral said. "Enjoy your leave. I don't think there'll be any need to alter plans at this stage. We'll reconvene in a week or so."

Thomas nodded. They'd been warned their ships would be redeployed relatively quickly, once the damage had been repaired and their magazines restocked, but there'd been few actual details. The Admiralty had something planned, yet...he shrugged as he rose, saluted and headed for the hatch. They'd be told in due time, he was sure. Until then...

"My wife would like the pleasure of your company at another ball," he said, when he and Captain Campbell were outside. "You'd be welcome to stay at the hall again."

"I think I can find time," Captain Campbell assured him. "It just depends on where I am at the time."

Thomas nodded. "I'll forward you the details," he said. "And you'd be welcome."

Admiral Onarina watched the two men leave, uneasily aware that Captains Hammond and Campbell hadn't *quite* managed to establish a professional relationship. Their reports were bland, but—reading between the lines—it was easy to pick out stresses and strains and disagreements between the two men. Hammond was conservative, cold and careful and generally unwilling to lift a finger unless he thought the odds were in his favour; Campbell was a hard-charging fire-eater who'd throw himself into anything, as long as it wasn't *quite* suicide. Together, they would make a pretty good team. As polar opposites, on the other hand, they were likely to start working at cross purposes.

The intercom bleeped. "Admiral, Admiral Mason has arrived."

"Send him in," Susan ordered.

She smiled as the hatch opened, allowing Admiral Mason to step into the office. "Paul."

"Susan," Mason said. The hatch hissed closed behind him. "Did the meeting go well?"

"I assume you watched the debriefings," Susan said, dryly. She keyed a switch, activating the privacy wall, then pressed her finger against the terminal to bring up a bundle of highly-classified files. "There's some friction between the two of them."

"How terrible," Mason said. "How much friction was there between you and Captain Blake of unhappy memory?"

Susan gave him a sharp look. "I don't think Hammond or Campbell are in quite the same league," she said. Captain Blake had frozen in combat, something that had forced her to relieve him of command. She'd been very lucky to survive with her life, let alone her career. Being a war hero had its advantages. "They're not cowards or fools."

"Good." Mason took a seat facing her. "The BioBombs worked."

"Well enough," Susan agreed. She would have preferred something that spread as fast as the virus itself, but it seemed she wasn't going to get it. Not yet. "And I think we can proceed with Operation Grand Slam."

"If you can talk everyone into going along with it," Mason said. "And not everyone will."

"I know." Susan made a face. "Paul, you've seen the figures. Are we winning the war?"

Mason shook his head. "No."

"Quite," Susan agreed. She brought up the figures and stared at them. "We're being ground down, piece by piece. The virus is pushing us, and our allies, to the brink. And if we don't find a way to take the offensive—quickly—we'll lose."

Mason met her eyes. "And if the operation fails, we'll lose quicker."

Susan smiled, humourlessly. "Then we'd better not fail."

THE END

HMS Lion and HMS Unicorn Will Return In:
Fighting For The Crown
Coming Soon.

If You Enjoyed *The Lion and the Unicorn*,
You Might Like *Debt of Loyalty (The Embers of War II).*

PROLOGUE

THERE WAS BLOOD ON THE CAPTAIN'S CHAIR.

Lieutenant Commander Sarah Henderson tried not to think about Captain Saul as she took his seat. Saul had been a decent old man, for all that he'd been a dyed-in-the-wool reactionary who'd been reluctant to promote colonials when he could promote a Tyrian instead. She'd learned a great deal from the older man, from starship tactics to how to manipulate the system...and, perhaps unintentionally, just how badly slanted the system was against colonials. She'd thought, when she'd joined the navy, that there would be room for promotion, that she might climb to a command chair of her own. Instead, she'd discovered that most command chairs were reserved for Tyrians. She'd been lucky to be allowed to stay in the navy after the war had come to an end. She wasn't blind to the simple fact that most of the officers who'd been placed on half pay, transferred to the naval reserve, or simply let go had been colonials. The old resentment had curdled long before the civil war had broken out. She was good enough to fight, to risk her life, but not good enough to be promoted into a command chair of her own.

She took a long breath as she studied *Merlin*'s display. The mutiny hadn't been planned, not really. Sure, there had been times when she'd *thought* about taking the ship for herself, but it had been little more than an idle fantasy. Where would she go? A *Warlock*-class heavy cruiser was designed for long-duration missions, but *Merlin* would need a refit sooner or later. And what would she do? She hated pirates too much to become one, and there was little else she could do. But now...

It had happened so quickly, so quickly that part of her still couldn't believe that it *had* happened. It had been sheer goddamned luck that she'd been manning the communications console when the message came in, sheer goddamned luck that she'd been able to copy the message to a datapad and erase all traces from the message stream before Captain Saul or his XO had been able to see it. The orders had been clear—and devastating. All colonials, all naval personnel who weren't from Tyre itself, were to be rounded up and held prisoner until they could be transferred to holding facilities on a penal world. Sarah had no idea what had prompted the message, not then, but she'd seen an awful truth in the cold, hard words. She could fight, she could take control of the ship...or she could go tamely to her fate.

And my ancestors didn't tame their new home by being tame, she thought. She'd linked up with a dozen others, put together a plan at desperate speed, and taken the ship. The remainder of the crew—Tyrians, or colonials she couldn't vet personally—had been put into lockdown, where they would stay until...She didn't know. She honestly had no idea where to take her ship, not now. *If I go home, what happens then?*

She felt a worm gnawing at her heart as she paged through the starcharts. They were committed now. They had been committed from the moment the mutiny stopped being a theoretical exercise and turned deadly. There would be no mercy if the navy caught them. They'd be lucky if they were merely dumped on a penal colony, with a handful of supplies; they'd be more likely to be put in front of a firing squad and shot, their bodies unceremoniously cremated and the ashes dumped in the nearest sea. She knew they were committed...and yet, what were they to *do*?

A hundred ideas ran through her head. She could take the ship to *her* homeworld, but what then? The planetary government wouldn't be pleased to see them. They'd have no choice but to hand Sarah and her comrades over to Tyre for trial and execution. And even if that hadn't been a concern, the only thing that linked her and her comrades together was that they were all colonials. They came from a dozen different homeworlds. In hindsight, she wondered if that had been deliberate. The navy might have intended to spread its colonial recruits out as thinly as possible, just to keep them from developing any sort of planetary camaraderie. They were united by their dislike and resentment of the Tyrians, but disunited by everything else. No one would agree on where to take the ship if she put it to a vote.

And we shot the command structure to hell when we launched our mutiny. Her lips twitched in bitter amusement. *Who would back me if I tried to impose my authority by force?*

Sarah gazed around the bridge. There were only four officers on duty, three men and a woman she'd known for the last two years...but how far could she trust them? Really? She hadn't been the only officer to want to climb the ranks, no matter how hard the authorities tried to keep her down. She was only the *nominal* commanding officer, even though she'd planned and executed the mutiny. She'd set more than enough precedent for her mutineers to mutiny against *her...*

Lieutenant Olaf, the communications officer, glanced back at her. "Captain, we're picking up a push message from the local StarCom."

Sarah felt her expression harden. "Another one?"

"Yes, Captain," Olaf said. "It's being pushed out *everywhere*."

"Show me." Sarah let out a breath. It had been a push message that had started the whole goddamned affair in the first place. "We may as well hear the bad news directly."

King Hadrian's face appeared on the display. Sarah watched, feeling a multitude of emotions. The king had been the strongest supporter of the Commonwealth, before and during the war; he'd been the only one fighting for the Commonwealth on Tyre while the dukes and duchesses had been trying to draw back as much as possible. Sarah knew—it had been on all the newscasts—that the king had been pushing for more integration, for more investment...for everything that would make the Commonwealth *work*. And yet, he'd lost more than he'd won. The House of Lords had been steadily cutting the Commonwealth's budget. The cornucopia of resources and investment that had been offered to the colonials during the war had dried up almost as soon as the war had come to an end. Sarah had heard the news from home. Jobs had been lost, businesses were failing, banks were collapsing...They'd thought the good times would never end.

But they did, Sarah thought. *We really should have known better.*

She listened to the king's message with a growing sense of disbelief. The king had been forced to flee his homeworld? The king had been declared an outlaw? The king had led his loyalists to Caledonia, where they had established a government-in-exile...a government that claimed to be the legitimate government? And hundreds of ships, hundreds of thousands of loyalists, were rushing to join him, to fight for their rights against the cabal that had captured Tyre? It was madness...

But she'd heard the rumors. She'd seen the signs that all was not well. Perhaps, just perhaps, the outbreak of civil war was a matter of time.

Had been a matter of time, she corrected herself. The message ended with an appeal to loyalists, inviting them to join him. *The civil war is already here.*

She supposed that explained the message, the one that had sparked the mutiny. The king's loyalists must have been seizing ships, if they hadn't been in command already. His enemies would have moved to stop him... She had a vision, suddenly, of superdreadnought bridges being torn apart by gunfire as loyalists battled for control of their vessels. *Merlin* wouldn't be the only ship that had been taken by mutineers. There would be others. She hoped there would be others.

"We have to go," Lieutenant Vaclav said. "Where else *can* we go?"

Sarah contemplated her options carefully. They were painfully few. She couldn't surrender, not now. She couldn't take her ship to her homeworld, not without risking a mutiny or being arrested as soon as she arrived. She couldn't abandon the ship without risking being caught the moment she passed through a bioscanner. She couldn't become a pirate or mercenary or anything else without...She looked down at the uniform she wore. She liked to think it still meant something, even though it was splattered with blood. The king wasn't just their *best* option. He was their only *realistic* option.

There was nowhere else to go.

"Nowhere," she said. She straightened up in the command chair. "Set course for Caledonia."

"Aye, Captain," Vaclav said.

And hope to hell we don't get intercepted along the way, Sarah thought as she felt her ship thrumming to life. *They could have set up a blockade by now if they had time to get organized.*

She kept her face impassive, keeping her doubts to herself. The StarCom network wasn't known as the net of a trillion lies for nothing. Even with the latest advancements in interstellar FTL communications, with messages relayed through a dozen nodes rather than simply radiating out of Tyre, it was still possible for *someone* to take control of the network...or simply use it to spread lies. There was no way to tell the difference between truth and lies, not from a distance. They were possibly flying straight into a trap.

But we have nowhere else to go, she thought. *We'll just have to do our best to avoid contact until we reach Caledonia.*

CHAPTER ONE

CALEDONIA

"TRANSIT COMPLETE, ADMIRAL," Lieutenant Kitty Patterson said. "We have reached Caledonia."

"Transmit our IFF codes," Admiral Lady Katherine Falcone ordered. She felt numb, too tired and worn to be relieved that they'd finally reached their destination. "And keep the vortex generator in readiness."

"Aye, Admiral," Kitty said.

Kat sat back in her chair, one hand brushing blonde hair out of her face. It had been a nightmarish voyage, even though the task force had avoided enemy contact...*enemy* contact, damn it. Thinking of her comrades as enemies hurt deeply. She knew there would be ships and crews that had remained loyal to the House of Lords, commanding officers who owed their positions to patronage or crews that simply didn't understand what was at stake...She knew it was only a matter of time before fighting broke out in earnest. The brief exchange of missiles at Tyre had made it clear, brutally, that the time for talking was over. The dispute could be settled only by war.

She forced herself to watch the display as more and more icons flashed to life, heedless of her churning thoughts. Everything had happened so *quickly.* She'd known trouble was brewing, everyone had known trouble was brewing, but she hadn't expected a descent into violence and civil war. She hadn't expected to have to make a choice between supporting her king or her family. She hadn't expected...

None of us expected this, she thought. *And perhaps, if we'd taken the possibility of war more seriously, this would never have happened.*

She gritted her teeth as her sensors picked out massive orbital fortresses, each one packing enough firepower to give a superdreadnought a very bad day. The king had been confident that Caledonia would side with him—he'd been pouring resources and investment into the colony world for years—but Kat didn't dare take it for granted. If Caledonia sided with the House of Lords instead...She shook her head. She wasn't blind to just how badly the colonials had been treated, even during the war. It was unlikely that anyone on Caledonia would feel any real allegiance to the House of Lords, whatever they felt for the king. She knew many of them would want to sit on the sidelines and do as little as possible for either side.

"They're hailing us," Kitty said. "They're requesting permission to speak to the king."

"Relay the message to him," Kat ordered curtly. "And order the fleet to hold position here."

"Aye, Admiral."

This would never have happened if my father had survived, Kat thought glumly. Lucas Falcone had been a stiff-necked old bastard, but he'd been a *man*. He'd understood the importance of winning the peace as well as the war, the dangers of constantly slashing budgets and cutting spending when people were desperate. He'd understood that desperation could lead to war. *And he would never have pulled ships out of the occupied zone until peace was firmly established.*

She let out a breath, feeling sweat prickling down her back. If there was one thing that had angered her, just one thing, it was how the House of Lords had played politics while the occupied zone had burned. She'd watched helplessly as chaos had swept across the region, planets collapsing into civil war or being raided by pirates or simply being hit with genocidal attacks by the remnants of the Theocracy. The war had been won—she'd emerged triumphant from the deciding battle—but the peace had been constantly on the verge of being lost without a trace. Every starship that had been pulled from her command, every marine regiment that had been sent back home...Everything she'd lost had meant more dead people, more destroyed lives, more hopelessness and desperation and...

We promised those people that we'd protect them, she told herself again and again. *And then we abandoned them.*

She felt a surge of bitter anger. She'd never got on with her oldest brother, but she'd thought better of him. He'd been an adult when she'd been born, a young man who had acted more like a third parent when he'd had time for her at all. She'd never realized that he would abandon the people the Commonwealth had promised to help. He'd sat in his chair, in their *father's* chair, and pronounced a death sentence for hundreds of thousands of people he'd never met and never would. And he'd done it because of politics. He hadn't had any personal hatred for the dead. They'd simply been collateral damage.

Her console chimed. The king's face appeared in front of her. "Admiral?"

"Your Majesty," Kat said stiffly.

"We're welcome here," he said. His handsome face betrayed no trace of the concern he must have felt. "Take the fleet into orbit, then join us for a planning session."

"Yes, Your Majesty," Kat said.

The king smiled, warmly. He didn't look *that* put out, for someone who'd been forced to flee his homeworld at very short notice. He looked every inch a monarch, from his handsome face to a perfectly tailored naval uniform. But then, Kat supposed he found the outbreak of civil war to be something of a relief. The endless circle of politics, the endless debates over the same issue, time and time again with no resolution in sight...over. He didn't have to argue for hours over the slightest concession, over something that could be withdrawn at a moment's notice. He could finally command his own ship.

"You've done well, Kat," he said. "Thanks to you, we will thrive."

"Thank you, Your Majesty," Kat said. "I have a small matter to attend to first."

She couldn't help feeling conflicted as the king's image vanished from the display. The war wouldn't just be waged against the House of Lords. It would be waged against her family, against men and women she'd known since she was a little girl...She wouldn't be the only one, she was sure, torn in two. How many people would be asking themselves which side they should take? And how many would try to steer a course between the two until neutrality was no longer an option?

And how many will be laying contingency plans for defeat as well as victory? The thought mocked her. She knew her fellows too well to have doubts. *The loudest among them, baying for the king's blood, will be planning how best to surrender if he wins the war.*

She stood. "Order the fleet to enter orbit, as planned," she said. "And then...order all off-duty personnel to assemble in the shuttlebay."

"Aye, Admiral," Kitty said.

Kat took one last look at the display—the orbital fortresses were sweeping space with powerful active sensors, but weren't charging their weapons or launching missiles—and strode through the hatch into her ready room. *Her* private space, perhaps the only truly private space on the ship. Everyone else was sharing quarters, doubling or tripling up as the king's staffers and allies crowded onto the ship. Even the king himself was sharing quarters with his fiancée, Princess Drusilla. Kat felt her lips twitch sourly. She didn't *like* the princess—her instincts told her Drusilla was trouble, but the king evidently disagreed.

She put the thought aside as she splashed water on her face, changed into a clean uniform, and studied herself in the mirror. The uniform was pristine, her face was clear...but her hair was unkempt, her eyes tired. She ran her fingers through her hair. She'd allowed it to grow out over the last few months, when she'd been stationed in the occupied zone, but she'd get a cut close to her scalp as soon as possible. She couldn't allow herself to grow lax. She'd done too much of that over the last six months.

And we were the most well-drilled unit in the postwar navy, she thought. *The rest of the fleet must be much worse.*

She scowled, feeling a pang of loss. It was terrifying how quickly standards had fallen once the war had been won. She'd seen too many officers neglect their duties, forsaking drills that taught their crews vital skills; too many experienced officers and crewmen had been pushed out of the service while inexperienced officers with the right connections had been allowed to keep their ranks. Kat had done what she could to arrest that trend during her last deployment. She dreaded to think how badly the other peacetime deployments had neglected the fundamentals. They'd been more concerned with saving money than saving lives.

Maybe William was right to get out when he did, she thought. *Leave on a high note.*

She wondered, as she walked through the hatch and down the corridor, just what had happened to her former XO. She'd taken him back to Tyre, but...He hadn't rejoined the fleet in time to leave the system. Where was he? Had he been sent back to Asher Dales? Or was he under arrest? William was, technically, her family's client. What would Duke Peter Falcone, Kat's oldest brother, have made of him? A hero? A traitor? Or someone who had merely been in the wrong place at the wrong time? Kat wished, in hindsight, that she'd kept William on her ship. It would have been good to have his support over the last two weeks.

A handful of crewmen were hurrying into the giant shuttlebay as she approached, their faces pale. There had been all sorts of rumors flying through the ship, even though there hadn't been any official announcement of...well, *anything*. A couple of the king's staffers had complained about the rumors; they'd even demanded she shut the rumormongers down, but Kat had merely shrugged. One could no more stop rumors than one could stop the tide by shouting at it. Sure, she could put a handful of loudmouths in the brig...but what then? That would simply suggest—to anyone who cared to look—that the worst of the rumors were true.

"Admiral." Captain Akbar Rosslyn was standing by the hatch, looking grim. "They're ready for you."

Kat nodded her thanks and stepped past him, into the shuttlebay. The giant deck had been cleared, the shuttles and landing craft pushed against the far bulkhead so the crew could gather as a body. Chatter hummed through the air as Kat took the makeshift stand and looked down at the gathered crew. There were hundreds of warm bodies in the shuttlebay, only a fraction of the superdreadnought's entire crew. The remainder would be on duty or listening in from the other shuttlebays. It took more than three thousand officers and crewmen to operate a superdreadnought.

Although we could do the job with fewer people if we didn't mind losing efficiency, she reminded herself. A marine sergeant bellowed for silence. *A small crew couldn't fight the ship once she started taking damage.*

She waited for quiet, studying the crew. It was strange to realize that the chain of command had been badly weakened over the last two weeks, even though there hadn't been any serious incidents. She'd studied history. Civil wars weakened the bonds between people, fragmenting society into smaller groups...She frowned inwardly. The only thing linking the various colonies together was the Commonwealth itself. If the Commonwealth fell, the colonials would fragment. A chilling thought. The association of worlds she'd sworn to serve was, in many ways, a victim of its own success.

"Two weeks ago, civil war broke out." Kat kept her voice calm, even though she knew she was giving voice to the worst of the rumors. "The dispute between the House of Lords and King Hadrian turned violent. It is unlikely that the crisis can now be settled by anything but force of arms. I, and this ship, have joined the king."

She paused, choosing her next words carefully. Some of her crew would fight for *her*. Others, colonials all, would fight for the man they saw as their ally and protector. Still others would do their jobs without thinking about the wider implications. And others...They wouldn't fight for the king, not against their own people. Or they wouldn't share the grievances that had kick-started the civil war.

"If you want to join us, to fight for the king, you are welcome. I won't attempt to influence your choice. You should choose your side for whatever reason makes sense to you. If you *don't* want to fight for the king, you can either go into an internment camp on the planet's surface or travel straight back to Tyre. We will make transport arrangements as soon as possible. You have my word that no one will be hindered if they want to return to Tyre."

A low rustle ran through the gathered crowd. She didn't give it time to build.

"Make your choice, whichever one you want to make," she said. "But whatever choice you make, stick with it. I won't fault anyone who wants to leave now. Afterwards...I need the crew to be united. There will be no chance to switch sides later, once the fighting begins in earnest."

And anyone who tries to switch sides later will be seen as a traitor, she mused as she surveyed the crowd. *And he'll be lucky if he only spends the rest of his life in the brig.*

"If you want to leave, let your section chief know and report to Shuttlebay A by 2100," she concluded. "The marines will transport you somewhere safe, at least until we can arrange transport. If you want to stay, just remain in your place and resume your normal duties. I will be happy to have you."

She stepped down and headed for the hatch, ignoring the chatter behind her. She'd meant what she'd said. She wasn't going to try to influence them, even though she knew she *could*. The Royal Navy had been an all-volunteer force from day one, when there had been only a handful of destroyers to protect Tyre, and that wasn't about to change now. Besides, trying to run a navy with conscripts was difficult and dangerous. The Theocrats had found that out the hard way.

And our crewmen are far from ignorant, she reminded herself. *A handful of resentful crewers could do a great deal of damage if they decided to rebel instead of submit.*

She winced at the thought. She'd never understood how the Theocratic navy had managed to function. There were limits to how far one could brutalize one's crews before the starships started to fall apart, if the crew didn't mutiny first. The Royal Navy had never made that mistake, thankfully. Tyre trusted its crewmen. But it also meant the crewmen couldn't be press-ganged into fighting for either side. Better to lose half her crew than risk having a mutiny at the worst possible moment.

General Timothy Winters met her outside the shuttlebay. "Admiral, we've borrowed a colonist-carrier from Caledonia for the…ah…*dissenters*," he said. "They should have no trouble getting home."

"Good," Kat said. A colonist-carrier had the great advantage of looking harmless. The defenders of Tyre might be jumpy after everything that had happened, but they were unlikely to slam an antimatter missile into a colonist-carrier, particularly one that was careful not to violate the planetary defense perimeter. "And your men?"

Winters looked impassive. His voice was disapproving. "We had a few desertions, Admiral. But most of my troops chose to remain."

"It's important they have a free choice, General," Kat said, although she knew saying it would be pointless. She'd done her best to keep her thumb off the scales, but she was uneasily aware that there would be people who would feel pressured into making a choice that didn't sit well with them. "We…This isn't what we signed up for, when we took the oath."

"No," Winters said. "But that doesn't mean we can change our minds when the shit hits the fan."

Kat shrugged. The Theocracy had been a serious threat when she'd joined up. Everyone—at least, everyone with a gram of sense—had known that war was coming. But no one had seriously expected a civil war, not back then. It was unreasonable to expect everyone to be *happy* with the prospect of firing on their own people. She would have been seriously worried about anyone who *was*.

"Don't pressure anyone," she said. "Just…give them the same chance."

She nodded, then walked down the corridor. The next few days were going to be very busy. She would have to reorganize everything from crew rotas to squadron formations, transferring officers and crewmen all over the fleet to fill the gaps in her roster. It was going to be a nightmare, even if she could pass most of the work to her subordinates. She wondered, sourly, what she'd do if her staffers chose to go home. She'd never really understood how important staff officers were until she'd been promoted. *Someone* had to turn the commanding officer's orders into reality.

Two of the king's personal guardsmen were on duty outside the VIP section. They checked her identity and scanned her for concealed weapons, then waved her through the hatch. Kat snorted at their paranoia, although she understood their concern. The superdreadnought was an alien environment, manned by crewmen who hadn't been thoroughly vetted. Who knew how many crewmen might try to end the civil war by murdering the king?

"Admiral," a quiet voice said as she passed through. A short man was standing by the king's cabin, waiting for her. "We need to talk."

CHAPTER TWO

CALEDONIA

KAT DIDN'T KNOW SIR GRANTHAM THAT WELL.

He was one of the king's privy councilors, one of his foremost advisers, but he and Kat had hardly shared the same social circles. He'd been knighted at some point, suggesting that he'd done the kingdom some service, yet the act hadn't made the news. Kat knew there was a lot that *didn't* make the news, of course, but she should have heard whispers if it was something classified. The fact she hadn't heard anything meant…*what*? She didn't know.

And she didn't really like him. She wasn't sure why. He was handsome, in a bland way that suggested he'd had cosmetic surgery rather than having his genetics engineered or relying on blind chance. His brown hair and wry smile made him look warm and friendly, although there was an edge to his posture that suggested it was an act. Maybe she was bothered by the hints of sycophancy, of a social climber trying to make his way to the top through any means necessary. God knew she'd met enough social climbers in her early life. She could have surrounded herself with a small army of sycophants from birth if she'd wished.

But he is completely dependent on the king, Kat reminded herself, as she allowed Sir Grantham to lead her into a small conference room. *He has no independent power base or wealth of his own.*

The thought stung, more than she'd expected. *She* didn't have an independent power base now, insofar as she'd ever had. She'd been her father's client, for all intents and purposes; now, technically, she'd betrayed her family by siding with the king. Her trust fund had probably been confiscated, at least until she gave a full accounting of herself and sought her family's forgiveness. The thought made her snort. Her brother had never liked her. He'd sooner see her starve than forgive her...

She rested her hands on her hips as she turned to face Sir Grantham. "What do you want?"

Sir Grantham looked, just for a second, unsure of himself. "We have to talk," he said finally. The hatch hissed closed behind them. "We..."

"Then *talk*," Kat said. She had too much to do. The fleet had to be reorganized, the crews had to be shunted around...She simply didn't have *time* for a long and pointless chat. She'd never liked high society's habit of using ten words when only one would do, and she had no intention of embracing it now. "What do you want?"

"You're sending half your crew back home," Sir Grantham said. "Back to the *enemy*."

The enemy, Kat thought. A month ago, everyone had been on the same side. It was hard to believe that the Commonwealth was now irreparably split in two, that they were about to start shooting at each other. *We're already thinking of them as the enemy?*

She kept her face carefully blank. "Yes. So?"

Sir Grantham flushed. "You're giving aid and comfort to the enemy!"

Kat took a long breath. "Would you rather I kept unwilling crewmen on this ship?"

"You shouldn't have sent them back to Tyre," Sir Grantham said. "I..."

"Let me put it to you as simply as I can." Kat met his eyes, silently daring him to look away. "Spacers, soldiers, marines...They're not *machines*.

None of them signed up to fight their former comrades. None of them. They joined to defend the Commonwealth or fight the Theocracy or simply because they wanted adventure and excitement...They didn't join up to fight a civil war. And we dragged hundreds of thousands of crewmen all the way to Caledonia without so much as *asking* if they want to join us."

"They should follow orders," Sir Grantham insisted. "They're paid to—"

"*Legitimate* orders." Kat cut him off. "There's no provision in the Articles of War for *civil* war. They didn't know they would be fighting their former comrades when they joined up."

"And so you want to send them back home?" Sir Grantham sounded astonished. "You should keep them here..."

"And then what?" Kat held his gaze. "There will be—there *are*—crewmen in this fleet who don't support the king. What am I meant to do with them? Hold mass executions? Throw them out the airlock? Dump them on a penal world? You know what? I don't even know which members of my crew might support the king! Perhaps I should just start shooting crewmen at random."

Sir Grantham flushed. "You know what I mean."

"I *don't* know what you mean," Kat corrected, coldly. "Please. Enlighten me."

"The crewmen you're sending home will join the enemy," Sir Grantham said. "You're *helping* them to..."

Kat let out a long breath. "First, it probably doesn't matter. The House of Lords is not short of manpower. We're not going to be sending entire squadrons of superdreadnoughts into their welcoming arms. They will have no trouble mustering a fleet, if we give them time, with or without the crewmen we're sending back. It simply does not matter.

"Second, and I want you to think carefully about this, what sort of message do you think it sends to everyone, the people on both sides, if we *don't* let our crews vote their conscience?"

She didn't give him a chance to answer. "I'll tell you what sort of message it sends. It suggests that we don't give a damn about the people who fight for us, that we are willing to press-gang crewmen into fighting for us...that we are dragging people who have nothing to do with our fight—who don't *want* anything to do with our fight, who don't give a damn who comes out on top—*into* our fight. That we are *forcing* them to fight for us. Do you really want a mutiny? Or someone trying to sabotage the ship?"

"They'll follow orders," Sir Grantham insisted.

"It only takes one person to cause a great deal of trouble," Kat said. "If we force people to fight for us, they will resent it. They will see us as the enemy even if they see our cause as *right*. The ones who don't really care about our cause will sympathize with the ones who see *us* as the enemy, because we press-ganged them into fighting for us. We cannot afford to treat our crew as *slaves*. Slaves can revolt."

She sighed inwardly, knowing he wouldn't understand. He'd probably grown up among the lesser aristocracy, at a guess, the ones who obsessed over status and social precedence, the ones who snapped and snarled whenever someone of lesser birth threatened to climb past them...the ones who clung to their social pretensions because they simply didn't have anything else. To them, the servants—their butlers, their maids, even their bodyguards—were just tools. The idea that they might have thoughts and feelings of their own was alien to them.

"I did what I had to do," she said, firmly. "This way, we know that the people who fight for us genuinely *want* to fight for us. And the remainder of the crew will know it too. It will be harder, much harder, for any dissenters to plot a mutiny or sabotage the ship."

"You weakened us," Sir Grantham protested.

Kat allowed her gaze to sharpen. "I would sooner take an undermanned ship into battle than risk having my crew turn on me," she said firmly. "And I will *not* betray my crewmen by forcing them into a war they didn't volunteer to fight."

"We have to win," Sir Grantham said. "And that means..."

". . . Not doing things that might cost us the war?" Kat strode past him. "I am in command of this fleet. If you have a complaint about the way I do things, take it to His Majesty. He can tell me what he thinks of your complaints."

She stopped by the hatch, slowly turning to face him. "And if you try to interfere with the off-loading, I will break you."

Sir Grantham purpled. Kat was sure he was trying to think of a response, of a crushing remark that would send her to her knees, but she didn't give him time. Instead, she turned back to the hatch and walked through. The hatch hissed closed behind her, leaving him in the conference room. She wasn't really surprised he hadn't tried to follow her. She'd put him in his place.

I sounded just like my cousin, Kat thought sourly. She'd never really *liked* Cousin Olivia, who'd married well and didn't let anyone forget it. *And she would have been a great deal nastier as she cut him off at the knees.*

Her lips twitched as she made her way down the corridor, passing a handful of open cabins where the king's staffers and closest supporters, the ones who couldn't remain on Tyre without being arrested or forced into exile, were making their preparations to disembark. Kat's crew would be glad to see the last of them. The superdreadnought was no *Supreme*, no interstellar liner with gold-plated bulkheads and staffers willing to do anything, anything at all, for a hefty tip. Kat had had to put one of the aristocrats in the brig for harassing a young crewman. The dumb bastard hadn't realized, somehow, that he wasn't in his estate any longer. Or, for that matter, that no one had to put up with his conduct. He'd been lucky not to have his lights punched out.

A pair of servants hurried past her, carrying a large trunk. Kat wondered idly what its owner had packed, then decided it probably didn't matter. The king himself had packed well—he'd been one of the few people to realize he might have to leave Tyre—but the others hadn't had much time to think about such eventualities. Kat had read the security reports. Some of the aristocrats had brought clothes and money, in a number of interstellar denominations; others, less practical or simply caught on the hop, had brought everything from shooting gear, as if they were going on safari, to works of art and other absurd comforts. She found it hard to believe that anyone could be so stupid.

But I suppose they could sell the paintings, if they desperately needed money, she reflected as she reached the final cabin. *They'd just have to find a buyer...*

She pressed her hand against the scanner and waited. The king's guardsmen had been horrified when it had dawned on them that it was difficult, very difficult, to keep the superdreadnought's crew out of Officer Country. The superdreadnought was no luxury liner, with firm lines between first-, second-, and steerage-class passengers. The guardsmen had wanted to seal off the whole section, but the king had overruled them. Kat rather suspected her old friend was enjoying his freedom, such as it was. He'd never sailed on a superdreadnought before.

The hatch hissed open, allowing her to step inside. The quarters, designed for an admiral, were palatial by naval standards, which hadn't stopped some of the aristocrats from openly wondering if they'd been dumped in *midshipman* cabins. Kat honestly hadn't known if she should laugh or cry when she'd heard the complaints. Midshipmen, even *aristocratic* midshipmen, could only dream of having a boxy compartment to themselves. They simply didn't have enough room to swing a cat.

And they have to share it with a handful of others, Kat reflected. She'd enjoyed her first cruise, but the lack of privacy had grated on her. *They would kill just to have the compartment to themselves.*

She looked around the compartment, feeling an odd twinge of discomfort. The quarters had been hers a couple of weeks ago. She'd moved into her ready room to provide space for the king, his princess, and his attendants. They hadn't changed the compartment much, she noted, save for the handful of boxes stacked awkwardly against the far bulkhead. The portrait of her father she'd hung on one bulkhead hadn't been removed. She wondered, grimly, what her father would have thought of the civil war. It was hard to believe that the situation would have spun so badly out of control if her father hadn't been assassinated at the end of the war.

The last *war,* she reminded herself. She'd never really been at peace, even after the formal end of the Theocratic War. *How quickly we forget.*

A hatch opened. She straightened to attention as the king stepped out of the bedroom, wearing his carefully tailored naval uniform. He looked good in it, Kat had to admit, although he'd never served a day in his life. His advisers hadn't either, she guessed; he might not know it, but he didn't *hold* himself like a naval officer. His posture was a little *too* sharp, his bearing a little *too* authoritative. But he'd look good on the holovid, she supposed, and that was all that mattered.

"Kat," the king said. "Thank you for coming."

"Your Majesty," Kat said.

She bobbed her head. They'd known each other since childhood, although the demands of their respective social classes had kept them from being too close. And she was a privy councilor in her own right. She had the right to call him by his first name, if she wished. But she knew better. They *had* to tend to the formalities, now that the established order was starting to fracture. They had to keep telling themselves that very little had changed. Who knew? Perhaps the pretense would be enough to make it so.

The king grinned. He'd always been handsome, with dark hair, dark eyes, and a roguish look that had melted more than one heart. Kat had heard the rumors about the king's girlfriends, although none of them had ever been confirmed. It was hard to take them on faith when she knew the rumors that the king had engaged in an affair with her were complete fabrications. Her lips twitched at the absurd thought. An affair with the king? She was sure she would have noticed if she'd had an affair with the king. She liked and respected him—not least because he was the only one who'd fought for colonial rights—but they'd never been more than friends and allies.

"I hear that you're disembarking some of your crew," the king said. He gave her a reassuring smile. "I *quite* understand."

"Thank you, Your Majesty." Kat kept her face impassive. "Sir Grantham has already tried to tell me off for it."

The king shrugged. "Some of my advisers feel that it is a mistake."

"Keeping them would be an even *greater* mistake," Kat pointed out, again. "We don't want people who haven't committed themselves to our cause."

She shook her head in irritation. She had little patience for politics, for endless debates over pettifogging issues when there were *real* problems on the horizon. Politicians seemed to produce nothing these days but hot air... while *real* people were robbed, raped, and murdered. Her father, at least, had been an exception. She wondered, bitterly, why he hadn't taught his oldest son the difference between important matters and petty politics before it was too late. The king might have been inexperienced, at least before the Theocratic War, but at least he had a good head on his shoulders. He knew not to waste time with nonsense.

"Quite," the king said. "There will be others who will join us, of course."

"Of course," Kat echoed. The Commonwealth had been fracturing into two camps well before the shooting had actually begun. Now...Everyone who wanted to fight would be heading to Caledonia. "Why do you keep him around?"

The king blinked. "I beg your pardon?"

"Sir Grantham," Kat said. She knew why most of the privy councilors had been chosen, but Sir Grantham was a mystery. "Why is he on the privy council?"

"He's a fixer," the king said, simply. "He gets things done for me."

"Ah," Kat said.

The king's smile grew wider. "I'll be transferring myself to Caledonia this afternoon," he told her. "The people down there"—he jabbed a finger at the deck—"have already laid on a reception, after which we will discuss reclaiming Tyre before our enemies rally their troops and prepare for war. You'll be joining us?"

"Of course," Kat said. "It would be my pleasure."

That was a lie. She would have preferred to remain on her flagship, but she knew it wasn't really a request. Besides, she would have to ensure that the king and his councilors didn't come up with a plan that looked good on paper but would fail spectacularly the moment someone tried to put it into practice. She'd seen enough problems caused by armchair admirals not to want to let the councilors dictate the course of the war. They were good people, in their way, but they were not experienced military officers. She shuddered to think how many lives had been lost, during the *last* war, because too many officers had never fought a real war.

"Very good," the king said. "I'm sure you'll enjoy it."

"We'll see," Kat said. She was pretty sure that was a lie too. "But I don't have much time to waste. I'll be needed back aboard ship fairly soon."

"We have time," the king said. He sounded confident, for someone who had never witnessed combat from the flag deck. "It will take them weeks, perhaps months, to organize themselves for war."

"Yes," Kat said. True, as far as it went. But her duty consisted of pouring cold water on his thoughts. "And it will take us a long time too."

CHAPTER THREE

CALEDONIA

CALEDONIA, KAT RECALLED, had been a surprisingly well-developed world when the Commonwealth's expanding border had washed through its system. Indeed, in many ways, Caledonia had been an *ideal* candidate for membership. The system had a small but growing industrial base, a thriving educational base, and a handful of freighters plying the spacelanes, helping to reinvigorate interstellar trade. But Caledonia had been hampered by the Commonwealth itself. Tyre had seen Caledonia as a rival, a potential threat; Tyre had manipulated the Commonwealth's structure to ensure that Caledonia would always be second-best. Kat rather suspected the move had been nothing more than petty, pointless evil. In the short term, it had worked; in the long term, an entire planet had become enraged and united against Tyre.

And the king was able to position himself as the protector of the small, Kat thought, as they finally, *finally*, headed for the royal residence. *The entire planet loves him.*

She didn't blame the planet for welcoming the king, their savior. It had been the king who'd insisted on establishing shipyards and industrial nodes at Caledonia, the king who'd invested *trillions* of crowns in the planet's infrastructure...the king who'd argued for the planet to be heavily defended, who'd pushed for defending *every* planet in the Commonwealth even though such measures prolonged the war. The contradiction amused her more than she cared to admit. Caledonia loathed Tyre but adored Tyre's king. He could literally get away with murder, as far as the locals were concerned. He'd worked hard to earn their goodwill.

Kat felt tired, a deep, aching tiredness that pervaded every inch of her body. She detested formalities, but ever since the shuttle had landed, there'd been nothing but formalities. An endless series of speeches from local dignitaries, all of which had blurred together in her mind, followed by a long parade, where everyone on the planet seemed to want to shake the king's hand or meet his eyes. She hadn't been the only one, surely, who worried about what a lone gunman could do when the king was in the open. A sniper could have put a bullet through the king's head with ease if he'd had the chance. The security cordon had been almost pitifully weak. She was relieved when they finally entered the palace, leaving the crowds behind. And yet, part of her wanted only to return to the ship. The latest set of updates had suggested she'd lost a third of her crew.

It could have been worse, she told herself as the staff showed them into the conference chamber. *We could have been stuck with all officers and no crewmen.*

She looked around the chamber, not bothering to disguise her interest. The space was quite efficiently designed, certainly in comparison to the conference rooms back home. The walls were paneled with dark wood, and a painting of the *previous* king hung on the far wall, but otherwise the chamber was strikingly modern. There had been no attempt to hide the holoprojector or the drinks cabinet, no attempt to pretend that the chamber dated back to a bygone age. Kat had always found the pretensions amusing, when they hadn't been awkward. There wasn't a person alive who remembered the days before FTL travel and high technology. She didn't think there was anyone on Tyre who'd been born on Old Earth.

A serving girl wearing a strikingly conservative uniform offered her a mug of coffee. Kat took it gratefully, nodding her thanks. The servants looked pleased to be fawning on the king—although, the cynical part of her mind noted, their fawning wasn't quite up to Tyrian standards. She wondered, as the servants were shooed out of the chamber, just how they'd cope with the king and his court. Too many people in his retinue were used to taking their servants for granted.

And he'll have to deal with it, somehow, she thought. The king might be popular and lauded, but that wouldn't last. If he wore out his welcome, the planet might turn on him and his followers. Kat had no illusions. Caledonia's orbital fortresses could blow the hell out of her fleet if they opened fire at point-blank range. *We'll have to do whatever it takes to keep them onside.*

Sir Grantham rose. "Ladies and gentlemen, the king!"

Hadrian waved for his councilors to remain in their seats, then leaned forward. "We are at war," he said. "The time for talking is over. The issues between us, between the Monarchy and the House of Lords, can only be settled by violence."

He lowered his voice. "The universe does not *care* who is in the right, my friends. The universe doesn't give a damn if our cause is just, if we are righteous souls; we do not have the strength of ten because our hearts are pure. There is no time, now, for debating the rights and wrongs of the situation. The time for talking is over. This is the time of war. Might may not make right, as many have argued; might determines what happens. The winners of this war will be the ones who determine what is *right*."

Kat shivered, despite herself. She knew he was right.

"There is no room for compromise," the king continued, coolly. "We cannot come to terms we, or they, would find acceptable. Either we win and impose our will on them, or they win and crush us. There is no middle ground. We will not negotiate with them on major issues, because there is no way to come to terms. We will discuss minor issues with them, such as trading our loyalists for theirs, but nothing else. I want everyone to be absolutely clear on this. We are at war. There is no room for half measures."

There was a long, chilling pause. Lord Gleneden spoke first.

"Your Majesty," he said. "Are you proposing that we fight an *uncivilized* war?"

Kat winced. Lord Gleneden had always struck her as being conservative, so conservative that she was surprised he'd remained on the privy council, but his expertise as an economist was unmatched. He'd worked closely with Kat's father when they'd prepared the Commonwealth for war. And he'd served the *king's* father, practically from birth. He might be conservative, but he wasn't disloyal.

Hadrian looked annoyed. "No. I am making it clear that we cannot reach a compromise that both sides can accept."

"And how far are we prepared to go?" Lord Gleneden pressed, sharply. "Because we may have an edge in the short term, Your Majesty, but *they* have the long-term advantage."

"Then we take advantage of what we have." Earl Antony thumped the table with one meaty fist. "We move now to retake Tyre and crush our enemies!"

Kat felt a flash of irritation. Earl Antony genuinely *did* have military experience, but it had been in the planetary militia. He'd never seen real action. And, like all people who didn't have experience, he underestimated just how difficult it could be in wartime to get the slightest thing done. He'd never had to worry about moving troops from one place to another, making sure they arrived on time and armed...He'd never had to actually *fight*, outside training exercises. He'd done well on the tests, Kat had to admit, but exercises always left out the *real* emergency. A platoon of Royal Marines would have wiped out a militia regiment before its commanders even realized they were under attack.

"We will fight according to the Articles of War," she said firmly. "It is important, particularly now, that we honor the rules. This war could easily spin out of control if we don't."

"The Theocracy didn't give a *damn* about the Articles of War," Earl Antony snapped. "You should have nuked Ahura Mazda to retaliate for what they did to Hebrides!"

Kat cocked her head. "And how many *billions* of innocent civilians would have died, if I had?"

"They were enemies," Earl Antony hissed. "They had no right—"

"I was there." Kat cut him off, her voice as sharp as a knife. "The average person on Ahura Mazda—male, female, whatever—had *no* power. They could no more have stopped the war and brought their leaders to heel than I could repeal the law of gravity! And they didn't deserve to be slaughtered simply because their leaders were utter bastards!"

She met the king's eyes, willing him to understand. "This is a civil war. The people we will be facing—the people we will be trying to kill, the people who will be trying to kill *us*—are our people, our friends and families and countrymen. We will have to live with them after the war comes to an end, whoever wins. We cannot hope to win by turning the homeworld, *our* homeworld, to glass. We have to put limits on what we are prepared to do to win.

"If nothing else"—she allowed her eyes to sweep around the table, silently gauging their reactions—"we have to convince them that they *can* surrender. That we *will* treat them with honor, if they come to terms with us. That there *is* a future with us...

"If we don't, they'll fight to the last. And they might win."

Another pause grew and lengthened.

"Anyone who fights for the House of Lords, against the king, is committing treason," Earl Antony growled finally.

"Technically, perhaps," Kat said. It might be true, but the issue would be decided by whoever won the war. "But if we start refusing to accept surrenders, or mistreating people who do surrender, they won't surrender. Why should they?"

The king nodded slowly. "We will fight according to the Articles of War," he said. "And yes, we will accept surrenders."

Kat allowed herself a moment of relief. Attitudes would harden, she knew. The war would make sure of it. Earl Antony wasn't the only one to argue that the Commonwealth should have repaid mass slaughter and genocide in kind, even though it would have been futile. She doubted the Theocracy's leaders would have cared if a handful of colony worlds had been glassed, scorched free of life; she knew, deep inside, that she would have refused to carry out such orders if they'd been issued. Perhaps she would have been relieved of command, with her successor carrying out the genocide, but…At least her conscience would have been clear. She couldn't have lived with herself if she'd wiped out billions upon billions of innocents whose only crime had been to be born on the wrong planet.

"And that means sending the guilty parties into exile, rather than putting them on trial and executing them," Earl Antony grumbled. "They…"

"If it ends the war sooner, with us victorious, it is a small price to pay," King Hadrian said. "And Admiral Falcone is right. We have to live with them afterwards." His smile thinned. "Lord Snow, where do we stand?"

Lord Snow took control of the display and projected a holographic starchart above the table. Kat leaned forward, studying it thoughtfully. Thirty-seven stars were blinking green, suggesting their planets had joined the king; twenty-two stars were red, indicating that they were either hostile or occupied by enemy forces. A handful of stars were blue, suggesting that they had declared neutrality and refused to join either side, but none of those were particularly significant. They were on the edge of the Commonwealth, too poor and primitive to tip the balance. Kat guessed their rulers were secretly hoping they'd have a chance to join the winning side, once the outcome became clear. Their allegiance probably wouldn't make any difference.

"We've been exchanging diplomatic notes ever since the shooting started," Lord Snow said, calmly. The king's diplomat seemed unconcerned by the prospect of all-out war. "A number of worlds have declared for us, although their ability to support our ships and troops is limited. We believe that Boskone and Yale *would* declare for us, given half a chance, but the House of Lords controls the naval bases in their systems. It might be… *dangerous*…for them to come over to our side."

"Probably," Kat said. "The House of Lords wouldn't have to occupy the planets to render them harmless."

Lord Snow nodded. "The majority of our *enemies* have strong ties to the House of Lords," he added, "and have no particular interest in switching sides at the moment. We're still exchanging messages, of course, but I feel we're unlikely to get anywhere, at least until we produce victories. Right now, Your Majesty, that means that a sizable chunk of the Commonwealth's industrial base is under enemy control."

"Then we have to take it off them," Earl Antony snapped.

"If we can," Lord Snow said. "I've sent missives to foreign governments, declaring the existence of a government-in-exile, but so far there haven't been any replies. I suspect that any formal recognition of our existence, either as a government-in-exile or the legitimate government of Tyre and the Commonwealth, will have to wait until we show that we can and do exercise power. Right now, foreigners have nothing to gain and a great deal to lose by offering recognition. Whatever our legal status, on paper, it is a simple fact that our enemies are in control of Tyre."

"The government rests in *me*," the king said, sharply. "I *am* the government."

"With all due respect, Your Majesty, that isn't true." Lord Snow took off his glasses and cleaned them with a small cloth. "Your person is *part* of the government, true. But, even in the best of cases, you are not *all* the government. Nor do you exercise effective control over Tyre. The post-Breakdown standard is to recognize governments that exercise control. You, we, do not."

And that means, sometimes, that we have to recognize governments we dislike, Kat reflected sourly. There were some planetary governments that deserved to be unceremoniously crushed, their armies disbanded and their leaders hanged. And yet, they had to be recognized. It was *they* who were in complete control. Nothing short of an invasion would remove them from power. *Right now, we're a motley band of refugees.*

The king's face darkened. "Do we *need* their recognition?"

"Not now, Your Majesty," Lord Snow said. "And, once you retake Tyre, you will have it by default."

"Good," the king said. "Are we ready for war?"

Lord Gleneden spoke first, snapping out points as if he expected to be silenced at any moment. "They control roughly two-thirds of the Commonwealth's industrial base, Your Majesty. There were...*difficulties*... caused by the postwar drawdown, as you are aware, but the House of Lords should have no real difficulties in getting the industrial base back online. In most cases, it will merely be a matter of switching back to military production. They will need some time to deal with bumps along the way, I suspect, but by raw numbers alone they will outproduce us by a fairly considerable margin."

"And parts of their tech base will be more advanced too," Lord Snow injected.

"Quite." Lord Gleneden glanced at Kat, his face unreadable. "If we don't win the war soon, Your Majesty, we will lose. The skill of our commanding officers and the valor of our fighting men will not matter in the face of overwhelming force. We will be crushed."

"We'll be in the same boat as the Theocracy," Kat said.

"Then we will take the offensive as soon as possible," the king said. "Can we strike Tyre? Now?"

"Not yet," Kat said. "We will need time to reorganize, to compensate for the crew who've left us and integrate newcomers from all over the Commonwealth. We do have an edge—my fleet was the largest single unit outside Home Fleet itself—but we will need time to gather ourselves before we can take full advantage of it. Right now, any attack on Tyre will be, at best, extremely costly."

"And if we lose the fleet, we might lose the war," the king mused.

"There's no *might* about it," Lord Gleneden said. "Without the fleet, we will lose."

"Quite," Lord Snow agreed. "Let us have no illusions. Our supporters will start edging away the moment it looks like we're losing. They will want to come to terms with our enemies, just to save their skins."

"Then we should gamble everything on one strike," Earl Antony said. "If we will lose if we do nothing, then we should take the risk."

"It would end badly," Kat told him. "Tyre is heavily defended. There's no way we can take and hold the high orbitals without losing much of our fleet. We would have to lay siege to the planet, which would give them time to recall their fleets to dislodge us."

Earl Antony glared. "So you're saying it's hopeless?"

"No," Kat said. "I'm just pointing out that we have to lay the groundwork *properly* before we gamble everything on one throw of the dice. We have a great deal of work to do before we can launch *any* offensive."

"Indeed," the king said. His voice was very calm. "What do you have in mind?"

"I have half an idea," Kat said. She did, although she knew she would have to consider the strategy carefully before she took it to the king. "But our first priority has to be to ready the fleet."

"And call for others to rally to our banner," Lord Snow said. "We *might* have more allies than we think. We've already had a couple of ships report for duty, after their crews rose up in the king's name. There will be others."

"Yeah," Earl Antony said. "And how many of them will turn out to be fair-weather friends?"

Printed in Great Britain
by Amazon

60826124R00267